MORNING STAR

MORNING STAR

by

JAMES LANSDALE HODSON

LONDON
VICTOR GOLLANCZ LTD
1951

NOTE

Every character in this book is entirely fictitious
and no reference whatever is intended to any
living person.

PRINTED IN GREAT BRITAIN BY PURNELL AND SONS, LTD. (T.U.)
PAULTON (SOMERSET) AND LONDON

For

U. L. H.

CHAPTER I

THE HISTORY OF our times has many threads, and many weavers of those threads. It is a rich and variegated fabric. Some of it is woven in bold colours, as in times of war. In those awesome days there is no danger of the broad pattern being mistaken or the outstanding persons and events overlooked. Indeed, the outstanding persons themselves usually see to that. The historians are not lacking, from the Churchills and the host of marshals, admirals and generals down to the, or up to the, official war historians who never finish recording one war before they, or their successors, are compelled to start all over again recording the next. And there are the minor diarists of the day who think it well to note for us such grey but illuminating fragments as when their cottage was destroyed by incendiary bombs or their son was first decorated in the Western Desert or later slain in Normandy. No, there is no danger of wars being overlooked or the mosaic lacking its blood-red, its black and its grey.

But in times of peace it is different. Now the tapestry is not so vivid; its principal weavers are cast in a less heroic mould, and the events in which they play a part are sombre rather than fiery. A multitude of those events, important in their several ways and throwing a ray of light on the scene, must always run the risk of being obscured and forgotten. In these circumstances the historian who is himself comparatively obscure may find that it devolves upon him to portray—with such faithfulness as he can—what was happening in a corner of the tapestry which nobody else appears to have noticed, or noticed with enough particularity.

Thus such an historian might have observed in the summer of 1947 that certain editors of the British Press were writing, with or without directives from their proprietors, of the Government's decision to cut newsprint and save a bare £2,000,000 when no other decisive attempt was, in their view, being made to reduce the nation's deficit of £450,000,000. Even sober and sedate journals whose guiding principle is "strong views calmly expressed" were writing that it must be said with regret that political motives, foreign to the spirit of a truly democratic party, seemed to be behind the Government's discrimination against newspapers. Other newspapers less meticulous saw in the cuts the shadow of censorship and an onslaught on Press freedom. This was, of course, as it might be, but was no less interesting for that.

The historian might have noted further, with his omniscient eye, that about this same time or earlier, certain ideas and resolves were forming in the celebrated head of Mr. Samuel Sedgwick, who was himself a notable owner of newspapers of varying repute, and that those ideas were not unrelated to what he firmly believed was the Government's inimical attitude, expressed or unexpressed, towards the nation's Press—that unquestioned bulwark of liberty.

Mr. Sedgwick pondered this now as he drove down from his house near Beachy Head, in what he liked to think of as the highlands of Sussex, towards Fleet Street, immortalised by Philip Gibbs as The Street of Adventure. And so it was. What other street in the Empire had raised so many commoners to the House of Lords? None. Every time Mr. Sedgwick drove down it, glancing at the huge cliffs of concrete and glass, that stood like castles among the horde of higgledy-piggledy provincial newspaper offices he was stirred with pride. Those castles and strongholds were the towers of the new journalism with its sales in millions; they were the strongholds of the Press's freedom. His own stronghold was equally large but stood nearer the Thames Embankment, and was sometimes mistaken for the Shell Mex Building, a mistake that was a source to him of mingled mortification and pride. He headed towards it now, sunk in the corner of his motor car, his chin deep in his stiff wing collar and touching his broad satin tie. His large ruddy face under its cranium, mostly bald, was solemn and in repose. His eyes indeed were closed, for he was thinking. These cogitations of his on the way to the office were a vital part of his day. From them explosions might spring, causing men to rise like rockets or, like rockets which have emitted their shower of stars, fall extinguished to be trodden underfoot. Which light among the Press magnates had said there is a touch of brutality about journalism? No matter. He, Sedgwick, would not have denied it. What was it Northcliffe used to wire to his northern editors as he started out for the industrial regions? "Approaching your territory. Awake!" He, Sedgwick, had employed the methods from time to time—not invariably, of course. No. Kindness mixed with acerbity—that was the thing. A pat and a punch, eh? Yes, yes. He opened his eyes for a moment and saw the burly blue back of his chauffeur and alongside him the six-foot ex-Commando Sergeant Winterton, whose style in opening and shutting doors was immaculate. If Cabinet Ministers whose fathers had been policemen and coal-miners employed a bodyguard, he, Sedgwick, could hardly do less. It afforded him a moment of amusement and of assurance every time he saw Winterton. It was well worth the money. One of these days the Communists might grow violent. He closed his eyes again and turned his mind to the newsprint cuts. He could stand them better than most for he had his own paper mills in Nova Scotia. It was what lay behind the cuts that was significant. Not only those cuts, but this Royal Commission on the Press—before which he would in due course give evidence—and which was already sitting. This Commission had, on the one hand, the ostensible object of furthering free expression of opinion through the Press, but, on the other hand, was to inquire into so-called monopolistic tendencies in control—which inquiry, if it meant anything at all, meant hostility to the very idea on which he founded his faith, namely freedom to be bold and enterprising, to grow and expand, to own not one newspaper but several newspapers—as, indeed, he already did. And now he was reinforced in the plan he had set afoot some months ago; it was manifestly wise and timely in the circumstances of the day and of this attack, veiled or overt, on the Press, to acquire one or two other newspapers while, as his old father the first James Sedgwick would have said, the going was good; for only heaven knew what this Royal Commission would recommend (far too many Radicals and Socialists on it) or what this misguided Government would do about those recommendations. But it was at the same time highly unlikely any legislation would be made retrospective. What was done was always difficult to undo. Moreover, quite apart from acquiring one or two more journals of repute he had long set his heart on, the devil in him—and he prided himself on it—would delight in flinging, so to speak, this gauntlet in the Commission's face—or, rather, the Government's face. After all, was England free, or wasn't it? Was a son who had in him the blood and spirit of his father to be allowed to complete the edifice his father had laid the foundations of, or wasn't he? Did England still hold to the hereditary principle of kingship, or didn't she? Well then. . . . There were kings of commerce, as there were royal kings. There were kings of newspapers, hereditary moulders of opinion, statesmen of the Press born to responsibility and affairs; and he was one of them. Why had men like Burnham, Northcliffe, Kemsley, Beaverbrook, Layton, Camrose, Rother-mere—and himself to follow in due course, he hoped—been made Peers of the Realm? It was because they were great servants of the State, men to be relied on in times of crisis and emergency, men whose loyalty to God, the king and the country was beyond dispute; certainly incomparably more beyond dispute than that of many leading Socialist politicians, some of whom had been in their time either avowed adherents of Communism, or fellow-travellers.

There were the envious and malicious who, of course, were wont to say that various Prime Ministers had bestowed these peerages to harness the Press to their chariot wheels, or with a lively sense of favours to come; that the honours were a form of bribery. Well, well, human nature was human nature and you couldn't prevent a premier trying to ensure that the great British public was on his side and that the Press, this very present help in time of trouble, had a good word to say for you. But—and Sedgwick chuckled to himself—how often the statesmen had found they had caught a tartar! What of Northcliffe and his attacks on Lloyd George? What of Beaverbrook and the dynamite he occasionally placed under the Tories? What of Kemsley, whose *Sunday Times* was a very independent journal? What of himself, Sedgwick, and his campaign for home rule for Scotland and Wales? What, on the other hand, of Baldwin, who said the Press were like harlots down the ages, desiring power without responsibility? No, no—politicians couldn't rely on the Press, any more than anybody else. Um. Well, not exactly that perhaps.

He put down *The Times* at which he had now been glancing in a desultory fashion, noticing the signatures to the letters with envy and asking himself why it was that men like Bernard Shaw gave to *The Times* for nothing what he, Sedgwick, would have been glad to pay good money for. Perversity, he supposed. Or snobbery. You had to admit that snobbery was deep-rooted in the English; very. He had always tried to give his papers tone by pretending that all his readers went to Henley and Ascot and dined at expensive restaurants. Well, if they didn't, they liked to read about those places. Took them out of themselves. Sex, royalty, religion, racing, war—the eternal, perennial sellers.

The poor reading about the rich. Fashion. Did not some of the most avid readers of *The Tatler* and the *Sketch* and the *Sphere* dwell in the mining villages? This was one of the fundamental mistakes of the Socialists, to imagine the working-class didn't enjoy the spectacle of fur coats and coronets, that all the coster-mongers envied the dukes. The world was filled with those who loved a title and delighted in worshipping at the shrine of privilege, even in the East End or the West Riding. His father, Old James, had made the mistake of his life when he refused a knighthood. Old James had said he couldn't live up to it—this because he started as a jobbing printer. Old James was a great man; but he had had one or two north-country obsessions—first, with wanting to *make* everything instead of acquiring it (news-papers, for instance; all the first James's newspapers he had actually created, and what a job it was, whereas he, Samuel, had bought one or two good ones ready-made); and, second, with refusing to go up in the world beyond a certain point. Old James never would own a Rolls Royce; and he declined to have a house in London. The furthest he would go was a suite at the Savoy—and a top-floor suite at that. "We want no feasts and famines in our family," he would say to his son. "So long as we have both feet firmly on the ground, we shall do. When I'm gone I suppose you'll do as you like. See you don't make away with it." And he would pull at his jaw, which had begun in old age to sag like a bulldog's.

Ah, pondered Mr. Sedgwick, what a triumph it all was!

His father in his early days had done some jobbing work for the *Yorkshire Times*, a paper, he was wont to say, more quoted than purchased and whose writers and contributors had found, strangely enough, as great a part of their reward in the pride and titillation experienced when reading their work in its columns as in the comparatively meagre addition to their banking accounts that had resulted. And then, lo! the time came when his father had had the audacity to launch a paper of his own, to set up in competition, so to speak, with that revered journal;

revered, yes, but not perfect, not in James's eyes. Not everybody, he imagined, wanted to read full reports of parliament in small type, or immensely long leaders in the intellectual mazes of which you could, as he said, die of exhaustion. No. People wanted a bit of fun. Alfred Harmsworth had realised that. And Harmsworth was, of course, right. His *Daily Mail* proved it. What was true of the south was doubly true of the blunt and racy north—so James Sedgwick had firmly believed. Nobody liked a bit of spice, a robust tale, a report of scandal, a handsome lot of sporting news—and, of course, all the news of royalty—and everything done to a turn—more than your Yorkshire Tykes. And James had seen to it that they got it. James had his critics, of course, men who cynically said that his original success was founded on a near-monopoly for printing pawn tickets coupled with a large business in printing religious tracts—for he was a strong churchman. But he could afford to ignore envious gossip of that sort. What nobody could deny was that he gave his readers value for money, including serials by those he deemed the best writers of the day—Hall Caine, Marie Corelli, Ouida and suchlike—and he ran *Wuthering Heights*, the Yorkshire classic, as a serial too, thus spreading good literature and achieving economy at the self-same time.

Ultimately he could say, half jocularly, as the owner of two or three papers, that he could afford to buy the *Yorkshire Times* up. His wife Carrie had replied: "You could—if they'd sell it. But you know what happened when you mentioned it to Mr. Perceval Blackwood, the editor—he bit your head off."

"It's true all the same," he had said. "And another thing—I'll back our Sam against his nephew Oliver any day of the week. A genius for newspaper finance, has our Sam."

CHAPTER II

A FEW WEEKS after this history begins, Mr. Sedgwick, who was enjoying being alone in his room for a brief while (for it often seemed that he was as busy as a Cabinet Minister), finished the sentence he was speaking into his dictaphone, replaced the speaking tube, and rang for tea. He had been working in his silk hat—he often wore one in his room as his father, in his later years, had often worked in a brown bowler—"my badge of office," the old man had been wont to say. He now removed his silk hat and sank a little further into his leather tub chair. His massive face was inclined to redden under stress, but at the moment it was, by comparison, pale; it was also immobile and content. For all his fifty-five years and all his combats, triumphs, and discomfitures, his face could be serene. Moreover, he had one peculiarity to which his unfriendly critics attributed the secret— the only secret, they said, of his success: he could stare for very long periods without blinking. He now glanced out of the side window of his lofty room on top of Yorkshire House—he had gone as high as he could to show the staff he was not afraid of bombing, should it come—after all, the Duke of Wellington would have done the same—and he saw the Thames running towards him from Charing Cross, smooth, inexorable, like his newspapers. Nothing interrupted their flow, he reflected, any more than the flow of London's mighty river. But whereas this river was of the south only, his newspapers were to be found also in the north and the east and the west.

And *his* river, so to speak, unlike London's river, was still acquiring fresh tributaries to strengthen the main stream. He glanced across the room to where hung, framed, the illuminated scroll he had received a year or two before when his native town of Bletchford had made him a Freeman. On that occasion he had declared—and it was, of course, profoundly true—that his newspapers were proud to serve their king, their country, and their fellow-countrymen of Britain. He liked to think, he said, that a man who worked on those papers was known for his bearing, his courtesy, his integrity and his accuracy; that he was true to the public and could always be trusted. The speech had gone down well at the time—larded with a few good Yorkshire stories told in the Doric—and his weightier remarks had impressed him more and more as time went on. So, when he framed the scroll, he had picked out in red and blue underneath the words that are quoted above. They looked uncommonly well, he thought. If there was a touch of rodomontade in them, well, well . . . Prime Ministers had to do it, too. Something for his young men to live up to—something to cling on to in this cynical shifting world, this England in a social revolution. Um! He was aware that the ribald lads of the reporting room were apt to extend his words and add—trusted to blow the gaff, or sink a pint, or get it wrong, or leave out the uncomfortable facts. But journalists were a cynical breed—they knew far too much. No use expecting *them* to parade their idealism, even when they had any. No. He was satisfied that the Sedgwick creed had had its effect, misquoted and bowdlerised though it was. He smiled to himself, stroked his jaw and put on his silk hat again. He had, he reflected, a good deal to be pleased about. This purchase of the *East England Daily Chronicle*, for instance.

The *Daily Chronicle* belonged to a very respectable part of the country; nonconformist, solid; the old London *Daily News* had had a strong following in that neighbourhood. The *Daily Chronicle* had been called The Bible of East England and he, Mr. Sedgwick, saw no reason why it should not be called that again. No reason at all. For he insisted that nothing salacious or pornographic or too violently controversial should appear in his journals; except, that is, when these Socialists or extreme Radicals had to be kept in their place. This nationalisation, for instance. Ruining the country.

He was pleased, too, that the editor of the *Daily Chronicle* was staying on. A sensible man. A bit difficult at first—had jibbed over accepting the syndicated London Letter and one of the principal leaders each evening, but he had been susceptible to argument. Yes, a sensible fellow. He, Sedgwick, didn't anticipate any real trouble with him. Why, indeed, should there be trouble? The fellow—Crabtree, was his name?—would get £500 a year more than he ever got before. A respectable sum. What his father James would have called "good money". So it was. Very good money. And security—complete security so long as Crabtree—it was Crabtree, wasn't it?—continued to be a sensible fellow and do as he was told. He, Sedgwick, had decided to give him a good deal of latitude on local topics. That was his invariable rule. "My dear Crabtree," he had said, "if the local river wants dredging and the Conservancy Board are neglecting their responsibility, I leave it to you—take a strong line if you feel like it. Or if you want to give three columns to the agricultural show, well and good, fine and dandy. You are the expert. I leave it to you. And letters to the editor—they are within your discretion. You will not overlook the fact, of course, that we are an independent paper with a respect for tradition and a love for the Empire and a deep loyalty to the king. Some people, of course, wrongly call us Tory. Tory we may be in contradistinction to these Socialists, who are bent on giving the Empire away, who pretend to be Puritans but are given to licence, who have no traditions and whose personal records as fighting men are—well, what are they? I do not say their speeches must be ignored. Far from it. But no pandering, no giving way to their eloquence, their zest for a grievance, their passion for disturbing and unsettling, their devotion to levelling. A few lines is enough; and in letters—well, extracts from letters—you know the sort of thing. Of course, Crabtree," he had continued, "when issues of vast national importance arise, you will receive advice. On these occasions the Sedgwick newspapers speak with one voice. It would be improper for them to do otherwise; it would be puzzling and might seem that our journals lacked sincerity of opinion and purpose if we spoke with one accent and view in, say, Plymouth, and another in Norwich, and a third in Leeds and a fourth in Edinburgh. You will appreciate that. It wouldn't do for a moment. The British public would not know where it was. The public expects a lead. Giving that lead is a duty that devolves upon us, and it is a duty we and our newspapers have never failed to fulfil."

Crabtree had seen the point—his new editors usually did. They were at complete liberty to enter into a new contract with him, or to leave him, as they chose. This was a free country—apart from the inroads of Socialism. He always told them that. But, yes, they usually stayed with him. They ran the papers with complete freedom—within certain prescribed limits, of course. They knew his policy and he could not remember having had serious trouble with any of them—not for long. No. Whether what he had in mind for his next acquisition would prove to be a different kettle of fish remained to be seen. The *Morning Star* and its editor, Oliver Blackwood, nephew of Perceval. Um. Might be a fight there. High falutin', the pair of 'em.

A discreet tap came to the door and his private secretary, Col. Watson, a tall young man with receding hair who was more at home with a fly whisk in Cairo than here in morning clothes, entered, walking soundlessly across the thick carpet.

"Yes, Watson?"

"Mr. Fortinbras is on the phone, sir."

Mr. Sedgwick, with an almost imperceptible frown, lifted an instrument coloured purple. "My dear Rupert, how are you?" he inquired, with his studied mixture of deference and familiarity.

"Sammie"—Mr. Fortinbras spoke the name in his thick fruity voice—"I'm sending you my speech—do what you can with it. Time we blew a mine under this arid Government. I've drafted a few notes that may be of use to the leader-writer, too. I say, Sammie, have we given up the Channel Isles or the Isle of Wight yet?" It was a blend of chuckle and growl. The voice then disappeared. It waited for no reply. It might have come from another world, so unheralded its emergence, so swift its withdrawal. From various parts of the country—and indeed from the Continent—Mr. Fortinbras made himself thus felt.

When this happened, Mr. Sedgwick was flattered, inspired, prodded, irritated—all by turns. Mr. Fortinbras was as liable to telephone at 2 a.m. as he was at 10 a.m. No time—or subject—was sacred to him. India, Palestine, the coal-miners, the Royal Academy, American films—his views on all were laid down with the firmness of foundation stones. Nothing shadowy about this member of the Shadow Cabinet. Mr. Sedgwick sometimes wished there was. And yet, to have this battleship behind you firing its guns, to feel in your bones that were Mr. Fortinbras to become Prime Minister at some future time your barony would be once again floating on the horizon—ah! He had only narrowly missed it last time; his spies had informed him that the sub-editors' room had rung with the joke—"If only Sammie would get his promotion to the lords and then we could knock hell out of the Cabinet again!" No truth in it, of course, because he hadn't the least desire to attack the then Cabinet. Loyalty—he prized that highly. During the General Election the Sedgwick newspapers had been immaculate in their crusade against the Socialists, and it was a blow when they got in—a blow in every sense. Had his organisation overrated its power? He was aware of the old jibe that if Sedgwick supported you in a by-election you were as good as done for; but he would have said that sheer weight of numbers of papers sold, read, perused, glanced at—call it what you like—

would have swayed the electorate. It hadn't been so—unless the fact was that had his newspapers *not* supported the Tories they would have been utterly destroyed. Well, well, these incalculable English. His father had always said you never knew when you had 'em. Even on humour you had to go slow—very slow. Irony? Out with irony. Satire? No place for that. The English didn't like being codded (his father's word). "You have to understand how the English work," Old James always said. "They're like women. They have a secret engine inside 'em which goes round and round. They pretend to be gentle—but they're really ferocious. They pretend to be good sportsmen. But did you ever hear 'em shouting 'Kick him in th' head!' at a rugby football match in Hull or Halifax when the visiting team was winning? They say they're not artistic. Why, nobody ever had any poets like ours. And your grandfather Isaac—why, he left his family stranded every harvest and went off with his bassoon and 'cello fro' one church to another—didn't care tuppence for his family; and if that isn't artistic, tell me what is! And this 'ere artistry is even in me— I know it is. I've had my inclinations to go over the traces—had to stifle 'em, stamp on 'em. You'll have 'em too, Sam— they're in the blood. Hold 'em down—well, that's to say don't let 'em interfere too much wi' the work in hand." And here his father had winked. "After all, if I hadn't been an artist—no newspapers, eh?"

Money was a great tempter, his father always said. And so it was. It was easier for a working man to go straight than for a duke or a lord, James had argued. Once rich, enticements were thrown in your way; folk delighted to kowtow to you. The world was divided into masters and servants, and the born servant got as much pleasure out of deferring and bowing and boot-licking, as some men did out of being the boss. "Therefore," said Old James, "don't preach, don't be censorious. Gets you nowhere. Let folk have their bit o' fun. What made old King Teddy so popular? His liking for a bit o' fun. Marie Lloyd knew all about that. A little o' what you fancy does you good, eh? Best song she ever sung."

Mr. Sedgwick, sipping his tea out of a delicate teacup he had brought back from Copenhagen, pondered these things.

It was at this point in his ruminations that Mrs. Polly Tremayne was announced. A sparkle entered Mr. Sedgwick's eye.

CHAPTER III

THE ENTRANCES OF Mrs. Polly Tremayne into Mr. Sedgwick's office were not as unexpected—or as brief in their tenure—as Mr. Fortinbras's by telephone, but they had this in common—Sedgwick never knew precisely what the outcome would be. More than once she had arrived for a moment's talk, perhaps a word of advice from him on whether he had a good tip to give her for the afternoon's racing, or whether he would get her a couple of seats for a play when the theatre swore there wasn't one left (well, you were not a Press magnate for nothing), and, the momentary business done, had carried him off for the whole day. It was thus, indeed, that she had carried him off, originally, not only for a day, but, in a sense, for the whole year that had preceded this particular afternoon. He often recalled their first day together. It was a turning point, in its fashion. His long and affectionate friendship with that admirable writer of feuilletons, Alice Collins, was being brought to an end by her decision to marry a banker. Sedgwick was both piqued and relieved—he had foreseen that the time must inevitably come when he could bear her absence with equanimity. In its way, this emergence of a banker was a stroke of Providence. Sedgwick was so pleased—or, anyhow, a part of him was, and his affection for her had been so real that he had bought her, as a farewell gift, a diamond bracelet that cost him considerably more than a thousand pounds. He had had it in his pocket when Mrs. Polly Tremayne called in response to an invitation he had extended to her at a cocktail party—how amusing she had been, this rather diminutive, somewhat rotund figure with dancing black eyes and a trick of almost pirouetting on her toes as she talked to you, intimate, exquisite, provoking. "Come and have a cup of tea one afternoon," he had said jokingly, for tea seemed the last thing she would wish to have. And lo, she had come; the first of a large number of calls upon him. The diamond bracelet that lay in his pocket that first afternoon had never, in the outcome, adorned the arm of Miss Alice Collins. True, he bought another bracelet for her, but somewhat less ambitious, less costly. For, after all, a gift that salutes a memory need not necessarily have the exciting—or expensive—qualities of one that salutes the dawning of a new relationship—or so it seemed to him. Moreover, Alice was marrying a banker, whereas Mrs. Tremayne was alone in the world—or as alone as a woman of her charm and wit ever is. Her wrist, dimpled, chubby, became that bracelet most extraordinarily well. She wore it within a week of their first encounter.

When, on this afternoon a year later, Watson had ushered Mrs. Tremayne into his room and withdrawn, she put her arms round Sedgwick's neck and kissed him.

"Where were you last night?" she inquired, taking off his silk hat and putting it on the desk.

"At the club—won forty-five shillings at bridge." He took up the hat and put it on again. "Don't sit on the arm of the chair, dear, I've got Pick coming in."

"Club indeed! And why do you send for Pick when I'm here, darling?"

"Safety precaution. Besides, I wanted you to hear what I'm up to. Will you come to Lancashire for a day or two?"

"If you make it worth my while, darling." She twirled round on her toes away from his chair and almost disappeared in a deep leather armchair and crossed her legs. "Was it to Lancashire we went once before?"

"It was. But this time it's Greycastle I'm going to, not Burnham."

She sighed. "Half the men we saw looked like Labour Members of Parliament."

"Come, not as bad as that." They both laughed.

"But why Lancashire again?"

"I'm probably going to buy a newspaper."

"Is that all?"

"All?"

"You don't need me for that, darling. Anyhow, I never read newspapers. They frighten me—you never know what they'll say. Jennie, my sister who writes novels, swears she had a breakdown because of the reviewers—she never reads a paper now. Though I must say it seems even worse for her to be told by her malicious friends what the reviewers have said." This was a long speech for Mrs. Tremayne and she closed her eyes and sank a trifle lower in the chair.

"Polly."

"Yes, darling?"

"I will bribe you."

"I adore being bribed. What with?"

"I will buy a play for you and put it on."

"I don't want a play—I want a film, Sam, a lovely film like *Life with Father*. A part with a lot of children." She sighed. "I am really a very domesticated woman. I am a mother gone wrong." She wriggled further into the chair.

"Freddy Pick will not approve of the sight of your legs, Polly."

"All you know"—and she chuckled.

"Sit up, dear, and behave like a lady."

"I will behave like a lady when you marry me, dear."

"I will never marry you. My life wouldn't be worth living. You boss me enough as it is, knowing you've no hold over me. Man is a monastic animal who is at his best on battleships. Why do you suppose naval officers are the handsomest men in the country?"

"But, darling, what is the use of all those good looks among men?—unless they are all—whatever you call them, with their exits and entrances?"

"That is a remark, Polly, more appropriate to two o'clock in the morning than five in the afternoon. Ah, here's Freddy."

Sir Frederick looked incredibly old and dried up, so that his face with its snub, cherry nose and wide mouth appeared to wear a perpetual smile. The reporters' room, which called him The Laughing Man, said he dated back to the firm's earliest days. Certainly, he had worked as a book-keeper for Old James and had learnt nearly fifty years ago the arts and wiles of reporters with their expenses. He had been borne aloft like ballast on the tail of the Sedgwick kite, having tied himself on securely and needing thenceforth to do little more than suffer himself to be carried along murmuring "Yes, yes," at the right moments. His knighthood sprang from the First World War when he had accompanied Old James to the United States on a purchasing commission. Old James, who had a soft spot for Freddy, had stipulated before they went that this must be Pick's reward. And the Prime Minister of the time, who was said to have his own price list for honours, had made no demur.

Sir Frederick bowed to Mrs. Tremayne and toddled over to Mr. Sedgwick's table.

"Well, Sir Frederick?" inquired Sedgwick with a touch of irony.

"I saw Molyneux." The voice was thin and high.

"You did, eh?"

"I believe he would sell, tho' he's worried about what people will say—an old independent paper joining the Sedgwick Group. I told him, of course, that the *Morning Star* would be on firmer ground than ever before financially, that as a newspaper it would be much improved—a more comprehensive foreign service, better pictures—I doubt for instance, if it ever had a telegraphed picture in the paper until five minutes ago."

"And he was impressed by that?"

"Oh yes, oh yes. Of course——"

"Go on."

"I don't think if it rested entirely with him, it would be easy. On the other hand, his wife——"

"Yes?"

"I gathered his wife has a great hankering after living in the United States—they went over there last year. She didn't like the bombing very much in the war——" Sir Frederick made this sound a surprising notion. "And then again, she's not over fond of the Socialists."

"She's not, eh?"

Sir Frederick moved a little closer. "There's another thing might help us—I don't believe, from what I heard, that she hits it off too well with Oliver Blackwood."

"Good! That's the ticket. But why? Has he refused to fall in love with her? You know what women are, Freddy." Sedgwick grinned at Mrs. Tremayne, who blew him a kiss.

Pick's face screwed itself up even further till it resembled a dried-up skull from Central America.

Pick said: "Blackwood has a wife of his own who's something of a tartar, I hear."

"Do I understand, Sir Frederick," inquired Sedgwick, taking off his thick horn-rimmed spectacles, "that the human element may play an important part in our acquiring this saintly newspaper?"

Pick put his tiny hands beneath the tail of his coat and tossed the coat up and down delightedly. "Wheels within wheels," he said.

Sedgwick put on his spectacles again. "How much did you offer Molyneux? Or was that delicate point never reached?"

"Oh yes, oh yes. I spoke of four hundred thousand."

"What did he say?"

"He allowed it to pass without any striking comment."

Sedgwick frowned. "I don't like that. Sounds a very good businessman. I hope he's not an artist in addition. They're always the worst. Remember our attempts to deal with Wells and Shaw?" Mr. Sedgwick almost groaned.

Pick said: "I took the liberty of saying you would be visiting Greycastle yourself in the near future. Was I right?"

"Never righter. It's a matter to be decided with some celerity. Because although this Press Commission can't interfere yet—— Well, do you think they might, then?" For Pick was looking grave.

Pick said: "The love this Government has for us could repose without difficulty on the edge of a threepenny bit."

Sedgwick said: "The freedom of the Press—Milton, Wilkes, and the rest of 'em. No, they daren't do it, Freddy. All the same . . ."

"I shall feel happier," said Pick, "when the *Morning Star* is yours."

"It's not a bad title," Sedgwick said, rolling it round his tongue. "Um. *Morning Star*—and a sub-title, 'For king and country—and the Briton who prizes liberty!' That will set it off."

"Set it off! It may blow it up," said Mrs. Tremayne, chuckling.

CHAPTER IV

ON THE AFTERNOON that has been described, a curious figure, who occupied an equally curious place in the set-up of the *Morning Star*, was bound for the office of that particular Lancashire journal in the seaport of Greycastle.

He climbed the tall flight of drab wooden steps to the over-head railway, thinking what a Victorian and ramshackle air it preserved. His long, loose and shabby jacket had pockets that were bulky with sandwiches, a wad of manuscript and two volumes—an Everyman edition of Pushkin's short stories and Waugh's *Brideshead Revisited*. His cap was pulled down, and its neb made, along with his sharp nose and pointed chin, a trio of projections. He stood on the high platform in the warm wind and turned his weak eyes towards the docks and warehouses that lay between him and the grey river beyond which caught a flicker of brown silver. He couldn't see very well, but his heart was lifted up every time he gazed, as he gazed now, towards the world of ships, flour mills, tobacco warehouses, of ancient loco-motives with their clanging bells, of ship-repairing yards, of timber stacks, of the vessels that sailed to New Orleans, Baltimore, Philadelphia, Boston, New York and a hundred other ports. He supposed he had never got over being a boy; he supposed he ought to have gone to sea—as he would have done if his drunken father had found the twenty pounds for his kit as an apprentice. Ah! what might he not have written then! Lancashire's own Conrad, eh? He grinned to himself wryly; he who had hardly kept himself in cigarettes out of his novels. Why the hell hadn't he written more about Greycastle, this sprawling port with its thirty miles of quays, its rich shipowners who waxed fat in the old days on carrying slaves in their noisome ships to America (and the Yankees still cursed us for it too, for having given them their negro problem), and its shipowners who today made a fine thing for their sons by handing their ships over to be managed by one company, and found in victuals and stores by a second company, and unloaded and loaded by a third company of stevedores—and made those sons directors of every one of those companies, a trinity in unity and unity in trinity, as the prayer-book said. And, talking of the prayer-book, what of this city with its two new cathedrals, the Protesant cathedral built by a Catholic and the Catholic cathedral built by a Protestant, and the money for the Catholic one paid for partly out of the dole in the great depression; what other city had two cathedrals the like o' that; and wasn't the Protestant one the biggest church in all England, and didn't its roseate sandstone become a beacon of fire when the sun caught it in the evening so that the Lord

himself must be exalted? Begob, he thought, there's so many
Irish in this town I'm thinking like an Irishman myself, and I
wonder if I am a bit Irish too, for my mother was the friendliest
soul and she had to be that and have a fancy-man now and then
with my father thinking more of his ferreting and pigeon-flying
than his labouring at the docks carrying the merchandise that
had crossed the seven seas. So maybe he, Richard Lovelace, was
really the son of a merchant from Rodney Street, and maybe he
had a touch of the slave trader's blood in him? Assuredly there
was nobody like him in the family; not a one of them would ever
dream of writing a ha'penny postcard except himself. Mr.
Lovelace sniffed the wind and liked the salt in it and thought of his
old friend Frank Tucker, the pilot, who used to go down to the
sea in ships and take his wife with him. Frank was the only man
Lovelace knew of who had read all his books. Frank had read one of
them, *The Stone in the Heart*, three times over, which was once
oftener than Lovelace himself. Where was Frank now?—aboard
that fat squat bluff old sea-lady coming up river as slow as a
stagecoach, or that jerrybuilt newfangled reconditioned Liberty
ship behind her, the sort that sometimes broke in half during the
war? Frank said there wasn't the brass made out o' ships in this
last war that there was in the first, but, by God, there was enough.
Aye, quite enough. What about the *Corybantic*, bought for six
thousand pounds and insured for a hundred thousand pounds and
mined off Sicily? What about Harry Stokes and Benjamin
Redroof who worked for nothing in the Ministry of War Transport? A-guinea-a-year men, was it? Did their firms do it out of
kindness of heart, no hope of a picking or a trifle of preferment?
When did they think we—meaning himself, Lovelace—came off
the barbed wire? He wouldn't mind betting——

"Howdo, Mister Lovelace, you're early."

Lovelace turned and peered at his interlocutor. He said:
"At my back I always hear, Time's wingèd chariot hurrying
near."

Two or three afternoons a week they caught the same train,
he and Joe Pembroke, a foundry-hand on the *Morning Star*. Joe
said: "Yo' mean what I call the buzzer."

"Time like an ever-rolling stream, Joe." Lovelace's eyes went
back to the river.

"You said it," said Joe. "Roll on two in the morning. Been up

half the night with toothache. It's old enough to know better
—had it turned forty-seven years." Joe gnawed his stringy sandy
moustache.

"The Almighty didn't make much of a job of us, Joe—your
teeth and my eyes."

"You said it," said Joe again. "We certainly wouldn't have
given him his card in our union—not the week he made my
teeth."

"Too bad, Joe. How's the pools doing this week?"

"Just missed it—one figure wrong—one bleeding figure. Hear
about the chap at Jones's rope works? You can just see the roof
yonder. Won nineteen thousand. Know him well. Johnnie Webb.
Spends one and nine a week on 'em same as me. But he ain't leaving
the job. Think o' that. Can you beat it? Ain't leaving. Why me—
see that liner there? the *Atalanta*. I'd be in the bridal suite." He
removed a fragment of cigarette that had stuck to his bottom
lip and ground it under his boot. "Nothing to 'em these days,"
he said. He dismissed cigarettes, this modern currency. After a
moment he delivered judgment on mankind. "Men's browned
orf," he said. "Austerity this, austerity that. If I'd my time to do
again, I'd be orf—South Africa's the place."

"Ah, you dream of gold, diamonds and ostrich feathers, Joe.
Your other name is Marco Polo."

"You said it," said Joe. "Look at us here. Look at this overhead
railway. Back number. Thought while I was away down South
they'd have ripped it up—or Jerry would have blown it down.
He might ha' done worse. As it is——" Joe eyed the approaching
train as if it were doom.

"Atom boy, atom boy," said Mr. Lovelace.

"Eh?" bellowed Joe, as the train swept past. But Mr. Lovelace
didn't add anything. They climbed into the train, and Lovelace
disposed himself so that he could watch the river. He thrust out
his long thin legs, making his feet in their big boots look as
clumsy and enormous as those of a dead man.

"You writin' a book agen, Mister Lovelace?" Joe shouted
above the din and rattle.

"Yes, as a matter of fact I am."

"In th' office, like?"

"Some of it, yes."

"It's a gift, I suppose," bellowed Joe.

29

Lovelace leaned over and spoke in his ear. "A man once said to me I looked more like a ratcatcher."

Joe eyed him carefully. "I wouldn't go as far as that," he shouted. "Not altogether, anyhow. Think I shall like it?"

Lovelace shook his head. "I wouldn't think so."

"I'm a bit of a reader, yer know. I like the *News o' the World*—tells you about life—choir-boys and married women an' that."

Lovelace looked solemn. "Can't compete with that, Joe."

"Pity we don't get more racy bits in the *Morning Star*," said Joe. "That's what I always say. None o' my pals ever read *our* paper, yer know. Find it dull—all this stuff about foreign politics. We got enough trouble at home. Woman in our street put her head in the gas oven last Sat'dy—nothing about it on *our* paper. Told 'em in the reporters' room, too. Tipped 'em orf. Not a word." Joe shook his head, wrote off the *Morning Star* and lapsed into silence.

Lovelace opened his Pushkin but he didn't read it. So long as the *Star* was edited by Oliver Blackwood, nephew of Perceval of the *Yorkshire Times*, it would remain a trifle austere—or more than a trifle. His weak eyes were staring towards the roofs of the warehouses and the occasional masts with their pennants poking above the roofs. He could see the powerful drayhorses straining at their loads of raw cotton, the broad motor-lorries bouncing over the rough cobbles and sunken railway lines, the little clouds of dirt and chaff scurrying before the wind. Yonder was the floating landing stage from which he had caused one of his heroines, Jennifer MacArthur, to throw herself into the grey swirling waters one winter's night. It had hurt him grievously to do it, but he had done it and the tears had gone dribbling down his cheeks. By God, did any other writer behave so foolishly, he wondered? Why, whenever a book was done he was empty; he would never write another book, he swore. The agony and labour was too much, and, anyhow, he had no more to say. The well was empty. But, of course, it never was. It filled up again. He supposed he would go on—scribble, scribble, scribble, eh, Mr. Lovelace?—till the end was reached; and he'd leave an unfinished manuscript behind him; and somebody would light the fire with it.

The train pulled up with a jerk at Litherland Street. He drew himself to his feet and Joe did likewise. Mr. Lovelace's mind, which had been occasionally lit with lines of poetry throughout the afternoon, now murmured to him: "But hark! My pulse like a soft drum, beats my approach, tells thee I come." Seventeenth century, that was the time to have lived. Why hadn't he been born then? But perhaps he had, perhaps he had. Reincarnation, that sensible notion. Certainly the times had something in common; both were somewhat out of control.

CHAPTER V

NOBODY COULD SAY the *Morning Star* building had moved with the times. It wore a somewhat Victorian air. It stood close by St. John's churchyard and you had to look spry not to miss it, for the entrance lay at the bottom of a courtyard that stood at right angles to the thoroughfare, a flagged courtyard sloppy in wet weather and slippery in snow. An old lamp, oil in its first days and electric now, was fastened to the brick wall over the door and bore the words "Morning Star" in chipped white on a blue background. It was not unusual for tipsy gentlemen to wander inside the office thinking they were entering a public-house or the police station. Inside the swing doors, which never quite closed because they appeared either to have outgrown one another or gone slightly askew, sat Wilfred Fletcher, who had waxed enormous since he lost a leg as an artilleryman at Passchendaele. Whether his bulk was due to lack of exercise or the fact that Wilfred ate and drank as much as ever but had less body to provide for, often exercised Lovelace's mind. Wilfred presided over a couple of brass tubes for pumping telegrams up to the subeditor's room, and although telegrams were fewer nowadays in the era of teleprinters and reporters who telephoned their stories, Wilfred still used the tubes. He enjoyed doing it. He would load a letter into the tube like a round into the breech and pump it up with a terrific clatter, the while humming

> Whiter than the snow,
> Holy Joe!

—a relic of his old artillery days.

Lovelace paused on his way to climb the stairs.

"Any messages, Wilfred?"

"Mr. Blackwood phoned to tell you he's gone to see Sir Thomas, sir. He'll be a bit late."

Lovelace went up the wooden stairs, past the oil painting of Sir Thomas Molyneux's father—florid-faced as a butcher and wearing hunting pink—walked down the badly lit corridor, known as the sacred region of the office, and entered the editor's room. The door always reminded him of the door into a magistrate's room—weighty, with a green curtain behind its opaque glass. The room was sombre but comfortable, like that of a club. In winter a coal fire burned there. Lovelace doubted if the room had changed much since the *Morning Star* was born.

Lovelace emptied his pockets on to a small and rather disreputable table tucked away in a corner of the room. At this table he acted as a mixture of adviser, minor leader-writer, secretary and general factotum. He said Blackwood kept him to answer the telephone when otherwise the room was empty. But the bond was close. They had been reporters together for a brief space thirty years earlier; they had soldiered together in the first war. Lovelace had been buffeted about a good deal in his time and this table represented anchorage. He began to roam and quest about the room humming to himself, sniffing the smell of last night's proofs, enjoying the sight of what remained of last night's battle. A volume of the *Encyclopaedia Britannica* was lying open as they had left it at 2 a.m. The *New Yorker*, *Humanité* and *Economist* lay there together with *Hansard*, one or two new Command papers, a pile of the London dailies, and leading provincial newspapers of the north and Scotland. A number of new novels, biographies and volumes of poetry had come for the editor marked "Personal". Lovelace sighed over them—that they should hope to win Blackwood's meagre time, and rare approbation, and that even if they did he would interfere with his reviewers' judgment! Vain, vain! Why, it was never certain his own novels would have more than a line or two devoted to them; they took their chance. The fact that his later novels had been written largely in this room on the *Morning Star's* copy paper didn't make a ha'porth of difference. He had to confess that he sometimes thought this was carrying integrity rather far, that a bit of good honest log-rolling would have rejoiced his old heart—

but the particle of a martyr in him said it was right; no half measures. Ah, it was good to be here. Home was the hunter, home from the hill. Aye. What crises in the life of the *Morning Star* had been faced and routed here; the night when the machine-room caught fire; the night when the police were on strike and the rioters hove stones through the windows because they didn't like the *Morning Star's* contents bills; the various nights when the private line from London went phut and the London Letter and Parliamentary stuff had to be taken down over the telephone; the nights in the war when the city was lit by fires and the docks were blazing and you could barely hear yourself speak for the bombers droning overhead—and Oliver writing away at his desk as if wrapped in the peace that passeth understanding; Oliver advising everybody to go to the rooms in the basement where the mighty presses were—but not going himself and leaving the decision to them, being a Liberal and wedded to the dignity of man. Aye, aye. He reckoned he and Oliver had enjoyed it, after a fashion. Oh, war was devilry and dirt, but it had something to be said for it; for it tumbled down money to where it belonged, low down in the scale. Aye, what this room had seen—what wranglings, arguments, swift decisions, denunciations, ironies, comedies, what oaths and prayers, what triumphs—for every issue of the *Morning Star* damp from the press was in itself a kind of triumph.

Lovelace lifted his nose from the *New Yorker* as he heard a step in the doorway. Seth Entwistle, the printers' overseer, bearing a galley-proof and wearing an apron like a cobbler, paused there.

"Will he be usin' this column o' letters tonight, Mr. Lovelace?"

"What are they on, Seth?"

"Herrenvolk, coal, black markets and whatnot."

"Nothing about watery beer and the price of victory being eternal queues?"

"We shall be havin' 'em," said Seth jovially.

"The voice of democracy," said Lovelace.

"I could write one myself," said Seth, "in case we run short."

"Subject, Seth?"

"Rudeness," said Seth with great heartiness. "This was a decent country while t' war were on. Gone downhill ever since.

Have to fight to get on a bus now. And as for chaps workin'—
they don't *like* work now—an' they don't mind sayin' so. I can
remember the time when I could have set up the *Star* all by
meself—an' not had so many literals, neither."

"It's the upsurge of the workers, Seth. Got to expect it."

"They've gone soft," said Seth, waving the galley-proof.
"I'm sixty-two an' I started when I were twelve, an' it's done me
no harm."

"Ah, Seth, who can tell? Who can tell? We've fifty Peers o'
the Realm who are turned eighty and nearly two hundred over
seventy."

"Work killed nobody," said Seth stubbornly. "But the lack
of it—ah!—you should ha' seen 'em in the slump—foldin' up
like kippers."

Lovelace said musingly: "I see them coming out of the workshops, Seth, and some of 'em have legs as bent as tho' they
carried both hemispheres on their shoulders. Atlas wasn't in it.
And their teeth—they might have chewed rocks."

"They're chewin' 'em now, if their butcher's same as mine,"
said Seth. "If I find a horse-shoe on my plate I shan't be surprised."

"Horatio Nelson could say the same, Seth. Horse-beef and
roast rats a delicacy. Food for heroes. Chaos and crisis have come
again."

"It's makin' a rare mess o' family life, I can tell you that,"
said Seth. "Why is the divorce rate up by leaps and bounds?
It's this rationin'. Monotony. It were bad enough to see the same
face opposite to you every breakfast-time, but to see t' same bit
o' dried egg or spam under your nose as well—human nature
can't stand it. Ay, ay, I know what you'll say, I know Mr.
Blackwood would remind us we're better off nor the Germans.
I say—so we should be too. We'd be havin' no dried egg but for
them."

Mr. Lovelace, whose nose had been down in his *New Yorker*
again, raised it for a moment: "We must preserve the liberal
spirit, Seth."

Seth grunted. "Our editor," he said, "is a great man, but
there's times——" he paused—"there's times when everybody's
right but us. I don't hold wi' it."

"Ah," said Lovelace, "roses growing on a stone wall."

This cryptic remark drew nothing from Seth for a moment. Then he said: "Too good for this world—I've often said so. Look at him over this Government."

"Ah!" said Lovelace again. "I thought *you* voted for 'em."

"Oh, I *voted* for 'em," said Seth. "What else could a chap do? I fathered my dowter Nancy, but I don't hold wi' her views on marriage—in an' out like a duck in water. Same wi' this Government. Scuttle, scuttle, scuttle, that's what I say."

"Are you referring to India, Seth, or is it coal?"

"That's another thing," said Seth, "coal. I can remember the day when coal was put into my cellar at four and sevenpence a ton, and colliers got sixpence ha'penny a ton for cuttin' it. And there was plenty of it. Now—I pay three pounds five, when I can get it; and the stuff won't burn."

"That's the revolution in action—war and peace—which is which, Seth?" Seth grunted. Lovelace added: "But we're on the side of the stirrers-up, eh?" He sat on the edge of the editor's table, perching himself gingerly to avoid showering papers on to the floor. "That was a great noise we made over that compensation case—remember?—the collier who broke his back and then in despair cut an artery with a carving knife and the judge held that the cause of death had nothing to do with his accident? Oh, we had a great leader that night beginning 'The quality of mercy is not strained . . .' We got very near contempt."

"And what happened?" asked Seth, tho' in truth he knew well.

"Nothing," said Lovelace, "except maybe the choirs in heaven sang louder that day."

"Another of our lost causes," said Seth sombrely.

"Are they lost? That's the point. Are they lost? Who can tell? A seed planted in a youthful breast, maybe. The old man's gone on for years pursuing the gleam in the dark, getting people's backs up, keeping 'em on the straight and narrow. And they don't like it, Seth. They didn't want to stop the halftime system in cotton mills, and they hate us for cavilling at four hundred thousand people being employed in the gambling racket when coal and cotton are starving for labour. Give us our football pools and let the country perish, they say. The great British public is reactionary, Seth. You and I are born reactionaries. Don't deny it! I like my beer and I like it strong and at all hours

of the day and night. Be damned to licensing hours! If I want to
put my shirt on a horse, who is any man to say me nay? If I
want to spit in the tram, why not? Now the old man is our
conscience, Greycastle's conscience, sometimes England's conscience. He's a prophet, a scarifier, a fighter for our souls, Seth.
Without him we're lost, practically burning in the pit this very
minute." He paused. Then, "He'd certainly have been burnt
at the stake if he'd lived at the right time."

"He's got the eye of the Holy Ghost," said Seth, catching
the glow from Lovelace.

"His voice is as the voice of the wind," said Lovelace. "It
can be as the cooing of doves and it can be as the thunder in the
valley."

"When his feet come along the corridor, the floor-boards
shake," said Seth.

"He gives us hell, Seth."

"He does, he does."

"And yet we love him."

"We do," said Seth—"when he'll let us."

"Does he overpay his men, Seth?"

"Ah—you've touched a sore spot there."

"Does he think anybody should have a day off?"

"They don't figure in his calendar," said Seth.

"The *Star* is his meat and drink," said Lovelace.

"Give him a boiled egg and an apple and a bite o' bread and
butter and he's good for eight hours' solid work," said Seth.

"When he lights a cigar it's like running up the storm cone."

"When I smell it comin' down the corridor, I crawl behind a
machine," said Seth.

There was a pause. Then Seth said: "How is he lately?"

"He'll do—made of fiddle strings and concrete."

"Nay, nay. That wound he got in the first war—I've seen him
nearly doubled up wi' pain. But you were with him when he got
it—*you* know."

Lovelace thought: "Yes, I know." For a moment or two he
was back on the sunken road near High Wood on the Somme
with Blackwood hit by shrapnel in the stomach and legs, and
himself, Lovelace, a stretcher-bearer then, lying out in front with
him, unable to move him lest the poisons from the intestines
should infect the wound and put paid to him. They were captured

and recaptured that night and the Germans had been good about it—hadn't tried to move him. By God, a lifetime gone and yet how clear it was.

Lovelace said: "If he's like he is with half his guts shot away what would he have been otherwise, eh? Churchill would have had to look out."

"He would an' all," said Seth. "By the way, what's the news o' our proprietor, the baronet, tonight?"

"O.B.'s gone to see him."

"Sir Thomas always looks apoplectic to me," said Seth, shaking his head. "Would you like a pull of his obituary?"

"Now, now, Seth, be charitable."

"Don't say I didn't warn you. Nowt like having the graveyard up to date—'specially the boss's tombstone." Seth took his departure, a couple of long galleys floating like a pennant from his chubby hand.

CHAPTER VI

OLIVER BLACKWOOD, SUBJECT of the foregoing conversation, was a man of medium height and, in his fashion, of considerable handsomeness. That is to say, his eyes were dark grey and very fine and sparkling and his nose aquiline with a touch of Roman in it. The brow was noble and square and the skin had an almost marble pallor. The mouth—what could be seen of it, for he wore a beard—was curved and sensitive; the rather sensuous bottom lip had been compressed so often and so hard that it had been drawn thinner and tighter than it had been meant to be. The beard itself was still mostly dark—it had been close to black— but the streaks of grey were now being added to year by year. In build he was lighter than his squarish figure and his beard led one to believe. In this sense he was rather deceptive. Perhaps it was not the only sense.

He was, for example, rather weary and exhausted when he left his house to drive over to Sir Thomas Molyneux, yet he showed little sign of it. He had laced his belt tighter that morning when he rose. This belt was ribbed with whalebone; he hadn't been without one like it for thirty years, it held him together in a very real sense, and the more troublesome the day that lay before him, the tighter he pulled it. (In much the same way he had been wont to lace his boots tighter when returning to trenches after rest.) Moreover, a tight belt did something to deaden the pain to which he was still subject—indeed, from which he was never wholly free. It was with him like a brother. The top right-hand pocket of his waistcoat held a phial of pills, one of which he sometimes took when the ache grew too intense or developed a sharp stab. It was astonishing, he would reflect, what you could grow used to. It was interesting too, in its way, to fight the battle not to take the pills; and yet, when the effort of suppression had been prolonged, he was familiar with the tremor that would run through him, on the odd instant, so that he vibrated like a steel wire in wind.

The causes of exhaustion now were simple enough. He had been later than usual at the *Morning Star*—they had remade the principal news page owing to a serious mining accident at White-haven—the shaft went under the sea—and he had stayed to see the page through and to do a short leader on it. He had driven home through a storm of rain—a sudden change in the weather which affected his old wound and gave him a restless night. And at breakfast Hannah, his wife, had let fall casually that she believed the *Centurion* had returned to be based on 'Greycastle, and was in dock. He had glanced at Hannah then, seen the half-smile playing round her mouth, the musing, faraway look in her eyes. He had asked: "How *is* Dryden?"—keeping his voice quiet and as level as the table; nothing in it to betray the thought: "Is this to begin once more, then? Do we put on our playactors' clothes, wear our disguise? What was it Congreve said: 'Let us be very polite and well bred—as if we have never been married at all . . .'" Hannah had said: "I think he's much the same." Blackwood hadn't inquired if she would be seeing Dryden that evening. The thought crossed his mind for an instant that at the time he would be writing his long leader on the complexities of Palestine or Communist infiltration into trade unions, Hannah might be dancing with Dryden at the Grand Hotel. The thought lent his mouth a wry twist for a moment; no more. Wasn't he steeled with the years? He had watched Hannah with perhaps greater attention than usual after she gave him the news—had realised she could still move him intolerably, had wondered for an instant at the mystery of it, asked himself why it was that Hannah with her heavy body and rather clumsy gait, her over-large mouth, her long and rather irregular nose, her grey eyes with their specks of yellow, should still stir him so profoundly. Asked himself? But he thought he knew well. It was, he supposed, the passion in her, the force, the sheer animalism, the delight in sea and wind, the zest for food and drink—all giving her, at her best, an immense radiance and sparkle. And till the war had made an end of part of him, he could match her, though in a different way. She had said he lit the flame in her; had given her the feeling that he was the framework of her being. Oh, she had loved him, she said, more than he loved her; a divine match, she had said it was. She had refused to let him go when he had told her in the hospital at Blandford in 1916 that his injuries made it better so. She had said: "You are alive, alive, and O God! I have dreamed so often you were dead. Alive, my love, alive! That is enough, that is enough. I will not leave you, or let you leave me!"

That was a long time ago; a long time. They had lived through a good deal of torment together since then. Hannah would have had to be a saint to bear it all, to live with equanimity the sort of life that was inevitably theirs. So life had worn them down and sharpened the edges of the relationship. Would he have poured so much of himself into the *Morning Star* if life had been otherwise? Maybe not. Maybe nobody but Hannah knew that. And Lovelace—the hard-drinking, Celtic Lovelace, variable as the shifting river? Maybe an inkling there.

What, he wondered, did Molyneux want to talk to him about? It would be in accordance with the rhythm of things if it touched on that sore subject—Molyneux's wife and her views on the *Morning Star*. Blackwood's mouth was compressed at the discomfort of his thoughts and at the pain in his loins. Not single spies . . . There were days born of the sun and days born of the dark. . . .

Sir Thomas Molyneux was in bed when Blackwood arrived, and was mixing himself a drink. The bedside table, inlaid to make a chessboard, was resplendent with bottles. Molyneux was less comely—he had not troubled to shave and both the stubble on his chin and the grey bristles on his head caught the light. A thick-set man, whenever he moved in the bed he threatened to topple over, and to avoid this had thrust out his stumpy legs in the shape of a V under the bedclothes. His voice, naturally thick, was husky with a cold.

He waved a fat hand to Blackwood. "Sit you down, Oliver. Have a whisky? You look as if you needed one. I certainly do. I'm glad you've been able to come. I couldn't get to the office—and there's something I want to talk to you about." He grew thoughtful, narrowed his grey eyes which were glazed, iridescent, like the inside of an oyster shell.

"I wanted to see you. How are you?"

Molyneux grinned. "Can't afford to die yet—not for five years anyhow. I've given a lot of money away to the wife and suchlike to dodge death duties. So I'm taking no risks, that's why I'm nursing this—must do the Government in the eye."

"Ah," said Blackwood, "the old complaint was that we were taxed *out* of existence—now you tell me the reverse. Would you say this is why we're becoming an older nation?"

Molyneux smiled. "I must tell 'em that at the club." He drank his whisky down and poured himself another.

Blackwood asked; "What were you doing to get this chill?"

"Shooting—boots let water in. What's happened to the leather? Those politician friends o' yours usin' it to repair their own hides, I suppose?" He paused to get his breath. "I liked your leader about defence. You're a rare bird, Oliver, a Radical fire-eater, lover of the Old Sweats." He lay there breathing hard. Then he said: "I keep on asking myself—was I right to encourage Godfrey to go into the Coldstream? I wanted him in the Guards—never occurred to me he'd get more dirty work to do than in a line regiment. Was I *right* to get him in the Guards?"

Blackwood said: "Yes; perfectly natural—even if they get the toughest jobs—and I think they often do. As for Fate—who can circumvent that? No, Thomas, I think you were right."

Molyneux said: "At first—I mean when he got killed—I stood it better. Other men were losing their sons and—the usual idea is that it bowls you over and then you get used to it—time, and all that. It's been the opposite with me. Time just—rubs it in. Goes deeper. Aye." He leaned over to the table and gave himself another drink. Then: "Nobody I care tuppence about to inherit." He paused. "I apologise for this. I didn't ask you to come for this." He looked for a moment a broken man, huddled up, sad, and remarkably ugly.

Blackwood said: "You've nothing to reproach yourself with, Thomas; outside your control."

Molyneux looked up. "If I'd acted sooner—more childer, maybe."

"Men can't always have them." Blackwood spoke sharply.

After a silence, Molyneux asked: "Yours all right?"

"Yes, he's all right."

"Bob's not much like you—flying his aircraft."

"That's the way children are."

Molyneux said, his tongue loosening with the whisky: "I can see a lot of his mother in him but I've never been able to see much of you." He didn't notice the frown that crossed Blackwood's face, but went on: "He's got his mother's build." He continued garrulously, "You're very dark and he's very fair—nothing of that look you have—a bit Irish or Italian—you remind me a bit of a picture I once saw of that Roger Casement—did I ever tell you? Spanish grandees in your family somewhere, eh? Or kings of Ireland?" Molyneux was now pleased with himself, lit with drink. He went on:

"I believe in family—keeps cropping out. My wife comes from the Crows—Crow was captain of the last slave ship. When she tells me she never knows why she married me, I tell her the reason—although she doesn't like it. She married me because ours is one of the oldest baronetcies in the kingdom—bought from King James for a thousand and eighty pounds in three annual instalments. She won't believe that, but it's true enough. Aye. Oh, family keeps cropping out right enough. Something in Fanny would like to use a whip on people—I tell her that too. When she gets on to me about my vulgarity, I tell her that." He wheezed and grinned and slumped down again.

Blackwood said: "You're talking too much, Thomas. Tell me what you want to see me about before you're too tired."

"I'm getting there by degrees. Give me time. Have another drink." He helped himself. "I need it—heart, you know." Molyneux looked slyly up at Blackwood, and took a fierce pull at the glass. Then: "Fanny hasn't forgiven me over Godfrey—

41

thinks I ought to have got him exempted somehow—and she wants to leave the town. So she drags Godfrey into it—never forgives, never forgets. 'Sell the paper,' she says. 'Let's clear out. It isn't as if Godfrey was alive.' Aye." He stared at the glass in his hand. Without looking up, he added: "She hated that leader you did about reforming the Lords, abolishing the hereditary principle. Gave her another excuse for goading me. But you wouldn't understand that—you being happily married." Molyneux looked at Blackwood, encountered his dark eyes clouded and inscrutable and turned his own away again.

Without further preamble, Molyneux said: "I've been approached to sell the paper again."

Blackwood said: "I see." It sounded like the comment of a judge. For the moment it aroused no great feeling in him. It wasn't the first time offers had been made.

"That surprise you?"

"No. It was the brewers' interests last time, wasn't it?"

"It's not them this time."

"I see."

Molyneux waited to be asked who it was, and after a moment, feeling a little disappointed, he said: "It's Sedgwick."

Blackwood moved in his chair. This was, he realised, a different kettle of fish. Lady Molyneux and Sedgwick together might be a powerful combination. He inquired: "Did you go to him or did he come to you?"

"Does it matter?"

"History may be curious." Blackwood smiled, and Molyneux mistook it for good humour. He went on:

"My wife ran into Sedgwick's man, Pick, at Lord Timperley's. How far Pick arranged that I don't know. He's what they call a fixer. Fanny brought a message—would I lunch with Pick? Met him at the Grand—private room. He'd a lot to say about Sedgwick and his newspapers—their crusades for the Empire and clean journalism."

Blackwood said: "Nothing about their astrologers, I suppose?"

Molyneux said: "No."

"Did he name a price?"

"Yes, after some time he did—round about four hundred thousand. Though he made it clear it wasn't simply a question of money—there was the crying need to win the nation back to

42

Conservatism. Spoke vaguely about Sedgwick being close to Mr. Fortinbras and my not being overlooked when baronies were conferred in due course. Hinted the country is in my debt already."

Blackwood said: "Had he mentioned the barony to your wife?"

Molyneux replied: "I'm afraid so. She'd enjoy a barony. Women do."

Blackwood said: "You didn't inquire if that consideration would be put in the legal documents if you sold?"

"No, I didn't—didn't think of that one. I wish I had. Well, by this time my vulgarity was in full swing and I said: 'Brass, Pick, brass, that's the thing. How much?' He then murmured something about the figure I told you of and asked would I see Sedgwick himself if he came up to Greycastle. I said I would— and that's where it stands."

"Thank you for telling me all this."

Molyneux sank back into his pillows, content with his afternoon's work. "I had to tell you. You'll have time to put yourself into a good bargaining position if I sell."

"You're seriously thinking of selling, Thomas?" Almost involuntarily Blackwood had invested the question with an edge, and Molyneux said more grumpily: "Depends what he really offers, of course."

From the river a ship's siren blew—a hoarse blare from a big vessel—probably a ship slewing in midstream. The sound had a warning note and it struck Blackwood how appropriate it was to this moment. He could see Molyneux's point of view—ailing, his son dead, his wife termagant, Sedgwick tempting him. All the same, it had to be fought, the business put into its right frame. He said, speaking reasonably, almost gently: "A newspaper like this isn't—merchandise, Thomas."

Molyneux sat higher on his pillows, roused a little: "You know how costs are going up—price of paper—printers' wages."

"It's paying five per cent, isn't it?"

"What's that—these days?" Molyneux spoke as if the plague were rampant.

Blackwood said quietly: "And there are other things. Your honorary D.L. at the university."

Molyneux flushed. "You mean you earned it for me?"

"I suppose the *Star* earned part of it. It would hardly have been —your shipping interests."

Molyneux said pugnaciously: "And you mean you're the *Star*?"

"Not altogether by any means—a lot of other people have done their share."

But Molyneux wasn't mollified. He said, as if it were a grievance: "Everybody knows who runs the *Star*. But *my* family started it—not yours."

"Certainly they did, Thomas. And I'd like them to go on owning it—till the day comes when it's turned into a Trust to see it doesn't fall into the wrong hands."

"I'll decide that—it's my property."

Blackwood, a trifle nettled in spite of himself, said: "Up to a point, yes."

"Up to a point? Your own shares are only a handful——"

Blackwood said: "Oh, that; I wasn't thinking of the shares."

"What then?"

"You were a colliery owner, Thomas. But the coal in the pits —and the quality of the seams—you didn't put that there?"

Molyneux growled: "This damned Radicalism again—that's another thing. You little know the ragging and abuse I get in the club."

Blackwood's voice was remarkably dry now: "The price of responsibility and privilege, Thomas. Remember the barony on the horizon."

Suddenly Molyneux asked: "What do you want me to do? You've done well out of it, haven't you? Made it a platform, a pulpit, crusaded for this and that, made a kind of name for yourself; and been well paid for it—paid like a bishop."

Blackwood smiled: "A suffragan bishop, Thomas."

Molyneux sat there growling like a dog.

Blackwood said: "You ask what I want for the *Morning Star*. As I said, I want you to make it a Trust—make it safe from the filibusters and adventurers."

"Safe for yourself, you mean. And what should *I* get out of a Trust, eh?"

"A fragment of immortality, Thomas."

Molyneux made an exclamation of disgust.

Blackwood rose. "A Trust—that is the thing, Thomas." He walked to the window. He could see the river from here, and on the far side the smoky blue mass that was Greycastle.

"I'll decide that."

Blackwood swung round. "Perhaps Greycastle will decide it."

"How will Greycastle decide it?"

"We shall see. This is a free country, Thomas. But we needn't discuss it now. I hope you'll soon be better; take care of yourself." He turned to go.

Molyneux leaned forward in bed: "I ask you again—What's it got to do with Greycastle?"

Blackwood turned back. "It's a strange thing, Thomas, but a newspaper and the town it's printed in—if the paper is the right sort—can become part of one another. Could *The Times* spring from Paris, the *Glasgow Herald* from Dublin, or the *Burnham Guardian* from Bristol? The *Morning Star* is Greycastle, part of the fibre of the place. In a way it's Greycastle's voice. Will the city, do you think, allow itself to be struck dumb?"

"Dumb?" echoed Molyneux. "Dumb? The paper would still come out."

"Sold to Sedgwick it would be one of a heap—a nonentity," said Blackwood. "I don't believe you could do it."

Molyneux half raised himself and clenched his fist. "Don't tell me what I can or can't do. It's my property—isn't it? My property."

Blackwood looked down at him. Molyneux was considerably dishevelled by this time. Blackwood said: "You own the body, Thomas—nine-tenths of it. The soul—the soul belongs elsewhere."

They stood looking at one another, Molyneux's thick fingers pulling at the bedclothes, his face puckered in a frown, unhappy, petulant; Blackwood troubled by the news of Sedgwick's offer, by Molyneux's sickness, by the man's loneliness. But he must steel himself—too much sympathy for Molyneux might be fatal at this moment. So all he added was: "Think it over carefully, Thomas. Your forefathers—and possibly mine—sold men into slavery. This could be much the same." Molyneux made no answer— just lay staring ahead of him as if he had not heard. Blackwood said quietly: "Good afternoon, Thomas. Let us have another talk soon." This time Molyneux nodded, but didn't speak, and after a moment Blackwood left him, went downstairs and let himself out into the garden, got into his car and drove down towards the river.

CHAPTER VII

Whenever Blackwood was troubled, as he was troubled now, he liked to cross the river to the *Morning Star* office by ferry. The journey refreshed him, brought him into tune with—what? The Infinite? He would strive to open his mind and heart to the heavens, and think both of the Divine compassion which enfolded him (as he firmly believed) and of the enduring quality of England, its age, its faith, its quality of standing fast. Was it easier to think thus near the sea and this river which was one with the heavens, unchanging, eternal and able to make him feel the transcience of his being? Maybe it was.

So now he headed his car for the ferry. He would park it close by and pick it up tonight or tomorrow. He had been more disturbed than his remarks to Molyneux had betrayed. That Molyneux could contemplate selling the paper almost as if it were an old tanker or a timberyard deeply affronted him. He felt—as he had hinted—that a part of himself was being put into the market; for the paper—for all he had said of the work of others—was stamped with his imprint. All that he was had gone into it; the lover who said "I am a coin for you, spend me as you will," had hardly been more devoted. They talked in Fleet Street about "marrying the job"; well he supposed he had done that, imprisoned himself for the paper; and gloried in doing it, seeing it grow, feeling it in his hands like a live boat in a strong sea.

He stood on the ferry, enjoying the stiff warm wind, enjoying the sight of caps on the dirty water, the sight of bluff boats breasting the chop, the scarves of cloud high today over the irregular skyline of Greycastle. A long low hooting came up the river from deep-sea vessels homeward bound. What was that device round the high wall of the Docks and Harbour Board— "They that go down to the sea in ships and do business in great waters, they see the works of the Lord and the wonder of His ways." Not only they, not only they. The ferry moved across the tumbling mighty river, Blackwood revelling in the feel of the moving deck, the sway of the vessel, the throb and tremble of her.

Just so the *Morning Star* could be alive and tremble as the great presses started. Something to do battle for.

Blackwood's heart had not warmed to Greycastle in the beginning. It had been in the 12th Greycastles that Blackwood had by the fortunes of war been enlisted. Those early war days of 1914 among the privates who had till lately been dock labourers, corner boys, warehousemen and shipping clerks—sprinkled, of course, with the unemployed—and who were treated as if they were convicts—for they lacked uniforms, were ill-fed, lousy, and fobbed off with two or three shillings a week pay—those days were still a lively and uncomfortable memory at the back of his mind. It was strange, in a sense, that it was to Greycastle that he had shepherded that first batch of down-at-heel recruits from Burnham, and that to Greycastle he had returned as editor. A great city undoubtedly. A vast port; a city old, built up on the slave trade; a city that had drawn to it hordes of Irish and Welsh; a city the most cosmopolitan in Lancashire, and with more fashion and style than the rest; a city touched and influenced by the stream of trans-Atlantic passengers going forth and returning. And yet by reason of its very qualities and virtues, a city lacking the Lancastrian timbre that Blackwood's native Burnham possessed. "Burnham men and Greycastle gentlemen," said the old saying. Blackwood didn't quarrel with that; he approved it—was tickled by it.

He could say to Lovelace: "You're one of the Dicky Sams, Richard, speaking that strange lingo that calls the pavement the *parapet*, hardly a Lancashireman at all."

To which Lovelace would answer: "I know, I know. But you can't deny it's a kind o' uniqueness. We used to say 'twas a great city for the rackets, and the Tammany Hall atmosphere, and there's as much hell can be let loose in Ireland Road on a Saturday night as there ever was in Belfast or Dublin, aye, or Glasgow. Do you remember Bloody Sunday when I finished my last message to the Press Association—'The troops are firing on the populace . . . end message'? And you don't forget either, do you, the days of the police strike, when the scruffy denizens of the courts and labyrinths came out and played pitch and toss large as life on St. George's steps on the Sabbath afternoon? Ho! show me a better place for a lineage merchant—I'd have been a wealthy man if I hadn't had a hole in my throttle to pour the liquid down."

"You might have had done better," Blackwood would say. "if you had stuck to your newspaper last instead of apeing the man of letters."

"Apeing is the word," Lovelace would say.

"You were the best reporter on the waterfront ever I knew," Blackwood would say. "Every time you went down to the landing-stage it was either a disaster or a romance you brought back. Do you remember the consumptive cotton operative who had a heroic wife who went out to New York to build a home for him over there?"

"Don't mention it," Lovelace would say. "As good a bit of honest faking as ever I did, and nothing but the grace of God prevented me from getting fired over it. For I invented it for one of the London dailies and they made a little splash of it and demanded the name of the woman so they could wire their New York man to get another story when the ship landed."

Blackwood would say, "No wonder you turned to fiction after that".

"It's like this," Lovelace would say, "the subs. always remarked that my reporting read like fiction and now the critics say my fiction reads like journalism."

"Good evening, Wilfred," said Blackwood, going past Fletcher's deal counter whereon innumerable copyboys had cut their names.

"Evening, sir. Couple o' letters, sir—just come in."

"Thanks, Wilfred. How's the leg tonight?"

"I'd say there was a storm comin' up, sir. Mr. Lovelace took some other letters up, sir—Lord Mayor's messenger brought one of 'em."

"Good." Blackwood thought: Another appeal, no doubt. Um!

Blackwood went upstairs and down the corridor towards his own room. A door on the right opened and he almost collided with a plump woman with black ringlets and a mouth permanently open over buck teeth—Lavinia Ward, who edited the woman's page, or rather half-page, for that was all the *Morning Star* accorded her.

"Ah, Lavinia—you were very kind to the Cabinet Ministers' wives." He paused.

48

Lavinia had been up to London to attend a reception so that she could inform her readers what the Ministers' wives were wearing.

She looked up at him gravely. "I had to be, Mr. Blackwood. For my old Sunday-school saw as much fashion. Those stories about Ministers' wives all having wonderful dresses and jewels— all nonsense so far as I could see."

He said: "You contrived to let a little truth shine through."

"Oh, Mr. Blackwood, did I? I did try so hard." Her eyes grew luminous behind her hornrims. She said: "I'm carrying that article on the dangers of excessive smoking. Is that right?"

"Certainly. Have you quoted those figures—families with an income of five pounds a week spending two pounds on cigarettes?"

"Yes, indeed, Mr. Blackwood. Oh, what a change it is from the *Comet*, where I had to submit every article to the advertisement director! He would have killed this one on sight—offending the tobacco firms. I can breathe here!" And she took an enormous breath which made her blouse excessively tight.

"Yes, yes, Lavinia. By the way, find out why it is I see so many women golfers carrying their own clubs while their burly husbands have caddies. You might start an amusing correspondence."

He walked off, while she stood murmuring: "Yes, how very interesting."

Blackwood glanced at Lovelace as he crossed his room to hang up his hat and coat on the old revolving hatstand.

"Well, Richard? Did you catch the last bus? Or did you decide to finish the chapter?" Blackwood was stooping over his desk, turning over letters, proofs and a medley of messages, seeing if anything vital and explosive awaited him there, half his mind on this, a particle of it on Lovelace. He sat down with relief in his oaken arm-chair and enjoyed the reassurance it gave him as his back fitted in.

Lovelace lifted his long frame, giving himself the excuse he wanted for ceasing to think. He said: "I finished a short story— one of those things I never manage to sell."

Lovelace was looking down at Blackwood, his weak eyes screwed up as he rolled a cigarette and dribbled particles of tobacco on to the worn carpet. He inquired: "How was the monarch?"

Blackwood looked up. "His blood pressure, I imagine, was rather high when I arrived—and no lower when I left." He said nothing about the question of selling the *Morning Star*: that could wait; not a topic to begin the night's work with. Instead he said: "I gathered that his wife doesn't like the Socialists any better. Do you observe, Richard, these signs in England of political animosity that is almost American in virulence? The Tories are shocked that the Socialists should behave like Socialists. And yet, Richard, there's the unctuousness of Labour."

"These cursed politics, Oliver."

"My favourite niece Charlotte said to me just after the election that, of course, Labour could not have the capitalist Press sabotaging the Socialist State. She thinks nothing short of extermination will do for the Liberals—judging by her letters from Oxford."

Lovelace said, smiling: "A bit of the Blackwood bluntness coming out in her."

Charles Greenhalgh, the chief sub-editor, came in, perspiring in a black alpaca jacket, torn at the front and greasy with spilt tea, his enormously blunt forehead freckled and red from daily golf.

Blackwood asked: "What's in the London letter, Charles?"

"Only half of it has come yet, Mr. Blackwood—more about Cripps's Working Parties—something about the Commons being overworked—and the gallery men, too."

"Ah! Our faithful Longworth making his protest. How does that middle-class cost-of-living budget look?"

Greenhalgh beamed. "Oh, very well. Bears out what I thought. Looks as if you'd have to give a professional man five hundred a year for every child to make it worth while having any."

"Worth while, eh?" murmured Blackwood. "The profit and loss account on children—how's that to be reckoned up, Charles?"

"I could put part of it into figures," said Greenhalgh, a touch of stubbornness creeping into his voice. "If you have a thousand a year and four children you're reduced to the level of a four-hundred-a-year man."

Lovelace thought: "Charlie can't forget he's had five while some of us have had none." But he didn't speak. Non-intervention was the rule when Blackwood talked to his staff. And Lovelace knew to a nicety when to withdraw out of the room and down the corridor.

Blackwood asked: "What's the best lead, so far?"

Greenhalgh said: "The coal debate is promising. Mr. Fortinbras has declared that when the Minister says there'll be no coal crisis he's a lunatic—that there'll be a coal crisis till we're exporting seventy million tons a year as we did in 1913."

Blackwood inquired: "Did Fortinbras suggest that a lot of us perform jobs that, compared with hewing coal, are not of much importance?"

Greenhalgh, a trifle shocked, said: "No, he didn't go as far as that." Greenhalgh withdrew. Between his going and the entry of Herbert Bryce, the chief reporter, Blackwood said to Lovelace: "You'd make a pretty good checkweighman, Richard."

Lovelace smiled. "My foot would be on the ladder to the Cabinet. Fourteen ex-miners in the Ministry, isn't it?"

Blackwood said: "The pendulum swings, Richard. There were two dukes and sixteen lords in Mr. Fortinbras's Caretaker Government."

Mr. Bryce, who was now standing silently in the room, resembled a shabby lawyer—a wing collar, striped trousers and a rimless monocle on a black cord. He waited, precise, important, deferential.

"Anything good tonight, Bryce?"

"I'm afraid not very good, Mr. Blackwood."

"No *Titanic* disaster to displace the coal debate?"

"No, sir." Bryce spoke sadly.

"The night is young, Mr. Bryce. Time for the tower to fall off the cathedral or a ferry boat to capsize. You must not delude yourself into thinking people buy the paper to read my leading articles. It is your department, my dear fellow, that keeps us going—the murders, floods, and scandals in high places. It is a mystery to me, Mr. Bryce, why we do not discover things before public events make them manifest. Consider the terrible state of England unveiled by the wartime evacuations—the children not even house-trained. England of the dark ages suddenly revealed. But why didn't we of the *Morning Star* know all about that before? Why are we taken by surprise? A good newspaper should *never* be taken by surprise, eh?"

Blackwood leaned back and tapped his strong teeth with the end of his spectacles.

Bryce polished his monocle. "I agree, of course—in theory. Indeed, I've made a small investigation today——"

"Ah!"

"Dining at the club last evening, James Butterfield, who manages the clothing factory, said to me there's a marked difference between the boys and girls he takes on. Girls splendid—boys young hooligans—no respect for law, or for their elders, or for sex. I followed it up—varied opinions, of course, but the balance on the side of the girls. The bishop has said something caustic about films undermining youth. A schoolmaster says he came across a group of his boys who are hopeless at arithmetic in school, working out in their heads with great facility the bets they had won or lost on horse-racing."

"Good. You've covered that flood in Cheshire?"

"Yes, Mr. Blackwood. We've got good pictures on that, too. I find that that village has been flooded every year for nine years."

"Excellent. Ask the chairman of the county council what the reason is—are they training gondoliers down there?"

Mr. Bryce still paused.

"Anything else?" Blackwood's tone was a trifle sharper.

"The city council are to discuss the concert hall with its stage for plays—the municipal theatre idea."

"Good. Do that pretty fully. Smite the Philistines."

Bryce waited another moment or two, then took himself reluctantly away. He had hoped he might be invited to write a short leader on some topic or other. He had hoped this for several months; but it had not happened.

Blackwood said: "I think, Richard, before I go to supper, I'll write something about the situation in the British Zone in Germany. Our Government policy goes back to the Luddite rioters." This was the signal for silence.

Lovelace settled down to his own writing with a stump of pencil. Blackwood dipped his pen in violet ink, his office trade mark; no doubt which were his own corrections on a proof. A violet ink correction was a "must". They hadn't been writing long before Greenhalgh came in and quietly placed a sheet of teleprinted copy close to Blackwood's elbow. He paused in his writing to glance at it.

It was a new paragraph of the London Letter beginning: "Mr. Sedgwick announced this afternoon that he has acquired the *East Anglian Daily Chronicle*." There followed some details of the journal's history and its editors, one or two of whom, in an early period, had been distinguished. The paragraph concluded: "There is speculation in Fleet Street on whether Mr. Sedgwick's ambitions as a newspaper-owner are now satisfied, but this is thought to be doubtful. He is known to have made approaches, in the past, to the owners of the *Burnham Guardian*, which is now, of course, a Trust. He has spoken frequently of his pride in his native north country and there are those who would not be surprised if he tried to extend his ownership there."

Blackwood murmured: "Thank you, Charles," and pushed the paragraph back.

"Shall we let it go as it is?"

"Yes. I'll probably do a short leader on it."

He went on with his writing.

CHAPTER VIII

Mr. Sedgwick travelled north by car; in short, by two cars. The petrol restrictions which applied in Britain at this time to private citizens who wished to see the glories the Almighty had dispensed over the land, or to visit their ailing and lonely friends, did not apply to him, any more than to Ministers of State. He got all the petrol he wanted. He moved by car. Nobody was likely to criticise aught he did. Dog did not eat dog (or rarely) and Ministers of the Crown were not so invulnerable in the matter of privilege as to wish to start a battle with those in high places on this pettifogging question of a few gallons of petrol, more or less. Certainly express trains—which everyone was supposed to use instead of motor cars—ran to Greycastle as they did to Burnham, and you could, on these British trains, which now belonged to each Englishman equally and by right, reserve a compartment or two, did you so wish. But British trains were not precisely a Rolls Royce car, nor did they carry the stamp—or the privacy. Mr. Sedgwick favoured a small entourage; usually two, and sometimes three, cars on these sorties into the provinces. This was the way army generals and foreign potentates moved, and what was he if not a prince and a commander? Moreover, he needed secretaries and expert advisers. On this purchase of the *Morning Star* he needed the impeccable Pick; and he required the services of Colonel Watson to give to his suite the requisite tone and formality; maybe to keep intruders at bay. For you never knew these days—communists and all that. So here Mr. Sedgwick was, travelling in the first car, accompanied by Mrs. Tremayne (who at this moment—three in the afternoon—was sleeping like a child), with the second car riding at a distance that showed respect but enabled it to avoid getting lost or unduly delayed, and carrying Sir Frederick Pick, Colonel Watson and Miss Agatha Price, who was equal, in Sedgwick's view, to half a dozen wire recorders or dictaphones. There were those who asserted he had had children by her, but this was not true. Indomitable as he was, he was not equal to that.

Although it was true that Miss Price was more than equal to a portable dictaphone, a dictaphone was still necessary, as on the present occasion. Mr. Sedgwick glanced at Mrs. Tremayne and saw her breast rising and falling with an engaging rhythm and her rosebud mouth emitting, once in a while, a tiny burble of air and moisture which, as he gazed at her admiringly, formed into a tiny iridescent bubble. He watched it burst with great pleasure. This would be something to plague her over—plague being a word he had inherited from his father. He would tell her she had been snoring. Affectionate badinage was one of the joys of life. Yes. He did not wish to disturb her but he knew she slept with great soundness (on occasion, that could be unfortunate) and he imagined he could do a little work without disturbing her. At all events, he would try. So now he began, with great circumspection and an air of terrible secrecy, to speak into the instrument words which Miss Price would in due course transcribe on to sheets of paper, and make known with becoming éclat throughout the Sedgwick kingdom. (There were those inside that kingdom who dusted the seats in the telephone boxes before they spoke to him.) He dictated as follows in his rich voice with a touch of the north country in it:

54

"Since leaving London this morning, I have been studying my papers closely. Stop.

"We did not make enough of the fact that at a South Yorkshire colliery, when a miner was killed, the pit shut down for the whole day entailing a loss of 3,500 tons of coal. We all deplore the loss of a miner's life but we deplore even more—no, cross that out—we deplore also the loss of the nation's lifeblood. For we cannot live without coal. Paragraph.

"Continue to draw particular attention to the fact that the first-fruits of the planned state are trickery, evasion and dishonesty. Play this up. Quote all bishops and chiefs of police who say we are not the honest people we were. Stop. It occurs to me we had better get some first-class interviews on this subject from prominent men all over the country of all parties, or none, provided they are willing to take our line, which is that controls make for dishonesty and that the Government favour controls for controls' sake. Paragraph.

"I was surprised to see that our literary editor had given so much space to the novel by Jeremiah Bentley called *The Sword of Damocles* in which the British Press is shown in an unfavourable light. The fact that the book is alleged to be humorous and satirical does not mend matters. The Press has enough enemies, especially in the Cabinet, and we cannot afford to cry stinking fish. No further references to this book or to its author will appear in my newspapers. Repeat no further references. I shall expect an explanation from the Literary Department. The notion that the arts stand divorced from politics or public affairs is untenable. Everybody knows that far too many novelists and dramatists have leftish tendencies. Remember Shaw and Wells. Paragraph.

"Circulate once again my instruction that a close watch must be kept to see that headlines do not give false impressions. This is our aim at all times.

"In addition, issue a new order: Never accept any statement of which there is the slightest suspicion. Never use a half-fact as a fact. Never turn probabilities or possibilities into established facts. Never exaggerate. Keep to the truth. Keep to the facts. This is the Sedgwick credo on which our success is founded. Paragraph.

"No references to my visit to Lancashire will appear in my papers until I authorise them. Stop. I wish to see all references, however, in other papers. Print in all papers on the main page the short leading article from the *Morning Star* on the subject of newspaper chains. But make no comment. This omission of comment may be relied on to intrigue the public."

Sedgwick carefully placed the speaking tube into its receptacle, glanced at Polly Tremayne to see if she was still sleeping—she was—and settled down to read this *Morning Star* leader once again. It read thus:

Newspaper Ownership

During the past half-century the number of British newspapers has seriously declined both in London and in the provinces. At the same time the ownership of newspapers has fallen into fewer hands.

Those who believe that the Press has a vital function to perform and that democracy as we know it will not work without a large body of critical and independent journals cannot look with any comfort or equanimity on the existing tendencies. Nobody would pretend that what is called the Newspaper Chain, that is, the ownership by one person or group of persons of a number of journals expressing one point of view, must be necessarily inimical to the public welfare, but nobody, either, could pretend that it does not contain the seeds of danger to the free expression of widely differing points of view. If all newspapers spoke with one voice—that of the Government or of any one particular individual—there would be an end of freedom of expression as we know it; and democracy would falter and, next, fall. If control of all newspapers would end freedom, how far can control go before freedom is endangered? There are those who believe that three newspapers—one morning, one evening and one Sunday paper—are as many as should be controlled by one man, or one group.

This whole problem of newspaper control deserves consideration at a time when more than one Press magnate is thought to be considering attempting to enlarge his kingdom.

Sedgwick put down the paper and stared at the higgledy-piggledy countryside near the potteries. There was a coal-pit on the right, and from the yard, with its medley of wagons and locomotives, a dozen puffs of white steam and smoke rose in bursts, as though soundless explosions were occurring. On the left were two small, dark conical hills of pit refuse, bearing a thin straggling vegetation. A number of slag-heaps were faintly smoking. The extremity of one slag-heap was rounded and red, very akin to a sore. How unchanged it was since he had first regularly seen landscapes like this! The same patches of water lying rusty red, the same stretches of water overgrown with reeds, the same stone-walls with broken-down shacks leaning against them, the same dank small fields wherein stood huts built of odds and ends—this "making do" which smelt of poverty. The same ugly Methodist chapels with their slate roofs and clanking bells. This was the beginning of the north wherein he was nurtured. It occurred to him that Oliver Blackwood probably attended such a chapel as that; Nonconformity, he was sure, was in Blackwood's bones. Who did he think he was? God? Did God repose in Blackwood's waistcoat pocket; was he on intimate terms with Him? Mr. Sedgwick reflected that his father, Old James, who did a little work for Blackwood's uncle, had never been able to endure the Methodists either. They were too Puritanical, narrow as a hen between the eyes. They had said racing and gambling were encouraged by his papers, and they had advised everybody to read the *Burnham Guardian* which published no racing programmes or results whatever. Neither—now he remembered the fact—did the *Morning Star*. Well, he would have great pleasure in remedying that omission, once the paper was his. No wonder it had no circulation to speak of. An abode of sanctity, austere, arid. How the Government must love it! Well, he, Sedgwick, would turn it into an abode of joviality and cheerfulness, the organ of men who knew that a little of what they fancied did them good, an organ of Merrie England! (Not too merrie, though, lest the public should grow content with the social revolution in progress. Let us say, he thought, mirth with a barbed shaft planted in the middle of the diaphragm).

He looked out of the car windows once again. He was now running past stacks of pig-iron billets that were pale-brown like faggots of wood. Yonder metal furnace with its old grey, sheeted-metal sides had half a dozen tiny gold lights shining like infinitesimal stars, and from various pipes plumes of steam issued forth. The blackness inside the shed was suddenly broken by a flare, a fountain of pretty sparks. Yes, this began to resemble the neighbourhood in Yorkshire where he was born: the place where men took their pigeons to be tossed into the grey skies; the neighbourhood where his father's sporting papers had given space to whippet racing, knur and spell, trotting, jumping with weights, catch-as-catch-can. Ah! That was the area. More people to the square mile than anywhere in the wide world. Where there's muck there's money. If his father hadn't coined the phrase—he always swore he had—he had lived up to it. What did Oliver Blackwood know of all that? Nothing. Blackwood ran campaigns for smoke abatement. Smoke abatement! Would Willie Lever ever have made a fortune out of soap if smoke abatement had been put into practice? Not for a moment. All this damned reform, taking the spice and flavour and richness out of life. Of course, these chaps running the country now were dead against making a fortune. Grind everybody down, stop anybody from rising. That was the idea. Where would his old father, James, have been in a socialist country? He would have been a compositor for ever and a day. True, they might have made him Father of the Chapel in his old age, they might have allowed him, Mr. Sedgwick, as his father's son, to rise to the honour of being a member of the typographical trade union—that is, if his father had put his name down early enough, for, by heavens, it was like putting your lad's name down for Eton College—you had to do it as soon as he was born—or was it conceived? They talked about the privileges and snobbery of the well to do. Not in it with that of the printers. He wouldn't dare to talk to a printer's labourer as the linotype operator did. He'd like to know how Blackwood got on with *his* printers. Hard as nails, no doubt. These damned Nonconformists usually were. What was this business of printing books by a kind of photography? He must look into that! What if the time came when you could do the same with newspapers? He'd have the laugh of one or two chaps then, right enough! Oh, right enough! His father would have been tickled at that idea. His father had been a pioneer, right enough. You had to get up mighty early to catch Old James. He had stopped the fire-engine more than once to ask them where they were going—unprecedented in his day.

It was his father who had coined the phrase, "Some folk think the smaller the print the greater the accuracy", when contesting the notion that the *Yorkshire Times*, was more reliable than his own journals. "The *Yorkshire Times*," Old James had said, "in leaving out the scandals and the police-court seamy side ain't holding the mirror up to nature—it's lying its head off, gilding the lily." Mr. Sedgwick, thinking of his parent, murmured to himself, "Thou shouldst be living at this hour." He was feeling very satisfied with that quotation—for he was not given to quotations—when Mrs. Tremayne woke up.

She said, in her voice full of sleep and enjoying that immense urbanity that an after-lunch nap always afforded her: "Hello, darling." She opened her eyes languorously and closed them again. "Kiss me," she commanded.

Mr. Sedgwick leaned over and kissed her, and at that instant the car's taking of a corner precipitated him upon her. She giggled and put her arms round his neck. "I love you," she said.

He raised himself and straightened the rug about his knees. "I had a dream," she said.

"I hope it was a nice one."

"It was a lovely one. We were married."

"Now, Polly, don't begin——"

"We were married and had several boys all very like you." She sat up. "It was astonishing how like you they were. They were all very red in the face and they all played rugby football."

"They couldn't *all* be playing rugby football, dear. How old were they?"

"It may seem very strange, but they were all about the same age. They were all about twelve. Several of them had been born at the same time."

"Anyhow," he said, "*I* never played rugby football."

She said: "But it is natural, darling, that your sons should enjoy some advantages you never had. After all, *your* father was never as well-known."

"No, that's true." He was not displeased at being reminded of that.

"And yet he had a son. You are more famous, and you have no son."

"Now Polly——"

"It is not right. I do not believe the king will ever make you a lord if he knows you will never have a son."

"Man proposes and God disposes."

"What do you say, darling?"

"Nothing, dear."

"It is not fair to put it on to God. You could have sons if you wished."

"Not without being married, dear."

"But *I* will marry you." She opened her eyes wide to indicate that no matter how daring this might be, she was prepared to do her duty.

"I have no desire to be married."

"Then what will become of all your estates and newspapers?"

"My nephew Harry will get 'em."

"It is not the same at all. You are flying in the face of Providence."

"You know the reason, Polly."

"I know what you say, that you were once very much in love and that she married somebody else, and that you hope her husband may die and she will marry you. I must say it does not sound very nice. Are you going to murder him?"

"I hadn't thought of doing so—not so far."

"You admit you have been in love since those days. You are in love with me, are you not?"

"Yes, dear."

"If you saw her now you would probably not love her at all. She will have grown very fat and matronly and have many children."

"Well, in your dream I had several myself—by you." He chuckled.

"Every time I speak of marriage you laugh at me."

"Yes, dear."

"But I am very serious."

"I know."

"If you do not marry me, I shall leave you."

"Yes, dear."

"I have no hold over you. How do I know what you are going to do? I never know. Even in this horrid place we are going to—Blackcastle——"

"Greycastle, love."

"It will be all the same—rain and slush, and there will be soot on my nose. Even there you may run into somebody you will fall deeply in love with."

"I shall be far too busy. Don't you realise I am going to buy a newspaper."

"That is what you say."

"I always do what I say I shall do."

"Sometimes."

"Always."

"I remember the night you said you would marry me."

Mr. Sedgwick groaned. He murmured: "With a woman it is never finished."

"What did you say, darling?"

"Nothing, dear."

"Your friend Lord Kemsley has many sons."

"Yes."

"He puts you to shame."

"I know. I am a sinful man, O Lord."

"I could redeem you."

"Darling, I am not an article in pawn."

"If you devoted half the time to me that you do to your newspapers, your life would be worth living."

"My life is very much worth living, dear. I would not be dead for any money. With you by my side———"

"You are a very strange man. Most men are not strange, most men are precisely the same—interested in only two things—but you are strange."

"Thank you, dear. What is coming now?"

"If Mr. Fortinbras becomes Prime Minister again will you be made a lord?"

"It would be very improper for me to discuss that with you."

"It will not be the first improper thing we have discussed, darling. Will you?"

"I cannot tell. I ought to be."

"Has he promised you?"

"Not exactly."

"Why don't you strike a bargain, dear?"

"Polly, there is a streak of indelicacy in you. . . ."

"You mean that that is not how it is done?"

"Yes."

"You men are so absurd. You talk of putting your cards on the table. You dine together to broach an important subject and you get so sozzled before you mention it that by next morning you cannot remember what you agreed on. Isn't that so?"

"Not a syllable of truth in it."

"You have told me yourself. Once you promised to marry me and then next morning you swore we had been sozzled and you had no recollection."

"That was the truth."

"You realise, darling, that we are married in the sight of God?"

"That is a matter for God."

"It is what Lord Nelson always said of his beloved Emma— married in God's sight, he said."

"I cannot come up to Lord Nelson—he was a national hero."

"Your responsibility equals that of Lord Nelson and you need a good woman's hand to guide you."

"You must admit, dear, that I've not done too badly up to now."

"You have hardly begun. You have never won the Derby, you are not even—pardon me—the lowest form of lord, you have no heir, nobody has put you in a stage play, the navy have not named a battleship after you, your newspapers make a lot of money but they have little political influence. Sam, that is what you always say yourself——" For he had begun to protest.

He said: "Are you suggesting, dear, that if I were to marry you the political influence of my papers would increase?"

Polly said: "*I* am capable of wielding immense political influence. There was a Cabinet Minister the other night who . . . However, I promised to be discreet."

He said: "It is no use, Polly. You cannot make me jealous. I know you are the soul of honour."

"I am nothing of the kind. My emotions are easily played upon. You know that yourself. You know how I could never resist you."

"Quite so, dear. That is why I have always found you enchanting. You have not the foolish coyness that spoils so many members of your sex."

"But," she said, "you must not suppose that you are the only man I have found irresistible. Not at all."

"That," he said equably, "was before you knew me, dear."

"No, darling."

"You mean that since you and I have been, as it were, be-
trothed——"

"Yes, darling."

"I am deeply shocked."

"I know, darling, and I am very sorry. But there it is. That
is why you should marry me. It would be safer for both of us.
I find it a great strain. Men are apt to grow passionate with me
and I need something to lean on. If I could repeat slowly to
myself as he kisses my hand—'Now remember, dear, you are
Mrs. Sedgwick' and were I able to cast my thoughts back to the
day you made me yours in St. Margaret's, Westminster, with
the organ playing Mendelssohn's 'Wedding March' and the
choirboys singing 'The voice that breathed o'er Eden' and Mr.
Fortinbras giving me away—my honour would be as safe as that
of my mama."

"Well, dear, that was deeply touching. And why was your
mama's honour so safe? Was she married in St. Margaret's, too?"

"No, darling."

"Why, then?"

Polly sighed. "It is really very sad," she said.

"My darling, what is the matter?"

"It is the way my sense of the ridiculous always undoes me."

"Oh?"

"You must admit that I was worked up to a high pitch of
romantic indignation."

"Were you, dear?"

"Certainly I was. And then I had to blurt out that about
mama."

"I should say that your mama, from the little I have seen of
her, was—in her day—even more enchanting than you are.
More Irish, for one thing."

"You needn't rub it in, dear. I have suffered from comparison with mama all my life. But at all events I have not had
her absurd reasons for living a highly respectable life and keeping
her lovers and admirers at arms' length."

"Beloved, I can hardly wait to hear."

Polly said: "The fact is that whenever she thought of running
away with somebody who adored her and whom she rather
adored in return, she got so excited that she had to spend a
penny. On one occasion, the cab was actually at the door when

63

she had to say: 'Forgive me, Gustav, I am not quite ready.' In the privacy of the smallest room in the house she confided to herself that she could never sustain an illicit love affair cursed by this weakness in her abdomen, and so, after keeping Gustav— who was a Swedish banker and a millionaire—after keeping him waiting for fifteen minutes she returned with her mind resolved and her tummy still rather queasy—and she sent him away."

"Did she tell him the reason?"

"Of course not, darling. She was always very haughty and accused them of trifling with the affections of a devoted and married lady, who had recovered her sense of duty just in time. They were deeply apologetic and sent her the most expensive gifts to heal her wounds."

"They don't sound up to much to me," said Mr. Sedgwick. "They obviously didn't come from *this* part of the world." He looked out of the window at the hideous outskirts of Northwich. "And they hadn't read the novels of Arnold Bennett, who understood women very well and who knew that appeasement is death and damnation."

"So that is what you think."

"That is what I think, love." And Mr. Sedgwick placed his arm round Polly's waist and drew her vigorously into his embrace."

"You are a brute," she said, when she could speak again.

He did not disclaim the compliment.

CHAPTER IX

It was two o'clock the next morning. Mr. Sedgwick and Mrs. Tremayne, who had enjoyed a brief ecstasy followed by a glass of champagne, were now fast asleep, a dreamless slumber of pure contentment. Dreams wherein she possessed seven sons and he owned all the newspapers of Britain could not have been more perfect than this limpid, dark oblivion. For them the world was as distant and silent as if their spirits had already left England and Greycastle and this suite at the Grand Hotel.

And yet, of course, the world was in fact very wide awake; or, rather, considerable parts of it were wide awake; the *Morning Star*, for instance. The *Morning Star* building was trembling slightly to the thundering of the presses in the basement. When you went down the stairs it was as if you descended into the engine-room of a ship. The place stank of oil—and paper. As for the *Morning Star's* editor, this was the time of day, or rather night, when he experienced a small glow of satisfaction, as a conqueror might. The first edition was on his table, a vestige of dampness over the pages and the smell of newsprint in his nostrils. He had read most of the paper in proof, especially the leaders, London letter and main news stories, but he now enjoyed looking at the finished thing, newly born, brought forth, delivered. He turned the pages and drank the tea Lovelace had made on the electric kettle. The signs of battle were about them both—proofs an hour or two old, pulls of odd pages, reference books lying open, one or two newspaper files on side tables, a general disarray. And out of the comparatively ordered chaos had sprung this tidy, symmetrical thing, its opinions as considered in tone as if they had been pondered for weeks or months. Out of this night when he had been a mixture of writer, printer and publisher, had come from Blackwood's mind or control something as weighty, in its way, as an infinitesimal book of history, a book of judgments. His mind suffered a pause there, an abrupt momentary check, for it recalled Sedgwick—the fact that Sedgwick had reached Greycastle, as Mr. Fred Cheshire, the late duty reporter, had informed him. Old Mr. Cheshire had made his customary round of the police, hospitals, fire station, and on this night, as he sometimes did, he had called at the Grand Hotel to have a word with the assistant manager Mr. Peabody and there had learned the news.

Blackwood poured himself out another cup of tea, and allowed his mind to play over the figure of Sedgwick. He had thrust the news aside when Cheshire had sent in his note; there were bigger issues than Sedgwick to be decided then—the leader he was doing on the decline of Britain's prestige abroad. But now ... Sedgwick. It was news, of course, of the arrival of the enemy. So might an old-time general have observed the fluttering of the enemy standards as they appeared over the horizon. In the sight of those banners there was both exaltation—and foreboding.

Sedgwick was apparently moving in this business with some determination; it was only two days since he, Blackwood, had learned from Molyneux what was afoot. Had Sedgwick seen Molyneux this last evening, he wondered? He would learn that during the next twelve hours, no doubt. He must see Molyneux again—he thought he could trust him not to sell without a good deal more reflection. He had heard no more from him since their talk and he himself had made no moves. He could hardly do so until he was presented with a concrete situation. Then, if it became a question of rousing the city—of finding money in a short time—what then? Could he do it? This was a wealthy city—even though it had hardly recovered outwardly from the bombing and although its Atlantic traffic was nothing like it used to be; and although the cotton market had been closed—something the *Morning Star* had much questioned at the time, for it smacked too much of doctrinaire action. Yes, still a proud and mighty city. He could think of a handful of men who might be willing to step in and help—Peter Stead the banker, Raymond Wilberforce the flour miller, Arthur Hesketh the shipowner, John Picton the marine engineer, Harry McGrew the timber importer—these came into his mind as men he knew something of, who had done public work or taken a stand on this or that or had written private or public letters to him, let him know they appreciated what the paper did. They weren't all on his side in politics by any means—most of them were Tories or Liberals moving to the right and Picton, he believed, had turned Socialist—but they were Greycastle men, outstanding in any cause, and, in former days, generous towards charities. How far they still were he didn't know. Who did? The springs of charity were being withered in the blast of taxation. All the same, the *Morning Star* was a business—paid its way. If it were worth four hundred thousand to Sedgwick it couldn't be worth very much less to somebody else—at least he hoped not. When you turned to the other side—letters, art, religion, politics in the broader sense—he imagined he could see doughty figures looming up there. The bishop, Dr. Brodrick, would hardly permit himself to be absent from the fight, this unofficial member of the Labour Party who was better at chastising than at blessing, who could be relied on to be uncompromising; and Mr. William Moffatt who looked extraordinarily gentle in his low stiff collar and wearing a gold ring on his white tie when he spent his Sunday afternoons in the poor boys' clubs but who had a scarifying tongue when he scented injustice. He would doubtless be in the offing too. The God of Brodrick and Moffatt was certainly a jealous one. Blackwood's thoughts were interrupted by Lovelace—would he have more tea? Lovelace came over and perched on the edge of the editor's table—something he was permitted to do at this hour in the morning.

Blackwood lit a cigar and leaned back. "Did you know Sedgwick has arrived, Richard?" Blackwood examined the end of his cigar and blew a column of smoke at it.

"No—what's the old devil after?" Lovelace stopped rolling a cigarette.

Blackwood looked at Lovelace quizzically. "The *Morning Star*," he said.

Lovelace finished rolling the cigarette, licked it, spat out gently and said: "The field will be strewn with corpses." After a pause, he said: "So the London letter par. was no fake."

"No fake, Richard."

"By God!" said Lovelace. He picked himself off the desk and walked to and fro, stooping and drawing hungrily at his cigarette. He paused, and a wicked, amused glint came into his weak eyes. "If I murdered Molyneux—that be any good?"

"His wife would be worse."

Lovelace grunted. "These women—no wonder those I draw all have complexions like cheese." He looked at Blackwood and thought how calm he looked and doubtless was. The Blackwood of the Menin Road again—quietest when things were at their worst. He asked: "What are you going to do, Oliver—or oughtn't I to ask?"

Blackwood said: "It's a bit early to say. I've done some thinking, of course."

"We might raise the town." A light came into Lovelace's eye.

"Perhaps not only the town, Richard." Blackwood put up his feet to the desk and pushed himself back so that he tilted on the rear legs of his chair.

"That's the stuff," said Lovelace, a grin coming over his face. "Do you know him—Sedgwick?"

"Only what I've read—and heard. I understand he apes Northcliffe in his bulletins to the staff. I shall be interested to meet him." Blackwood tugged his beard gently and bit into his cigar.

Lovelace walked about again. "By heavens, I'd give a week's wages to be there! You'll want somebody to take a note o' what goes on, Oliver—he's bound to have some o' them hangers-on with him—fair enough to take me—fair enough. . . . Oho, a month's wages, Oliver, six months' wages. . . ."

Blackwood smiled. "We'll see."

"I could immortalise it," said Lovelace. "I could write it in impeccable prose. I should be inspired. I can feel it coming on. 'Mr. Sedgwick wore a red carnation'—or should it be a green one?"

"Your powerful imagination might work better if you're not there, Richard." Blackwood added drily: "It's never hindered you yet."

"Aye, aye. I know, I know. All the same . . . I could remind him of when I worked for his late lamented father, Old Jimmy. He was a corker, was Old Jimmy. I did the police courts and rugby football for him just before he died. I go back to the days of messenger pigeons, Oliver—pigeons tossed up from the reporters' box with the half-time score, three-quarter-time score and special titbits in between. Old Jimmy used to send up decoy pigeons to lure the enemy pigeons flying to our hated rival, the *Evening Sentinel*. Oh, a bobbydazzler was Old Jimmy! I had to write on art, drama, literature, politics, catch as catch can wrestling and sport of all kinds. No extra pay, neither. No wonder we started a trade union. Old Jimmy used to say: 'Go home? What d'ye want to go home for? Go to the pub, aye, go to the tripe shop, go to the Press club, but go home? Why? You won't find Marie Lloyd there, will you, or somebody being murdered? We provide you with more life in a month than bank clerks get in a year. I ought to be paid for giving you elbow room.' We called Jimmy's papers Eye-openers. All the same . . . he had the feel of it. He loved it—the seamy side, life in the raw— the blood-and-thunders, the tipsters, vaudeville. He said what people liked was to glance into the room when the gas was lit and they'd forgotten to draw the blinds—and that a really good paper did this for you. He had a week-end paper that could make your hair curl—I made many an honest penny subbing on that paper, writing up all the week's dirty cases from the courts; luscious stuff."

Blackwood said: "You're incorrigible, Richard."

"I am, I am," said Lovelace. "The incorrigible rogue and vagabond. Every artist is a vagabond at heart, Oliver. Respectability—by God, that's death."

"Well, Richard, if Sedgwick takes over the *Morning Star* maybe you'll have all the chance you want to be a vagabond again." Blackwood bit a pencil between his teeth and left his teeth-marks in it.

"Aye, Oliver, you do well to remind me. Were you ever in at the death of a paper?"

"That has not been added to my manifold experiences—yet."

"It's murder, Oliver, plain murder. I was on the old *Gazette*— born in reaction and lived on putrefaction, that's what we used to say. Never a good word for the men in a strike. The comps used to swear over their pints in Dirty Dicks that they wouldn't set the bloody stuff; but, of course, they did. Couldn't afford not to set it. And then—I'll never forget that night—we didn't know till two o'clock in the morning. Ben Lovatt told me—the chief sub. Ben whispered it to me, and the tears started rollin' down his face. We'd cursed the paper, sworn we'd chuck it, and now— when the news got round—like a funeral it was."

"You showed a very proper feeling, Richard."

"Like hell we did," said Lovelace. "I suppose"—a wry smile crossed his face—"in the main, I suppose we were like the woman whose old man died and the neighbours sympathised. The wife said: 'Aye, you can say what you like—but there's thirty-five shillin' a week lyin' upstairs.'"

There was a silence.

Blackwood said: "I was thinking, Richard, it would be a strange thing if the edifice built in part on that stuff you once wrote were to take us over. What is it?—'Better to be lowly born than wear a golden sorrow.'"

Lovelace said: "By God, let me ring him up and tell him that one over the telephone." His face was lit up again. "I could ring him up every half-hour—all through the night—torture—like they do in mid-Europe. I could make his life a hell. . . ." He paused. "Or does every man do that for himself?" He looked down his hatchet face at Blackwood.

"The latter, I should say, Richard." Blackwood looked at his watch, rose, and put on his light overcoat. Almost at the same moment his telephone rang and a voice from the lodge said Mrs.

Blackwood had arrived with the car. He put on his soft green hat and gave it a hard pull, down at the front. "You're in the mood for a great chapter, Richard. Draw the great sword. Have at thee, chicanery, falsehood and the double-cross. Tell Charles he can ring me at home in three-quarters of an hour if anything crops up that matters. Good night, mon vieux!"

He went out, and as he did so his face took on a graver cast.

CHAPTER X

BLACKWOOD'S HEART GAVE a small catch when he saw Hannah at the wheel of the car. The sight of her could still do that; and on this occasion there were other reasons, too.

He had tried to dissuade her from coming for him—Lovelace, he had said, would drive him back in his friend's ancient Baby Austin, held together with string and black lacquer. Lovelace liked nothing better, and Blackwood enjoyed it too. There was enough of the artist in him to like being close, at times, to those without money; he'd never had too much himself. Lovelace would talk romantically of how, when they were both very old, they would set off round the world, if Blackwood would come, seeing the sights they had never seen, the Seven Wonders of the World, studying in the evenings those obscure mathematics so that they would discover how the universe was built, learning Russian (which Lovelace said was the future world language— that or Chinese), exploring Tibet and governing as the Grand Lama for a while (he, Lovelace, would make an ideal high priest to Blackwood's Lama, he said) or sitting at the feet of the fakirs of India. Oh, Lovelace had it all mapped out; and although they knew it would probably never happen, they allowed their imaginations to roam on those early-morning drives at the witching hour. At that time Blackwood was a different man.

So he had been sincere enough when he asked Hannah not to bother fetching him. But there was Hannah's evening with Dryden, too. Was it never to end till his life ended, this pang, this torment, this failure to reconcile something, that was neither his fault nor Hannah's—nor indeed Dryden's? Providence, the Fates, God—call it what you would—had fashioned it thus, and it was part of the torment that he saw it largely as a failure in himself that he was not more philosophical. It was, he told himself from time to time, natural enough that Dryden, who had never married and who had come into Hannah's life and his own within a year or two of their wedding, should have an enduring regard for her, for the unbreakable link was there. And yet, of course, he had always hoped that when Dryden had served his purpose—for Hannah had chosen him, not he her—he would disappear. Not an unreasonable hope, perhaps. For Dryden was a seaman, the world his domain. Travel, long voyages, foreign ports—these were his future. That other women would come into his life was certain; with one of them it might be expected that he would make his life, settle down. But that had not happened. When it did not, and in due time the Second World War came, the thought had crossed Blackwood's mind that Dryden might be lost at sea. It was an inescapable thought—and one he could turn over with great equanimity. The merchant marine was in the very forefront—ships were blown up, mined, torpedoed— and Dryden was in the midst of it, sometimes in convoy, oftener out of convoy cutting his way across the oceans doing his sixteen knots, sailing alone. The war might have done a lot of resolving of this business—Dryden on the high seas, himself and Hannah in Greycastle, which had been a considerable enemy target—but it had not. There were seamen—perhaps rather more of them than some of the newspapers led the public to suppose—who, apart from nervous strain, saw little or no trouble while at sea. A charmed life in an inviolate ship—that had been Dryden's fate. He had been given an O.B.E.—as the *Morning Star* had reported. Blackwood had made the sub-editors use a small photograph of the man. He remembered seeing it lying on his desk, portraying this fair, fresh-faced man, very English in his fashion, rather sulky round the mouth, his cap worn at what used to be called "the Beatty tilt", eyes staring and bold and a little too close together. Some stupidity in the face, no doubt, but— as his record showed—courage with it. Gossip at the time said he drank too much. So did many a man. He had been a dashing young fellow right enough when Hannah laid, as it were, her finger on him, and he had been complaisant; as who would not?

He, Blackwood, ought to have been grateful; as he was—for a brief while. Oh, how brief the gratitude was; and how he had failed to rise many inches above jealousy and a mind racked! How much did Hannah know of that? Hard for him to say. Blackwood had kept his torment as secret as he could. Whenever she had spoken of a continental holiday he had said she must go, helped her to make plans. As to who her companions were to be he never inquired; she did not entirely belong to him; she had another life. When, in the beginning, after an evening with Dryden, she would return having drunk far too much wine, he, Blackwood, strove to match her gaiety, had another drink with her, indeed drank two for every one of hers, that the tossing mind of his might be stilled, and her heavy mouth and sulky satisfied look might not offend him. For why should it, why should it? She had half-ruined her life for him. She had plunged into she had known not what, and she suffered now because she had loved him in the beginning too much, been faithful too well, challenged her spirit in a fashion that was beyond her. He, Blackwood, was the rightful one to take the blows—not her, not her, not her. So—let it be.

For a moment, as he approached the car, she didn't see him. Then, as he opened the door, she gave him her left hand. He said, unthinking, "You ought to be in bed, dear"; and an instant later the words smote him. The car moved out past the church and trembled slightly on the rough cobbles. A constable at the corner, recognising the car, gave them a salute, and Blackwood raised a hand in reply. Hannah's face was a greenish mauve in the new lighting which turned everything in Lord Street into a shade of death. Her large mouth was not quite closed and her eyes, he thought, looked large and fixed, as though she were overtired. She might, from her look, have been suffering from dope or hypnosis, but he couldn't think that was so. He frowned, and a spasm of pain crossed his face in the darkness. He took a cigarette and, pausing before lighting it, asked: "Shall I light you one, darling?"

"Yes, please, dear." Her voice was steady but toneless.

He lit the cigarette, carefully moistening it with his lips so that it would not stick to hers. He had often done this for her in the past and now it afforded him, he realised, a momentary feeling of comfort—of permanence, was it?

They drove for a while in silence. He always enjoyed this time of morning, the city mysterious and still save for a distant rumbling of carts or the sharp hum of a car going by on some strange errand or the hooting of a ship down river. You could feel a trifle remote and godlike at this hour; remote from most men and women who were asleep. Thus, as they drove, he grew calmer—almost as if he were faintly anaesthetised, and he was able to ask with perfect quietness:

"Had they had a rough voyage?—I saw that another arrival, the *Empress of China*, had some casualties."

"I think it must have been one of the worst summer storms they've ever had. Rex didn't leave the bridge all one night."

He heard even that as though it came to him from a long way off. He heard himself asking: "Is he—well?"

She said, and he thought she was smiling to herself: "Before I left him he almost went to sleep as we talked." She added: "Age coming on."

"Yes." He thought: "He's younger than I am."

She said: "He's getting very florid."

He said, the judicial quality in him having sway for a moment: "I always thought he stood the war well."

She said, sensing this standing together of men: "Oh, *he* enjoyed the war—like a lot of other men."

Blackwood knew what she thought of that masculine trait, and they drove on in silence for a while. Then he asked if Dryden would be likely to be based on Greycastle long, and she answered that she thought for several voyages. He said: "He'll enjoy that," and, when he had said it, realised it must sound ironic. Hannah made no comment, thinking that Blackwood was entitled to deliver a thrust if he wished. She could have preferred, at times, that he would let himself erupt more than he did. She had no such control over herself as he had, and while she admired it to some extent, she resented it a little, too, and thought it betokened some lack of humanity—or was it only lack of frailty? Blackwood, at this moment, was thinking that it would be a good thing if he could live these coming months always at this hour of the morning, when life and the world were much less real than usual and he could, in a sense, look at himself and Hannah from a distance.

They were driving through the river tunnel and neither of them spoke. The grey-yellow tiled walls rushed by and, with Blackwood, the feeling of queerness persisted.

But part of it was dispelled when she said, soon after they had emerged and were running towards High Shields, the road lined with oak and beech: "Bob's coming tomorrow." It was always to her the news of Bob came, and for her sake he was glad of that, glad she and her son were so close to one another. A small glow spread through him, for Bob's vitality and abounding spirits filled the house when he came, striding about in his flying uniform, talking of the fine meals he'd had in Munich, or the Iron Curtain atmosphere of Prague where a Czech would pick up an English paper and hide it under his jacket as if he'd be scalped if found with it; Bob, who'd never been known to put pen to paper if he could avoid it.

"How much leave has he got?"

"Doesn't say, but I should think four or five days. He's probably coming to try out the second-hand Bentley. How many's this—the fifth since the war?" She added: "Where does he get this passion for change and spending money from?"

He thought he knew well enough; Bob's working life had begun in the war—not conducive to sobriety in any sense. He said something of this and she said she wished they knew more of where he was flying to; when he was away on duty they heard almost nothing—no idea whether he was in Rome, Madrid or Stockholm. "It's almost like the war over again," she said. He said: "No, not as bad as that"; and he put a hand over hers affectionately. He had advised during the war, when Bob was flying Lancasters, that they should not inquire too closely into his movements. He had said to Hannah then: "Suppose you do know he's going to Berlin tonight—you'll tear yourself to pieces listening to the eight o'clock news in the morning—wondering if he's among the missing. No, no, darling, better not know." She had answered with a touch of bitterness, "It's easier for you." "Yes," he had granted, "it's easier for me."

They drove on again in silence. How often he had driven up these same roads during the war—at five or six in the morning, after a night made hideous with destruction and anxiety, probably the telephone wires down and no means of ringing Hannah to learn how she was—whether she was still alive. It seemed a long time ago now. Not much of those days left except—except that Hannah, who had learnt to drink a good deal then to take the edge off her anxiety and loneliness and her fury at a world devoted to war, still had a drinking bout sometimes. But they had grown rare now; and she had begun to sail her boat again and paint her landscapes—a good sign. He drew in his breath sharply. And now Dryden harbouring at Greycastle again; a kind of hard bargain driven by Fate, a giving and a taking. . . . Fate, he thought, had a trick of doing that; in his own life it seemed to occur and recur.

He asked: "Is Bob motoring up through the night?"

"Sure to be, dear. He loses no time."

"So he'll be on the road now. I hope this Bentley doesn't leave the road and take to the air."

"Don't worry, dear. He drives more carefully now."

"Years of discretion." He spoke very quietly.

She replied more sharply. "He's seen too many people killed." She added: "I curse the newspapers sometimes," speaking for a moment as if they were not his business. "The air crashes they publicise—their big headlines." He thought: So it's the mortality of flying since the war, not during it, that is in her mind now. Just so. His own too. Every time the news of an air disaster came into the office he looked quickly, with apprehension, to see if the pilot were Bob.

Hannah added, with another touch of bitterness: "Of course, I know newspapers think they have to do it—the competition. The front pages which depress us today—war clouds gathering— and lift up our hearts a fraction tomorrow—clouds dispersed. A nerve war."

He said: "I know that's how it must seem sometimes."

After a moment, she said: "I'm sorry."

He said: "No—that's all right. I've thought the same. But that's how the world is behaving at present—swinging to and fro, or seeming to—and by the time you've been faithful to what comes on to the news desk . . ."

As they drove through the iron gates of Fielden Lodge—a brick house whose upper part was half-timbered, overlooking the links —she said: "You have a stern creed, dear. If somebody you loved got into a scrape, I wonder what you'd do with the news. . . ."

He didn't answer that. He sensed she was on edge again. He said: "Let me put the car away, darling." She opened the door on her side and went up the steps. She murmured something, but he didn't know what it was. He watched her go. She opened the studded door and entered and the door closed with a click after her. He hoped this was accidental but he wasn't sure. He slid into the driver's seat, enjoying the warmth she had left, turned the car and ran it into the garage.

CHAPTER XI

IT WAS ABOUT five a.m. when Hannah heard Bob's car enter the drive. She had been sleeping lightly, expecting him. He was never far out in his E.T.A. However erratic he might be in money, or his relationships with young women, his movements by road or air were precision itself; so far as weather allowed. He was in the hall taking off his uniform raincoat when she came down. He put his arms round her and kissed her on both cheeks. "Off you go back to bed," he said, "and I'll make up a cup o'."

"No, darling, I'll do it."

"Spoiling the troops," he said. "Here's some cheap cigarettes —I remembered mama!"

He threw two or three packets on to the hall table as if they were dirt. He didn't smoke and couldn't understand why anybody did. Beer, now—beer was a different matter.

"I've some stockings in the bag—or don't you wear them, love?" His banter was common speech.

"Time you had some other young woman to give them to," she said, leading him into the large kitchen.

"No fear," he said.

"How long has it taken you?" She knew he was keen on that, the time element.

"About five hours," he said, affecting carelessness. "I seem to have been passing heavy lorries all night—doing their regulation thirty an hour, which, with the wind behind them, or in front of them, means about fifty. Good show. How's father?"

"He's very well, dear."

"Working himself to death as usual, I suppose. Pity it doesn't run in the family. Look at me, flying twenty hours a month and going strong for a pension."

Hannah watched him as he sat in a wooden armchair. His eyes were rather narrow with tiredness, his brow a little furrowed, his body sunk far back, filling the chair,—big, fair, his flaxen hair coming low on the wide forehead and to a point; he'd a row of war ribbons, led by the D.S.O. and above them the gilt and silver wings. The parting of his hair was growing wider, the hair leaving it. He had grey hair round the ears, not easy to see, so light was he, but she had seen them, oh she had seen them. The mark of the war again, a violent hand on her husband and a finger on her son.

She remembered Oliver once saying he felt he had lived on borrowed time since the First World War when so many of his friends were killed. She herself had felt she lived on it since 1935 or 1936, when England started to rearm. Was Bob living on it now at high speed—for where would he be if a third war began? Dropping his block busters again? Or would it be atomic bombs next time? He wasn't really demobilised—still on reserve; everybody on reserve. His comings on leave now were strangely like those of the war—especially at this hour of the morning—except that his uniform now was a darker blue. She could easily imagine this was a quiet spell between the raids. She asked him now if he had been to Germany lately—what was it like?—was it changing much? This question nagged her—she'd sworn during the bombing of the port that she'd never speak to a German again.

Bob yawned and said he didn't see much difference—our private soldiers lived at the rate of about two thousand pounds a year, selling their cigarettes at a terrific price, getting their sex life for almost nothing—a couple of cigarettes—and enjoying chamois hunting. He gathered that venereal disease in our army was now higher than in either the French or the American. When Hannah asked why that was, he said, speaking in the old R.A.F.'s satirical fashion: "No discipline, dear. Ours is the most democratic army in the world, dear, we don't compel them to use prophylactics, dear, and there's no punishment for V.D., except some loss of pay if they're ill too long, dear. You know what this Government thinks of discipline, dear—and you should hear what some of my R.A.F. friends think about them, too, dear. But there it is. Have some more tea, love."

Hannah said: "Time you were in bed, darling. I suppose we shall spend all these millions on setting Germany up—and then . . ."

He said gruffly: "It'll certainly cost a lot to set up what we knocked down—we certainly wrote a lot of it off, my gallant friends and I, dear. The general notion now, I gather, is that we shall need Fritz to help us wipe out the Russkis—in God's good time, dear, in God's good time. Unless, of course, Fritz and the Russkis gang up together, dear—in which case we shall have had it, dear." He got up and kissed her lightly on the cheek. "I should think we've got about six years in front of us, love—which at one time would have seemed a million years. However, I daresay father is more optimistic than I am, being a wiser person and knowing that man has lived a long time without being extinguished. Come, dear!"

They went upstairs very quietly to avoid disturbing Blackwood and Hannah lay awake for a long while, her mind refusing to be still. Bob under this roof, and, a few miles off, Dryden on his ship. Neither in the town for months and now, both. Very strange. Dryden had asked after Bob but she hadn't told him Bob was coming; she hadn't made up her mind whether she should allow them to meet this time—that was, if she could prevent it; she wasn't sure enough of Dryden's discretion—in drink he could be unreliable. It was a pity she hadn't known more about him twenty-odd years ago—and of herself. They had all changed—almost imperceptibly, but how irrevocably. Life, somehow, had seemed so short a thing when she married Blackwood; they had been living through months when every day might be the last for those you loved; and if you saw a few months ahead, why, that was time enough, that was a lifetime. If she had seen the long years stretching ahead and this incomplete marriage persisting—would she have thrown herself into it? But no use asking that now, no use, no use. Why, at that time it wasn't certain he would survive the war at all, and, besides, she was young enough, idealistic enough and unawakened enough to be ignorant of what the future might mean. It was only as the months went by and proximity to him and her great love for him and the frustration of that incompleted love made her stricken to the soul, that she knew what life was going to be like. They had their own rooms from the beginning, which the servants—you had your servants then—found odd. She had even gone to the subterfuge of deceiving the servants by tumbling the bed, making it a disarray—the first harmless subterfuge. Since then, there had been deceit piled on deceit;

sometimes gay, with Bob very young, and herself delighting in the pleasure she had in him; Oliver himself delighted by him, finding her own looks and traits in him, able to thrust aside (he strove to believe) the awkward truth. That Bob was even half her was enough for him, he said; environment was the thing—the home the boy had, the thoughts around him. If Bob bore no resemblance to himself—what of that? Wasn't that common enough; when did men have sons who were like them or had inherited their bent or their sorts of brains? And in those early years Dryden was a visitor; they played lawn tennis together, swam, sailed the boat; it all seemed a success. And then—as though a wind shifted, as though the sky suffered a change, one hour bright, the next obscured—hardly a precise moment in time when the change occurred—the relationship turned a little sour. Incidents, true: one day Dryden came to see them unheralded; and he had drunk too much; said he wanted to see Bob, who was in bed; and Oliver had told him coldly that that was impossible. She had tried to ease the situation, brought out the drinks, talked of anything that came into her head—of the regatta, the Lennox Robinson play at the repertory theatre, and Oliver had made an effort and Dryden had gone away amicably enough. But the stain was there. And then, at the grammar school Bob was just about the most unintellectual boy they had; good-natured banter followed between the headmaster and Oliver —how odd that the boy should be so utterly unlike his father, and so on. And later, the scrape over money—Bob in debt to a money-lender, money he'd spent in taking a gang of other schoolboys on a trip up the coast, insisting on paying for them all, a kind of wild boasting; harmless enough and yet . . . foreign to the very nature of Blackwood. Hannah had seen Dryden emerging in that, and other things: Bob's recklessness, his dash, his temper sometimes ungovernable—or did he get that from her? And his cynicism— was that from her too? She wasn't sure; the world was different now; the young were more embittered, harder, more critical of their elders. The young people of today had not ever, she thought, been quite so young as in her day and cynicism had come earlier; and why not, why not? Charlotte, Oliver's niece, who stayed with them sometimes could call Bob, when they argued together, a "Fascist type" and be half serious in doing it; Bob retorted that Lottie's half-baked internationalism would get us nowhere—

except to give our atomic secrets to the enemy and lose us the only advantage we possessed. "Fly over Europe," he said, "and see how much brotherhood of man there is." Bob was scornful. Lottie, to him, was like the politicians who knew how to run the world, including the yellow and black races, but had never themselves been further afield than Southend. She, Hannah, was much nearer to Bob. In God's name, she asked herself, what good had it all done, this pretence that we and the Chinese and the French and Germans were brothers? This bringing the world closer together—this flying across the world in a day or two, this incessant talking of fifty nations together at U.N.O.—did the world ever hold so much hatred as in this new age, was war ever so monstrous a threat? The more peoples get together the more danger there appeared to be of slaughter and the universe itself flying apart? What was that Lottie—who was a science student—said about our tampering with the very forces that held the whole thing together? There were scientists, Lottie said, who had thought that the whole world might splinter when the first atom bomb was dropped—disintegrate, one explosion, then nothing. If only one could lock the door, thought Hannah—shut out the world, shut it out, shut it out. She buried her face in the pillow. And Oliver; Oliver presided over the arguments like a judge—tolerant, wise, pointing out this wasn't quite so, that that wasn't quite accurate; the world couldn't go back; just as man had it in his power to blow everything to pieces, just so he could make the desert blossom and put food into hungry bellies as never before—it was all in his own hands, simply up to him. Which road was man going to take? The tears came into Hannah's eyes as she lay there, sleepless, her mind spinning. She had heard it all often enough—so reasonable, so wise, so sane, holding the balances so fairly; and meanwhile the world was getting more and more hideous; and her moments when, as during the war, she felt men were so wicked as to deserve to be blotted out—these were returning. What were those lines—Lonely and afraid, In a world I never made . . . ? And that other thing—it was all mixed up in her mind—O for the wings of a dove—and something about—O that I might fly away and be at peace—like a bird, like a bird. But O liver would never fly. There must be parts of the world, surely, where men could be at peace—far-off—if that was what you wanted. There was, she had read, a part of New Zealand's coast inhabited by men and women who had given up the world, passed it up, written it off, decided its values were hopeless—old fellows who had been chemists, doctors, lawyers and the rest and who now had run away from it all, who tilled a bit of ground, ruminated, sat and thought in the sun, didn't give a damn, lived on tuppence, did odd jobs, took in one another's washing, told tales of how they got there, sat in the gallery watching the crazy world still fighting and battling—for what? Just tell them, for what? And just tell her, Hannah Blackwood, fighting for what? Oh, it would have been fine to go to a place like that if—if she and Oliver had had their own children, been really happy . . . that is if ever people *were* happy. . . . Were they, were they? Adolescent to expect happiness? Call no man happy. . . . How many married women did she know who were happy or happy for long? She had divided her love into two parts—was that true? Could you divide love—split the mind from physical love? Could men and women love yet never be one flesh, these twain never one? They had striven hard enough, she and Oliver. I have been faithful to thee, Cynara! in my fashion. . . . Oh, they both could have said that! For many years, yes, even until now; though it was true Oliver's absorption in his work had been profound but that had come later, much later—since he found in it recompense. No completed love—and what might have gone to make that love beautiful and fine, thrown into his writing, his tempestuous mental energy, his equipoise. Part of her own life thrown into that newspaper? She didn't know. Oh, heavens, how much she didn't know! Thus and thus her mind had raced before, seeking ways out towards serenity like a bird imprisoned in a room. And she had never found it, never found it.

She sat up of a sudden; rose, and groped her way, half blind, to the cupboard where she kept whisky and aspirin.

CHAPTER XII

It was ten o'clock when Blackwood awoke. He dimly heard somebody moving in the room and opened his eyes to see Hannah putting a tray on the table by the bed. As usually happened, the sight of her gave him extraordinary pleasure; in the half light she looked to him beautiful in her print dress and heavy fair hair, which a thin beam of light from the curtain caught as she moved. He murmured: "Hullo, darling"; and she answered: "Hullo, dear. Did you sleep well?" He said: "Yes, darling, did you?" "Yes, dear," she said, lying resolutely.

He felt remarkably steady and quiet within, though his head was heavy and aching slightly. He had taken a sleeping pill and this was the result, this aching head. But it was worth it. He was long past the day when he hedged on the subject of sleeping tablets or felt guilty if he took one. He had felt strangely disturbed last evening in the half-hour before he got into bed, and he'd had no intention of being at his worst this morning. Sedgwick—and Bob —and Dryden—and Molyneux. Well, given seven or eight hours' oblivion he could carry all that.

Hannah asked: "Shall I draw the curtains or will you sleep again?"

"Draw them, darling. Has Bob arrived?"

"Yes, dear."

"Is he well?"

"Very well, dear."

"Is he asleep?"

"I expect so."

"What time did he get here?"

"About five?"

"Did you see him?"

"Yes, dear."

Blackwood looked at her. "So you've had a wretched night."

Hannah didn't answer that. She said: "Let me give you some tea."

He asked: "How much sleep have you had?"

She said: "I don't need much sleep."

Blackwood got up, went to the dressing-table and brushed his hair and beard, crossed to the high Georgian windows. It had rained in the night and drops still sparkled on the railing outside: As he watched them they shimmered, threw out radiations like stars, turned from aquamarine to yellow as the sun caught them. When he raised or lowered his head an inch or two the drops became emerald, gold, almost ruby. He called Hannah over and she, too, came and saw the miracle. He thought: "All you

82

cutters of stone, you creators of the ornaments of kings, you never achieved anything so fine as this." What he said was: "Wonderful what morning sun and drops of water and a dash of wind will do."

Bob's voice behind them said: "Sounds like an R.A.F. lecture I heard years ago. How are you, father?" Bob was in his dressing-gown, carrying a cup to share the tea as he had done when a boy on holiday.

They shook hands, Blackwood trying to break Bob's grip and failing, of course. The days when he could do it were gone.

"You've no business to be up, either of you," Blackwood said. "No discipline in this house." He felt, for the moment, very gay. He went back to bed, and Hannah and Bob sat on the edge of it, drinking their tea. These first meetings always had a glow about them. It was queer, Blackwood thought, that the glow didn't per-sist longer that it did. When Bob was young and he and Hannah returned after an absence, Bob was exuberant in his delight, climbing all over them—but in an hour or two he was off, the novelty over, ready to part with them again. Ah well, here was the glow, and let them rejoice in it. So they gossiped lightly about Bob's plans, about theatres, made a date for golf together, talked of when Bob would take them out in the Bentley. They chaffed him about his women-friends, but Bob was elusive as ever. Those of his friends, he said, who were married with wives working were getting unmarried—divorces or separations—to save income-tax, and were still living together—did the righteous Cabinet realise how they were driving people to live in sin? The talk turned to flying. Blackwood knew Bob had no high opinion of their air-craft as compared with the American machines; had Bob and his friends got any new types yet? Bob shook his head. "They're all right, of course, provided the pilots are good." He grinned. "Actually, I suppose we've got about the worst aircraft in the world. We refuse to buy the Yankee stuff and we use our own. Fine, but it means I fly aircraft that can't rise much above ten thousand feet without discomfort to passengers—can't go much above twelve thousand, anyhow." Bob paused there as if that explained everything.

"Does that matter, Bob?"

Bob said Yes, it did; the air up to ten thousand feet contained just about all the rainstorms and thunderstorms there were.

Very few of their pilots of experience had failed to have their aircraft struck by lightning. The American aircraft, by contrast, shot up to twenty thousand feet and stayed there, serene—virtually no storms. In a few years' time the British, too, would be flying up there. Till then . . .

Blackwood said, his eyes glinting: "Do I understand that we British, then, have just about all the air in the world up to ten thousand feet because nobody else wants it?"

Bob said: "Well, that's not far wrong." He got off the bed. Blackwood thought: "I'll have an investigation made into this."

Hannah asked Bob: "Have *you* been struck by lightning?"

"Yes, I was struck last week." The reply was laconic.

Blackwood asked: "Anything happen?"

"No, nothing really—she took it extremely well. Question of luck, of course."

"You couldn't see the storm coming?"

"Not this one, no. If you know, you go round."

"Nature still incalculable? And the met. imperfect?"

Bob said he guessed so. The foreign met. chaps were seldom as good as our own.

Blackwood's sense of justice and reason coupled with his journalistic instinct was aroused. He had never, since the First World War, been without a feeling in his bones that the English had a way of expecting their young men to perform great feats with poor tools. He himself had sat in trenches in 1915 wearing a cloth cap under bombardment of *minenwerfers*, and with no mortars or rifle grenades to hurl back. Never go in to bat early on the English side, said our generals, for you'll never have the wherewithal to do the job. Um! So now he asked whether Bob thought the poor met. overseas caused any accidents. Bob said it was hard to say—"I think discipline should be tighter. The world seems to be running down." He stared out of the window moodily, his shoulders hunched.

Blackwood waited for him to go on. He knew how strong Bob was on service discipline, remembered the casual but contemptuous things he had let fall during the war about crews which didn't go to the target—crews who turned back when the flack was too heavy for them—dropped their load elsewhere—in the sea perhaps. Bob's view was that the public-school pilots were more likely to hammer their way through than the others—or,

84

putting it the other way, were less likely to turn back; their sense of duty, he thought, was higher. That was his experience, anyway. Blackwood had reminded Bob at the time how many V.C.s and other decorations were won by rankers—no class had a monopoly of courage. All the same, given equal numbers, Blackwood himself thought it likely the public schoolmen would throw up a higher proportion of good leaders—it would be strange if they didn't, springing from families mostly leaders in some walk of life or other. When a cadet-school colonel had been sacked for expressing some such opinion as that Blackwood had written a leader defending him. Did people pretend, Blackwood had asked, that there was nothing whatever in heredity, or in the firm inculcation of responsibility and public duty? But while Blackwood wrote that, he was writing also that all air pilots should be commissioned—that it was wrong for bombing aircraft to be captained by sergeant-pilots (as they sometimes were) with officers serving under them; men doing the identical job should bear the same rank whatever schools or families they came from—so he had argued, but without apparent success.

All this ran through his mind as he waited for Bob to go on. He knew he and Bob didn't see eye to eye on this. But Bob said no more. He turned and looked at his mother, and said: "Time we were pressing on." It struck Blackwood that Bob had suddenly realised his mother must hate this talk. Maybe he, Blackwood, ought not to have raised the subject, although he had a belief that it was better to talk freely about troublesome things rather than bottle them up. It was later, at breakfast, when they were discussing their plans for the day, and he said he thought he must see Molyneux, that he told them of Sedgwick's visit to Greycastle and what its purport was. They both took it quietly, partly the quietness of incredulity; they had regarded the *Morning Star* for so long as synonymous with Blackwood. For almost as long as Bob could remember, this had been the way things were—his having to keep quiet in the mornings while his father slept; this paper being written, talked about, in his home; books and papers of all sorts coming into the house; members of the staff, and especially Lovelace of late years, coming to the house to work or confer; Lord Mayors, bishops, magistrates, Members of Parliament visiting Blackwood at home to talk privately; an occasional dinner-party at the week-end—scarcer during and since the war under the new austerity. But the paper overshadowing everything. This new threat was, to both Hannah and Bob, in some obscure way, undefined but no less real or malignant, further evidence of a world out of control, and the England they found somewhat unsatisfactory —something that couldn't have happened before the war. When they spoke of this Blackwood was impelled to point out that this latter thought was misconceived—the threatened sale was a minor evidence of private enterprise in operation, the private enterprise that had been at its zenith long ago; it was under private enterprise we had had three million men on the dole; it was under private enterprise that the number of morning papers in Britain has been reduced by two or three scores—papers gone, sunk, vanished like ships gone down—and London evening papers fallen from six or seven to three. What Sedgwick and Molyneux contemplated doing was the apotheosis of freedom, the doing precisely what you liked with what you owned, even to the point of destroying it.

"All the same, they should be shot down in flames," said Bob. "Is Sedgwick the man whose father was a jobbing printer?"

Blackwood said he believed he was.

Bob grunted, and added he gathered the gentleman was not exactly a ball of fire. "His father did some work for the great Perceval, didn't he, at one time?"

Blackwood said yes, he thought he did.

"Water ought to fall on him from a great height," said Bob— "through a tundish. You say he's already arrived in this place? Natives hostile. No reason why he should get away with it. . . . Give me some more coffee, mama."

Hannah, whose mind had been turning to what Oliver would do if he left the paper, now said: "Well, Oliver, if you did leave the paper you could write books of your own instead of helping Dick Lovelace to write his." She had always believed Oliver was the inspiration—he was obviously so much cleverer than Lovelace.

Blackwood said he didn't really help Lovelace with his books except to find him office room and the smell of ink and some cheap paper to scribble on.

"You save him from the workhouse," Hannah said.

Blackwood said no, not quite—Lovelace had that jewel in the toad's head that made the difference between writing leaders and being a bit of a Dickens. He had it, and most writers didn't have it.

86

"I like old Lovelace—looks like a housebreaker," said Bob. "Why is it that all reporters look the same? I see 'em on the tarmac, and even if there wasn't a celebrity they were running down I'd still know them in their flop-eared hats—even before they start calling me 'old man'. . . ."

Blackwood was thinking he could add to that: something about sensitive men who had grown hard-skinned, who had taken on a colouring that was a mixture of the bombastic and the ingratiating, the winning and the arrogant—the best of whom within an hour or two would get the bones of a story—investigate, appraise, dress it up, make it readable. He said: "You must look on them as a special breed—artists, detectives, judges, vagabonds, cleansers of public life, all rolled into one; and impoverished, of course."

The telephone rang and Bob went to answer it. Blackwood said he thought it might be Molyneux. Hannah thereupon asked how he was. Blackwood said he hadn't liked the look of him when he saw him last. Hannah said drily: "Nobody could, dear." Blackwood went on to say he thought one day Molyneux might explode—a sort of widespread thrombosis.

Bob returned saying: "The baronet would like to speak to you, sir. Extremely civil to me—I suppose the old scoundrel is feeling guilty."

Blackwood asked them to excuse him and went into his study.

CHAPTER XIII

WHAT SIR THOMAS Molyneux said to Blackwood over the telephone was that he wasn't feeling too good, that he had seen Sedgwick and that he thought he had better see Blackwood again pretty soon—in double-quick time, was the phrase. But he used it dispassionately.

As Blackwood motored round he wondered whether Molyneux thought he was not long for this world and how he himself would take it if that fact were borne home regarding himself. It was a long while now—as this modern world went—since life had been lived

for the day or the week. But when that had been so, he had grown
accustomed to it. And he had had one or two moments in his life
quite unrelated to wartime, when his relationship with Hannah was
so strained that he could have looked on lying down to sleep, knowing that he would not awake, with equanimity. That was the sort of
truth that would have astonished all who knew him, as he was well
aware. How little we knew of others; how inscrutable we were to
ourselves also! In the secret places of the heart what depths un-
fathomed, what regions unchartered. When he learned of a judge
found shot with a fowling-piece between his knees, or of a distinguished novelist who filled her pockets with stones and flung herself
into a rushing stream, or of an ambassador or a Minister of State
who was found dead after taking too many sleeping tablets, he
thought he understood how, like fine crystal that can be shattered
by a powerful chord in music, they had trembled so violently in the
torment of this world, and especially this postwar world, whose
convulsions and threats were unusually brutal, that their very
lives had been shattered into fragments. So far as he was concerned,
he had no condemnation for them. The spirit which could distil
fine poetry from life, which found enchantment in the scent of a
flower or the shape of a cloud, could hardly be expected to square
up to the truth about concentration camps and steel whips as
easily as did an army corps commander. It had occurred to him
sometimes, too, and the thought crossed his mind now, that a
man's span of life could have its own artistic length and that the
man was fortunate who died at the right time, his work finished.
If a man who saw nothing ahead of him but idleness and poverty
and ill-health decided that the time had come to make an end, he,
Blackwood, knew he would find it hard to condemn him. Not in
every man was the stuff of which martyrs and heroes are made. He
found it strange that those who looked on war and the slaughter of
young people as something that must be borne with fortitude and
as something in the way of the world, should look on the voluntary
termination of an old and finished life with horror and re-
pugnance. His old friend Nathaniel Hawthorne had jokingly said
the other day that he'd be in an awkward fix if he lived more than
two years longer—his savings wouldn't run to it. "I shall have to
see what the chemist can do for me if I go on longer than that,"
Nathaniel had said, his old eyes dancing. That, of course, was
another problem altogether—living longer than you expected.
88

plus the rising cost of living. But old Nat got a lot of fun out of life with his viola and his roses; nobody could say old Nat was finished. Thus and thus Blackwood's mind went running on as he drove, indulging his ruminations, enjoying the countryside. Here, within four or five miles of Greycastle, were sandstone walls and copses, occasional gorse in the fields, ponds with water-fowl, half-timbered houses much like his own and others that were whitewashed, and some of these rambling. Of such was Molyneux's, overlooking the estuary. Molyneux's wife had led him a rare dance, shifting him from one house to another, urging him to build this or that, but by the time trees were planted and gardens made she was eager to be off again. She was sitting with Molyneux when Blackwood was shown into him—a large, bustling masculine woman who leaned across Molyneux's bed to shake hands; but she said nothing about being pleased to see Blackwood, nor did he. She sat herself firmly down as though entrenched for this meeting.

Molyneux appeared to Blackwood's eyes to have shrunk, and when he spoke it was in a smaller voice than usual. Before he had said many words, his wife interrupted him to give him his medicine, holding him up with one powerful arm and giving him his spoonful of cough mixture with the other as if he were a recalcitrant small boy who would certainly avoid this experience if he could. She made no apology for interrupting him, spoke no words, just ladled a spoonful into his gaping but unprotesting mouth. Molyneux swallowed it, pulled a face, and resumed. Sedgwick had been to see him, he said—"A very fine man," interrupted Lady Molyneux firmly. Sedgwick had said how proud he would be to take over the *Morning Star*. "He seemed to think it was a very fine paper," again interposed Lady Molyneux, as though this was a little surprising and something she had never been at all certain about. "Go on, dear." Molyneux said he had told Sedgwick that he had been thinking of turning the paper into a Trust. Molyneux looked up at Blackwood at this point with a flicker of the eyelid which Blackwood took to be as near as Molyneux thought was advisable to a wink—and went on, that being so, it was not merely financial inducements that would have to be considered. "Although," added Lady Molyneux, in her masculine voice, "they could not be ignored. I made that very clear."

"Yes, love, you did," admitted Sir Thomas.

Blackwood inquired if these remarks had had the desired effect —a question which caused Lady Molyneux to look very hard and suspiciously at him. Molyneux coughed—and it was difficult to say how involuntary the cough was. When his wheezing was over, he said that Sedgwick had explained that he had been going into figures and he thought Sir Frederick Pick had underestimated prices today. Here Molyneux again cocked an eye at Blackwood, as though to warn him something was coming. He went on to say that Sedgwick had remarked that he imagined a fair price would be in the neighbourhood of half a million.

Blackwood said: "So Sedgwick has advanced the offer by a hundred thousand within a few days?"

Molyneux said yes, that was so.

Blackwood said that on this evidence Mr. Sedgwick was showing considerable determination. Blackwood was wondering how far the two parties were working in concert; the higher the price became, the more difficult it would be for him, Blackwood, to find an equal amount. If Molyneux's conscience were uneasy, it might suit him well enough to have enormous sums spoken of, bandied about, in the hope that Blackwood would give up the ghost; and Molyneux might then, by arrangement with Sedgwick, accept a much smaller sum which had, all along, been agreed on. Or was he, Blackwood, being too subtle over this? Molyneux looked genial and honest enough at the moment

Blackwood said, with a slow smile, "Delaying tactics seem to be profitable." He was looking down at Molyneux, who had seemed glad at the pause in the conversation and was staring unblinkingly across to the window. It occurred to Blackwood that perhaps Molyneux was not deeply interested; that whether the paper were sold or not was of no great consequence to him after all. If he were sick enough, well. . . . Lady Molyneux had been watching her husband, too, and she now said: "I want to get the matter disposed of—you know that, Tommy." The use of this diminutive struck Blackwood as bizarre, but it was in keeping with her attitude towards her husband. But Molyneux waved a hand almost negligently, as if he were fending her off, waving her words out of his hearing. She frowned and seemed about to speak, but at that moment a nurse appeared and said Lord Timperley was on the telephone. So soon as Lady Molyneux had left the room, Molyneux turned eagerly to Blackwood, beckoning him to bend closer.

90

When Blackwood had done so, Molyneux spoke like a conspirator: "I promised him nothing—told him he must see you. You spoke of the town when you were here before—what Greycastle would do? Well? Would it, do you think? Could you find the money?"

Blackwood felt his spirits rise—a moment of elation stirred him. How long was Molyneux prepared to give him, supposing Sedgwick made a firm offer? he inquired.

Molyneux gasped: "Oh, it'll be firm enough."

"Then how long will you give me? Three months?"

Molyneux shook his head doubtfully. "You see what she's like," he said, nodding towards the door.

"But you'll give me time?"

Molyneux whispered: "If I'm here—yes; but——" He pulled a face. "I get very short o'—o' breath." As if to emphasise that, he began a wheezing bout and Blackwood put an arm under him and lifted him higher up on to the pillow. The body sagged and had surprisingly little strength in it, Blackwood found. The thoughts he had had as he drove over recurred to him. But he asked: "When are you seeing Sedgwick again?"

Molyneux looked up almost slyly: "When *you've* seen him. He'll be inviting you. You'll go?"

"Oh yes. After that we'll see him together one day—we might arrange a game of golf." He must try and put life into Molyneux.

"I'm afraid my golfing days are over, Oliver."

"No, no, Thomas—a good rest—take a voyage."

"A man knows when he's finished. . . ."

"I was once sure I was going to be killed—in the war—but I was wrong. So you see, Thomas——"

But Molyneux shook his head, not altogether sadly—half whimsically, as if he didn't really mind, found it tinged with amusement.

Molyneux said: "We shall see. She"—he nodded towards the door again—"she's got a notion, too. I could"—a smile crossed his mouth that was never now shut—"could leave a note—in the will, eh? I might give you a month, eh? Sh-sh!" He had heard his wife returning. He lifted a finger in warning.

Lady Molyneux bustled in as if she had been charged up afresh by her talk with Lord Timperley. "Why are you so keen on a Trust, Mr. Blackwood—I don't understand what it means—what is a Trust?—is it a *Socialist* idea?" She used the word Socialist as if it were pestilential.

Blackwood said: "*The Times* is a Trust—and the *Observer* and the *Economist*—and the *Burnham Guardian*. They are not, of course, Socialist."

"But I don't understand——"

Blackwood said as gently as he was able, holding himself down: "Trusts vary. The one I have in mind would be formed by three or four leading citizens—the bishop, the vice-chancellor of the university, the Lord Mayor, and so on—to see that the paper didn't get into wrong hands and that its policy of liberal independence didn't change."

"But," she said, "I think its policy *ought* to change. I should like it to be Conservative."

"Now, Fanny," said Molyneux, "the paper's always been Liberal——"

"But there aren't any Liberals today," she said. "Or if there are, they've no business to be . . . spoiling everything." She rose. "I'm sorry, Mr. Blackwood, but that's how I feel. And I must say I didn't like what you wrote about hereditary honours. Sir Thomas is a baronet, and if Godfrey had lived . . . "

Blackwood rose, too, partly in politeness, partly because he felt the time had come to go. He said: "I'm most deeply sorry, Lady Molyneux, about Godfrey, and I quite understand your feelings about the hereditary principle. I respect them but I don't share them."

She said: "I think you have too much power." She stood glowering at him, her bosom rising and falling quickly.

"Yes," he said, "I gather that."

She said: "Well, then. . . . " After a moment, she added: "I hope you won't keep Sir Thomas too long."

Blackwood pursed his lips but didn't answer that. She paused another second or two and then, saying to Molyneux she would be back presently, she went out.

Molyneux looked up at Blackwood, the quizzical look returning to his eyes. He sighed, and murmured he was sorry.

Blackwood said: "I'm sorry, too, Thomas. I hope it doesn't upset you."

"Oh no—I'm used to it. She'll be better with it off her chest."

"Anything you'd like me to do for you in Greycastle?"

"See Sedgwick."

"I'll do that."

"And tell me the result."

"I can do that now."

"He may offer you a mint o' money. I'd like to be there."

"I wish you were to be. Look after yourself."

"Not much chance of getting into mischief now—and I've nearly done wi' walking about to cheat Cripps."

"No—no."

"We shall see."

They shook hands.

Molyneux said: "I'll drop a line to my solicitor about it." He put a finger to his lips again and winked.

"Thank you, Thomas. Very kind of you. Give me as long as you can."

Molyneux whispered huskily: "As long as you pay as much brass as t' other chap, what does it matter—to her?"

Blackwood smiled, nodded and took his departure. It occurred to him that Sir Thomas was finding great pleasure in doing his wife what was called in Greycastle "a thick 'un"—always provided he, Blackwood, could raise the money—yes, always provided that could be done.

CHAPTER XIV

MR. SEDGWICK PREPARED for the visit from Oliver Blackwood by having an extremely busy day. He had decided to play himself in, so to speak. Not, of course, that he was in the least perturbed about this meeting. After all, he had invited Blackwood to come, had he not, and, like a sensible fellow, he had accepted. He, Sedgwick, had himself written a diplomatic note, of course—almost charming, in fact, with the beginning and end in his own hand and the type itself large and formidable—very similar to that used by the Prime Minister from Downing Street.

"My dear Mr. Blackwood," he had written, "I wonder whether during these few days that I am in Greycastle (where I am reading your paper with immense interest and no little profit) I might have the pleasure of meeting you. There are several things I should enjoy discussing with you, I am sure, appertaining to our great craft—and its future. Perhaps, if you fall in with this, your secretary could telephone mine? Yours very sincerely, Samuel Sedgwick."

Unexceptionable. That phrase—"and its future". Masterly, almost. Intriguing. And when in due course Blackwood's secretary had rung, and his, Sedgwick's, impeccable Colonel Watson (this put him at a decided advantage, of course, the male over the female) was able to inquire in his bass voice: "When would it be convenient for Mr. Blackwood to call?" That pretty firmly decided who should call on who, didn't it? Blackwood's secretary had indeed made no difficulty.

Was the affair a shade too easy? Sedgwick had wondered. Did it signify anything? He would have liked Blackwood to have written a personal note in reply. It would have been—well, courteous. But, of course, these northcountrymen who stayed in the north . . . wrong to expect it, no doubt. Anyhow, the fellow was coming. That was the important thing. He, Sedgwick, would have a busy day—take Blackwood in his stride, sharpen his mind on other people first, give himself no time to cogitate too much.

So he had a very busy day indeed. He rang up London nine times before three o'clock. The telephone operator thought she had hardly had so busy a day since Mr. Carlos Szforsa, the film producer, had come to Greycastle in mistake for Newcastle and decided to change the location and bring everybody else to Greycastle also. Mr. Sedgwick's stream of callers—ranging from the reporters of the branch office (this gave, he thought, an admirable impression of interest in the journeymen of the profession) to various editors and specialists from the midlands together with northern celebrities —was uninterrupted, save, that is to say, for the entrances and exits of Mrs. Tremayne. The whole scene was unquestionably impressive. Never less than two people were waiting at the same time, and if they happened to be men who were each jockeying for position—even the other's position—in the Sedgwick kingdom, well, that was no bad thing. A reasonable wait, coupled with secretaries flitting in and out, and a loud imperious word or two of command ringing in the air—this could induce a proper frame of mind. Generals and admirals knew it had to be done, and was not he, Sedgwick, a field-marshal of civilian life? The same rules really applied—of precedence, dress, ritual and all the rest of it. If Mussolini, fool as he had shown himself to be, had done nothing else, he had displayed perception when he sat at one end of a long room and made his visitors walk across an enormous and slippery floor to get to him. Sedgwick had nearly fallen when he himself crossed that floor. Damned disconcerting. Well, he, Sedgwick, had learnt one or two of the tricks. Even the new Labour peers were picking things up; some of them were actually using a Latin quotation on their Christmas cards—men who knew no more Latin than they did Japanese; coronets on their envelopes, too. He must really ask Blackwood, this great Liberal, whether he approved of *that*. The peerage was certainly not what it was. Latin tags—and their wives still bending over the wash-tub. And the men themselves fellows who never took any regular exercise. A poor business.

Blackwood, now—Blackwood must be a strange character; he couldn't be making much money, here in this comparative backwater. And yet—no apparent desire to move, no real ambition. Molyneux himself didn't seem to know him really well—allowed him to have all his own way editorially—always a mistake, that—bred arrogance. Blackwood sounded like a scholar—almost a bishop—aloof—overlaid with integrity. The Press a holy crusade. Dear, dear. What would his father, Old James, have said of that? And yet . . . Molyneux had let fall hints of queerness in Blackwood's ménage but had refused to be at all explicit. . . . Blackwood's wife was a tremendous character, he said—an *exciting* woman; exciting. Um. And Blackwood full of integrity. Integrity. He got sick and tired of the word on the lips of these northcountry people, especially the spinsters who wrote to him personal letters concerning the influence of his newspapers—we must preserve the young generation's integrity at all costs, they said. Quite true. After all, his papers were cleanliness itself—absolutely. What was the phrase Mr. Fortinbras had used of a wartime committeeman who came from the transport industry, and who was a nonconformist? —"That impeccable busman." Well, the north seemed to be littered with impeccable characters; and Blackwood sounded to him, Sedgwick, very impeccable indeed—nauseatingly so. Quite clearly he overawed Molyneux a bit. Well, he, Sedgwick, was in no danger of being overawed by Blackwood—no more than Old

James had been overawed by Blackwood's uncle, Perceval. After all, he could buy Blackwood up, as they said in the north—and he was proposing to do so, in fact. He chuckled to himself at his joke. Mrs. Blackwood, too—he must get to know her—sounded interesting. If he could persuade Blackwood to come into the Sedgwick fold —he would tell him he could practically draw up his own contract— life might have its added interest. No doubt about Blackwood's ability—the *Morning Star* was remarkable—remarkable—those leaders every day—putting the world right—pronunciamentos on China; the five-day week in the mines; Palestine; equal pay for women; the situation in Western Germany; the future of Japan— how did he do it? Virtually no money to speak of—not as Sedgwick newspapers had money. He supposed Blackwood had half the professors at the university working for him for next to nothing —maybe old ambassadors in retirement, too, and former Ministers of State, and Chiefs of Staff—all delighted to turn an honest penny and to be able to let fall a hint in the club that they were behind this or that article. By heavens, while the war was on Sedgwick's impression was that he himself had half the bowler-hatted gentlemen of England on his pay-roll. One old general had even offered to deputise for their tame astrologer—he had indeed. Sedgwick gave himself a very good lunch, himself and Mrs. Tremayne, followed by a glass of port to aid his fifteen-minute nap; and he firmly resisted any thoughts of dalliance.

Blackwood, on his part, approached the meeting with his mind composed; it needed no making up on a matter of this sort. To him Sedgwick's attempt to take over the *Morning Star* was no better and, indeed, considerably worse, than Northcliffe's acquisition— temporary, fortunately—of *The Times*. He had been quite sincere when he had spoken to Molyneux of the paper's soul; he considered every paper had one; the *condition* of the soul was a different affair. It was no new thing, of course, for newspaper proprietors to attempt to acquire the souls of their men—every editor who slavishly toed the line had parted with a goodly part of his; but it was a miserable business. Blackwood knew perfectly well how it came about—the economic screw, ambition, the social position to keep up, the pressure—probably unexpressed—of wife and children, the rating of the craft too low—reducing it to the role of barrister speaking to a brief. All this was familiar. If the *Morning*

Star were sold and some members of his staff went over with it, he wouldn't condemn them—there was writing to be done on a newspaper which needn't be affected much whoever the owner was—a railway disaster or a football match could be described with perfect honesty and skill as well for one journal as another. It was true, of course, that even a reporter or sports writer could often write infinitely better for one paper than another—that by one paper he was encouraged or inspired and by another depressed—and yet was it so strange, since a man wrote from the pit of his stomach, from his subconscious perhaps. Men came on to the *Morning Star* and surprised themselves; the notion that men wrote only for money was disproved every payday. The fact was that if Blackwood had possessed all the money in the world he would still have paid his men moderately, believing money was, ideally, fourth or fifth down the list of things in life that were most important. No, there was not likely to be anything that Sedgwick could offer that he, Blackwood, would consider worth a moment's thought. The loss of complete independence of mind—that was outer darkness, alongside which wealth and technical resources were meretricious. But it would be interesting to hear what Sedgwick had to say; it might even be entertaining.

Blackwood spent the latter part of the morning on the links, practising pitching and putting. He could walk straight on to the links through the wooden door at the foot of the garden. Through that door the world was expansive—half a mile away beyond the sixth hole the skyline was a low ridge of mounds and dunes, and beyond them the sea—not the busy river estuary, but the true sea. The deserted links, the vast dome of grey sky, the wind sweeping in from the ocean, this flat grey sea with a low piece of land lying like a submarine in the water—this could bring peace to his spirit. Low land, a tall sky, emptiness and loneliness, and earth, sea and sky a wash of grey—these were, for him, akin to great music in the quelling of tumult. He walked across to the sea and watched it for a while—silvery, motionless, soundless, shipless. Sedgwick, well, well. . . . This earth and sea and sky put Sedgwick—and most else—in their right dimension. He turned and went back towards a green and began practising. He was pleased by the way he came down on to the ball as if he would slice a piece of it off. Ah! that was the way—hard, crisp, bite in it. The club felt no weight at all. And the putting, too—smooth, the ball rolling up to the hole as if on wheels. Only the pain in his stomach as he walked back reminded him he was not whole.

Blackwood had chosen five o'clock for the meeting. Afterwards he would go straight on to the office. Colonel Watson received him with deference, and Blackwood stood for a moment or two in this room, with its white curved chairs upholstered in magenta, looking out over the river. It was a windy afternoon; the smoke from the ships dispersed as soon as it left the funnels, the pennants fluttering hard, the sky dirty with rain; a day that suited his spirit, put him in mind of the power that lay in Nature's hands; reminded you that a man's lifetime was a fleeting, ephemeral thing.

Sedgwick had placed his table with its back to the light and turned this sitting-room as near to an office as he could, had its furniture arranged as much like his office in London as he could. He was alone. Sir Frederick Pick was within call, but Sedgwick had judged this talk would be better extremely private—as one editor to another. He liked to call himself editor sometimes. He was wearing his black coat and waistcoat—a waistcoat with a lapel; if he looked, wearing his silk hat, like an old-fashioned Cabinet Minister of the early Lloyd George period, well, there it was. England was sadly lacking in style these days; whatever gesture he could make . . .

"It is kind of you to come," said Sedgwick, rising to shake hands.

"I looked on our meeting as inevitable," said Blackwood easily.

Sedgwick smiled. "As between the two foremost newspapermen in this part of the world?"

Blackwood said: "That may be putting it rather high."

"Our families have been prominent for two generations," said Sedgwick.

"You mean editorially, or on the printing and business side?" The inquiry was gentle in tone, but Sedgwick flushed a little.

"I mean in both—on *my* side," he said roughly.

Blackwood said: "I see."

In the pause that ensued the curled head of Mrs. Tremayne came round the door on Sedgwick's left and exclaimed: "Darling! Oh! I'm sorry—but are we dressing tonight?" She took in at a glance this dark, bearded man she had been determined to see, and decided he looked fascinating. She looked at him long enough for Sedgwick to feel his title and all it implied in the nature of courtesy, demanding he should behave more politely than he felt like doing at that precise moment—this compulsion could be rather a nuisance at times—and he thereupon said: "Polly, this is Mr. Blackwood—you've heard me speak of him. Mrs. Tremayne."

Mrs. Tremayne advanced on Blackwood, beaming. "But I know—Mr. Blackwood is one of the most distinguished editors in the country. How do you do? Your paper once gave me a lovely notice."

Shaking hands, Blackwood said gravely: "I doubt if we did you justice."

Mrs. Tremayne said: "No justice for me—mercy is what I prefer. Sam usually allows me to write my own notices in advance, don't you, Sam?—which places a great strain on his integrity. Will *you* let me do that, Mr. Blackwood, when yours is one of the newspapers Sam owns?" She said this very winningly indeed, filling Sedgwick with a certain amount of consternation, so that he was impelled to protest and apologise, but Blackwood waved it aside, saying with a smile: "When mine is one of Mr. Sedgwick's newspapers, you may do just what you like."

She said: "Oh, thank you, Mr. Blackwood."

"Not at all," murmured Blackwood.

"You see, Sam?" she said.

"I see," said Sedgwick.

She withdrew with a gay smile, saying: "Do let's dress, Sam"; and Blackwood bowed to her.

Sedgwick, recovering his sense of humour, said: "Well, that may be said to have cleared the air, I suppose. You will be aware, I daresay, that I have had some talk with Sir Thomas Molyneux?" Sedgwick raised his eyebrows in interrogation.

"Yes."

"And that it would give me great satisfaction to have the *Morning Star* within my group?"

"No doubt," said Blackwood, biting off the words. There was a pause.

Blackwood inquired: "Do you mind if I smoke a cigar?" He pierced it and lit it carefully in the silence. When he had it going nicely, Sedgwick said: "Our industry is passing through difficult times."

"It reflects the world."

"We are disliked by this Government."

"Some of us," said Blackwood. "But that is hardly new."

"You don't detect a certain vindictiveness today in cutting down newsprint imports, for instance?" Sedgwick was a little impatient.

Blackwood said: "I discern something rather foreign to the spirit of a truly democratic party."

"Ah!" Sedgwick uttered an exclamation of satisfaction.

"But," continued Blackwood, "I said so in a leader two or three months ago. Did you?"

"More," said Sedgwick, "much more. We said that if this tendency went on we should have a censorship in peace exercised by means of withholding supplies."

"You mean *you* said?"

"Every single one of my newspapers said it," said Sedgwick triumphantly.

"Every one of your editors wrote that?" The question sounded innocent.

"Certainly"—very firmly.

"Of his own volition?" Again the question was mild.

"Of his—what do you mean?" Sedgwick frowned.

"Or did he receive a directive?"

"That," said Sedgwick, "is a word I never use." His mouth had grown thinner.

"I see," said Blackwood. "I should have thought it a suitable word, though I agree that 'order' would be better. I assume that's what it was—that the editor was not permitted any discretion in what he wrote?"

"Listen, Mr. Blackwood." Sedgwick placed his elbows on the table and cupped his face in his hands. "Are you suggesting—" he repeated the phrase with distaste as if the thought were lunacy— "are you suggesting that on national questions such as this it would be right for one of my papers in the Midlands to be saying one thing and for one of my papers in Sussex to be saying something quite different? Eh?" It seemed to him unanswerable. "Eh?" he asked again, the Yorkshire in him emerging.

"Mr. Sedgwick." Blackwood paused there. "This is the crux of it—the essence of the difference between us. If an editor always does what you tell him, he is not an editor but a rubber stamp, a gramophone. Why call him an editor—why not call him a secretary or an office boy?"

Sedgwick sat back again and put on his silk hat, which he had removed when he spoke about censorship. He spoke now more blandly, as to somebody who needed a little instruction. "I am familiar," he said, "with this old-fashioned idea about the position of an editor—that he is a person who has the divine gift of knowing everything and seeing into the future as into a glass darkly—I think that is the literary phrase?" He was pleased with that and allowed a suitable pause.

"You think it old-fashioned," said Blackwood, "to allow an editor to form his opinion for himself, and to pass that opinion on to his readers?" He was examining the end of his cigar.

"Omniscience," replied Sedgwick, "is antediluvian. Consider the topics that arise—from the price of fish to the wars in China. Is he expert on them all? So my newspapers have their panels of experts who decide the policy; and that policy is uniformly followed. You see?"

"I see. So that the voice of Edinburgh, let us say, is the same as the voice of Exeter?"

"Of course," said Sedgwick. The fellow seemed to be seeing the point at last.

"Poisonous," said Blackwood.

"Eh?"

"I said—poisonous."

"Rubbish," said Sedgwick. "Do you realise my papers sell ten or fifteen million copies a week?"

"So many? A heavy responsibility."

"Exactly. Ex-act-ly. And you think I can have every Tom, Dick and Harry up and down the country determining what his policy should be?" The voice rose.

Blackwood said: "Do I take it you mean that the more papers you own the more uniform should be the point of view expressed?"

"But how could it be otherwise? Tell me, how could it be otherwise? The public wouldn't know where they were—a Sedgwick paper here saying this and yonder a Sedgwick paper saying the opposite? Unthinkable."

"So that if by some great good fortune you owned *all* the newspapers in England, it would be even more desirable they should express one opinion?"

Sedgwick leaned forward again. "Now," he said, "now you're taking up an absurd position. No question of my owning *all* the newspapers. You know that very well."

"Impossible certainly, but would you think it undesirable?"

Sedgwick didn't answer—just smiled broadly.

"You think mine would be enough to be going on with?" said Blackwood.

"Yours might—conceivably—be the last I should acquire. The very last." This, Sedgwick seemed to indicate, would put a stamp of immense distinction on it.

"And the principle would be the same, of course—it would express the same views as your journals in Birmingham, Edinburgh, Bristol, Leeds—and all the rest?"

"I should give you considerable latitude—as I always do."

Blackwood said: "But on major questions I should obey the order?"

No hiding the touch of acidity now, but Sedgwick hardly noticed it. He said: "I should be willing to listen to what you had to say—I always listen; I'm always approachable. We should have our private wire—from me to you and you to me. Why should there be so much difference in our point of view?" He leaned across his table, speaking confidentially. "*You're* not a revolutionary. *I'm* not a revolutionary." He seemed to imply that no difference could remain.

Blackwood knocked the end off his cigar. He said: "If you'll forgive my saying so, you remind me of Henry Ford when he said, 'You can have your motor car any colour you like so long as it is black.'"

"Ah," said Sedgwick, "good! I like that." He felt more comfortable—Blackwood had a sense of humour.

"In the same way," said Blackwood, "I can write whatever I like so long as the content, the argument, the message keeps to the general line?"

Sedgwick liked that less again—damn it, the man ebbed and flowed all the time. It occurred to him he was not making remarkable progress, but at all events the conversation was proceeding; and he still had guns to fire. He now asked: "Do you *trust* this Government? Do you believe what they say when they attend dinners to Press benevolent funds or things of that sort? Butter wouldn't melt in their mouths. But hark at them when they're in the wilds of Wales or Durham—what then? We're the most prostituted Press in the world—pouring out our daily dose of poison. What do you think of that?"

"That," said Blackwood, "is adolescent vituperation—writing on lavatory walls in rather a different form."

Sedgwick warmed to that.

"But," said Blackwood, diminishing Sedgwick's glow, "you'd have to admit that the prying of Fleet Street into whether the Ministers' wives are buying fur coats, and the keeping watch with cameras on the private houses of Ministers—even on their windows, is equally contemptible."

Sedgwick shook his head. "No—oh no! These men are levellers—they've denounced wealth and privilege—and when they fall from their lofty perches, tumble out of their pulpits, they deserve to be stigmatised. Let us have the truth about what they do and how they behave and let the people judge." He truly thought at that moment that that was what he stood for. "My own papers have been very moderate on this," he went on. "We could have done much more than we have. We could rake up their past speeches on Communism and print it day after day—keep it set, in fact. We could print the actual details of what these Cabinet Ministers did during the First World War—it's a very varied record, I assure you—I've had it gone into—there's a remarkable scarcity of D.S.O.s—I don't think you can find even one. We could print every day that the Prime Minister draws four thousand pounds a year free of tax—something new in our history, and this at a time when most people are feeling the pinch damnably. We could publish at regular intervals the jobs faithful party hacks have got in the nationalised boards and elsewhere, and compare their salaries with the wages they drew before—some of them are drawing five to ten times as much as they ever earned. We could make a point of always using their worst photographs—and there's considerable precedent for that." Sedgwick paused; it was difficult to prevent a feeling that he was really a kindly and merciful man.

Blackwood inquired: "You think all that would be justified? And, I grant you, I've drawn attention myself to the elevation of so many trade union secretaries."

"Yes—why not?" The reply was decisive.

"Why then have you not carried it out?"

Sedgwick growled: "Too English—too English—I suppose that's it. Mind you, I've done a fair amount—quite a fair amount —on the links with Communism."

Blackwood said: "You haven't been influenced by the English sense of fair play—knowing that if you overdo the attacks they'll recoil on you? Or is that what you meant by being too English?"

Sedgwick looked puzzled. He felt at times like a witness under cross-examination. It was almost good practice for being in front of the Royal Commission on the Press. He said something of this— which made Blackwood like him—and then inquired what Blackwood thought of the Commission. It didn't spring from the Government's love of the Press, did it? Blackwood agreed it didn't, although he welcomed it. The Press could no more expect to be free from criticism than any other influence in public life.

"Don't you see," said Sedgwick suddenly, "that the way things are going—this Government vendetta against the Press, coupled with the rising cost of paper, the shortage of it, the growing power of trade unions, the demands for higher and higher wages—that the only *safe* place for a paper like yours is inside an organisation like mine? We've *got* our own paper mills overseas—and if we're shut down in one place we can print in another. A dozen voices need a lot more silencing than one. If you stand alone, you may well be extinguished, economic forces may crush you."

Blackwood said: "But if I came into your group I should *certainly* be extinguished. It would be exchanging what I agree may be a struggling and troubled life for certain death."

Sedgwick made an exclamation of disagreement and incredulity.

"I mean death of the spirit," said Blackwood.

"But even supposing," said Sedgwick, "that under my control you didn't get *all* your own way—that the paper's policy became an amalgam of your ideas and mine—and, by the way, has it occurred to you—I must confess it has only just struck me—that you might exercise a profound influence on *all* my papers?— would you regard that as being worse than having no paper at all? After all, who among us gets all his own way all the time? Life, my dear sir, is a compromise."

Mr. Sedgwick was very pleased with that speech. It seemed to him the height of liberality and reason.

Blackwood smiled. "I can well understand," he said, "that if I were to sail under your flag, it would be advisable, even from the lowest motives—which I am not attributing to you—that, in the beginning, my leaders and the paper's tone should not be markedly different from the past. You would want to lull the public—tell them that the firm remained under the old management, that you were really only a benevolent owner, almost a sleeping partner, an absentee landlord; that nothing would be changed. And then—imperceptibly almost—a new note dropped in—the old radicalism toned down—the strong liquor powerfully diluted—the reader's beliefs shaken—undermined. Under Mr. Fortinbras's inspiration——"

Sedgwick looked up quickly and down again to the carved bronze paper-knife he was playing with.

Blackwood went on quietly: "—and if I were amenable—or dismissed—you would be able to swing the old arguments into a new channel, and presently some of our readers would give up the paper in despair—and others, less discerning, would be swallowing the slightly poisoned medicine and wondering why they felt so decidedly unwell—so unsure of everything."

Sedgwick grasped the heavy paper-knife and held it like a short-sword. "You make me sound like an assassin," he said.

"Call it a would-be executioner," said Blackwood.

"I am throwing you a lifebelt," said Sedgwick.

"You are handing me a cup of hemlock," said Blackwood.

Sedgwick said musingly: "I should be sorry if, when the paper is mine, you were to resign."

"You are still determined to acquire it—if you can?"

"That is why I came to Greycastle."

"You are a patriot, Mr. Sedgwick?" This was only the second time Blackwood had addressed him thus formally, and Sedgwick noted it.

"As you are—I trust."

Blackwood ignored that. He went on: "And you think the purchase of the *Morning Star* by you would be in the public interest?"

"My papers are a bulwark against subversive elements—and if a thing is good, there should be plenty of it."

105

"The silencing of an independent voice—my voice—would be a good thing, you think?"

"I should not silence you."

"You mean I should only be muted?"

"If you put it like that."

"But you know, in fact, that so far as my journal goes, I *should* be silenced—for I should not be there. I should have departed."

"I should regret that."

"Regret it or not, you will not hesitate to do it——"

"If a man behaves unreasonably, I cannot help it."

Blackwood rose. "We shall have a considerable fight," he said. "I regard you, to some degree, as an enemy of free speech."

Sedgwick rose also. "You know very well," he said, "that I stand for the freedom of the Press."

"Your *own* freedom—freedom for you to publish—freedom for you to suppress what you don't like."

Sedgwick said: "But every editor is in the same boat. Selection—selection—and again selection—how can there be any other basis?"

"And your black-lists?" Blackwood dropped the term in suddenly.

"My what?"

"The men—or women—whose names are not to be mentioned? Those who have offended you? The authors whose books are a disturbing influence? The public men who take an awkward line—or attack your newspapers? I'm told your sub-editors have a song—'On and off the black-list, Oh, he's been on before'. No truth in all that?"

Sedgwick flushed. He didn't answer for a moment. Then he said: "If there's a troublesome fellow who every time you report what he says complains you've got it wrong and demands corrections? Or threatens you with libel if you write about him? Or goes out of his way to vilify you and other owners of newspapers—what do you do? Advertise him, treat him like a friend and a brother? You know as well as I do that the wise thing is to keep him out of the paper altogether; it's the only safe way. So you put his name up in the subs. room saying, 'Steer clear of this man.' And then some ill-disposed journalist spreads the tale of a black-list. Tell me, what do *you* do?"

Blackwood said: "If a man attacks us, and he's the sort of man we should report in the ordinary way, a man of consequence—we still report what he says. I agree we handle warily those who always say they are misreported—as one or two Ministers of State do. But we've never had a list of them. We go on treating them on their merits. We never say, 'This author must be left alone'; or 'This speaker must never be reported'." He smiled. "Perhaps we've never had enough enemies—not yet. Fair treatment begets fair treatment—or don't you think so? We try not to have preconceived ideas. We don't send men out on investigations and tell them before they go what we expect them to find. Do *you*?"

Sedgwick said blandly: "When I investigate, I have a point of view. If I am told a grave abuse exists and then find, on looking into it, that the charge is not true, I drop the matter. No point in wasting space on a nonexistent thing."

Blackwood asked: "You wouldn't think it worth while pointing out that charges are being bandied about that don't stand up?"

"I might or I might not. But I'm not producing newspapers that send people to sleep. My papers must be keen, interesting, amusing, exciting, surprising." Ah! That was rather good!

Blackwood said drily: "How disappointed you must be."

"What do you mean?" asked Sedgwick warmly.

"I mean that I, unfortunately, find most of your journals so extremely dull. I read the large headlines which make all the pages resemble roads under repair, and look as if the type had experienced a violent explosion; but so much of the stuff underneath is like dry chips in the mouth—tasteless." He paused and continued:

"Oh, I don't just mean absence of fine style." A smile covered his face. "You must be aware of those secret factories where all the flavour is extracted from railway food before you get it? Your sub-editors' rooms appear to work like that—they appear to cut out the flavour, the authenticity of how people talk, the small touches that make all the difference. I suppose what has happened is that they've cut out a good deal of the truthfulness and, with it, the life. Most pages read as if the same man had emasculated them, and taken some dead language—abrupt, violent and crude—and written all the stories—not with a pen, but on some machine made of hammers."

Sedgwick's face by this time was a confused red.

He said: "You are very impolite, Mr. Blackwood."

Blackwood said: "I am being frank. I don't think politeness arises. After all, your visit to Greycastle has hardly a polite intention—not so far as I am concerned. You are really here to murder me. As for my criticisms of your journals—you don't write them, do you? You are not a journalist, are you?—I mean no more than as a figure of speech?"

Sedgwick thrust out his large face. "I am a journalist by hard training—and long practice. I control my papers as firmly as you control your"—he hesitated—then, "your paltry *Morning Star* which sells fewer copies than any one of my papers. Why, you sell hardly more than my father's first venture."

"Ah!" said Blackwood, "I remember—it was first set up on my uncle's cast-off machines."

"And I am proud of it," said Sedgwick.

"Why should you not be proud? Your father was most enterprising."

"Not only *in*genious, but a true *genius*," said Sedgwick. "He created something that finds employment for a host of people."

"True," said Blackwood. "Willie Lever, the soap manufacturer, could have said the same."

"Are you now comparing our journals with soap manufacture?" asked Sedgwick with temper.

"Not altogether, but *I* thought you were judging them by the numbers they employ—by which standard I agree they would count more than by other standards."

Sedgwick said: "I find it amusing—I really find it amusing. Here you are—in a provincial town—a backwater—editing a paper you do not even own—thinking the words that fall from your lips are oracles—scorning an offer——"

"Spurning," said Blackwood.

"You will see," said Sedgwick. "You will see. On the day I take over your paper——"

"Has your astrologer predicted the date?" inquired Blackwood quietly.

Sedgwick turned away.

"I refer," said Blackwood, "to those gentlemen who tell the millions of us who are born on the same day that on Tuesday of next week, let us say, we must be careful with our financial transactions. I often wonder what the poverty-stricken who are born on that day make of it. I understand that during the war you had a weekly conference when you instructed the soothsayers what they must predict that week—victories or withdrawals."

"By God," said Sedgwick, turning round, "it must be marvellous to be so righteous—so full of rectitude."

"Not at all," said Blackwood. "I marvel on my side at the way Nature carries on the ingenuity from one generation to another. Your father never thought of astrologers, I think. On the other hand, I always understood he struck a remarkable vein in coupling the printing of religious tracts with the printing of pawn tickets, thus taking care of two important traits in human nature at the same time."

"Both of which I suppose you equally despise," said Sedgwick savagely.

"You do me an injustice," said Blackwood. "You must not imagine I am a Puritan. I know that you cater for a very large public and that your wares are no more inimical to the public weal—and perhaps even less so, let us be quite fair—than the films of Hollywood which are put over to the people by at least one man of the strongest religious principles. No. My quarrel is that there is, so to speak, rather too much of you—that you are rather too widespread—that you tend to grow tedious—and that it would be a good thing if there was infinite variety in the Press— as in the person of Cleopatra. I have never had any passion for superb mediocrity."

"Have you nearly done?" shouted Sedgwick.

"Almost," said Blackwood calmly. "I would only add this: You may buy a newspaper but you can never buy what makes the newspaper great. You might take over members of my staff— but I doubt if they would ever be able to write for you as they have written for me—for writing is a matter of the spirit. Their pens might well fall from their palsied fingers."

"By heavens," said Sedgwick, striding a pace to and fro, "you ought to be spouting in the cathedral—or, I should say, the Nonconformist chapel."

"Oh no," said Blackwood, nonchalantly crushing the butt of his cigar. "It happens that the pen is mightier than the pulpit and print more enduring than the voice." He looked up. "In passing, that is a sobering thought, Mr. Sedgwick—all your papers filed in the British Museum, an enduring monument to sport and crime—and your leading articles sparkling like soda-water too long opened."

Sedgwick strode over to his desk and impatiently pressed a buzzer on it.

Blackwood said: "I am sorry that my views—which you desired—should have discomposed you. But I wanted you to feel as certain as I do that neither I nor the *Morning Star* could ever occupy a place—however close to the throne—in your kingdom."

Colonel Watson appeared inside the door and stood waiting, like a gaoler.

Mr. Sedgwick was glad to see him. An audience for what he was about to say, was fitting. He straightened himself and took a breath that was less quiet than he could have wished. He said—and not without dignity—"You have had a lot to say, Mr. Blackwood. Now let me tell *you*. I have never taken over a newspaper without improving it—most of them were dying on their feet and would have perished but for me. I have put life into them—raised their circulations—given them a better foreign news service—better pictures—more up-to-date machinery—and paid better wages to the editorial staffs. And I will do the same with the *Morning Star*. I will transform it—as you will see, as you will see. Goodbye, Mr. Blackwood." And Mr. Sedgwick dismissed him. Indeed, Colonel Watson opened the door.

But Blackwood was in no hurry. He said, speaking with immense deliberation: "You have assumed control of many papers, Mr. Sedgwick—and you have, in doing so, slain some other papers. Those that exist tend to be like mausoleums, holding the dead bodies of those they have amalgamated. If the day were to come when you controlled the *Morning Star*, your touch would wither it as surely as the sirocco withers the rose. Against that I will strive as I would against domination by Mr. Stalin —for the death of independence would be precisely the same."

Blackwood's pallor had deepened a little as he spoke and he sought Sedgwick's eyes and, having found them, held them for a moment. He said no more, but turned and walked out of the suite, moving with something close to a limp. Colonel Watson he never noticed.

Sedgwick stood looking after him, thinking that somehow he ought to have had more control of the talk. These fanatics, these damned fanatics!

CHAPTER XV

THE REPORTERS' ROOM of the *Morning Star* discussed the situation at six o'clock in the evening. This was an interim period—afternoon engagements were being written up, evening ones had not begun. You could gossip, you could pontificate, you could argue, you could indulge in persiflage. The secret history, the scandals, the stuff that never got into the paper because of libel, or because you had been told in confidence—all could be held up to the light here. These day-to-day historians revealed it, impaled it, dissected it. Men who spent a good part of their lives behaving outwardly with immense discretion, and some of whom had developed that ingratiating manner common to those mortals whose lives are dependent on procuring something from other people which those individuals are not anxious to part with—commercial travellers and demonstrators of vacuum cleaners are almost blood relations on this point—can, in the reporters' room, behave like kings, lay down the law like judges of the King's Bench, and give rein to their idealism, if any, like evangelists. In short, they can blow off steam and be their true and mighty selves.

On this occasion the subject of the paper's future was raised by Frank Knowles. Mr. Knowles was a large man, very near-sighted, who always wore a cloth cap and stammered his way to the heart of trade-union politics and terrible statistics on man hours. He headed his pieces "By our Labour Correspondent". Frank, it was always believed, could have settled any strike on the docks within forty-eight hours given a free hand and liberal expenses. He had never as yet, of course, had either. Mr. Knowles now stood before the tiled, cracked, fireplace and gazed round at his colleagues. It was an old room as much like a large vestry or company boardroom as anything else. Behind him and above the fireplace there was actually a small stained-glass window—some *jeu d'esprit* of the architect—which depicted Mr. Shakespeare (some said Mr. Blackwood, since both had a beard) leaning thoughtfully on an elbow with a scroll in his hand. The room had a motley assembly of tables and desks, as if each reporter had brought his own. There were square tables, round tables, a baize-topped table on which bridge was sometimes played, and a roll-topped desk at which sat the notable Thomas Spence when he wrote his music criticisms, which he coupled with being a horticulturist. Mr. Knowles was filling his hooked pipe, and he now said, without looking up: "What are you chaps going to do when you find yourselves working for the new boss?"

Just as those who spend their time abusing others are themselves excessively pained when they themselves are the subject of abuse, so are the calm purveyors of news of disaster and sudden death mightily stirred when their own destinies are at stake. There was no lack of interest now. The recording of great and small events stopped at once. Mr. Knowles, having to do with organised labour, was accepted as one who would know about these things. Perhaps the trade unions had told him.

The clatter of typewriters, noisy, or so-called noiseless, mostly ceased. It's true that Brenda Smith's went on for a moment or two and that she then asked: "Has our Herbert got the sack?" Herbert being the chief reporter, Mr. Bryce, who has his own room round the corner. But her remark was taken as no more than a demonstration of the toughness which distinguished this young woman who had joined the paper originally to write from the woman's angle, but now was turned on to any subject.

"Nay, nay, Brenda," said Mr. Knowles. "I mean the chap who stamps our insurance cards. Don't you ever *hear* any news, any of you?" Mr. Knowles's face assumed a look of pain.

A man with the rubicund face of a bishop and a bishop's aloof manner, said languidly: "Don't rake up that ancient *canard* about Molyneux selling out to the brewers, Knowles." The unruly grey hair went back over his machine and he tapped out another word, slowly.

"The brewers?" said Knowles, in deeper pain.

There was now a chorus of voices and two or three figures wandered over to him—Ridgway, a spectacled youth not long down from Oxford who had hoped to do dramatic criticisms but was assigned to the municipal calls, and finding the life tame compared with what he had expected; Forsyth from Glasgow, who was a crusader for journalists' rights, and did his reporting almost as a sideline, so active was he in the journalists' trade union's work; Vincent de Ferrers, a plump, dishevelled figure, whose speciality was shipwrecks and who, on behalf of various papers which had employed him at different times was said to have bought most of the tugs on the waterway so heavy were his expenses in hiring them; Clifton Prince, the aforesaid bishop-like figure whose name might or might not have been his own. Prince was something of a mystery: he had worked both in Paris and New York, stepped off in Greycastle, as it were, during a journey across the Atlantic, and gravitated to the *Star* office. Nothing moved Mr. Prince, nothing stirred him; if the river had run dry he would have devoted an item to it. The chief reporter's ability to get excited over a fall of snow struck him as madness. In addition to these members of the reporting staff who, in general, moved over the surface of Greycastle with an air of boredom as befitted the superiority of the journal which employed them, there was Fred Cheshire. Mr. Cheshire was almost a legendary figure—he was referred to in his absence and over half pints of mild-and-bitter as "The Man who Ate the Railway Smash"—this because on one occasion, when working as a sub-editor in Durham, he had been in such a highly nervous state that he had devoured the whole telegram. He had at that time developed the nervous trick of tearing off corners of the telegrams he was subbing and popping them into his mouth. On that awful afternoon there was nothing of the fateful telegram left by the time he had finished sub-editing it, and his paper went to press without a word of the railway smash in it. He had, of course, been fired. Mr. Cheshire had been fired from innumerable papers, and during the long years had fallen from posts such as chief sub-editor or chief reporter to what he now was—the "late stop" reporter, coming on duty at six o'clock in the evening and going on till two or three in the morning. He was supposed to be an authority on crime, but as the *Morning Star* thought but little of crime, Mr. Cheshire's lack of sparkle was of no great consequence. Mr. Cheshire, his rheumy eyes blinking and his stained moustache drooping over his watery pipe, shambled over to Mr. Knowles along with the rest.

113

"What will you do, Fred, if Mr. Sedgwick buys the paper?" inquired Knowles.

It wasn't often Mr. Cheshire had a flash of wit or perspicacity, but he had one now. "I suppose," he said, blinking at the group, "I suppose I should get the sack again." He added, if any explanation were required: "His father sacked me years ago."

"I guess we'd all get the sack," said Forsyth. "If he didn't sack us, we'd be sacking ourselves in next to no time. You couldna work for a journal the like o' that."

Mr. Forsyth glowered at the rest of them as if challenging anybody to refute that, and searched out the face of Prince, who was a back-slider in paying his union subscriptions. But Prince merely remarked: "A lot of people seem to—people exceedingly well known. They flash past me in motor cars." He opened a small rusty tin, took out a cigar that was half smoked, relic of a town-hall lunch, and carefully lit it.

Forsyth rejoined fiercely: "Do you mean ye'd enjoy having stuff syndicated intae half a dozen papers for the same wages—juist to spread your name aboot?" He made this sound a very low proceeding.

"Notoriety and money," said Mr. Prince, "are inseparably locked together."

Brenda Smith, who was a Tory Reformer, now turned to Forsyth: "Weren't you once on the Press Association—sending your stuff into every office in the kingdom? How many men were *you* doing out of a job?"

Mr. Forsyth looked disdainful. "Not the same thing at all," he said. "The P.A. sticks to the facts—not this garbled rubbish—and ye canna get extra publicity oot o' the P.A. with a fat cigar, neether."

"Order, order," said Mr. Knowles, drawing circles in the air with his pipe. "The position is that there's an attempt going on to buy the paper. You've read the various bits we've had and you can put two and two together—or don't you read your own paper? Well, Sedgwick has been stopping at the Grand Hotel for the past two days——"

"How do you know that's what he's here for?" asked Brenda.

"Spies, love, spies," said Knowles. "Joe Belshaw, their Labour man from Leeds, has been over. Joe and me had a couple o' pints together. His lordship has been receiving streams of callers, Lady

Molyneux, wife of our revered boss, among them. I had a word with the hall porter at the Grand—me having your interests at heart." Knowles suddenly dropped his tone of semi-banter. "It's a serious business, I'm telling you. It's a bad time to be out of a job—small papers and big staffs. And I'm saying nothing about the honour and glory of the old *Morning Star* as it is today."

The mood of the group changed. They all saw it as readily as Knowles.

"Sedgwick usually keeps all the staff on, doesn't he?" It was the aloof Prince who spoke again.

There was a silence. Then Knowles said: "I believe he does—but as far as I'm concerned, I couldn't see me writing the labour stuff *he'd* want, usually weighted on the employers' side. Of course, I don't say everybody else would be in as bad a position as me." His gaze travelled to Pritchard-Jones, who had entered the room since the talk began. Pritchard-Jones was the specialist on religious matters, a man who wore a bowler hat and stiff stand-up collars in the manner of a bygone period. Moreover, he had six children. Pritchard-Jones said: "I hope like all the rest of uss, the paper will never be sold, but I haf heavy responsibilities—and if I am not required to tell lies, I doubt if I could afford to resign. Is that what you are suggesting, Frank, that we should all resign if it happens, man?" Pritchard-Jones looked over his pince-nez.

Mr. Knowles, feeling this was travelling much too fast, giving no decent time for negotiation, so to speak, said: "Not necessarily, no—this is early days. Serious, but early. Mind you, solidarity is always a good thing."

Forsyth, who had been simmering, said: "It's the *only* thing. Bring out the unions—we're all together, aren't we?—writers and printers? Don't *set* the bluidy paper, I say, if Sedgwick buys it. Make that clear. That 'ud stop it being bought."

Miss Smith asked: "What becomes of freedom, then? Would you be saying the same thing if the T.U.C. wanted to buy the paper?"

Forsyth said: "The T.U.C. *doesn't* want to buy the paper. Why drag in that hypothesis?"

De Ferrers said darkly: "There are fellas who think the Press should be nationalised."

"Better *be* nationalised than owned by the Press magnates," said Forsyth doggedly.

Miss Smith said: "So there it is. I thought so."

Fred Cheshire, who had been nervously running the stem of his pipe along his moustache and staining it more yellow than it was already, now blurted out: "There's one who'll never allow it to happen."

Pritchard-Jones, whose thoughts readily flew to the Almighty, said: "You mean God, Fred?"

"No, no. Oh no," said Mr. Cheshire. "Somebody on the spot."

"God *iss* always on the spot," said Pritchard-Jones gravely.

"I mean Mr. Blackwood," said Cheshire desperately. "Nobody can buy *him*."

And suddenly the meeting saw how true that was. It was like a revelation.

"Good for you, Fred," said Mr. Knowles heartily. "Good for you, lad."

Thus encouraged, Mr. Cheshire gave rein to his imagination. "He'd raise the town," he said. "The very stones would cry out." Then he looked quickly at Pritchard-Jones, realising he had trespassed on biblical preserves.

De Ferrers cried: "Jolly good, old boy," and smote Cheshire on the back so that he stumbled forward. "I'd been standing here," said de Ferrers, "my tongue cleaving to the roof of my mouth, seeing the time when not an expenses sheet stood between me and starvation, and now . . ."

Miss Smith said: "We all know Mr. Blackwood lunches at Downing Street sometimes. . . ."

Ridgway said: "After all, we're almost a national institution. . . ."

Knowles said: "If money can be found for dam' silly films . . ."

Pritchard-Jones said: "God answers prayers—I am sure of that. I could arrange for prayers in all the chapels."

On this emotional note the discussion looked like ending for the moment, especially as the clock over the roll-top desk chimed the half-hour and they were reminded that work waited. But now Mr. Prince, who had felt unspoken thoughts crying for utterance and who abhorred sentiment, said: "One moment. I am an ignorant and heartless man who has always written as he was paid to write, loyal at one time to the Tories and at another to the Liberals, seeing himself as no more than the barrister of the

Temple he actually is——" He paused for a moment here to allow this to sink in. "—holding a brief for his employer, thinking even the murderer has a right to be defended. I know how wrong this is, especially in the eyes of members of our union, none of whom, of course, have worked for the Press magnates they denigrate, or written a syllable without their hands on their hearts. Or am I wrong?" He glanced at Forsyth blandly. Prince went on: "I have at other times, when my imagination took flight, seen myself as an artist, free to move from one patron to another—and with my patron equally free, unfortunately, but surely justly, to dispense with me. Now I am aware that in the Welfare State where the point has been reached when many amateur rugby footballers will not play in matches unless they are insured against accident, this is a sorry state of mind for me to be in. But, as I said, I am a wicked man. Now, ladies and gentlemen, I have an appointment in a moment or two at Sam Sharp's dive, round the corner, where, if my financial advisers are agreeable, I will buy the modest gill for anybody who cares to accompany me. But before I depart, may I leave this thought and query with you: How is Mr. Blackwood—whom God preserve—this arch upholder of liberty in this still comparatively free country, going to prevent Sir Thomas Molyneux, this low form of royalty, from selling what he owns—if that is what he decides to do?"

There was a silence.

"Unless, of course," added Mr. Prince genially, "we all club together and provide Mr. Blackwood with the wherewithal to raise the bid." He took half a crown out of his trousers pocket, spun it and caught it, offered an arm to Miss Smith who accepted it with a bow, and they went off together.

"And he owes three months' bluidy union money," said Mr. Forsyth bitterly, glaring at the door through which they had gone.

Mr. Knowles was conscious of an anticlimax. But suddenly he had an idea, and he knocked out his pipe with an air of immense resolution. "He's not so daft as he sounds," he said. "That bit about raising money. Now if Brenda sweethearts that shipowner of hers—the chap who made millions out o' the two wars and is in his dotage—— By God, quite an idea! Aye."

He picked up his cloth cap and strode after them.

CHAPTER XVI

IT WAS NOT until they were driving back from Lord Timperley's late that evening that Mrs. Tremayne cross-examined Mr. Sedgwick about Mr. Blackwood and the *Morning Star*. Mr. Sedgwick was in an excellent humour. He usually was at this hour of the day. He was in a glow with good food and wine, his host and the guests had made a fuss of him, treated him as a powerful figure—as, of course, he was—asked him to use his influence with Mr. Fortinbras to get this abominable Government turned out, and had laughed immoderately at his Yorkshire story—a story of how he had been visited by an impecunious young man who had come to borrow money and who when asked for security, replied that he, the young man, was the security. "I opened the door of my safe," Mr. Sedgwick had said, "and I said, 'Step inside, young man, *this* is where I keep my securities'." Yes, Timperley thought that was very good, very good indeed. So did Sedgwick—built him up as a tough card. Kept these fellows from presuming. Some of those blue-blooded chaps thought you were fair game—doing you a favour by borrowing a hundred pounds. But not from him, Sam Sedgwick. Oh no, oh dear no. He wasn't Old James's son for nothing. His thoughts were idly turning these things over, living his moments of triumph again, his right hand idly caressing the velvet coat that Mrs. Tremayne was wearing over her evening frock. It occurred to him that within forty-five minutes they would be enjoying the ecstasy that is too deep for words—and he was suffused with warmth and delight at the thought. It was at this moment that Mrs. Tremayne inquired: "Darling?"

"Yes, love." He spoke the words with extraordinary tenderness.

"When is Mr. Blackwood starting to work for you?"

"I don't know, dear." He felt a little disappointed that the subject was so matter-of-fact.

"Didn't you fix it today?"

"No."

"Why not?"

"Well—there are several things to be decided."

"Do you want my help, darling?" She snuggled further into his arm.

All the same, he replied: "No, dear."

"I'm sure I could give you help."

"What are you thinking of?"

"He has a lovely beard."

"I see," he said.

"King Solomon had a beard."

"So I have always understood."

"And four hundred wives." She laughed.

"Are you suggesting that one attribute follows on the other?" Mr. Sedgwick took a tighter grip of the velvet jacket. He inquired: "How many brandies did you have?"

"Two, darling," she answered demurely. "How many did *you* have?"

"Two."

She sighed happily. "Then we're quits, aren't we?"

"I thought you had rather a lot of champagne," he said.

"But you like me best when I have had champagne."

She turned to him and kissed him.

"Now about Mr. Blackwood," she said.

He sighed.

"Yes, dear."

"Is he being awkward?"

"A little awkward."

"Are you going to dismiss him?"

"Not until I have engaged him, dear." He chuckled.

"You think I have no head for business."

"I think—for some kinds of business—you have a very good head indeed, love."

"Now you are saying I am mercenary."

He chuckled.

"I am sure Mr. Blackwood would never laugh at a thing like that."

He said: "I don't believe Blackwood has a laugh in him."

"Ah!" she said, "he is a poet."

"Oh? How do you know?"

"I could see it in his eyes—grey opals—deep—eloquent—passionate."

"You took in a lot, dear, in so short a time."

"I may be impetuous, darling, but I am never wrong. Did I not recognise you the moment I saw you?"

"That is very flattering, dear. And have you recognised Mr. Blackwood in the same way?"

"Not in the same way, of course. But still—he is one of the few men in Greycastle who look as if they have—potentialities."

"You make him sound like a generating station, dear."

She replied calmly: "That is what he is. That is what all men are—who are endowed in the customary way. That is why it is so sad that you and I are not married, for we should have had many children."

"I think we get on very well as we are." He turned his head and kissed the nape of her neck.

She said: "Happy is the man that hath his quiver full of them. That is what it says in the Bible. When you consider how many Russians and Indians and Chinese there are, it is not right, the way we are neglecting our duty. After all, the British are the finest race in the world—that is what your newspapers always say. . . ."

"No, darling, we never say that. The Americans wouldn't like it."

"You say the British are the world's policemen. I have read that many a time."

"That is rather different, dear."

"And you, Mr. Sedgwick, have not produced a single policeman. Is that *right*?"

"Well, dear, I am in the same boat as Mr. Shakespeare, Bernard Shaw, Abraham Lincoln, Leonardo da Vinci . . ."

"I do not believe you know for certain about Leonardo da Vinci."

After a pause she said: "I understand Mr. Blackwood has a son."

So it wasn't finished, after all. "And a fascinating wife," he said—and it came out like a cork out of a bottle.

"What did you say, dear?"

"A fascinating wife." He spoke a trifle louder.

"Have you *met* her?"

"No, dear. Have *you* met his son?"

"Darling, you are not getting testy, are you?"

120

"Not in the least."

"How do you know she is so fascinating?"

"That is Molyneux's opinion."

"Oh—do you regard him as a judge?"

"I don't see why not."

"I always understood his own choice was so remarkably unfortunate . . ."

He said, with a touch of desperation: "Ugliness across the breakfast-table can sharpen a man's eye when he looks elsewhere."

"I must say, darling, that is a very strange remark. Are you speaking from experience?"

"I have lived a considerable number of years."

"Not with me, dear."

"No, darling, *not* with you."

"I have always wondered how many ladies poured out your morning coffee before—before I did." Mrs. Tremayne's voice trembled a little.

Now how, wondered Mr. Sedgwick, have we got to this pitch? It was a moment for firmness. He said: "Darling, it cannot be of the *smallest* consequence who, as you say, poured out my morning coffee *before* you did. All past and done with. One of the most delightful things about you is that you are a woman of the world. . . ."

"I do not feel at all like a woman of the world," said Mrs. Tremayne burying her face in his shoulder, and with a delicate snuffle going on in her nose.

He placed his hand more firmly round her, and his fingers encountered the delicious softness of her bosom. Was there ever such a charming creature? So bewitching, so changeable, so like a spring day of sunshine?

"You need a son like Mr. Blackwood's," she said.

Mr. Sedgwick thought to himself that if he had been a weaker man he would have groaned. As it was he merely exclaimed: "I hope he resembles his mother more than Blackwood —for the boy's sake."

"I believe that is true."

"Oh? How do you know?"

"You will not be angry, darling?"

"Why should I be angry?"

"I know you dislike my allowing strangers to speak to me."

"You cannot always . . ."

"Thank you, darling. I had no intention, of course, of striking up an acquaintance. I was buying an evening paper in the hotel—and I found I had no money. And an officer in naval uniform—I think it was naval—offered me the three-halfpence—such a small—and inconvenient—sum. But there it was. He asked was it a Sedgwick paper? I don't know why. And I said unfortunately it wasn't because, of course, they were the best . . . and one thing led to another. He said he knew one or two editors . . . and it seemed he knew Mr. Blackwood *very* well, and his wife, too, and the son . . . knew them *extraordinarily* well . . . *quite* extraordinarily . . . something almost strange about the way he spoke of them. I mentioned I had seen Mr. Blackwood that morning. . . . He has a great admiration for you—said the country needs men like you——"

"Blackwood said?"

"No, dear, the naval officer—Captain Dryden. He likes the slogan you print on the front pages: 'For king and country'."

"Good."

Mr. Sedgwick experienced a small glow. This was the artist in him, he reflected. No matter how many millions of copies you sold, no matter how much you prided yourself on being indifferent to letters of abuse—or praise—you couldn't withstand the word of appreciation. After all, you did need reaction—otherwise it was as if you threw the papers every morning into the Thames. Or this great river here in Greycastle; for they had now left the roads of Cheshire behind and had entered the purlieus of the seaport. The moon, in its misty wreath, which he had been enjoying, whenever his preoccupation with Mrs. Tremayne allowed him to cock an eye at it, was beginning to be obscured by tall buildings, some of them most uncommonly black. All Blackwood's campaigns for smoke abatement clearly had had no effect whatsoever. None. He couldn't help being pleased about that. These damned reformers. . . .The English put 'em in their place.

Mrs. Tremayne, after a thoughtful pause, was saying: "It struck me, darling, that if Mr. Blackwood is intransigent——"

"He is, he is—and a Nonconformist, I'm sure."

"A small dinner-party, darling—along with the Molyneuxs. . . ."

He said: "Molyneux wouldn't be fit to come—and his wife—an ogre."

But Mrs. Tremayne was not to be dismayed. "Well, the Blackwoods, dear . . . you are the perfect host. Ask them to bring their son."

Um! He had, as a matter of fact, been turning over Blackwood—what to do about him. To take over the *Morning Star* without Blackwood wouldn't be half the score—not half. The agreement to differ on certain things—the whittling down—urbanity—men of the world. Well, well, it might be done. He said: "Polly, you are in a dangerous mood. You want to see Blackwood again—bring him under your spell. . . ."

She giggled. "It's his *wife* who is fascinating, dear—those were your words. And remember . . . "

"Yes?"

"You catch more flies with oil than you do with vinegar."

They would be at the hotel in a moment or two; but she lifted up her face and he kissed her rather hurriedly in the circumstances, but with immense zest. Really, this woman—how unpredictable!—and how delightful, how capable of making this love seem constantly and exquisitely illicit—as it was, of course, but not every illicit love remained so exciting. . . . How foolish to contemplate—what was it the actress said?—turning the hurly-burly of the *chaise longue* into the humdrum double-bed? No, no! No. He helped her out of the car with elaborate gallantry, and with the liveliest expectations of what lay ahead—he had an impulse to lift her up and carry her—up the half-dozen steps. He knew he could do it—he had carried her from one room to another more than once. However, he took her arm and they walked sedately up and into the hotel, across the hall and into the lift, with greetings fit for royalty floating about them, hovering over them—salutations—almost incantations—or whatever you called it. Very pleasant. You never quite became indifferent to it.

They walked down the quiet corridor—silent—soft—and she looked up and smiled at him. He squeezed her arm. Really . . . and fancy her remembering that saying of his—"You catch more flies with oil, et cetera"—and how true it was! If she ever wrote a book of memoirs—what a book it would be! In how many different cities—suites—had they made life memorable! . . .

It was an hour later that he finally acquiesced to her inviting the Blackwoods to a dinner-party. He was in no position to refuse her anything.

CHAPTER XVII

FROM THE TIME when Blackwood had first learnt that Mr. Sedgwick had made an offer to buy the *Morning Star* he had given thought to his own plan of action. His second conversation with Molyneux, in which Molyneux had made it clear that so far as he was concerned Blackwood could have a period of time in which to raise a sum equal to Sedgwick's offer gave Blackwood, in his judgment, freedom of action. He was spurred on, if he needed any spur, by his talk with Sedgwick. He would begin to sound men of substance who might be willing to invest money; a considerable sum would be needed—fully half a million pounds, for Sedgwick might possibly raise his bid again when he knew what was afoot.

But before that happened events were occurring in the newspaper world which called for comment, notably the publication of the written evidence of the Institute of Journalists presented to the Royal Commission. This document followed one drawn up by the National Union of Journalists published some weeks earlier. The institute's was much the milder of the two, but even this spoke of reports from its members in one or two areas of a steadily increasing tendency towards monopoly control; and said that in another county its members were strongly opposed to chain newspapers, fearing that such changes would limit free expression of opinion and lead to news distortion. In a further paragraph headed "Editors' freedom cramped", the institute said that a "cramping factor would be present in any policy which sought to secure identical expressions of opinion on national affairs in a number of grouped newspapers. Such a policy would impair the free expression of opinion which has traditionally belonged to the editor and which is assumed by large numbers of readers still to be his prerogative."

This view was, of course, in line with Blackwood's own, and in the leader that he wrote he said so. But he went deeper into it, recalling that the concentration of ownership had now reached a stage when five important groups controlled over one-third of the daily newspapers of England, Scotland and Wales, and that on one occasion at one stroke of amalgamation between two Press Groups, when three daily papers died, over one thousand five hundred newspaper workers had been thrown out of work. During the past twenty years, he wrote, the number of daily papers had fallen by thirty, and in London alone since 1906 the morning papers had been reduced by five and the evenings by four. "What does that mean," he asked, "except that variety of opinion and independence of opinion is being diminished?" He reminded them of the stunts that newspapers had indulged in to raise circulation—the insurance schemes, the beauty schemes, the gifts of all sorts of articles from Shakespeare to wringing machines, and the employment of mystery men to give away one-pound notes. Even newspapers of repute had been stampeded into copying these methods in order to prevent their readers being stolen by other journals less scrupulous. He went on: "The newspaper war is a very real one. This journal is one of a dwindling number which stands completely alone, which is not linked even with an evening paper, and whose editor has complete and absolute control over editorial policy and what is printed in its editorial pages in comment or news. This editorial authority and discretion is rare, and becoming rarer. In groups of newspapers where a common policy is laid down and followed, editors as remote from one another as London and Cornwall can be found expounding precisely the same arguments in almost identical phrases, and speeches by politicians and other public men are reported fully or sparsely as the minor dictator sitting in London has decided. An editor in those circumstances is little more than a ventriloquist's doll.

"Almost any independent newspaper may draw upon itself sooner or later the attention of one or other of the newspaper groups who may be seeking fresh allies to their kingdom. This newspaper is no exception. Newspaper proprietors who see small difference between the purveying of news and the sale of boots or bedsteads have made attempts to acquire this journal, and will no doubt do so again. We believe we shall carry our readers with us when we say that it would be a misfortune were they to succeed. Fifteen years ago in the city of Bristol a paper was founded—after a newspaper war had proved mortal to two or three contemporaries —bearing under its title the words: 'The paper all Bristol asked for and helped to create.' This identification of a city and its people with the newspaper published there, can be genuine and real. We believe this is so with Greycastle and this newspaper; and that this situation which has now lasted for nearly a hundred years will long continue.

"But the threat which, in our judgment, would result to true freedom of the Press were independent newspapers such as this to fall under the control of a group of newspapers whatever political views they held, is not confined to control of that nature. It could come from the restrictions which a jealous Government, or a Government hypersensitive to criticism, could place on supplies of newsprint which is the raw material and life's blood of newspapers. Without newsprint Press opinion would be silenced. With seriously limited supplies of newsprint, newspapers would be unable to perform their proper functions; they would be as men trying to run a race with one leg badly lame. A lamed Press must suffer some inevitable lowering of influence and prestige. Moreover, a Government could allow a situation to develop when newsprint was gravely short not so much because they were deliberately wishful that such a position should arise, as that they were careless and unmindful and had cared little whether the newspapers got their supplies or not, being unsure of the Press's importance or, alternatively, while being sure, resenting that importance. Newsprint supplies are undoubtedly short and how much is the result of ministerial blundering or ministerial intent is difficult to say. The charitable view is that there has been blundering. Those who have the interests of freedom of speech and writing at heart will continue to watch the position very closely."

During the time Blackwood had been writing this, a copy-boy had brought a note to Lovelace in somewhat uncertain pencilled writing and on disreputable paper saying: "Could I see you for a moment? F. Cheshire," and Lovelace had risen and gone out. He had found Cheshire in the reporters' room, alone except for Pritchard-Jones, who was writing his religious notes for the

Saturday edition. Cheshire indicated his wish that they should converse remote from Pritchard-Jones and they moved to the fireplace and stood beneath the bust of Mr. Shakespeare.

"I thought I'd better tell you first," said Cheshire, running his pipe stem along his moustache.

"Yes, Fred." Lovelace stooped over him like a hawk, his pointed nose only a foot from Cheshire's own. "Take your time—the edition won't go down for an hour or two."

"It's not that. You see—I've been making the early calls—police and that. I picked it up at the police. It's young Captain Blackwood."

"Bob Blackwood?"

"Yes—Mr. Blackwood's boy."

"What about him—is he hurt?—had an accident?"

Cheshire looked round towards Pritchard-Jones who, however, was oblivious of them, engrossed in a piece about a new organ for St. Matthias's Church.

Cheshire looked up, his brow crinkled: "He was arrested," he said. "But he's been allowed bail."

"What in the name o' God's he been doing?" Lovelace's fertile mind revolved at once. Embezzlement? Or some racket or other—surely he couldn't be mixed up in the troop rackets in Germany? Anyhow, the chaps had got away with it—no prosecutions so far as he was aware. Or had he killed somebody in his car? "Come on, Fred, what is it?"

Cheshire took hold of Lovelace's watch-chain and pulled him an inch nearer. With his hooked pipe stem he prodded Lovelace's waistcoat, heedless of the spots of saliva he was leaving there. "He'll be charged with assault—probably unlawful wounding. The man was taken to hospital—but allowed to go home. Lives up Ireland Road."

Lovelace said: "And he probably deserved all he got. What happened?"

"The police *say*—the police *say*," said Cheshire, "that Captain Blackwood, who was in his car, ran this man into the kerb so that he came off—the man was on a motor-bike. Captain Blackwood told him he must apologise for reckless driving, and when he wouldn't, knocked him down; and the man caught his head on the kerb."

"Was he a *big* man?"

"Don't know." Mr. Cheshire's heart immediately failed him a little. Why hadn't he asked that?

"Didn't you find out?" Lovelace fixed him with his eyes.

"I'll give them a ring now," said Cheshire.

"Wait now. Have you written anything?"

"No—that's why I asked you——"

"Right! Don't. Will the other papers pick it up? Bound to, I suppose."

Cheshire's face was working hard, a small bone in his cheek going up and down, as it was wont to when he was excited. "That's another thing I wanted to ask—shall I try to get hold of the boys to see if they'll keep it out?"

"Don't do anything—just sit tight. I'll talk to O.B.,—I'll talk to him now. Hang on now—take it easy."

Blackwood looked up as Lovelace re-entered the room. "Did you see, Richard, that a miner's leader says it is really the Press which is responsible for the loss of half a million tons of coal in the Grimethorpe strike? Rubbish, of course, but keep it by you. Collect some other extravagant charges against newspapers— may give you enough for an amusing 'short' one evening."

"Yes, I'll do that." Lovelace walked across to Blackwood's table and stood with his fingers outstretched touching it. He didn't speak for a moment.

Blackwood, seeing the long taut hand, asked: "What is it, Richard?" He knew the signs when Lovelace wanted to speak. Lovelace said: "Cheshire's picked up a thing at the police."

"Yes? Something good?"—the journalist's lightness in the voice. They wouldn't be mentioning it to him unless . . .

"Well . . . it's Bob . . ."

Blackwood put down his pen. "Yes?" The lightness was extinguished; he felt like a judge now.

Lovelace said: "He's been involved in some sort of a fracas and got himself arrested, but has been released."

"I see." Dryden, Dryden—was this that side of Bob emerging again? After a pause, Blackwood said: "You'd better let me see what Cheshire's written."

"He's written nothing."

"Why?" The voice was harder.

"He wasn't sure if he ought to—he asked me. I told him to wait—until, anyhow, I'd spoken to you."

128

"I appreciate your solicitude, Richard, but Cheshire must write as if—it were somebody we don't know."

He spoke with precision, coldly. Then he saw the gravity of Lovelace's face and threw a half-smile across his own. "Come, Richard," he said, "tell me what happened."

Lovelace looked at him, saw the Blackwood he was familiar with in tight corners—the glint in the eye, the mouth pulled a trifle to one side.

When Lovelace had finished, Blackwood asked: "Is that all we know?"

"I think so."

"Not very complete. Cheshire still there?"

"Yes."

"Have him in."

Mr. Cheshire entered with some trepidation. He felt that, somehow or other, he ought to have already tried to fix it with the other reporters doing the police calls to keep it dark. But this subject Blackwood did not even refer to. What he wanted to know was whether the police thought his son was, in any degree, justified in the action he took.

Mr. Cheshire said he didn't know.

"What had the cyclist, in fact, been doing precisely?"

"They didn't tell me." Why was he himself so honest? Cheshire asked himself. Minnie, his wife, always said to him: "What's the good of being honest? Gets you nowhere—except into the street." And here he was again. . . . He could hear Minnie at him: "Why did you. . . .?"

Blackwood was asking: "Who struck the first blow?"

"Captain Blackwood."

"You sure?"

"Well, I took it . . ." Come to think of it he wasn't sure. Why hadn't he asked? But (in despair) they wouldn't have told him, even if they knew.

"I see. You don't really know." Blackwood spoke gently, but Cheshire saw menace in the gentleness. Blackwood continued: "Is my son charged with being drunk, in addition?" The question was so obvious, yet Lovelace (who was also now accusing himself) had never asked it.

"I don't think the word 'drunk' is used."

"You are not sure?"

Es

"Y-es. I should have remembered that."

"You didn't copy the charge?"

"They—they shut up if you take too many notes."

"Very well, Mr. Cheshire. Go and write your paragraph." But Cheshire hesitated. "Mr. Blackwood——"

"Yes?"

He blurted it out. "Your son once came to a 'do' at the Press Club—towards the end of the war it was—he was very popular. The boys wouldn't want to put it in the papers—not if it was left to them. I could probably do a bit of——" He stopped there, floundering under Blackwood's eye.

"How long have you been on this paper, Mr. Cheshire?"

Cheshire thought, "Now I've done it. I've done it now all right." He said: "Five years, Mr Blackwood."

"It ought not to have taken so long to get to know us. Go and write your paragraph—on what you think are its merits—and safe from libel." Cheshire began to withdraw as fast as he could. "And, Mr. Cheshire . . ." The voice stopped him abruptly.

"Yes, Mr. Blackwood?"

"Thank you all the same for what you had in mind—but it won't do, you know."

"Th-thank you, sir." It was all right, then, it was all right. He hurried out, his eyes watering with relief.

It was not a very remarkable paragraph that Mr. Cheshire produced and a while later laid with a delicate and tentative hand on Blackwood's desk. It said:

In an argument that arose between a motorist and a motor-cyclist in Manchester road, Greycastle, last evening, blows were exchanged and the cyclist was treated for injuries at St. Bartholomew's hospital and later went home. The motorist, Captain Robert Blackwood, D.S.O., of St John's Wood, London N.W., was arrested and will be charged this morning with assault.

Blackwood read it twice and then asked Cheshire: "Did the police tell you he had the D.S.O.?"

"No, Mr. Blackwood—but I knew. Ought I not——"

"Leave it with me."

Cheshire withdrew, again troubled over what he had done.

Blackwood called Lovelace across, pushed the paragraph over to him.

Lovelace said: "I heard what you said about the D.S.O."

"Yes. I don't think we are entitled to use that—doesn't emerge."

"No. I agree."

"I have been thinking, Richard . . ." Blackwood took the sheet of paper and held it up.

"Yes, Oliver?"

"In the ordinary way we should take out the motorist's name—to be on the safe side of libel."

Lovelace felt warmer inside.

Blackwood struck out the name. "We can't bend over so far backwards that we become unjust, eh?" Blackwood looked up at Lovelace, creasing his eyes.

Lovelace was thinking: "By God! you'd think he was enjoying himself—the president of the Inquisition at work." He said: "There'll not be much left of the paragraph now—it's hardly worth——"

"Oh, I think we'll let it go now."

"Is it a *must?*"

"No. Greenhalgh can use his discretion."

"If he sees Robert's name crossed out——"

"Rewrite it, Richard, yourself."

As Lovelace was rewriting the paragraph, Blackwood said: "I think, Richard, I'll have a word with the police myself."

Lovelace took up his telephone:

"Shall I try and get the superintendent on?"

"Yes, do."

Blackwood went on working till Lovelace had made all the explanations, and said: "Here's Superintendent Giles now."

Blackwood took up his telephone. "Superintendent?"

"Yes, sir."

"This case of my son—was the injured man much hurt?"

"No, sir—he'll be fit to be at court in the morning."

"What time?"

"Half-past ten, sir. Stipendiary's court. Will you be there, sir?"

"Yes."

"Very good, sir. I'll look out for you. Will your son be represented, sir—legally?"

"I don't know. Do you regard the case as complicated?"

"No, sir—not on the evidence we have."

"Did the police see what happened?"

"A constable saw the latter bit of the fight, sir."

"Has my son any witnesses?"

"Not sure, sir. There was somebody with him in the car."

"Was it a man or——"

"Captain Dryden, I believe, sir."

"I see." Of all people, Dryden . . . involved in this. . . . Blackwood asked: "Will he be called?"

"Well, that's a matter for your son, sir."

"Did Captain Dryden get mixed up in the fracas?"

"Not really, sir—he seems to have had difficulty in getting out of the car."

"I see." (Pause.) "I understand my son alleges the man drove recklessly. Is there evidence of that?"

"No police evidence, sir."

"I see. Thank you. Oh, one thing more—is my son up on a *police* charge?"

"Yes, sir."

"Will he be in the dock?"

"I'm afraid he will, sir."

"Thank you, Superintendent."

"You're welcome, sir."

Blackwood put down the receiver. "You gathered something from that, Richard?"

"Yes, Dryden—he might be a good witness for Bob."

"He might. And now I think I'll go to supper."

Blackwood put on his hat and pulled it sharply down.

Lovelace asked: "Are you coming back?"

"Yes—I'd like to see a proof of that leader there for one thing"—he pointed to what he had written earlier. "All about the integrity of the Press, Richard." He fingered his beard, and for an instant smiled wryly again. Then: "By the way, speak to Bryce—he'd better cover the court specially tomorrow—nothing fancy, but I want a full note—good straight stuff, so that if I decide to run it . . ."

"Run it?" thought Lovelace. "Good God. . . ."

With that, Blackwood went, briskly, as if he were light of heart. Lovelace walked slowly over to his own desk, holding up

Cheshire's paragraph to his weak eyes, muttering: "I wouldn't print a word of it—not a bloody word."

CHAPTER XVIII

BLACKWOOD PUT HIS head into the warmth and fiddling clatter, like that of metallic insects, of the composing-room, on his way out, and told Seth Entwistle he could get the leader off his table. Seth, standing in his partitioned little cubicle, pushed up his spectacles on to his forehead and said: "Thank you, Mr. Blackwood, I'll see to it." Seth smiled in expectation; he liked to read the leader before it was set; one of his nightly enjoyments. The harder the clouting, the better Seth liked it. Blackwood went down the corridor, unlocked his private lavatory and took a drink of water with a pill, for his inside was aching. In crises he could be brisk and swift. But his other method was to become more deliberate, as if his movements were rather more weighted. In this mood he would carry out small pieces of routine with more meticulous care than usual, as if he were running up a flag signalling, "I am not to be hurried". It was with deliberation he set off towards the Athenaeum Club, that ugly gothic granite building black with soot and age.

He paused in the courtyard of the *Morning Star* and looked up at St. John's clock, with the tip of its big finger broken in the blitz and never repaired; a symbol, in its fashion, of England battered and bruised but still going on. Seven-thirty, said the old grey face which badly needed a wash. Behind the square clocktower the sky was pale blue and green with scarves of cloud. Ah, that was lovely; serenity and beauty beyond realisation. If he were a painter, he thought, he would paint nothing but the sky, never two days the same, never less than a manifestation of the gateway of heaven.

He resumed his way pondering.

Now how easy it was, he reflected for the hundredth or thousandth time in his career, to put the world to rights, to tell statesmen and politicians and town councillors what the wise and right thing was—and how difficult to order your private affairs with becoming wisdom and justice; even more, to preserve the right relationship with those near to you; to be tolerant and forbearing, neither being too harsh, nor yet too relenting, so that you weakened their fibre; nor yet being irritated by that which you knew ought not to cause a ripple of irritation. He foresaw that the situation between him and Bob would be difficult and might be tense; for the gulf was emphasised by a certain inarticulateness on both sides when feeling was involved. Extraordinary how difficult they could both find it to explain themselves; the more remarkable because Blackwood by his nature and training was accustomed to see all round a question. He had sympathy with Bob over this unfortunate business and yet it ought never to have occurred. Bob should have been more discreet, more in command of himself. He was a public servant, in Government employ, a man to whom passengers, among them people of the highest distinction, entrusted their lives. Airmen were often daredevils, and the best fighter pilots had usually a certain amount of devilry in them; but pilots of civilian aircraft, captains of airships, were a different breed—they must be steady, reliable, cautious, safe—above all, safe. He knew, of course, that Bob had some of the qualities of the fighter pilot in him; it had been as much pure luck as anything else, the spin of the wheel, which had sent him into bombers rather than fighters in the war. Being there, he had made good—but only as he would have made equally good in fighters, had he survived long enough. He had ended the war in Pathfinder Force, flying Mosquitoes, putting down the markers on the German cities which were to be destroyed—"written off" was Bob's phrase. "We certainly wrote them off," he had said. Two or three times he had acted as controller, directing the attack from his Mosquito, directing the markers, and the bombing force, telling the Lancasters when they could start dropping their bombs, and when they could go home, the town duly blazing and turned into hell. He knew enough from talks with Bob, mostly dragging it out of him, to gather what it was like.

Down below you the hideous inferno and destruction and slaughter that didn't bear thinking of—and, in fact, you didn't think of it much, Bob said; and round about you the crumping of flak, the streams of incendiary bullets from night fighters you were busy corkscrewing away from, and the occasional horror of watching Lancasters go down in balls of fire—maybe the engine and wings flying on for a second or two when the tail had been shot off—going on and then shooting down as a flaming torch to extinction; or watching a Lancaster explode in midair, disintegrate, *whoof*! Well, thought Blackwood, as he walked to the club, you went through all that thirty, forty, fifty times, and then it was over. Lo, it was over, and you were supposed to be no different, you hadn't changed one iota, it was supposed, from the quiet, peaceful fellow you were prewar. Your values now turned a somersault back to peace; you hadn't got to lay hands on a fellow now, even if he were a scoundrel, whereas five minutes ago you had to exterminate children if they happened to be born on the wrong side of a frontier. . . . Bob hadn't said all that, not in so many words, but Blackwood suspected that underneath the crust of him things went on; how could they not? The surprising thing was that the volcano beneath the crust of man was as quiescent as it was, and that in many a man it was extinct. Well, it wasn't extinct in Bob. The war had left behind, as Blackwood had grown aware, an ingrained cynicism which Bob's close contacts with France, Germany, Denmark, Italy and Sweden had reinforced. For in all of them he had run into pessimism and despair; a belief that World War Three was round the corner and that in it they would be overrun, turned into battlefields, probably this time destroyed utterly. Bob had spoken to Blackwood of finding England's comparative calm, complacency and obsession with welfare, higher wages and shorter hours infuriating, remote from the brutal facts; he saw all that obsession as delusion and sham. Allied to that obsession and running alongside it was a decline, as Bob saw it, in authority, an undermining of discipline in the country especially among civilians, but in the services, too; as witness the rate of venereal disease in the army in Germany. Blackwood's talks with Bob had laid bare much of this and hinted at more. So that he was troubled quite a good deal about Bob's state of mind as he walked to the club. There was another point, too: why had Bob not got into touch with him, sent him a message? Surely he had enough confidence in him, Blackwood, to do that, even though they didn't see eye to eye on discipline. This parent and child relationship again . . . the most difficult thing in the world even in the ordinary way; and here . . .

He went straight to the club telephone to try and speak to Bob, not expecting him to be at home. But he was.

"Bob . . ."

"Yes, father." The voice was more toneless than usual.

"I've heard about this business in court tomorrow."

A short pause. Then: "Well?"

"Do you want to be represented?"

"I can say my piece."

"Do you want an adjournment—for witnesses or anything?"

"No—I don't think we want to go to this target twice." Blackwood sensed the grim smile behind that.

"Have you told your mother?"

"Not yet—she's out."

"All right. I'll be home early—ten thirty or so."

"Fair enough." (Pause.) "I'm sorry for all this."

"All right. These things happen." (Pause.) "Where did you find Dryden?"

"In the American bar at The Grand."

"I see."

"I suppose the papers will make quite—a thing of it?"

"I don't think they'll be able to leave it out."

"Nor *The Morning Star* either?"

"No."

"Mother will think you ought to, I dare say."

"Yes, she may."

"I'll have a word with her."

"Leave it, Bob,—don't get yourself across with her just now."

"It's sure to crop up when I tell her."

"The publicity will depend on what emerges—and what line of defence you take."

A pause; then, "Yes."

"We'll have a talk about that."

"Yes."

"All right, Bob. See you later."

"O.K."

Blackwood went in to supper wearing a frown that started over his eyes and seemed to him to go down to the pit of his stomach. He sat at a table alone and made one or two notes for a leader on the Petkov murder. Afterwards he buried himself in an armchair and slept for fifteen minutes.

136

Wilfred Fletcher said as Blackwood went past his lodge in the office: "Mr. Sedgwick's secretary brought a letter, sir—a few minutes ago. I sent it up."

"Thank you, Wilfred. How's the leg tonight?"

"Better, sir. In for a dry spell."

"Good—we can do with it."

Now surely, he thought, as he climbed the stairs, Sedgwick hadn't heard already about Bob. The letter was on his desk. It ran:

My dear Blackwood,

I wonder whether, before I leave Greycastle, you and your wife and son—if he happens to be at home at the moment—would do me the honour of dining with me and Mrs. Tremayne here one evening? We should very much enjoy meeting your family and there would, of course, be no business questions discussed.

I am sending this round by hand because tomorrow night would be convenient for us, if you could manage that. But I quite realise that this notice is short. Unhappily, so will be my stay in the city.

Yours very sincerely,
Samuel Sedgwick.

PS. No hard feelings over what passed between us. I always appreciate frankness.

CHAPTER XIX

Before Blackwood had returned to the office, Seth Entwistle brought the proof of Blackwood's article as Lovelace was alone, writing. Seth wore his apron and his cap that was too small; his sleeves were rolled up. Seth placed the proof on Blackwood's writing-pad, putting it down almost with a touch of reverence. He took off his steel spectacles and put them on again. He looked across at Lovelace, feeling in his bones this was an important occasion. He said: "You've seen the leader, tonight, Mr. Lovelace?"

"Yes, Seth." Lovelace leaned back and thrust his long legs out so that his big boots projected through his desk.

"I'm not in love wi' the sound of it, Mr. Lovelace."

"No?"

"A lot o' wars and rumours o' wars come on to my desk out yonder—but they don't seem as important as this."

"Ah!"

"Professor Einstein has written a letter to UNO sayin' only the General Assembly can banish the threat of extinction that hangs over humanity—come on my desk a while ago."

"Yes, Seth."

"But it doesn't have the importance o' this threat to the old paper."

"No."

"No. It comes right home, does that. Is it the Sedgwick crowd who's after us?"

"I believe it is."

"These bloody combines—monopolies—cartels—like a plague o' leeches after your blood."

"That's it."

"If you're a good little property they won't leave you alone."

"True, lad."

"My brother-in-law had a grocer's shop. They gave him no peace—till he gave in. Quite a tidy sum he got—and what good were it to him? Nothing to do now. Fancies he's got every ailment under the sun, and if he hasn't he soon will have. You should hear my sister on combines."

"The women know."

"They do. What does the baronet want to sell for?"

"He may be trying to dodge death duties, Seth."

"If you give your stuff away, do you dodge 'em?" Seth smiled. "Must be a terrible thing to have a bit o' brass these days, and the Government chasin' it."

"Not to be borne."

"But my heart doesn't bleed for 'em as it should, Mr. Lovelace."

"On that we're at one."

"That's a lack in us, Mr. Lovelace."

"It is, Seth, it is. No charity, no feeling, no loving-kindness."

"It gives me a warm feeling, a glow, to let th' owd devil in me have his fling sometimes."

"I wouldn't say you're unique, Seth."

"When I hear o' somebody payin' nineteen and six in the pound income-tax it doesn't give me a sleepless night."

"Do I understand you've no pity for the poor rich?"

Seth chuckled.

Lovelace went on: "That the Socialist onslaught on them gives you a kick, pleases the malicious envy in you?"

"I'm a sinful man, Mr. Lovelace."

"And that therefore we shall be saddled with the Socialists for ever, pandering as they do to the worst side of us?"

Seth considered that. He said: "I think it's the women will put 'em out. Women, Mr. Lovelace, are the real Tories. My wife remembers when my weekly wage were less than thirty bob and on that she brought up the kids; and she saved a hundred pounds in the Co-op, and she even made me start buyin' a house on the never-never. And she wants to know why others can't do the same—she doesn't hold wi' makin' things too easy. 'Not when I've worked my fingers to the bone,' she says. 'What are the childer like nowadays?—all impudence and walkin' about with the key of the house tied to a string round their necks while their mothers are proppin' up the bar in the Dog and Duck, all ginned up, like they learned to do in the war when they were on munitions makin' more brass than was good for 'em.'"

"Would you say the workers are their own severest critics, Seth?"

"You've hit it, Mr. Lovelace. When these Cabinet Ministers come round butterin' everybody up, the chaps know they're talkin' rot. They want to know what's the good o' tellin' a chap who's not pullin' his weight that he's a hero? What's it in aid of? The men know we'd too much o' that durin' the war; in them days every man in the merchant marine was a hero—and if there was one place they knew it wasn't true, it was here in Greycastle. The truth—that's what people like, Mr. Lovelace."

"I wonder . . . I wonder."

Seth began to look solemn. "They respect it, anyhow," he said.

"They don't *buy* it—not to any extent."

"*I* buy it—when I can get it," said Seth.

"There's papers, Seth, in which very nearly the only thing you can rely on is the date—and they sell in millions."

Seth was silent.

"And then there's us, Seth, lucky if we sell seventy thousand."

"Aye," said Seth. "Aye."

"And practically every paper in the country of our quality is a parasite."

Seth looked startled. "Nay, nay. . . ."

"A barnacle, Seth, living on the back of its evening paper—kept afloat by it—and the evening paper living on racing results and the Saturday football or cricket editions. . . ."

"You make it sound a bad lookout for us, Mr. Lovelace. I'd best be off—or you'll have me jumpin' off the landing-stage. Sounds a miracle we keep goin' at all."

"That's what we are—a daily miracle."

"Will the Press Commission make things any better?"

"If it did, that would be the greatest miracle of all, Seth."

"You mean our only hope is in our right arm?"

"That's it, Seth."

"Well, when I read that leader tonight"—Seth pointed to the proof lying on Blackwood's table—"I said to myself: 'This is the flag of revolt,' I said. 'We're running up our colours,' I said, 'nailin' 'em to the mast.' Was I right?"

"Dead right. Never righter."

"That's enough for me, then," said Seth. He glanced towards the proof again. "I could have wished he'd have socked 'em a bit harder. But maybe that'll come?"

"Give it time, as Queen Lizzie used to say."

"Did she? Aye, well, she was a corker too." He cocked his ear. "I think I can hear him comin'—that stride—the way he puts his feet down."

Seth stood near the door to let Blackwood enter, said: "The proof's on your desk, Mr. Blackwood," and made a rapid exit.

Lovelace looked up when Blackwood entered and waited as Blackwood stood over his desk for a moment, read the letter from Sedgwick, picked up the proof of his leader and ran his eye over it.

Presently Lovelace said: "Fraser, news editor of the *Mercury*, rang me up about Bob's arrest—asked me what we were

140

doing with it. He said they didn't mind keeping it out. I told him what we were doing. He said he guessed they'd do about the same."

"Thank you, Richard. Did you thank Fraser?"

"Yes, I did."

"This leader looks all right. It can go."

"Good. It will make us a few more enemies, no doubt, but you won't mind that."

Blackwood, now sitting down in his chair and feeling the reassurance of familiarity, said: "We're moving into a period, Richard, when we shall make a lot of enemies, I dare say—and possibly one or two friends. We may even find out which is which."

He was thinking how extraordinarily—and comfortingly—cut off one felt in a newspaper office—akin to a miner down a pit. On his way up he had looked into the subs.' room where Charles Greenhalgh sat at the head of the long wooden table—presiding over his men, who sat on both sides as if they were dining; as, in a sense, they were, sampling the news, tasting it, cutting it, rewriting it, accepting this, rejecting that. Gods of events. There, the passing world was appraised on its value as news—you were quite inhuman about it. It was a good story if fifty men were killed in a pit accident; it was an even better story if a hundred were killed. Uproar in the Commons with a member suspended was better news than if the debate were dull and orderly. But the strange thing, or rather the wonderful and exciting thing, was the feeling of community in the office, of being a brotherhood, remote from the world—in a sense estranged from the world, a select band weighing the world, blaming it, praising it, putting it in its place. You were, so to speak, isolated, beleaguered, in a fortress. Messages came in and went out, but you didn't readily admit anybody to the brotherhood; everybody who wasn't a journalist—and a journalist on your own paper—was something of an outsider, possibly a spy. For here in this citadel sacred to news there were secrets—secrets first of all of what you knew and did not print, but secrets too of that which you would presently divulge with a bang, with a dramatic announcement, with headlines in appropriate type. And this citadel at this time of night was roaring with activity. In Greenhalgh's room sub-editors were bawling: "Boy! Put this up!" to youngsters usually ill-clad and of small education who pumped the sub-edited copy up pneumatic tubes to the composing room. Boys were hurrying round the table, picking up the folded telegrams and written copy. Sub-editors were rising in a rush from the table to hurry upstairs and make up their pages; reporters even walking in to deposit their stories at the side of Greenhalgh; boys were bringing jugs of tea to the subs. who were due to take a spell and eat their sandwiches at the desk. Greenhalgh, his face red with work and stress was watching the clock as if it were an enemy which would destroy them if it could (as indeed it was). All this was meat and drink to Blackwood. He had something of a scholar in him, a recluse, but he was equally the man who exulted and revelled in the heat and noise of the nightly battle. He was a commander moving among his men, giving encouragement, cool judgment, implicitly inviting them to seek his advice, reading a piece of sub-edited copy and approving or suggesting a headline. Here was Swindells the foreign sub., nervy, stammering, so short-sighted that he cannoned into you, who spoke to you in whispers as if the Kremlin would hear; here was Simpson, swollen to fatness, his waistcoat bursting at the back, a green eyeshade fastened with elastic round his bald head, the paper's whale on handling the splash; yonder was Chick Wadham, enormously tall with a bush of fair hair, ill tempered and rather stupid but passionately devoted to accuracy, and spending a good deal of time taking stories back to the reporters' room and demanding further information; Llewellyn, the Welshman, who knew to a nicety which Welsh correspondents were, and were not, reliable and how many times the goldmine near Barmouth had been rediscovered; young Smithers, smiling and boyish so that you wondered how he had got here; Godfrey Nichols, who was learning how it was all done before he took over his father's paper at North Shields; Webster, who drew cartoons of them all while he nibbled his sardine sandwiches; Crankshaw, who spent all his spare moments working on the competitions set by the London weekly reviews. They stared at the copy before them as if spellbound, pondering like chess players on what to do with it; they slashed the copy as if they hated it; they took another batch from Greenhalgh as if it would poison them; once in a while they sat back and smiled when they had achieved a headline that pleased them or some piece of news came in to sole and heel a former piece. To one side the tape machine ticked out its stream of perforated news from all over the world; through the glass door the telephoto apparatus was glinting and glowing, its bulbs burning, as if it were an infernal machine; and at the far end, somewhat isolated, youths sat with headphones on, tapping at noiseless typewriters as they listened to correspondents from a few miles away, or scores of miles away, dictating their messages. Overhead was whirring the copy carrier so that Blackwood stooped to speak in Greenhalgh's ear: "Anything better than Parliament to lead on?"

"Not yet. Longworth's stuff's not too bad, though."

"The Petkov murder—good enough for the end column?"

"Yes, I think so. Are you doing a leader on it?"

"Yes—a short one. The archbishop on the danger of planning carried to excess so that it robs people of initiative—quite interesting, but . . ."

They smiled at one another. In former days the "but" would have meant "keep it short". Now it hardly needed saying. In the clicking noise and the ejaculations of subs., Greenhalgh indicated the piles of copy. "One long execution," he said. "Quarts into eggcups."

Blackwood smiled again: "Like writing poetry—compression and again compression." He straightened himself. "I shan't stay late tonight. Lovelace will be here—and I shall be at home if anything breaks loose." He added: "Lovelace, by the way, will send you a paragraph about an arrest—a motorist. . . ."

"A 'must'?"

"No—as heaven decides." It tickled him to leave it to destiny.

In the corridor on the way to his room he had looked in on Charles MacGibbon, an Irishman from Belfast who looked after books and did dramatic criticism, a man who talked so fast and so Irish that he was hard to understand; and on Noel Longstaff, stabled with him, who had started life in a Yorkshire foundry and now edited the special features and wrote curt notices of films—notices which sometimes contradicted the views of their London film critic who had had first bite at them. Next door was Randolph Exeter, who had lectured in modern European history but who, having punctured a lung, had retired to the life of writing he had long coveted. Exeter, a hunchbacked man who had much cause to be sour but wasn't, had lighted, some days earlier, on a definition of the duty of a Communist which had impressed him: "Who fights for Communism must be able to say the truth and not to say the truth, to fight and not to fight, to keep a promise and to break a promise, to get into danger and avoid danger, to be known and to be unknown. Who fights for Communism has of all the virtues only this—that he fights for Communism." How much longer was it wise, Exeter had asked Blackwood, to hold to the principle of giving to Communists freedom to spread their doctrine, to stir up dissension in workshops and factories? They discussed it now for a moment or two, Exeter so low on his desk that his head looked decapitated, a head speaking in a soft sweet voice, mildly. "In time of war," he was saying, "we clamp down on this treason or near treason. But in this time of peace, which is no peace but another sort of war, we permit it."

Blackwood said: "Perhaps, Randolph, we need a fresh set of rules for the transition period."

"Yes, I'm inclined to think so."

"Will they allow ambassadors who're our potential enemies to go on enjoying diplomatic privileges, sending out secret bags containing knowledge gained by espionage?"

Exeter smiled. "And attending our manoeuvres and visiting our armaments factories?"

Blackwood said: "And what about the journalists? Isn't every good journalist in a foreign country something of a spy? But all this cuts both ways. Or doesn't it?" He was stimulating Exeter to go on.

"Not quite," Exeter said. "How much do our diplomats discover in Russia? Or our journalists? What do we get from Moscow?"

Blackwood said blandly: "We get descriptions of the ballet and the five-year plan."

Exeter said: "My neighbour at home who commanded a Guards brigade thirty years ago and now spends his time observing nuthatchers, says we are being strangled by an international ju-jutsu and that our defeat is just round the corner."

"He may be right."

"He may."

"It doesn't disturb his bird watching, I suppose?"

"No."

"Well, Randolph, try doing a piece on whether we need a new set of rules to run in harness with this sort of war. The change-over is a question of timing. People must be geared to it, ready for it." He was goading Exeter again, who responded:

"They must be led," said Exeter.

"Now you are in the mood." And with that Blackwood had left him.

He had wanted to drop into his routine after the minor upset of Bob's arrest. And now he had done it. He forced himself to carry out public engagements, sat on the court of the university, was a governor of the Blue Coat School, was a vice-president of various literary and antiquarian societies. But doing those things was an effort. He spoke well enough when he had to, after taking immense pains. But it was a vast labour. Here, in this editorial chair, was where he belonged. He said pensively: "Sedgwick might sack you, Richard."

Lovelace picked himself up, slowly, in fragments, and lumbered across. "Mind you, Oliver," he said, "I've known men who made a fortune by getting the sack from one paper, taking three months' money and walking across the road into the rival office. My tragedy is I was never clever enough to do it—I've regretted it all my life." He grinned.

Blackwood said, pulling his beard: "I foresee, Richard, I shall have to take you with me—wherever I go. And you'll die in a newspaper office. You'll stagger down on your last night, and you'll write a great piece, feeling bemused and ethereal. You'll set down what it feels like when you've passed over and the choirs are singing and the angels are flying round you in salutation. It will be the real stuff at last. And in doing it, you'll die. And I shall walk over, and pick up the sheets of paper—and alas! there'll be nothing written down there. It will be a mighty work —of pure imagination."

"By God, Oliver—you're right—that's just how it will be."

"Well, better write it now, Richard, while I do this short leader on the Petkov murder before I take myself off."

A silence fell as they both began to write.

CHAPTER XX

IT WAS TEN-THIRTY o'clock when Blackwood left the office. By soon after eleven he would be home. He could take a look at the sea before he went in. Yes, he would do that; the sea had a great influence on him; maybe he ought to have been a sea captain; maybe, if he had had a son, the boy would have been a seaman. If he had had a son. . . . What would he have been like? Lithe and dark and quick and full of fire? Or lumbering and fair and slow and playing rugby football for Cheshire—a country solicitor, or a cotton broker—no, hardly a cotton broker —the Labour Government had knocked that profession on the head. A junior partner in a shipping business?—one of those men he saw at the golf club, hearty, boyish, minds fixed in one channel, accepting everything Mr. Churchill said. A son three parts Hannah, with himself squeezed into the background; a son something like Bob? Yes. He might have been, in many ways, like Bob. The thoughts ran through his head as he was driving along, diving into the tunnel like a mole, emerging into the pale dark night, smoky-grey, past the ship-repair yards where vessels perched aloft like enormous toys, their screws looking fearfully naked—and on into the countryside growing rustic. But again, his thoughts continued, suppose fortune had given him several sons—for, although he was an only child himself, he thought it unwise to limit a family to one child unless Fate willed it so.

It would have been a fine thing to have half a dozen sons— doing all the jobs he would have liked to do—a sea captain, an actor and playwright, a country doctor, a judge of the High Court, a landscape painter, a scientist working on the cure for cancer. He would like to be born again six times over and do all those things. Each son with a particle of him, Blackwood, in him. His immortality. Hannah would have been a happy woman if that had happened—a woman born to have children. She had once said, when they were first lovers, that she would like to work in the fields and have a child every year. And this, and this, was how it had proved to be; this was the best that could be done. Bob could say, "I am all the sons of my father's house . . ."

No, he could not even say that. The day would come when Bob would learn the truth. . . . Or would it come? Would any purpose be served? Tomorrow . . . with Dryden in court . . . Bob and Dryden together . . . the same look about the face . . . the obstinate lip and jaw, the low forehead, hair coming to a point . . . . But he wouldn't think of that. No. Too much imagination, the conjuring up of devils, the witnessing of the drama before it occurred . . . useless, useless. And yet, and yet . . . forewarned . . . the awkward question parried in advance, so that when it came it struck no surprise, the reply calm, thought out, assured . . . something in that.

By the time he got out of the car and faced the sea, the wind was rising. The breakers were coming in, forceful, as if they were attacking the coast, delivering their blows, sullenly.

The house was silent when he entered it. The room was silent in which Hannah and Bob were. Bob was stretched out in a chair, his face moody and morose. Hannah was sitting with a book in her lap but she was not reading. They both looked up when he entered, but for a moment neither spoke. Then Hannah asked in a small voice, listless: "Can I get you anything?" Bob moved and rose and walked across to the window and looked down the garden, darkened now, towards the sea.

Blackwood, deeply aware of the charged atmosphere but determined to fight it, said: "I think if we all had a whisky and soda and a bite of something, that might do us no harm."

Hannah, rising, said in her heavy, slow voice: "You wouldn't think champagne was the right thing?" But she didn't wait for an answer. She went out and Bob turned in the window and said: "I thought I'd better tell her before you came."

"Yes, Bob—right."

"I can't make her out. Seems to be upset more by Dryden being mixed up in it than anything else."

Blackwood thought: "That's going to make it no easier." He said: "I wanted to ask you about that—about calling him as a witness."

Hannah returned with a tray and listened as Bob said: "Dryden was pretty tight—the police saw that."

Blackwood said: "But wasn't he competent to see the man's bad driving?"

147

"Yes, I think he was. And the police took his name. What he actually said was that the fellow ought to be shot or castrated."

Hannah said: "Why drag him into it?" She spoke harshly.

Blackwood said: "It's a question of corroboration. There's no police evidence of this dangerous driving."

She said: "If they say Dryden was drunk—suppose they turn round and say that about Bob, too?"

Blackwood looked at Bob. "That's not likely, is it? Nobody has suggested you were intoxicated?"

"I was asked if I had had anything to drink. I said three beers."

"You see," said Hannah. She was drinking her whisky in sips, looking into her glass as if she were among enemies.

Blackwood said: "Three beers don't make Bob drunk, and, anyhow, Bob's driving isn't in question. All that matters is the degree of provocation Bob had."

"Keep Rex out of it," she said again.

Bob asked, frowning, "Why are you so anxious to keep him out, mother?"

Blackwood thought: "Ah, is this it—now?"

But Hannah still looked into her glass. "I have my reasons," she said.

Bob glanced from Hannah to Blackwood seeking enlightenment, and Blackwood, knowing Bob was looking at him, continued to stare into the fireplace, avoiding Bob's eyes. He hated all this, felt a little ashamed, felt, as he had felt on many another occasion, that he would be immeasurably relieved, shake off a burden, if he spoke the truth. But—as often before—this wasn't the right moment. So he spoke as if nothing deeper lay beneath, mentioned the obvious harm to Dryden's career if his drunkenness were talked of in court, but added that, as they all knew, he had risked his reputation many times, and if they had to choose between damaging Dryden's career and damaging Bob's by trying to protect Dryden, then the right decision wouldn't be difficult to make.

Hannah said bitterly: "This is a decline from your strict impartiality, isn't it?" He didn't answer that, and she went on: "Has your—change—gone far enough to keep the news out of the paper?"

A stone was beginning to grow in his heart. He said: "You must know perfectly well, Hannah, that the news will be treated on its merits—neither more nor less. We shall publish a paragraph tomorrow——"

She interrupted: "So that's how deep your protection goes——"

He finished his sentence: "But there'll be no name in the paragraph."

"Having it both ways," she said. "I wonder if Mr. Sedgwick would print something that might injure his son?"

Blackwood said, as patiently as he could: "I'm sorry about it, Hannah—but there it is. What Sedgwick does, or would do, is his own business. Our paper couldn't behave in that way."

"So I suppose we may expect a full report of the court proceedings in the *Star*?"

"A report—certainly. How full—depends on what happens."

"No matter what it does to Bob's career, of course."

"What we do will make no difference to that. The others——"

She said: "You could get the others to keep it out—or print just a few lines—if you tried hard enough. You know that's been done often enough."

"Not by us; any more than a judge can acquit his guilty relatives."

She said stubbornly: "Dog doesn't eat dog."

Bob said sharply: "It's no use, mother. It's fair enough. I told you earlier on."

"Ah!" she said, "the men—standing together. So we shall be pilloried for the sake of—integrity—or something or other."

She poured herself nearly half a tumbler of whisky, and Blackwood saw that her hand was trembling. She picked up the glass and turned to the door. "I shouldn't call Rex Dryden if I were you," she said. She gave them no time to reply.

As Blackwood was about to get into bed, his door opened and Hannah came in. He was startled not only by her abrupt entry but the fact that she had only half prepared herself for bed, her hair brushed but her makeup still on. She looked distraught. She hardly looked at him but asked in a low urgent voice: "Would you be printing it all if Bob were your son?" then turned and went swiftly.

He sat on the bed, pondering, tormented. O Christ, if he were whole, how easy the solution would be! Yet something must be done. He rose, put on his dressing-gown, went to her room, closing the door behind him. For a moment he stood there, silent, grave, solemn. She was sitting on the bedside, and holding a glass of whisky. She looked up without any surprise in her glance and then down again.

"Hannah——" He spoke tensely but quietly so that the house should not be disturbed.

She looked up, but didn't speak, and down at her knees again.

"—what do you expect me to do? You know perfectly well that what there is between you and me—over Bob—makes no difference to this case. In fact, it would be easier to print it if he were my son. We haven't lived together all these years without you knowing that."

She didn't answer.

He said: "We've both lived through a—good deal of hell. Must it go on? Would it be easier for you if I—cursed you when you go on like this? Or if I were violent? Is that what you want— what you're short of? By God, you know I could do it sometimes." A tremor ran through him and the pain in him was fierce all at once.

She looked at him and now her face broke and she started to cry. He stood there, torn and despairing but in a moment or two his anger had turned to sorrow. He crossed to the bed and put his arms about her. Fumblingly she put the glass down on the bedside table and crumpled into his arms, weeping, at first quietly but soon convulsively.

It was a long time before he went back to his room.

CHAPTER XXI

It was a radiant morning when Bob's case was heard; a morning of sunshine bright enough to catch the dust and illumine it, bright enough to put a sheen of lead and silver on the river, bright enough to help the Press photographers to secure some excellently sharp pictures of Bob and Blackwood as they approached the court. Blackwood, who was feeling very tired and rather irritable, saw them with distaste; he hadn't expected this.

He glanced at Bob, but Bob's face showed little. He was wearing his uniform, his gold braid, his gold-and-silver wings, his medal ribbons—all catching the light. Blackwood had not expected the uniform either, but he had not commented on it. Perhaps Bob had thought that if he were to be described as Captain Blackwood the magistrate had better know why. Anyhow, it was for Bob to decide. Bob looked older today, assured, rather stern; as if he were taking over an aircraft. (Blackwood had flown with Bob once or twice and had noticed that he was a somewhat different man on these occasions—more abrupt, more decisive in movements. So it was now.) They had spoken little as Bob drove them down in his Bentley. He had asked: "Will the magistrate be a professional—or one of the spare-timers?" Blackwood said the case was pretty sure to be in the stipendiary magistrate's court.

"Is he any good?" asked Bob.

"Quite sound, I think—Gervase Tebbutt, K.C. Doesn't get reported much—except his advice to erring husbands and wives not to expect perfection." The words struck at him as soon as he had spoken them.

"How do they get these jobs—politics?"

Blackwood found relief in explaining: "I don't think so. Of course, the Lord Chancellor is concerned, and he's a politician, but I imagine he's just as likely to choose a man from the opposite party—to prove his impartiality."

There the conversation had ended. It struck Blackwood that Bob might be turning over in his mind his own theme of indiscipline, but he hoped not, and he thought it wisest not to raise the topic. As they walked down the sunlit street with the photographers performing their ugly little ballet of dancing forward into their path and then sidestepping away, Blackwood saw Dryden standing near the court. No mistaking him, this jaunty fresh-faced man, wearing a double-breasted blue blazer and grey trousers. He had a straw panama hat on, too, cocked rather on one side. He might have been bound for a trip by river steamer judging by his clothes.

Dryden's greeting was hearty, almost as florid as his fresh face. "Hullo, Oliver. Hullo, old boy"—this to Bob. "Feeling all right?"

Bob replied: "Yes"—shortly; adding: "Thank you for coming."

"Oh, that's all right. Going to call me?"

"Not sure. I won't if I can avoid it."

151

"Oh, I don't mind, old boy."

Blackwood thought: "You haven't been drinking already, surely." Dryden seemed to be quite unaware that his tipsiness at the time of the accident would be likely to emerge if he were called.

Dryden added: "Better get inside, I suppose. The beak"—Blackwood almost winced at the word—"won't want to be kept waiting." Dryden began jovially to elbow his way through the small crowd of bookmakers' touts, drabs, dockers and spivs, one of whom, as Blackwood noted, had a bowler hat, a black satin tie and a face hideous and raw, as red and purple as if he had been boiled in steam. "What you call the hoi polloi, Oliver," said Dryden over his shoulder.

Inside the door of the court, Superintendent Giles greeted them, first showing Oliver Blackwood and Dryden to the solicitors' table, where Blackwood carefully chose the side opposite to Dryden. That done, Bob surrendered to his bail to an old inspector near the dock, and was then escorted by a young constable wearing the D.F.C. ribbon to an ante-room.

" 'Fraid you'll have to wait in here, sir, till the case is called," he said.

Bob nodded. This was the form, and that was that. He eyed his fellow prisoners with interest, and when his eyes were off them, they stared back at him. He certainly lent tone to them, these young toughs with their coloured pullovers and wide trousers, the old girls with bedraggled hats and skirts and faces ravaged and seamed by the map life had drawn there.

In the court-room Oliver Blackwood was glancing about him. The reporters' pew was crowded. The *Morning Star* had sent Forsyth, looking brisk in his metal-framed spectacles, his light hair brushed in a quiff, giving him the look of a terrier. At the solicitors' table you felt hemmed in, as Blackwood realised, for the tiny court-room, about the colour of a Nonconformist chapel, its woodwork a dirty yellow, rose in pews at various levels. You looked up to the magistrate's chair with its embossed leather—once maroon but now faded and cracked with age. To the magistrate's left was the witness-box towards which a hand crudely painted on the wall pointed in a somewhat menacing fashion. Behind the solicitors' table was the square dock with its iron rail and iron knobs. Over the top of the pews, heads bobbed along and policemen's eyes peered over at you and vanished again. Over the court-room hung the faint stale odour of officialdom and the insufficiently washed. Dryden leaned over to Blackwood and said, nodding backwards and using his eyebrows: "That's the fellow—behind the Press."

Blackwood saw him—certainly no beauty. Blackwood took in the low brow, short nose, high cheek-bones, long upper lip, jutting chin. One eye was darkened with a bruise. Blackwood's mind went back to his own days in the Greycastle Regiment; his platoon had contained several such men as this.

"Silence!" The court rose. Mr. Tebbutt, the magistrate, came in and bowed—a small, neat man in rusty black, bald, with thick black eyebrows. The clerk to the court, who was beneath him, got up and engaged him in a short earnest conversation. Then the drunks and disorderlies were called—three of them, one an old woman turned sixty who looked like a quiet grandmother but who was charged with biting a constable's hand.

"I wouldn't do such a thing, your Worship," she said indignantly.

"I warned you last time you were here," said Mr. Tebbutt patiently. "What am I to do with you? Why do you drink this Red Biddy—you know it's poison?"

"I hadn't got my teeth in," she said, still denying the bite.

"The constable had to have his hand dressed," said Mr. Tebbutt.

"You couldn't do it with these new Health teeth," she said.

Mr. Tebbutt sighed. "Seven days," he said, speaking to his notebook.

"Seven days!" called the gaoler in a loud voice.

The clerk to the court bobbed up again and had a word with Mr. Tebbutt, sat down and said in a small voice: "Put up Robert Blackwood."

"Robert Blackwood!" cried the gaoler in a ringing shout.

The anteroom door was flung open and the young D.F.C. constable said: "They've given us the green, sir." He ushered Bob into the dock through a door at the side. Bob was now on a level with the magistrate, elevated. Blackwood, watching him, thought he looked an impostor standing there—so handsome, and finely turned out, startling against that hideous background.

153

The clerk read the charge, which was one of unlawfully and maliciously wounding William Gallagher. Did the accused plead guilty or not guilty?

"Not guilty," said Bob in a clipped, staccato voice. He was staring about him stubbornly.

"Witnesses out of court!" cried the gaoler.

When Gallagher entered the witness-box Oliver Blackwood saw that he was over six feet; the back of his head bore a piece of sticking-plaster. His was the story of a much abused and astonished man, told by a sullen one. He had been motor-cycling home, he said, when this man—the accused—came after him and nearly ran him down and shoved him on to the sidewalk. He got off and this man started shouting at him and asking for his name and address, and when he asked him what business it was of his at all, then the man let fly at him and without any warning landed him one in the eye. He overbalanced and fell and caught his head on something—and that was all he knew about it.

He had a remarkably plausible and soft voice for so uncouth a face. "Is that all you want to say?" asked the clerk.

"Yes, sir."

The clerk turned to Bob. "Do you wish to ask the witness any questions?"

Bob said quietly, "Yes, I do." Then in a loud, commanding voice he cried: "Gallagher!"

The whole court stirred; expectant. Gallagher was startled and turned towards Bob, his scowl deepening. They stood eyeing one another like a pair of duellists. Then Bob said, with a nonchalant contempt:

"Will you tell the magistrate, Gallagher, why I knocked you down?"

Gallagher flushed a darker colour. "I wouldn't know that."

"Do you remember nearly crashing into the woman with the perambulator who was crossing the road at the corner of Formby Street?"

"No, I don't."

"Did you hear the woman scream?"

"No, I did not."

"Are you deaf?"

"No more than you."

A rustle passed over the court.

"Never mind me. You shot across the road in front of her missing her by no more than a yard. Remember?"

"It's a lie." This was in a lower tone.

"What speed were you doing?"

Mr. Tebbutt, who had been leaning back as if he were withdrawing from the case as far as he could, now suddenly leaned forward: "Gallagher—you are not bound to answer questions about your speed in such a way as to incriminate yourself. Yes, go on"—to Bob.

Bob repeated his question: "What speed were you doing?"

"About twenty-eight."

"When did you work that one out?"

No reply.

"After the magistrate spoke?"

Silence.

"What's the fastest you've ever done on that cycle?"

"I wouldn't swear to it."

"You were doing at least fifty-five up Manchester Road, weren't you?"

"I was not."

"Swerving all over the place?"

"No."

"Did you know I was pursuing you?"

A pause. Then: "I knew there was somebody hootin' and drivin' like somebody crazed."

"At a high speed?"

"Terrible speed."

"But you still kept ahead?"

Gallagher, cornered, looked round a little wildly. "To—to keep out of the way of you."

"Doing twenty-eight miles an hour?"

A rustle went over the court again. Dryden leaned across to Blackwood: "Good show!" he whispered, but Blackwood irritably motioned him to be quiet.

Dryden, however, was delighted. His head went from Bob to Gallagher like a man watching lawn tennis.

Bob asked: "Where had you been that evening?"

"Ridin' about."

"Been at work that day?"

Pause. Then: "I'd a day off."

"What's your job?"

"At the docks."

"Dock labourer?"

"Yes."

"But not that day?"

"No."

"Having a little absenteeism?"

"I don't work seven days a week."

Oliver Blackwood was now listening in deepening depression. He ought to have warned Bob more sternly. Bob was going on:

"How many days *do* you work?"

"As many as is necessary."

"Three or four?"

"It varies."

"You work week-ends?"

"Many a time"—triumphantly.

"Double time for that?"

Pause. Then: "The same as anybody else."

"What did you do during the war?"

"At the docks—in the bombing."

"Never in the army or anything of *that* sort?"

"I told you—at the docks."

"Making good money?"

"We didn't work for nothing, dirty cargoes and that."

"Double pay for a bad smell in the hold?"

No answer.

"If you worked throughout a week-end, you could make twenty pounds in those two days—while men in the forces worked several weeks for this amount?"

Mr. Tebbutt coughed. "I don't quite see, Captain Blackwood, what this has to do with the case."

Bob said: "I was going to ask if the cycle is paid for."

"I don't see the relevance."

Bob said: "My point was, sir, that if he was trying it out before he paid for it he would be going very fast to see what it would do."

"We are not hearing a summons against him for dangerous driving—and as I have pointed out to him, he's under no obligation to answer questions about his speed."

Bob said, frowning: "But it was his speed, sir, and his reckless driving that led to the whole business."

Mr. Tebbutt said: "That is your contention, perhaps, but it doesn't affect his liberty not to answer. Go on, please."

Bob turned to Gallagher: "When I spoke to you, you resented it, didn't you?"

"Maybe I did."

"Said we were not in the so-and-so army now? and that you had finished with all such poxy-nosed bastards as me?"

No reply.

"But you never had been in the army, had you?"

No reply.

"Was the army a symbol of any kind of discipline which you resent?"

Gallagher looked round, a little bewildered. "I took you for a Fascist," he said.

"Because I told you you ought to behave yourself and not rush about endangering people's lives? That was it, wasn't it?"

Silence.

"Are you a Communist, that you use the term Fascist so readily?"

"I never was."

"What did you expect me to do when you called me a bastard —embrace you?"

"You took me unawares—or——" Gallagher stopped.

"You mean you were thinking of letting me have one, and I got in first?"

"I didn't say so."

"It isn't the first time you've been in a scrap, is it?"

"No"—reluctantly.

"You usually come off best, don't you?"

Gallagher shifted his weight from one foot to the other, turned to the magistrate. Mr. Tebbutt, however, vouchsafed no help. The court waited; Mr Forsyth had his pencil poised in delighted expectation. Then the boastfulness in Gallagher won.

"Yes, I do." He said it savagely.

"Ever used a razor blade?" As Gallagher paused, Bob added: "I don't mean on your own face—on somebody else's?"

"What are you gettin' at?" Gallagher turned to Mr. Tebbutt again, who said: "I don't think you need answer that—unless you wish."

Gallagher breathed heavily in fury, but kept silent.

Bob was silent too. After a long pause, Mr. Tebbutt inquired "Have you any further questions?"

Bob said: "None—that he would be likely to answer—in view of your ruling, sir."

Blackwood sighed. Thank heaven this part of it appeared to be over. But why did Bob have to say some of these things? All well.... He glanced at the reporters. They were writing furiously

After a constable had told how he saw the later part of the fight, with Gallagher rising from the ground, trying to strike Bob and then going down a second time and knocking himself out on the kerbstone, Bob himself went into the witness-box and was sworn. The court stirred, shifted in its seats in anticipation. By this time Blackwood was apprehensive of whatever Bob was about to say, but his first statement was concise and straight forward enough. When he had finished, Mr. Tebbutt leaned forward over his enormous notebook. He spoke with gentleness but insistently, glancing at Bob as he put his question and then looking quickly away at nothing in particular. He had found the trick effective in higher courts than this.

"Will you tell us," he asked, "why you took the law into your own hands?"

Bob answered readily: "I thought he would get away with it if I didn't."

Back went Mr. Tebbutt's gaze. "Get *away* with it?" he repeated, as if this were spoken in a dialect of New Guinea. "You mean that the law would not discover his alleged offence?"

"Yes, so far as I could see, no policeman had observed what happened."

"Could you not have taken the number of the cycle and reported him?"

"Not without overtaking him first, sir."

"Yes, admittedly you had to do that. But that wasn't difficult was it?"

"Yes, quite difficult. He must have been doing about fifty five."

"In those main streets?"

"When he got *out* of the main streets."

"So to overtake him you must have been doing well over sixty?" Mr. Tebbutt looked away more studiously than ever as he asked that.

Bob said: "You can hardly overtake unless you go faster, sir."

"You knew you were far exceeding the speed limit?"

"So does a speed cop."

There was a titter in court and a cry of "Silence!"

Mr. Tebbutt was not perturbed. He went on: "You felt spurred on by him?"

"I had no alternative, sir, if I was to catch him."

"You say he took risks trying to get away?"

"He took risks *before* he knew I was after him—he took plenty *after* he knew."

"And that incensed you?"

"Yes, sir."

"The more risks he took the more incensed you became?"

"Probably."

"Do you say he endangered people—their lives—as he went careering on?"

"He made several dangerous swerves."

"To avoid people?"

"Yes, but he might easily have skidded into somebody else."

"And from time to time you sounded your horn at him to make him stop?"

"Yes, sir."

"And he took no notice?"

"Oh yes, he went faster."

Another titter and another cry, "Silence in court!"

"And later, as I understood you to say, when you got out of the car, confronted him and demanded his name and address, he refused to give it?"

"Yes."

"He became abusive and used the term you mentioned earlier?" He refreshed his memory by glancing at what he had written down, pouching his lips. Mr. Tebbutt continued: "So the reason, you suggest, why you took the law into your hands was that you were angry at his bad driving of his cycle, and on top of that he became abusive, and because of those two things you assaulted him?"

"Yes."

"No other reason?"

Oliver Blackwood was watching Bob closely, praying he would leave it at this. But Bob did not answer "No", which

159

would have disposed of it; he stood puckering his brow, feeling for words, knowing that in his heart there was more to it than this—and Oliver Blackwood could have groaned inwardly.

Bob said: Well, sir——"

"Yes?" Mr. Tebbutt looked up. He had not been expecting anything further.

Bob said: "I suppose I looked on it as typical of the indiscipline in the country."

Mr. Tebbutt said: "I don't quite understand. . . ."

Bob said abruptly: "Unofficial strikes—disrespect for authority—increased lawlessness—we all know about it."

Forsyth looked up, pulled a face, and wrote like mad. So did the other reporters.

Mr. Tebbutt said: "I am not sure that I see the connection—between the bad driving you allege and unofficial strikes. Are you saying this man Gallagher was on strike?"

"No, sir." Bob was scornful.

"Well, in that event——"

Bob said: "I mean, sir, he's typical—typical of a country with many of its standards slipping—shoddy work—men breaking agreements—a general hatred of authority—he seemed to me to typify it—his driving—his language when checked. And I had a desire to deal with it—as it ought to be dealt with. And he was there—and he got it." Bob stood there defiant.

The court was astonished: in the person of Mr. Tebbutt who pouched and unpouched his mouth; in the person of the reporters who thought this almost too good to be true; in the person of the gaoler in his little cubicle who kept repeating to the rustling court, "Silence! Silence!" and looking round in an ill-tempered way, as if he had himself been attacked.

Oliver Blackwood felt the impact forcibly. This was what he knew he had dreaded. He looked at Dryden, who was sitting opposite. Dryden had turned his head to look at Bob and was silently applauding, his mouth slightly open, his eyes sparkling.

When the rustling had died down, Mr. Tebbutt asked Bob if he had any witnesses to call. Bob said he had thought of calling one to corroborate his own view of Gallagher's driving. At this point Dryden eagerly rose from his seat, thinking his time had come, but Mr. Tebbutt, glancing from one to the other said gently: "If your father's evidence——"

Bob interrupted: "He is not my father. . . ."

Dryden's smile appeared, in Oliver Blackwood's eyes, to widen into a grimace.

Mr. Tebbutt said: "I beg your pardon. . . . If this gentleman's evidence is concerned solely with his opinion of the complainant's riding of his motor-cycle I don't think it is important, though of course you may call him if you wish. Did he witness the—er—assault?"

"Only from inside the car, sir. I was not calling him on that."

Mr. Tebbutt said: "I don't think—unless you——"

"Very well, sir."

"Kindly return to the dock, then."

When Bob again looked down from his small eminence, Mr. Tebbutt said: "Robert Blackwood, there is no doubt in my mind that you are guilty of wounding William Gallagher; indeed you have not denied it; you have only sought to justify it. You appear to have seen yourself as one called upon to take action against what you regarded, rightly or wrongly, as the complainant's unsatisfactory driving. That was all very well up to a point, in fact commendable in the sense of taking the number of his cycle and reporting him to the police. That is, of course, what you ought to have done. Beyond that, you had no right to go. If we all took the law into our own hands we should no longer have law in this country, but anarchy. You seem to hold strong views on the subject of discipline and what you are pleased to describe as the lack of discipline in the country at this time. Whether your opinions are right or wrong is not the concern of this court. But it seems to me that your own behaviour is itself a striking example of a want of discipline in yourself. You have taken it upon yourself to condemn it in others and I must condemn it in you. You will be fined five pounds."

Mr. Tebbutt removed his gaze from Bob and began to write in his ledger-like notebook.

Bob asked in a loud, clear voice: "Will Gallagher be summoned for dangerous driving, sir?"

Mr. Tebbutt looked up and answered coldly: "That is a matter for the police."

As Oliver Blackwood and Dryden moved out of their seats, Dryden muttered: "It's a dam' shame!" But Blackwood had no

Fs

such comfort of indignation. He knew that if he had been on the bench his judgment and remarks would have been much the same as the magistrate's. He rose with a grave face, avoiding Forsyth's questioning glance, walked round to the dock door to meet Bob and accompanied him to the clerk's office to pay the fine. He took Bob's arm, giving it a friendly squeeze, but finding it difficult to say anything. He foresaw this case rising—a further ugly barrier—between him and Hannah.

CHAPTER XXII

MR. SEDGWICK READ a report of the case against Captain Robert Blackwood in the early editions of the evening papers. There was a column and a half of it, racy, lively stuff with headlines bringing out Bob's allegations about the country's lack of discipline. Mr. Sedgwick was drinking tea with Mrs. Tremayne at the time. He asked: "Do you see this story about Captain Blackwood, dear?"

"I didn't know he was a captain, darling."

"Polly, this isn't your Mr. Blackwood. This is Captain Robert Blackwood, D.S.O."

"What a lovely name. What's he done?"

"Spoken several home truths and got himself fined five pounds."

"Seems rather unfair, darling. You speak home truths and you become a great public figure."

"Not for speaking home truths."

"You don't mean for *concealing* home truths, dear?"

"Perhaps a bit of both, love. But never mind that. Here's a young man after my own heart—speaks of shoddy work, people sitting back—too much money and not enough work."

"Universally applied, dear, that would be heaven on earth."

"Polly, you are being perverse."

"Perverse and foolish, oft I stray."

"What's that?"

"That's a hymn, darling. If you've forgotten that, dear, it's time we went to the cathedral. I have suggested it more than once."

"I am not happy with you in cathedrals and churches, dear."

"You mean it reminds you of your unfulfilled duty?"

"Not at all. But listen now—if this is Blackwood's son, it will be nice to meet him."

"Have you had a reply to your letter?"

"Not yet, darling."

"That is very remiss of Mr. Blackwood. I shall ring him up and tell him so."

"Polly, if this is his son he must have been very preoccupied."

"You can rely on me to put it very delicately, to be charming to him."

"That is what I fear."

"My intention was to speak to him in your presence, dear. It occurs to me that Mr. Blackwood may have decided that his wife is suffering from a diplomatic illness so that he may visit us alone."

"Why on earth should he do that?"

"He may have heard of your reputation, darling."

"*My* reputation?"

"As a man who is not without an eye for a remarkable woman and not without a certain dynamic magnetism."

"Tut, tut, Polly."

"On the other hand, he may think that if he is un-accompanied——"

"You make him sound like a male-voice quartette, love."

Polly went on: "—if he is unaccompanied, any slight tête-à-tête he may enjoy with me will go unremarked."

"So that is what you have in mind—a tête-à-tête."

"Only in so far as my influence might be used in your behalf to bring the *Morning Star* revolving within your orbit."

"Polly, are you well? You are speaking in the phrases of Mr. Fortinbras."

"I know. I read a speech of his this morning. It is fatal. I wish you would stop reporting him at such length."

"There are three reasons why I cannot do that, dear—first, the country would go to the dogs; second, I should be deprived of a large amount of first-class copy which costs me nothing; and third, that he would make my life a misery."

"And you would never become a viscount."

"I may never be a viscount, anyhow."

"Why not, darling?"

"Because—because—has it occurred to you, my dear, that it is possible we may never have a change of Government?"

He lifted the telephone.

"What are doing, dear?"

"I am going to speak to Blackwood. Blackwood is a serious man and I am in a serious mood. Watson, get me Mr. Blackwood of the *Morning Star*. Now, dear, if the Blackwoods can come, shall we invite anybody else? What about this other poet you met?"

"Poet, darling?"

"Mr. Dryden, or whoever he is? Shall we?"

"On second thoughts, darling, I think a *little* party— intimate——"

"Not too intimate, I trust, Polly. Excuse me, dear . . . . Is that you, Blackwood? . . . Good afternoon. Was that your son in court this morning? . . . I congratulate you. . . . No, I think it needed saying. We should like to meet him—Mrs. Tremayne and I—and to meet your wife, of course. Can you come along tonight? . . . No, I haven't had the note yet. . . . You can? Excellent! . . . Whatever you feel like. . . . Yes, the ladies do, I think. Black tie, then? . . . Good. . . .Yes, I know. Well, stay just as long as you can. . . . Good. A quarter to eight? Look forward to seeing you. 'Bye. . . ." He put down the receiver. "That was your Mr. Blackwood, dear."

"He sounded charming."

"The mention of your name made all the difference."

"We shall have champagne?"

"Well, dear——"

"Nothing brings you out, dear, like a bottle of champagne— and the presence of an attractive woman—even more, of two women. I have seen it so often."

"Polly, you make me sound old—you imply that I need a lot of stimulation."

"Not at all, darling. But in those circumstances the ruthless northcountryman is utterly transformed."

Mr. Sedgwick was not altogether displeased by this reminder of his two selves. But he said: "Polly, when have I ever been ruthless with you?"

"It would be unbecoming of me to say," she said. "And I am not complaining of it when it happens. A time for everything, and everything in its place, my mama always said."

"I do not understand what you mean, Polly."

She rose and kissed him lightly on the head. "Let us have champagne," she said. "And now I shall go and rest a while." She paused. "You should rest, too, dear."

"Do not remind me once more that I am a middle-aged man," he said.

"We do not grow younger by increasing our exertions," she said lightly.

"You are growing terrifyingly wise, Polly. But I must do some work."

"Work?"

"I am going to write a leader—a short one." He spoke into the telephone. "Send Miss Price in. . . . Mr. Blackwood, Polly, is not the only one who writes leaders; and I do not want to be at any disadvantage with regard to him tonight."

"Goodbye then, darling."

"Goodbye, my love."

When Miss Agatha Price was ready with her notebook, he dictated as follows:

"This short leader will appear in all our papers tomorrow. Stop The heading is Discipline. Stop The leader is as follows. Quote A good deal of sympathy will be felt with Captain Robert Blackwood, D.S.O., who was fined five pounds at Greycastle yesterday for assault. Captain Blackwood spoke of the decay of discipline in the nation. Whatever the merits of the particular case there is no doubt of the justice of his remarks applied generally. The high increase in the rate of divorce, the rise in juvenile delinquency, the fact that the prisons have never been so crowded, the prevalence of black-markets and under-the-counter business, the appalling rate of road accidents, the frequency of unofficial strikes, the decline in church-going, the failure of recruiting for the armed forces, what does all this mean but a lowering of the tone of the nation? For all this the Socialist Government, by its lack of leadership, its insistence on unnecessary controls which lead to shortages, and on a crippling rate of taxation which is the highest in the world, has a heavy responsibility. We need many more voices like that of Captain Blackwood to draw attention to the dangers of what is happening. These newspapers, for their part, will never hesitate to speak their minds Unquote."

If that, he reflected, didn't get on the right side of Mr. Oliver Blackwood, nothing would.

CHAPTER XXIII

HANNAH LOOKED QUITE lovely that evening, Blackwood thought. She had slept during the afternoon and now her eyes were large and sparkling, and her heavy yellow hair, her full figure, her grey-green eyes, deepened by the jade necklet and ear-rings, the touch of gold in her dress, all lent her a slumbrous richness that made his heart ache. Beside her, Mrs. Tremayne looked diminutive, a robin redbreast of a woman—black curls, a red satin jacket over a white dress, her bosom high and explosive. They dined in Sedgwick's suite, which allowed them to walk from the sitting-room to the dining-room and out on to the balcony, from which could be caught a glimpse of far-off ships' masts and the noise of sirens down the estuary. Sedgwick had brought Sir Frederick Pick to balance the party—it amused him to have this gargoyle teetering about with cocktails and acting as an echo to whatever he might say. Sedgwick had looked forward with genuine eagerness to meeting Mrs. Blackwood. He had no doubt at all that she was one of the finest women he had ever seen— one of the finest. He felt younger at once—the fact that she hardly spoke and merely smiled inscrutably did not diminish her attractiveness for him. He was courtly as he bent over her hand. Polly watched him with a touch of trepidation as well as of amusement. She knew the manifestations. For her part she was delighted to see Oliver Blackwood again, this man so quiet and composed, who seemed to her to give forth a strange power. He was more like an early Victorian Cabinet Minister, a Melbourne or a Cecil, than a modern. And Captain Robert Blackwood—ah! how like he was to somebody she had recently seen—but who she couldn't remember; and how unlike Blackwood. The mother was in him, yes, but, somehow, part of the quality lost, the fineness gone. As for the dark fire of Oliver Blackwood—nothing. The greetings went on, Sedgwick telling Hannah how much he had admired what her son said in court, Blackwood answering Pick's inquiries about printing costs and the misfortune that London evening papers were not three-half-pence as they were here. "I remember," Pick said, "when the *Daily Mail* started its revolution by being a ha'penny—and the cry from the old-fashioned was, 'It's a ha'penny—but it's not cheap!'" And Sir Frederick cackled in enjoyment.

Polly sat at dinner with Bob on her right and Sir Frederick on her left; opposite to her sat Sedgwick, with Hannah on his right and Blackwood on his left. When the white wine was served, Sedgwick at once said: "I should like to drink a glass of wine with Captain Blackwood and congratulate him on his cross-examination and his concluding remarks." He lifted his glass. "Hear, hear!" said Sir Frederick. The others raised their glasses, too. "I'd love to have been there," said Polly: "a dock labourer as the modern butterfly on the wheel."

"The country needs leadership of this kind," said Sir Frederick. He turned to Sedgwick, "As the article you've written on the subject, sir, says." He added to Hannah: "It will be in all our papers in the morning—up and down the country." He smacked his wrinkled lips.

Hannah turned to Sedgwick and said in her slow voice: "That's more than kind."

Sedgwick glowed: "Not at all." He turned to Blackwood: "It occurred to me that you might find difficulty in applauding his act in a leader yourself."

Blackwood, toying with his glass, said: "Yes, I'm afraid so."

Hannah and Bob glanced quickly at him.

Sedgwick went on: "So I dictated a few lines. I hope they hit the nail on the head."

"In your inimitable style," said Polly, raising her glass to him.

"Thank you," said Sedgwick.

"With a sledge-hammer, dear," said Polly.

"You see," said Sedgwick, "how unappreciated my writing is. What I admire above all things is the editor who sits tight on the local powder magazine—the man on the spot, valiant, giving blows and taking them. The salt of the earth, pride of our craft." He looked at Sir Frederick.

"Hear, hear!" said the latter. "Our editors—a grand team—united—loyal—with one aim and object." He did not say, however, what that was, and nobody inquired. Suddenly he added: "And all equal—in this loyalty and unity." There was a short constrained silence.

Blackwood observed lightly: "I understand the Turks have an interesting saying on the subject of equality—something about all being strangled by the same silken cord." He smiled.

Sedgwick said: "You could apply that to the Welfare State, couldn't you?"

This remark caused a spurt of talk about the state of the nation; which brought the conversation round to discipline again.

"It struck me today," said Sedgwick, "—I think I said so to you, Polly—how venal the country would become unless we get a change of Government soon. The number of officials and civil servants has increased by scores of thousands, nay, hundreds of thousands—all of them with a vested interest in the party in power. If this went on for any great length of time we should be close to the regimes of Hitler or Mussolini or Stalin. The first two were notoriously corrupt and the third can hardly be less so—if you're a Red general I understand you have a seat kept for you at the opera permanently whether you're there or not. We should—without a change of Government—eventually become a nation of lick-spittles, no hope of preferment except from the party in permanent power. Don't you think so, Blackwood?"

Blackwood said yes, he thought the same party in permanent office, whether Socialist or Tory, would be gravely perilous, indeed mortal. But it wouldn't happen because we should refuse to tolerate it; we should put up with it so far and then not an inch further—the Goverment would be thrown out.

"You mean—it can't happen here."

"Yes"

"You've more faith in human nature than I have. Look what's happening now—half the trade-union leaders intriguing for jobs in the nationalised boards."

"I know. I don't like it. But the Tories have usually done very well for themselves in the City and in conferring titles."

Sedgwick looked from his partridge and gripped his knife fiercely: "It is my conviction that under the cloak or behind the figure of our mild little Mr. Wimpole at Number 10—who is

168

himself quite innocent—things are going on that are undermining our national integrity. Yes, Polly—crooked things he knows nothing about"—for Polly had made signs of dissent. "You cannot," went on Sedgwick, "deal in these fantastic sums of money—thousands of millions—concentrate so much power in a few hands, without gross inefficiency leading to jiggery-pokery. We talk about the twelve men in the Kremlin; soon—if not already—it will be the twelve or twenty men in Downing Street holding unlimited power over us."

He looked round, his face red and grim. Blackwood was sipping his champagne. He said: "I should like to see you writing something on those lines. It would be a valuable contribution to your newspapers. I should be happy to comment on what you had to say."

"Adversely?"

"Not altogether. I favour vigorous statement whether I agree or not. I think you dramatise it—no bad thing. But, of course, a certain amount of dictatorship isn't new. Churchill wielded enormous power in the war—did things sometimes and got Cabinet approval afterwards."

"We were at war," said Sedgwick. "A vastly different affair."

Blackwood said: "There's a sense in which we have never stopped being at war. The executive has too much power. Most of us are agreed on that. Happily, the Cabinet is often seriously divided—I gather some of their meetings are like a dog-fight."

"I'm delighted to hear it," said Sedgwick heartily. "I hope they use knuckle-dusters." He looked across to Bob. "How does it look to the men who won the war?" he inquired. "The young men?"

"I'm afraid some of those I meet are rather cynical, sir."

"Cynical?"

"Some of them say we'd better *lose* the next war, judging by what happens when we win."

"Don't like the Socialists, eh?"

"Don't like *any* politicians much, sir."

"What about Mr. Fortinbras?"

"They think he's a bit old, sir."

"And the Press—what do they think of the Press?"

"Well, sir——" Bob stopped and smiled. "One of my friends who went up to Town said it was curious Fleet Street had been so little damaged by enemy bombs—seemed to think it rather a pity."

Polly laughed. "You asked for that, dear."

"It is the fate of the Press never to be appreciated," said Sedgwick, smiling but stubborn. "You go to the Continent, I understand. What do they think of us British *there*?"

"Well, sir, in Germany a lot of them think Mr. Fortinbras is the best man we've got——"

"They do, eh?"

"And that he ought to be Prime Minister."

"Good. Very good. Excellent."

"They can't understand why, having won the war, we've allowed ourselves to be on such short commons—think we must be bunglers."

"Trust old Fritz! Trust old Jerry! Would *he* have been on short commons? Do you see any of them starving over there?"

"Yes, but not if they've any money, sir."

"Just as I thought—just as my men over there tell me. What did Northcliffe say?—'They will cheat you yet, these Junkers.'"

Blackwood said mildly: "But I understand Mr. Fortinbras's case is that we must make friends with them—get them into Western Union—that's one of the reasons the Germans like him so much."

Sedgwick said: "That's different. I say: Let us make use of them by all means—let us line them up with us to fight the Russians, if need be—but don't trust them too far—watch them. I don't believe they love us." He spoke as if that were a rare and surprising opinion. He then abandoned Germany, having disposed of it. He turned to Bob again: "What about the other countries—Sweden, Denmark, Holland? Are *they* going to fight with us, if it comes to it?"

Bob answered: "In Copenhagen a few days ago, I had a talk with a Dane—tipsy enough to be frank. He apologised for not speaking English very well—said he learnt it all in the British Army, where he was interpreter in German. 'I have my uniform,' he said, 'ready for second war that is coming, yes. We, Denmark, would prefer war now, isn't it?—than wait three, four, five years till Russia is ready with atom bomb. If another war I go England because Russians have my name for serving British Army and, anyhow Denmark will be occupied again. A United Western Europe, oh yes! But we can do nothing, too small, we shall be front door for next war. It is coming, oh yes!' That is what he had to say."

"And the Swedes?"

"Oh," said Bob, "the Swedes I run into think Western Europe should unite but—but they have been neutral in two wars and so . . . Western Europe should be strong, they agree, but, all the same . . ."

"But leave them out of it, I suppose," said Sedgwick. "Fifty nations—but most of the dirty work to be done by Britain and the United States. The price of internationalism is pretty tough—on *us*." He looked at Sir Frederick, who promptly said: "Our role has always been the world's policeman. And small thanks we have had."

Sedgwick looked round the table with a challenging look in his eye: "One of our former Ministers of State wrote me recently from Washington, where he's been stationed, saying he hasn't the slightest faith in internationalism of any sort—as a result of his experience." He pursed his lips and looked at Blackwood.

Blackwood said thoughtfully, a hand twisting his glass, at which he gazed, his voice quiet: "If there were no United Nations, you'd have to create it. It's faulty, disappointing, of course—heartbreakingly so—but what's the alternative? There is none. Do we want Britain, or even the Commonwealth, to stand alone? Britain is tired, impoverished, feeling old. For many years during the war we were preaching the creed: No difference of race, creed, colour or class. The Christian says: All men are equal in the sight of God—every man a soul to be saved. Our Socialists at home say: Fair shares for all. The teeming millions of India and China ask: What, then, of fair shares for *us*?—or they're beginning to ask it. They say: You said—No difference of colour or class. Admirable. When do we eat? You have over two thousand calories a day in England, and very much more in America. We —in India and China—have a half as much or a quarter as much. We are your brothers and sisters, you say. Good! When are you going to eat less that we may eat more?" Blackwood raised his head and looked at them. "What is the answer to that? Are we to say: 'We are sorry: we misled you; we didn't really mean what we said. After all, there was a war on—nobody speaks the truth in war. You took us too seriously. There isn't enough food or good things in the world—not yet—not for many years—for you to live as well as we live. You'll have to wait—possibly a long time. Moreover, there are far too many of you. Your religions, which encourage you to breed—and oppose birth control—they are cruel. Why bring into the world children which cannot be fed and whose portion is going to be poverty, disease and starvation? Before we taught you the rudiments of hygiene, cleanliness, and irrigation, famine and disease slew you in vast numbers. Perhaps we have erred in teaching you those elementary rudiments, for now you multiply more and more and we cannot feed those whom we have, in a sense, created. Perhaps we have interfered with Providence's method of keeping a balance.'

"We have not, of course, said those brutal things to them—and we could not say them—certainly not all of them. Meanwhile we are striving to give them a little more—and we are going a trifle shorter ourselves; and in this business of giving, the Americans are generous—more generous than we, as they can well afford to be. But have we the time we need? And can we do enough? Because, while we do a little, the Communists are saying to them: 'Brothers, the land is yours—take it! You shall eat and fill your bellies. The people of the West have been battening on you for generations. Out with them!'

"And this mighty uprising comes upon us after two world wars have enfeebled us; after two wars in which, against great odds, we have overcome the European enemy that would have destroyed us; and when, that task accomplished, a third enemy even more powerful has usurped the place of the other two. Only by such unity as we could achieve at home and in Europe were the first two enemies overwhelmed. Only by a similar unity do we stand the remotest chance of overcoming, or withstanding, the third. Only by striving to understand the surging millions of the Far East, helping them when we can, making such concessions as we must, can we hope to gain the time, buy the time, to give us and them a chance to come to terms without such a conflict developing as will put an end to us. Any doctrine that preaches retiring within our shell, standing alone, abandoning internationalism, giving up faith in a unity of nations and ultimately in One World —is really suicide."

The table was silent. Sedgwick thought: "He puts it clearly enough—but I don't see how his wife can stand too much of that sort of stuff. I know I couldn't. I don't think any woman, at bottom, is an intellectual." He looked at Hannah and thought how superb her figure was, and what a delight it would be to embrace her. He said to Blackwood: "Well, do you really think we shall get the time you speak of?"

Blackwood said: "If there is a Divine purpose in the world—and I think there is—yes."

"You mean," said Sedgwick, "that the English are a chosen people?"

"I think they have been an instrument—one of many. Of course whoever or whatever holds this world in thrall may have decided the British have served their end, and that the torch shall now pass to some other race. Events will tell us."

Sedgwick said, as the brandy was served and he and Blackwood lit their cigars: "I daresay everything you say is right—but—we didn't do a bad job in India. Not a bad job at all. Chaos when we arrived—and chaos and murder as soon as we left. Probably we got out too soon. Look what's happening in Kashmir. However. . . ."

Polly said: "I found Mr. Blackwood's speech fascinating."

Hannah smiled in her fashion that made Sedgwick think of —and it seemed to him a flash of inspiration—Mona Lisa. Ah! he must tell her that—when they were alone. His mind toyed idly with the phrase—"She is a woman therefore she can be wooed—she is a woman therefore she can be won." The brandy was running into his veins and the blood seemed to be charging into his head. But it was not an uncomfortable feeling. Hannah had smiled again but said nothing—Sedgwick had smiled back at her, and Polly threw out a question about bridge or dancing. But Blackwood murmured that in a few minutes he would have to return to the office.

Polly, instantly sad, went to him as they moved into the sitting-room, saying: "But you cannot go," and laid a hand on his arm; and when he replied that he must, liking her and showing by his glance that he did, she asked softly: "We shall meet again? I want to."

He said: "Yes, of course."

"Here—or in London?"

"Whichever you wish."

Sedgwick, when he was alone with Blackwood for a moment, and they looked into the blue night from the balcony, pulled from his pocket, not without pride, the leader he had written on Bob's court case.

Blackwood, knowing what to expect, read it reluctantly, thanked him and said it was very interesting. Sedgwick, piqued, a little hurt, asked: "Don't you approve of it?"

Blackwood, feeling cornered, was bound to say: "Not altogether, I'm afraid."

Sedgwick, worrying the point like a terrier, asked: "What I've said or the way I've said it?"

"It was kind of you to write it, but I don't share the opinion."

"Doesn't share the opinion," thought Sedgwick. "Good God! —and his own son. What are they made of, these puritans, these radicals?" He said: "If you were to write a leader backing up the magistrate, that would be a remarkable thing, wouldn't it?"

Blackwood didn't answer that for a moment, and, as Sedgwick waited, it was Hannah's voice from behind them which said: "But then, Mr. Sedgwick, my husband is a remarkable man."

It was almost the first time that Sedgwick had heard her voice so plainly—certainly the first time she had spoken with such clarity as this. It was a voice in keeping with her withdrawn, secret smile, and it was hard to tell what she meant. At that moment Polly and Bob joined them, and, without anything further of importance being said, Blackwood bade them good night and begged them to enjoy themselves. Sedgwick, taking Hannah's arm to guide her lightly back into the room, was aware of an exciting glow moving slowly over him. He watched the departing back of Mr. Blackwood with enormous satisfaction. "Your husband," he said, "is devoted to his paper. That is what I like to see. That is what I *always* like to see." He administered to Hannah's arm an infinitesimal squeeze.

CHAPTER XXIV

"You must be very proud of your son," said Mr. Sedgwick as he danced with Hannah. He was thinking how delicious this moment was but was making a powerful effort to talk soberly and with dignity.

Hannah smiled and nodded, and glanced across the room at Bob. Mrs. Tremayne was in Bob's arms, looking up at him, as they swung boldly, lithely, more swiftly than others, round the floor. What Polly was saying was:

"I've seen somebody the image of you—quite recently—and I can't remember who it was."

Bob said: "Common type, you know."

Polly puckered her brows. "I shall remember soon—I always do."

"Probably a gargoyle in the cathedral," said Bob. He added: "I can't say I've ever seen anybody very like you."

"Is that a compliment?"

"Very much so."

Polly laughed. "It's a large world."

"Yes?"

"And I've seen only a bit of it."

"Well," said Bob. "*I've* got the transport."

"I might get a world-wide season ticket. Is there such a thing?"

"Not yet, but there ought to be."

"Could we fix it?"

"The Press," said Bob, pretending to be grave, "has great influence. I'm sure Mr. Sedgwick——"

"Oh," said Polly, "I wasn't thinking of him at that moment." She laughed up at Bob and they both looked towards Sedgwick and Hannah. Sedgwick, holding Hannah very firmly, was tracing solemn and slow patterns over the floor. He was a strong adherent of Arnold Bennett's dictum that the dance was one of the few moments in life when a man has a woman thoroughly under control. Moreover, proximity to Hannah was delicious——. He might hold her almost as tightly as he wished—in this flood of lights—and he did, in fact, now hold her a little more tightly—and nobody was in the least aware of it—except himself and Hannah. And Hannah made no sign that she was aware of it.

He said: "Yes, I should be proud if I had a son who did what yours did in court today."

"You have no children?"

"No." He shook his head. He seemed to indicate that the Fates had dealt most harshly with him. It was unfortunate, therefore, that Hannah should now have inquired if his wife had died young.

"No." he said, "I have never been married. Some men search the earth for the right woman, and alas!" He relinquished her slightly as if he would make an appropriate gesture, but he didn't; as if in contrition he gripped her even more firmly.

They danced for a while in silence. Then he said: "Happily, most happily, in your case it is different. Are you sorry your son isn't a writer?"

"Oh no."

Hannah answered so quickly that he was sure he understood how she felt. What a trial Blackwood must be! He said: "I agree. One writer in a family is sufficient."

The music stopped, and they halted, but he went on talking, feeling inspired.

He went on, moving from irony into rodomontade and hardly knowing which was which. "Your husband is a man in a thousand. If the world is to be saved, it will be saved largely by journalists —they are at all the outposts—they are sentries—listening. They warn us—they make known the dangers—they tell us what to do to avoid disaster."

"But Oliver," said Hannah, with an air of mild deprecation, "has never been a foreign correspondent. He has seldom left Greycastle."

The music began and Sedgwick opened his welcoming arms. He felt he could take Hannah and all her problems and doubts into his capable hands. "Your husband," he said, "like all great editors—has ears most delicately trained. He doesn't need to travel the world. Just as the sheepdog can hear a whistle miles away—even a whistle that makes no audible sound" (really, he thought, it was quite true what Polly had said—what could not champagne and a pretty woman do?) "so the true editor— and I train all my editors in this art—can hear the distant whisper, can sense the earth's distant tremor. He is at once a seismograph, a hydrophone, a—a radar station such as saved us in the Battle of Britain. Would you care to sit down?"— for Hannah had lost a particle of her buoyancy, or so it seemed to his percipient arms, and, anyhow, it was not entirely easy to be moved to this degree of eloquence and to dance at the same time. When they were seated at the edge of the dancing floor and he had ordered two brandies, he went on: "I look at it this way: My men abroad are Britain's ambassadors. But whereas the ambassadors' dispatches are known only in Whitehall—and, I assure you, often buried unread in the archives—my men's dispatches are the property of the nation, of every citizen, making the people well-informed, adult. If the dispatches of journalists had been heeded in time, the last war might never have happened—the dispatches, I mean, of men like Gedye, Ebbutt, Reed, and the rest." If none of these enlighteners, as it happened, worked for his papers, his praise only showed, he thought, a certain catholicity and generosity of mind.

"So," he went on, "with this responsibility resting on me—with this powerful machine under my control, can you wonder that I should be glad to welcome your husband's assistance? The Commander-in-Chief needs a Chief of Staff; and sometimes"—he leaned forward confidentially—"the Chief of Staff is the more powerful of the two. Remember Ludendorff and Hindenburg!" The brandy came and he leaned back in his chair and sipped it. He regarded Hannah with immense delight and approbation. She was a joy to look at—mature, resplendent, abounding in her charms, and, he would swear, not indifferent to him—for had he ever put a case better?

Bob, watching Mr. Sedgwick, said to Polly: "I suppose he is a millionaire?"

"What makes you think so, dear?" Polly now called him "dear" as easily as does a Cockney stallholder, and with a similar warmth of heart.

Bob smiled. "All Press magnates are, aren't they?"

"Are you thinking of the day when your papa may work for him, dear?"

"He never would, you know."

"He'd pay him very well, dear."

"I don't think my old man cares much about money."

"Perhaps if he worked for Sam and got a huge salary, he could make you a very handsome allowance, and then . . ." She smiled radiantly at him.

"And then," said Bob, "I could buy you a season ticket."

"And if your papa worked for Sam, you and I would be almost members of the same family, dear."

"Almost"—and Bob gave her a little squeeze.

"If you see what I mean, dear," said Polly.

"The bomb doors would be practically open," said Bob.

"Oh!"

"What's the matter?"

"Nothing. Nothing to do with what you said. Something's broken my—not exactly my dream, but what I couldn't remember. You know what I mean?"

"No."

"The person you're like."

"Oh, that. Why, what's happened?"

"That man over there—with a red carnation in his dinner-jacket—do you see?"

"Oh yes—you mean Dryden."

"That's the name—a sea captain or something, isn't he?"

"Yes. Why? Do you know him?"

"Not really. I had a glass of sherry with him one evening."

"Trust Rex!"

"You know him?"

"Yes. He was in my car at the time I ran after that fellow."

"Don't you think he's like you—in a strange kind of way?"

"Could be, I suppose."

"Don't you *like* him?"

"Oh, he's all right."

"Does your father like him?"

"Well—I don't think he's exactly father's cup of tea."

"I see, dear. Well, I'm glad I've remembered—it always bothers me when I've something on my mind. Shall we go and have a drink with Sam and your mother? I could do with one, couldn't you, dear?"

They danced round to Sedgwick's table. Polly said: "Sam, dear, we want a drink, please."

It was while they were drinking a second glass that Captain Dryden approached their table and bowed to them. He was in that extremely affable condition that can smile its way through a sheet of armour plate. After Bob had introduced him to Mr. Sedgwick and he had bowed to each of the ladies separately and with a seraphic smile on his face, he said to Sedgwick: "This has been a great day, sir—in my opinion. I was proud to be present in court this morning—and to have been with Bob when it happened. A blow struck—for the right things, sir." This little speech having been delivered and received with polite murmurs of agreement, Dryden bowed to Polly and asked if she would honour him in a dance. It was, at the moment, almost easier for him to dance than to walk—the dance lent him something of the movement of his ship. Moreover, he was not captain of a vessel carrying a handful of passengers for nothing—he danced uncommonly well, so that although Polly had risen with no marked alacrity she could not forbear to enjoy the waltz in which they were now engaged. She thawed, and in her good-humoured fashion began to make a little conversation.

She remarked pleasantly: "When you came into the room tonight, you resolved something in my mind!"

Captain Dryden beamed. "Wonderful! Was it—something to do with me?"

"Oh yes."

"Of a—kind I should like to know about?"

"Well—neither one way nor the other, I expect."

"I see. You—in-intrigue me, Mrs. Tremayne, you really do."

Polly said nothing further for a while.

"You have—excited my curiosity, Mrs. Tremayne. Won't you tell me?"

"Oh, it's just that I thought I had seen somebody remarkably like Captain Blackwood—and couldn't think who it was—and then when you came in—I saw it was you."

"Yes. Yes, and then you saw it was me." He looked very knowing.

"Does that surprise you?" She was quite gay.

"No—not altogether. No, after all—why should it?"

"People have remarked on it before, you mean?"

"Well—I suppose they must have done. If you have, others must have too, wouldn't you say?"

"Are you a distant relative—I suppose it sometimes happens, this . . ."

"Not very distant—no. Not *very* distant."

"You mean—you mean you are a close relative?"

Dryden's mind was beautifully bemused. He was smiling, swaying slightly to the music. The questions were coming to him from a thousand miles away.

"I could—I suppose—be called—*very* close. And, of course, I'm proud of him."

"After the case today?"

"Oh—not only today—proud of him all the time. As I have—have reason to be. Every reason to be. No—no man has a—better reason."

Polly was now uneasy but driven on by a curiosity beyond her power to control.

"You mean—I don't understand—surely his own father has more reason."

"That," said Dryden airily, "is what—is what I do mean. That—that is the great secret which must never—never be divulged—never be divulged. Top secret! Don't you agree?"

"Yes—of course—yes—yes—of course." Polly, startled, a little frightened, almost breathed the words.

They danced the dance out, he escorted her to their table, she thanked him graciously and he bowed himself off.

"What's the matter, dear?" asked Sedgwick. "You are looking pale all of a sudden."

Polly said: "It's nothing, dear, I'll just take a sip of wine."

She was looking at Hannah and thinking: "My God, just imagine that. What a situation! Poor Mr. Blackwood."

They sat there chatting for a while longer, the departed figure of the carefree Captain Dryden—who had already forgotten what he had said—hovering, so to speak, like an apparition over them, occupying the minds of Hannah, Bob and Polly—the first two a little uneasy wondering what the volatile gentleman had done or said, Polly watching Bob afresh and imagining she discerned Dryden in him more and more clearly. Mr. Sedgwick noted the silences, and made no determined protest when Hannah thought it time for them to be getting home. What he was longing for was a moment or two when he could enjoy her society alone. He contrived it when they returned to the sitting-room to pick up her wrap. He managed to arrive there with remarkable speed for a man of his years and took her on to the balcony for a moment or two before Polly and Bob arrived. He helped her on with her wrap, taking rather longer to do it than was strictly requisite. Taking her arm, he led her on to the balcony.

"What a beautiful night," he said, sighing rather heavily. "I shall never forget this night. Memorable, memorable!" He linked his fingers with hers and exerted a delicate but firm pressure. A hoarse blare came from the river. "If I could take you across the world," he said, "how enchanting that would be! How enchanting! A ship's deck at night—under the Southern Cross, a ribbon of moonlight across the water, the sea green and grey and lilac——"

"Lilac?" queried Hannah suddenly.

"Yes," he said, "lilac, dear—a most suitable colour for romance. . . ." His thick arm, tight in its sleeve, stole for a moment round her waist and pressed her to him. He glowed at the thought that she had not made any sort of protest, and that his more or less deliberate use of the word "dear" had gone unremarked. How natural it would be if she should long for some—well, change—from the impeccable Blackwood. He heard the tinkling laugh of Polly from the room behind and turned, his face beaming with satisfaction.

"What a romantic night!" said Polly, coming on to the balcony. "Bob—may I call you Bob?—Bob and I would like to stay up all night—go bathing or something."

And on this note of unfulfilled delight with promise of favours to come Mr. Sedgwick and Polly parted from their guests.

CHAPTER XXV

As Mr. Sedgwick was taking off his evening tie, and, catching tantalising glimpses of Polly as she trotted to and fro in and out of her bathroom, he pondered on the evening's events and decided that the affair had been a success.

Polly said: "I liked Bob Blackwood, didn't you?"

Sedgwick turned to reply but saw no more than a disappearing ankle in a slipper with a yellow feather on it. He decided that Polly was not anticipating a reply and did not make one. A voice came out of the bathroom mingled with the hissing of water. He could make nothing of it and called: "Yes." That, he had found, was a fairly good answer to most such vocal sounds which at moments like this usually expected acquiescence. Meanwhile he examined his face in the mirror. Was this another ridge near the ear—one of those damned ridges which, in some

181

curious fashion, like the rings in the sawn-off trunk of a tree, told of age with mathematical precision?

Polly tripped in at this moment perfectly naked. He was unlacing his shoes, one foot on his knee, his stiff shirt billowing in front of him like the sail of a yacht in high wind. He looked at Polly with appreciation but concluded that, taking her all in all, she was more attractive with a certain number of clothes on. He was pondering how long he had been able to regard her form in this coolly appraising fashion and whether, like the lines close to his ear, it could be used as a measurement of time, when Polly inquired: "How did you like Hannah?" As she said it, her pretty figure was curved like a boomerang and, like a boomerang, she shot out of the room again clutching one of those mysterious porcelain receptacles with which women's rites are performed. It was a pity, he reflected, that Mr. Shakespeare had not let himself go on the seven stages of a love affair, as he had done on the ages of man: the first stage all elusiveness and mystery; the second, the instincts of the hunter thoroughly aroused; third, the pursuit, the quarry advancing and retreating, coy and provoking; fourth, the capture and the delicious surrender; fifth, the summer of ecstasy and exaltation; sixth, the passion merging into mere affection; seventh, languor and boredom with a tendency to slumber even in the loved one's presence, but with one eye involuntarily opening whenever a fresh quarry crossed the horizon. There now! He was in the vein this evening, was he not? A pity Polly was in the next room or he would jot all that down on the wire recorder. Notwithstanding how intimate one's relationship was, there still remained secrets. No matter, the seven stages of love were bound to recur to him, life—and ladies —being what they were.

Polly now returned wearing a blue-silk wrap, her face refulgent with grease. Before going to her dressing-table she advanced upon him and pouted her lips for the most infinitesimal of kisses, which he bestowed on her. And yet, even as he did so, he thought here was a thing: Would she, at a much earlier stage in their union—what a horrible nonconformist word that was, union— would she, during that first week they had dwelt together in Paradise—the place was Biarritz—would she have permitted him to behold her thus? It was very sad; it was evidence of the in- exorable passage of time, and man—puny, fleeting—could not withstand it. Nay, the situation was worse; he knew that, had this incident of the shining face happened at Biarritz, he would have been enchanted by it, seen it as proof that she knew their devotion to one another was so profound that she need not dissemble in the slightest degree before him. Whereas now . . .

"You are taking a long time to undress, darling," she said, massaging her face.

"Yes, dear."

"What are you thinking about?"

"I was thinking that these are among the day's most delightful moments."

"Yes—lovely."

"We have before us nearly eight hours in which we have nothing to do."

"Nothing to *do*, dear?"

"A little sleep, a little slumber, a little folding of the hands to sleep."

"What is that?"

"That is Proverbs, chapter six, verse ten. A commodore friend of mine, after his convoy reached port, once sent that message to the destroyers. I have never forgotten it. That is why the navy is so great. The senior officers believe in God." Mr. Sedgwick leaned back in his braces, which were ornamented with the heads of horses, and twiddled his bare toes luxuriously. He added inconsequentially: "Blackwood, on the other hand, probably does *not* believe in God."

Polly inquired: "Are you going to have a bath, darling?"

"Why, dear?"

"You needn't unless you wish. There are those who say that the olfactory organ is predominant in selecting the lovely one."

"You are not, I hope, placing Monsieur Coty or Monsieur Chanel higher than the Almighty in this matter?"

"Perhaps He works through Monsieur Coty."

Mr. Sedgwick rose. "I shall take my pencil and pad to the bath in case I think of a suitable answer. Meanwhile, what did *you* think of Hannah Blackwood, dear?" And without awaiting a reply he trotted into his bathroom.

Polly climbed slowly into bed. What, indeed, did she think of Hannah Blackwood? Brave beezum? Sly seducer? Gadfly and go-getter? Wife and wanton? Mother and monster? Oh dear! She must talk to Sam. She picked up her bedside book, Logan Pearsall Smith's *All Trivia*, and an amused smile spread like a benediction across her face.

When Mr. Sedgwick returned in his red-silk pyjamas and smelling violently of lavender, he crossed to her.

"Hullo, darling," she said, "are you coming in for a moment?" She smoothed the pillow.

"No, darling."

"Not even a friendly visit?" She pulled a little face.

"You've had a tiring day."

He kissed her and got into his own bed. He said: "No wonder the country is badly governed. I understand most of the Cabinet get only about five or six hours' sleep. Bad conscience, I suppose." He stretched himself.

"What do *you* think of Hannah Blackwood, darling?" she asked.

"I think Blackwood is a lucky fellow."

"Isn't it strange! It just goes to show."

"You mean the Lord evens things out, giving him a nonconformist's conscience and a lovely wife?"

"No, darling. Are you listening?"

"I am agog, dear."

"I believe I have made a discovery."

"In that case I shall put out the light so that you will not witness the look of consternation on my face."

"No, don't do that, darling. It will seem like a nightmare."

"Really, dear. You will have to write me a feuilleton. But pray begin."

Polly said: "I have reason to believe——"

She paused and he said: "Go on, dear. You sound like a policeman at Bow Street."

"I have reason to believe," said Polly, "that Mr. Blackwood is not Bob's father."

"You mean she's been married before?"

"No, dear, she hasn't."

"You mean he's been cuckolded?"

"Must have been, dear."

He said. "Good heavens! If that is true, it ought to cause me infinite distress, but I am afraid it doesn't. When did you turn detective, dear? Or are you from M. I. Five?" He sat up and turned his great red face upon her like an evening sun. Then he leaned back. "How gratifying it is," he said, "to discover that the man who takes a high moral tone is no better than he should be——"

Polly said: "It is not *Mister* Blackwood who has been faithless, dear."

But Sedgwick was going on, "How delightful it is to find that when you take the white sheet off him, he is piebald like the rest of us. Oh dear, oh dear, these radicals, these seagreen incorruptibles!"

"But why put it all on to him, darling?"

He said: "Listen, love. My experience of life teaches me to suppose that when a woman errs and strays like a lost sheep, there is something radically wrong—and how curious it is that the word radical should be found in that ancient saying—radically wrong with the *man*. Either he is drunken or mean or no longer cares for her—or is impotent. Ha!"—an exclamation of triumph.

"Yes, dear, go on."

"We can rule out drunkenness, and from the way his eyes dwelt on her he still cares for her. That leaves meanness and impotency. Now every radical, my love, is by nature somewhat mean with money. She must therefore have long grown accustomed to that shortcoming and would not stray from the straight and narrow on that account. Do you follow me, dear?" His voice by now possessed an edge of excitement.

"Yes, darling, although I do not necessarily agree with you."

"Therefore, dear, using the deductive process, the man is impotent—the great Blackwood is no better than Mr. John Ruskin was—indeed, I should judge they were both of the same kidney."

Polly, however, who was unwilling to permit herself to be other than fascinated by Mr. Blackwood's beard and general appearance of mystery and melancholic power, said: "You cannot argue, darling, that because a man has no children that Nature was ill-disposed to him in a certain direction, because——"

"Yes, darling?"

"Take yourself, dear."

"But I am not married, dear."

"You are married in the sight of God, dear."

Mr. Sedgwick groaned. This was, so to speak, where they came in.

He said: "My love, I am not a member of the Crime Club for nothing. When you have a man masquerading as the father of a son, it is plain that he is not particularly averse from children. Ergo, we may suppose that he would have had children if he could. And if he could not——"

"He may have changed his mind," said Polly. "People do."

"I think, if I may say so, dear, that that is a little thin."

"He may have insanity in his family. A learned physician once told me that we all have insanity in the family if you look deep enough. Most royal families have it, for example. It is quite distinguished. Cowper, the poet, Mary Lamb, George the Third —or was it William the Fourth—and——"

"Polly!"

"Yes, dear."

"I am being reluctantly forced to the conclusion that your scales are heavily tilted in favour of this man Oliver Blackwood; that you will not hesitate——" He paused. "I am not sure that I should pursue that."

"Go on, darling, I long to know what I will not hesitate to do."

"No, Polly, the hour is too late. I was only going to say that you will not hesitate to take the view that his wife Hannah is to blame. . . ."

"Undoubtedly," said Polly.

"Whereas I attribute the fault solely to him. My Roland for your Oliver."

"What did you say, dear?"

"I'll wager he would have been as inconstant as the moon his name is sometimes likened to—had he been able to be so. Which reminds me——"

"Of what, dear?"

"It is simple for a eunuch to be virtuous."

"You mean, dear, that no matter how affectionate a woman's friendship with Mr. Blackwood became, it would be absurd for those devoted to her to harbour the least apprehensions?"

Mr. Sedgwick sighed. "You are putting words into my mouth, dear. By the way"—a thought struck him—"have you discovered who Bob's father actually is?"

"I have no proof, darling."

186

"Come, Polly, do not, after swallowing the hook and the line, grow fastidious over the sinker."

"I have always understood—and been very glad of it—that likeness is not accepted as evidence in a court of law."

"And this brings us to . . ."

"Captain Dryden."

"Polly, you are a genius. You are, I am quite sure, Mr. Freeman Wills Croft in disguise."

"You agree they are very alike?"

"Alike? They are like an old and young walnut. And what, Polly, are you going to do with this piece of social history?"

"Nothing, dear. But I am sorry for Mr. Blackwood. He has had a very raw deal."

"At the hands of the Almighty, perhaps, darling?"

"At the hands of his wife."

"No, no. She has been hardly done by."

"You are inclined to be sentimental about women, darling."

"I know, I know. However, I shall be on my guard. Don't allow your penchant for beards to become too strong, dear, or——"

"Yes, dear?"

He chuckled. "Or I shall have to grow one myself."

"You would then look like a German admiral, darling. And, darling——"

"Yes, Polly."

"Hannah Blackwood is a dangerous woman. I am certain of that."

"The alluring stigmata of your sex, dear."

"She lay in your arms as you danced like a voluptuous mermaid reclining on the bosom of a kindly sea."

"That is very good, Polly. I like that. I have been likened to many things in my time. A kindly sea is good."

"So beware, darling."

"Many brave hearts lie asleep in the deep. Good night, dear."

"Good night, darling. I wonder what Mr. Blackwood will be doing."

"He will be working, dear—I hope. I hope he will be working very hard. That, I am sure, is what he is best fitted for. I might even say all he is fitted for." Mr. Sedgwick stretched himself luxuriously.

CHAPTER XXVI

WHILE THE SEDGWICK dinner party was but halfway through, Mr. Lovelace was confessing to himself that he would be relieved when Oliver Blackwood returned. Before him lay a proof of the court case—a full column of it, and nobody could say it didn't make good reading. The more spicy questions and answers were there verbatim, Bob's remarks on discipline and the magistrate's comment. The report was cold, deliberate—no descriptions of what anybody looked like (the evening papers, however, had repaired that omission), but the dialogue was enough by itself.

Greenhalgh came in and looked round. "Not back yet?"

"No."

"I think it ought to go on an away-page."

"It ought to go on the bloody spike."

"He'd never do that."

"The evenings have run it to death."

"All the same, it's good stuff——"

"We're tight for space tonight."

"Always room for——"

"That's a sub. all over—no heart, no bowels of compassion. Why don't you *lose* the stuff—you've lost a scoop many a time, haven't you?" Lovelace spoke with the old reporter's mixed contempt, raillery and savagery for the inside men, the butchers. "The mechanical department—that's what Northcliffe called you."

"I know how you're feeling, lad," said Greenhalgh. He turned to go. "Give me the wire if he comes."

Lovelace stared moodily at his desk. He couldn't understand Blackwood going to dine with Sedgwick, either—not after what had passed between them at their previous encounter, and what Sedgwick was trying to do. A knife in his ribs, that's what he wanted. Maybe he himself was jealous—yes, that must be it; the feminine streak in him. He hadn't been asked to go to court; Blackwood hadn't asked his advice about the dinner; he didn't even know if Blackwood intended to write a leader about Bob's case. Hell, he knew nothing, was asked nothing, told nothing. All this damned tomfoolery about strict impartiality. Where did that get you? Did anybody like it, approve it, love you for it? Not a damn' bit of it—you just made enemies; they said you were lacking in red blood, were wishy-washy, liberal. Why, if the *Morning Star* cut out all reference to Bob's case, he'd wager his last half-crown they'd be saying in the pubs: "That darn paper's become human at last." He looked up as Seth Entwistle poked his head round the corner.

"Not back yet? I wondered if he'd be doin' another leader——"

"On the court case, eh?"

"Well, I——"

"You're like a lot o' ghouls. I went into the reporters' room—they were having a cabinet meeting about it—full-dress debate—how many columns ought we to give of it—what the Royal Commission on the Press would say if we didn't give it a splash. To hell with the Royal Commission!"

"I agree with what the lad had to say."

"You do, eh?"

"I do. My own lad was bein' bitten to death by mosquitoes and bein' bombed by the Japs—all for five bob a day—when those dock labourers were gettin' ten times as much for sleepin' in their own beds and bein' told by Cabinet Ministers what marvels they were—you'd have thought they were savin' the country. You should have heard my wife on it."

"Did your lad come back?"

"He came back—what was left of him. But he hardly speaks now. Can't get a word out of him. Somethin' happened to him in Burma. Don't know what it was. Never told us. But he's a changed man."

"You could go to the machines and set a leader on this subject from blank paper, Seth."

"By God, I could! Well, I'd best get along."

"All right, Seth. Up the Lancashire Fusiliers!"

Seth departed and Lovelace took a thick pencil and eyed with venom something he had been scribbling. It ran:

> Squander not your love in tears
> Remember all the lonely years
> Before we met. When we must part
> Time enough to break your heart.

Love is birth and pain, we know
In love there's hate, yes, even so ;
But we must seek it who draw breath,
And when the seeking's o'er, 'tis death.

I will love you knowing torment,
Anguish, joy, in the same moment,
Glory in the wounds you deal me
Knowing that your love will heal me.

Now why in God's name did he go on wasting his time in this fruitless way? Why the hell didn't he get on with the novel? Always this cussedness in him, this shooting off at a tangent, this hopeless quest. The time had gone when any woman would look twice at him. No more would any woman's eyes light up when he entered the room, never again would a woman want to be made love to by him—not for his looks anyway. When he glanced at himself in the glass, he saw that his face had fallen to pieces, that his eyes lacked lustre, that his hair was like grey straw—what was left of it. In the morning the mirror told him that overnight Nature had had her way with his face. It took him half an hour to regain control of his features, to restore his gaping mouth to some shape, to put a grain of determination into his eyes. So if ever he made love to a woman again it would be because he was buying her favours—with money or with his reputation as a novelist. Ah well, thank God women were susceptible to a little success, like the stray dog the battalion picked up, the dog that went from the privates to the sergeant-major and from him to the company commander—a regular social climber. Why, if he won the Hawthornden prize, he might get somebody worth having even yet. What was it Lavinia Ward had said over a bottle of stout in The Mitre?—any man, no matter how ugly he may be, can always get a woman. She had said it with great feeling, too. Lavinia—ah, with what adoration he had seen her looking at Blackwood, with what a look of the disciple eyeing her prophet!

The unmistakable footstep in the corridor. Time, too, time, too. Blackwood came in and, as usual, Lovelace felt galvanised—his disgruntlement vanished, he was lit up.

"Anything doing, Richard? Cabinet not resigned yet?" Blackwood squared up to his papers, a half-smoked cigar in his mouth, glad to be back here, an awkward evening behind him.

"Charlie wants to know where to put the court case—fancies tucking it away."

Blackwood took the proof and held it up. "End column, splash page," he said. "Charles is losing his judgment."

He handed the proof back and took his pen. "Yes, Richard?"

"Seth came up to see if there's another leader."

"There will be. I'll do it now. What's the time?" He took out his half-hunter gold watch and looked at it. "Tell him he can have it in three-quarters of an hour."

"Not on the court case?"

"Yes—Richard—on the—court—case." He was already writing. He wrote the heading, "Discipline"—then crossed it out and changed it to "Disunity". He went on: "The significance of the police-court case at Greycastle yesterday in which a former R.A.F. pilot was fined for assaulting a dock labourer, lies not so much in the assault itself, or the actual events that led up to it, namely alleged reckless driving by the labourer. Nor will anybody quarrel with the magistrate's decision or the comments he made. No. The significance lies in the disunity in the nation that was revealed, the gulf that exists between those who served in the armed forces in the last war and those who did not. That gulf, in the event of a grave emergency arising, could be dangerous.

"It is a trite remark that in the Second World War everybody was called on to serve in the capacity wherein he was of most value, that even civilians at home were in the front line, that there was nothing to choose between the heroism displayed by the man in submarines, in the aircraft, in the tank, and the man who continued to work at his munitions lathe or to carry merchandise off ships at the docks. It is not, of course, quite true. The ordeals of men in the true front line were, with notable exceptions, usually greater than those of civilians. To begin with, the bulk of towns in Britain were never bombed at all. The Murmansk convoy, the desert tank battles, the fighting in the jungles of Burma were far worse than ordeals at home which, grave though they were in a handful of cities, Greycastle among them, had compensations in the proximity of wives and families. Equally important, in the case of men who continued at their old jobs, they were infinitely better paid. In time of war in Britain those in the powerful trade unions become something of a privileged class. It has been so in both world wars. Often enough, their rates of pay are higher in war than in peace-time—while their next-door neighbours who drove pens perhaps are now sent forth to drive tanks or aircraft at far less rates of pay than they formerly received. Those men usually suffered in loss of pay, they commonly suffered in loss of promotion in the battle of life. In the case of small, one-man businesses, they frequently saw the work of years reduced to ruin. In the First World War, many a soldier home on leave from France was glad to return to the trenches having been sickened by the profit-making, the luxury he saw in England, a place which often seemed not a hundred but a thousand miles removed from what he had left behind him in France. High profit-making in the Second World War was, on the whole, less, but still existed. A lot of people did well out of the war, among them the munitions workers, hard though the majority of them toiled; not all, by any means. A fair amount of slacking, the maintenance of rigid lines of demarcation between one trade-unionist's job and another which hindered the war effort—this never wholly ceased. Ministers of State went about the country praising indiscriminately. It was difficult, of course, to do other-wise when the enemy would have been comforted by condem-nation, but it left a bad taste in many a mouth.

"It is extremely difficult to achieve more than rough justice between soldiering and not soldiering. The skilled artisans, the coal-miners, the mechanics, the cotton and wool workers, the farm workers—these are in a sense the Brigade of Guards of the Home Front, as vital in their way as the soldiers, airmen and seamen. The work must be done and it is sensible to keep them in their jobs, doing what they can do better than others. But they are privileged, they are fortunate, they have, so to speak, won the toss.

"But it also happens that they are among the principal sup-porters of the Government now in power, the Labour Govern-ment, which, since the war ended, has been heaping more privileges on them to the comparative despite, often enough, of the men—middle-class men or the clerks, warehousemen, and the like—who bore the brunt in the actual front line. The officer class are in the main middle-class, whose standard of living has fallen by at least 25 per cent. In war they bore much of the heat and burden of the day—carried immense responsibility. They have been described by some of those who stayed at home as 'vermin' or those who 'don't matter a tinker's cuss'. To use these words was unjust and unwise; it was a disservice to the country almost criminal in creating disunity.

"Another important fact remains: The men and women who served in the armed forces have been demobilised; they are all on Class Z reserve. They can be recalled at any time and, we must suppose, in the event of emergency would be the first to rejoin the colours. There are about four millions of them—four millions who not uncommonly gave up several years of their lives in our service. They escaped death or maiming once, a host of them by the narrowest margins. They will ask themselves whether they could hope to do so again.

"If war should come, are we to wind them in on the end of our official string again—while those who were comparatively undisturbed and safe last time remain so once more? Are we going, for a third time, to pay high wages to those in the workshops and see men made poorer who carry the rifles and fly the aircraft?

"Men know what war amounts to now. The glory has departed from it. God forbid that this generation should have to face the dread ordeal again. But if it comes, two things are essential—first that the sacrifices necessary should be called for—as far as possible—by men who have themselves faced the greatest dangers, hardships and burdens in the past; and second, that we succeed better than hitherto in spreading the burdens and risks justly. Money is not everything, but it is one of the few compensations that can be given to the men who stand most chance of being killed or wounded. It is far too inequitable that men who have won the toss should draw the biggest pay packets.

"This is the significance of the case heard at Greycastle yesterday. There is a rift in the nation, and it is time we began thinking how to heal it."

Blackwood had not long finished the leader and passed it to Lovelace when, as he was reading the proofs of the main news articles, his telephone rang. It was Lady Molyneux. The voice was high and disturbed. "Could you come round, Mr. Blackwood—at once?"

"Is Sir Thomas——?"

"Much worse—very much worse. It's almost like a stroke. But he asks for you. He may not last very——" She broke off, in distress.

"Yes, of course. I'll come at once. Anything else I can do? The doctor——"

"He's on his way. Do come quickly."

"I will."

Blackwood rose, and Lovelace with him. Blackwood said: "It sounds as if this might be it, Richard."

"By God, it never rains . . ."

"I know. However—there it is. See to that leader, Richard."

"Yes."

"And look over the obituary—Charles had better have it ready. I'll telephone you."

"Yes. You really think he may be for it?"

"Yes—I've never heard her sound like this . . . so human."

"You'll take the office car?"

"Yes. Ring down for it as I go. I think that's all for the moment. I think you'll agree with that leader—for a change, eh?" He squeezed Lovelace's arm and went. By heavens, not in single spies but in battalions. . . .

CHAPTER XXVII

THE NIGHT WAS now cool and Blackwood pulled his light coat round his knees and sat far back in the corner of the car. He was not altogether surprised at the news Lady Molyneux had given him, but this arose as much from an earlier impression that fated events were occurring, as from the foreknowledge that Molyneux was ill and had had his own premonitions that he was not long for this world. Blackwood was now preternaturally calm, calmer than usual. He was no stranger to this feeling, either. He had encountered it at various crises in his life, especially in war. When a situation was more than usually grave, when the end of things—of life itself—looked as though it were in sight, then he had on many an occasion appeared to enter into an antechamber of another world and become an onlooker at the scene, possibly a somewhat disembodied onlooker. After death, would it be thus? —or when he was very old? Would there, in old age, be an imperceptible moving from one world of consciousness into the other, as one journeyed sometimes into the realm of sleep? And as age deepened, would the dwelling in the other regions— ethereal, fanciful—grow longer in time and the returning to this world be more and more reluctant, until there came a moment when returning was no more? When his old comrade Edward Vine had recovered from his dangerous illness after his life had been despaired of, he had written saying that it was a recovery in spite of himself, that he had put up no fearful struggle, had been content to cross the Styx. Blackwood had found this a little strange, for Edward Vine was a man of singular courage. Could one grow so used to the thought of death that death were as close as a brother? His thoughts ran on in this vein recalling how country folk could speak with great cheerfulness of their hankering after a special corner of the churchyard as if it were a new house of which they spoke; he remembered that Nelson had built for himself a coffin from the mast of a French ship captured at the Nile; he knew that Lancashire folk relished, as they said, a funeral. The method in war of wrapping a dead soldier in a groundsheet and disposing of him reverently if possible but assuredly without fuss had always seemed to him the right fashion. Cast me to the winds and let me blow, Lovelace would say. But there had been nights near Guinchy and Festubert when he, Blackwood, had done his share in carrying dead comrades out of trenches and burying them within gun-range as the starshells drew arcs with fiery pencils in the dark sky—and on those nights he had been intolerably moved.

It was a stony-eyed butler who opened the door to him at Sir Thomas Molyneux's house, and took his hat and coat. The house was hushed, and looked enormously large and ugly on this night.

The butler led the way up the broad, old-fashioned staircase with its mahogany balustrate and thick Turkish carpet, its stained-glass windows shutting out the world, typical in their way of a house nobody had had the heart to bring up to date —a childless house, since Godfrey had been killed in the Coldstream. A line came into Blackwood's head from the prayer-book: "We came into the world with nothing and we shall assuredly take nothing out." The bedroom door was opened noiselessly after a discreet tap and the butler had breathed his name. Blackwood stepped inside.

Sir Thomas was high on his pillows. The ruddiness was long since gone and the skin, in the few days since Blackwood had seen him, had yellowed like parchment. His face was strained and fixed, and only one eye, the right, swivelled to look at Blackwood as he came in. The other half of his face was immovable. Molyneux tried to speak but the words were hardly audible— certainly Blackwood could not catch them.

Lady Molyneux came round the foot of the bed to lay a hand on Blackwood's arm and murmur: "He cannot talk—not clearly—but he'll be glad you are here."

Blackwood said: "I am most desperately sorry—I wish I had come earlier. The doctor——?"

"Yes, he has been." She shook her head and her eyes filled with tears. "Nothing we can do—but he will come back."

In these few seconds, Sir Thomas's usable eye had been fixed on them, and Blackwood now took a step nearer to him and took the hand lying outside the coverlet in both of his. The half of Sir Thomas's face twitched convulsively. Blackwood sat down in the bedside chair and continued to hold the hand, and presently he felt a small pressure exerted and the face twitched again. A current of emotion swept through him and his stomach contracted so that the normal ache he carried there was increased. He was, after a fashion, glad of this, since it gave him something to battle with. The three of them remained thus, silent, for what seemed a long time, Lady Molyneux standing by Blackwood's side, Blackwood holding the sick man's hand, and Sir Thomas lying immovable, his eye staring at Blackwood's face as that of a child sometimes does, solemn, questioning, almost rebuking. Downstairs a clock chimed the half hour, most loudly. Soon afterwards, Sir Thomas's face made great attempts to move and the hand in Blackwood's emitted little spasmodic clasps, and sounds, half-formed words, issued from the side of his mouth.

Lady Molyneux bent over him and said: "Yes, Tommy? Yes, Tommy?" The babble of sound went on for a few seconds, like that of a child which is understood by its mother but nobody else. When it ceased, she said: "He says—it's all right—he's put it in the codicil." She paused. "Do you understand?"

Blackwood's heart smote him with gratitude and he could have wept. He conquered himself and said, nodding both to her and to Sir Thomas: "Yes, I understand. Yes, I understand. Thank you, Thomas, thank you." He pressed the hand in his and a warmer light came into Molyneux's eye for a moment or two as though indeed a current of light had been turned on; then it faded and died. The eye continued to stare at Blackwood, steadily, unwinking, and now seemingly unutterably sad. Blackwood, on an impulse, turned to Lady Molyneux and asked: "Do you think he would like me to speak something—a poem perhaps if I could remember one?" She nodded gratefully and Blackwood then began to say, in a low voice, his speech half choking him, but after a moment or two more clearly and distinctly, Bridges'—

> Whither, O splendid ship, thy white sails crowding,
> Leaning across the bosom of the urgent West,
> That fearest nor sea rising, nor sky clouding,
> Whither away, fair rover, and what thy quest?
> Ah soon, when Winter has all our vales opprest,
> When skies are cold and misty and hail is hurling,
> Wilt thou glide on the blue Pacific, or rest
> In a summer haven asleep, thy white sails furling.

As Blackwood spoke, the eye flickered and closed, opened again and closed again, and the pressure on Blackwood's hand relaxed. Sir Thomas lay infinitely still.

CHAPTER XXVIII

THE GENERAL OPINION among the reporters and sub-editors of the *Morning Star* was that Sir Thomas Molyneux could not have died at a more opportune time; that if they had small cause to thank him for what he had done in the past (it was astonishing how little most of them felt beholden to him for having enabled them to earn a livelihood) they could certainly pass a vote of thanks to him for becoming the dear departed now. His death cleared the air, said Frank Knowles. It clarified the issue, said Forsyth. It would soon show them where they stood, said Charles Greenhalgh. There will be a fight over the ownership of the paper like that of vultures, said Prince. Brenda Smith thought that if they had a woman proprietress her own opportunities might be enhanced; but she kept this view to herself. Fred Cheshire opined to de Ferrers that he anticipated getting fired again. Mr. Cheshire expressed this opinion with a touch of bravado over a first half-pint of beer, but two half-pints later he held the same view in the depths of melancholy and had much ado not to have tears dribbling into his glass. De Ferrers, who was a cheerful and generous soul, promptly laid Cheshire three to one that not only would nobody be fired but that they would all receive increases in pay—"because O.B. will buy the paper himself and hand over the financial side to Dicky Lovelace, and we all know what Dicky is with money".

But Mr. Cheshire was not to be convinced. He'd been sacked, he said, for doing things that other chaps had been promoted for. For instance—"Two more half-pints, Harry lad"—there was a time when you could get little scoops out of the police by tipping 'em a golden half-sovereign; you lolled on the police-station counter and you rolled half a quid to and fro and then it fell off on the sergeant's side—and a while later he produced a titbit. But the chief constable, said Mr. Cheshire, got wind of the dodge and complained to his Burnham editor, and the editor, who had winked at this way of getting news—didn't he keep twenty gold sovereigns in his safe for the purpose?—had put on the garb of sanctity and fired him. Oh yes! After that, said Cheshire, he had held his own integrity very high, very high indeed. And one day when he was working on a murder story, some smart crime reporters up from London had contrived to put a packet of French chalk in the chimney of the house where the murder was done and had thereafter persuaded an old skivvy to search that chimney. Of course she had found the packet and told the police, and the London reporters had got the local police to send it to Scotland Yard for examination. Oh, it made quite a good front-page story next morning—quite a splash!

"But I got into a hell of a row for not sending the story," said Mr. Cheshire. "Of course, I told 'em I hadn't really missed it—I told 'em it was a fake and I wouldn't *send* a story like that. Was ours a decent paper, or wasn't it? Was it lies they wanted?"

"And what did the blighters say?" inquired de Ferrers.

Cheshire shook his head sadly. "The news editor said it was a dam' good story, fake or no fake, and he said I was throwing it down simply because I'd missed it—and they fired me. But I hadn't missed it. You believe that, de Ferrers, don't you?" Cheshire turned his bleary, wistful eyes on de Ferrers.

"Of course you hadn't missed it, old boy," said de Ferrers. "They were a lot of dirty old sods. Don't I know? Here—have something short—it'll cheer you up. And never forget you're on a damn, decent paper now—no faking, no twisting, no letting blokes down when they tell you something off the record. . . ."

Mr. Cheshire smiled wanly. "Like being in the church isn't it?"

"It is that," said de Ferrers, "and just about the same amount o' brass in it. Lead in your pencil, Fred."

Sir Thomas Molyneux's death clarified the issue for Oliver Blackwood, too. For it was true what Molyneux had hinted at as he lay dying; he had, in leaving the *Morning Star* to his wife, stipulated that she must not part with it for one month after his death and that if Blackwood made an offer equal to that of Mr. Sedgwick, Blackwood's offer must be accepted. Sir Thomas had even mentioned the sum—£500,000. He had ruled out any opportunity for Sedgwick or anybody else to go on raising their offers to put Blackwood out of the running; £500,000 was the sum. If Blackwood could find it, the paper was his. If not, Lady Molyneux was at liberty to do as she wished. Lady Molyneux, in disclosing to Blackwood this paragraph in the will, had said: "You have had great influence over him, Mr. Blackwood." She spoke with a certain coldness. The room was ponderous with gloom, the curtains half drawn, evening light and sun excluded. Sir Thomas lay upstairs in his coffin and she had no desire that anybody should remain unaware of the fact. "You had great influence over him." She spoke as if the influence were a little malign. The warmth that had flowed between her and Blackwood for a brief while on the night Sir Thomas had died had now evaporated.

Blackwood said: "Thomas and I had many talks in the long years of our work together."

"And he has done what you wanted over the paper's future. You have got your own way, which, as you know, was not *my* way."

"I am sorry we do not see eye to eye," he said.

She went on: "Unfortunately, you will probably raise the money, for my husband's paper has a great reputation—a very great reputation."

"I am glad you feel that."

"Don't you?" She flashed it at him, but he merely murmured: "Of course." A remark of which she made little and which did not mollify her.

"You will realise," she said, "that it is very probable that in fixing the sum of five hundred thousand pounds my husband has deprived me of a large—additional sum."

Blackwood said gently: "I understand that was the largest figure Mr. Sedgwick mentioned."

"He would have been prepared to increase it."

"I wonder."

"He told me so himself—yesterday."

"Mr. Sedgwick is a diplomat—in addition to being a business-man." He tried to keep the irony out of his voice but he did not altogether succeed.

"Are you suggesting he was lying to me?" She struck her knee with her fist, her wide mouth very open as her words left it.

"No—but it occurs to me that it is a statement that cost him nothing to make—and which cannot now be tested."

"Which suits you very well, Mr. Blackwood."

He did not answer that.

She added: "But I suppose you are thinking that it makes no difference to me either way because this Government you give your support to will take about four-fifths of it from me."

He said very quietly: "My support, Lady Molyneux, as is clear in the paper, is intermittent, given only when they deserve it. That is one of the reasons why the paper enjoys the reputation you spoke of."

"But you agree with them taking eighty per cent of my money."

"No—I think it is too much. But——"

"Yes?"

"Money has to come from somewhere."

"Oh yes," she said, "for all this waste—false hair and false teeth for everybody, and medicine poured down the sink."

"And also," he said, "for reducing our infant mortality to the lowest we've ever had and for sending record numbers to the universities." She rose. "I can see, Mr. Blackwood, we should never agree about anything."

"I should be sorry if that were so," he said, rising also.

"It is quite—quite impossible." She crossed towards the door. "I hope that during this next month you will keep your radicalism within bounds, because——"

He was constrained now to interrupt: "I am sorry you speak in this way——"

"—because"—she flung it at him—"my friends know that I am now the proprietor and I do not want life to be made a nuisance by having to try and defend a lot of——"

Blackwood paused at the door. "You will be wise to make your position quite plain to them, ma'am—it will save you a lot of trouble—namely, that under the terms of my contract, which is nearly twenty years old, the policy of the paper is left in my hands; that on the *Morning Star*, as on the *Burnham Guardian*, the editor is really the editor. Good afternoon, ma'am."

She did not answer; they did not shake hands. She watched him down the hall as the butler opened the door for him, hating him and suddenly hating Thomas, too, for making her powerless. She went upstairs with tears in her eyes.

At the funeral, which Blackwood attended, she had not spoken to him, had merely bowed to him. She had written saying she trusted the funeral would be adequately reported with quotations from the principal wreaths, and the bishop's address given in full. She added that she had thought the leading article on Sir Thomas was extremely brief. Blackwood sent an acknowledgment of the letter and placed it in his private file, but he did not propose to act on it. Mr. Sedgwick had attended the funeral and, as Blackwood saw, had some conversation with Lady Molyneux. She had been marked in her cordiality towards him. Sedgwick, when they were all entering their cars, had hurried across to speak to Blackwood. He would like, he said, to have a few minutes' talk with Blackwood before he himself left for London. If Blackwood could—— Blackwood had interrupted to say he was going straight to the office; if Sedgwick cared to call there, he would find time to see him. He was curt, for he did not imagine the visit sprang from friendliness.

The meeting had duly taken place, both men in their stiff mourning clothes and the atmosphere formal—at first. Sedgwick had begun by saying it was sad that Molyneux had died so suddenly but that he supposed he must congratulate Blackwood on having won this month's respite.

Blackwood didn't answer that at once. He took a cigar out of his case, pierced the end, eyed it critically, and, just before he lit it, said: "Thank you." He stared across at Sedgwick interrogatively, and waited.

Sedgwick said, glancing about him: "I am bound to say there's a nice old-fashioned flavour here."

Blackwood inclined his head in agreement.

Sedgwick said: "The atmosphere of printers' ink—of books—of standing on the edge of literature—which is so becoming to a small newspaper office."

"You think so?"

"I do." Sedgwick stretched his legs comfortably and lolled back.

Blackwood asked: "Is this why you have visited me, to enjoy a refreshing change from Yorkshire House, which I am told is often mistaken for the headquarters of a chemical combine?"

Sedgwick drew in his legs. He said: "That old story—my enemies keep busy. In fact, of course, a vast organization like mine—my people number many hundreds up and down the country—cannot get along without its G.H.Q. You will realise that our capital—my capital—runs to millions; that I control over half a dozen papers——"

"Only too well," said Blackwood.

Sedgwick waved that aside. "—so that—and this is my point—five hundred thousand pounds is not the large sum to me—that it is to you."

Blackwood said: "A statement certainly more irrefutable than many that appear in your leading articles."

"And, moreover," said Sedgwick, sitting forward and assuming an air of great earnestness, "while I could guaratee my shareholders a reasonable dividend on their money—throwing in, so to speak, the *Morning Star* along with the rest of my papers and pooling results, you will never be able to guarantee *anything*. This paper has paid only the most modest return on a small capital. What sort of a showing will it make on a sum nearly twice as large—and a paper standing alone?"

Blackwood said: "If I were you I should not worry my head about it. None of your money will be involved."

Sedgwick continued: "Your integrity—your integrity will be strained—won't it?—in deciding what inducements you can offer to those you seek the money from."

Blackwood put his elbows on the arms of his chair and locked his fingers. "Mr. Sedgwick," he said, "you are beginning to strain my instincts of courtesy. Have you said what you came for?"

Sedgwick wafted some cigar smoke aside. He said: "I did not intend to be less than plain. You are a writer—a journalist—who is about to adventure into another world—that of finance. I want to warn you. You would really be wiser not to do it. The City of London is not for you. You think you know almost everything—most journalists do. You are probably contemptuous of the business and financial side of your paper. It's no good. Without us, you writers are sunk. Much better stay in your ivory tower—be an oracle—go on putting the world to rights—but don't adventure into the jungle of money and big business. You will lose your way."

"Is that all?"

"That is most of it."

"What you're after, I suppose, is that I should say: 'My dear Sedgwick—give me the money—take the paper. . . .'"

"That would be wise—certainly."

"Well—nobody can accuse you of not being persevering."

"But you will take no notice?"

"No!"

"It is what I expected. By the way——" He got up and stood leaning on his black ebony stick.

"Yes?"

"Your son—who is so remarkably unlike you in so many ways —if he should find himself in difficulties with the Government's air services which employ him—I dare say I could find him something to do—something more lucrative than what he's got now."

"I'll let him know."

"You wouldn't object to him working for me?"

"That's a matter for him."

"I like him. I imagine some of his ideas are more in keeping with mine than yours. Hardly a chip of the old block, perhaps—not in that sense." Sedgwick smiled. "One thing more: would you give my kindest remembrances to your wife? I can't help—well—envying you. I hope when you are both up in Town you will dine with me."

"I'm afraid we are not often up together."

"Well, Blackwood, goodbye. Our paths will keep crossing, I dare say. No use my saying I hope you'll find the money. I hope you won't. But you may, of course, tap some unexpected sources. Quite unexpected. You'll have to be careful none of the money is tainted—won't you?" He held out his beefy hand.

Blackwood took it, saying: "You've done one thing for me, at all events——"

"I'm glad of that. What is it?"

"You've strengthened all the convictions and beliefs I held before we met."

"No surprises?"

"None."

"Well, that's fortunate for you—very. Let's hope—for your sake—that none await you in the future."

Sedgwick executed a little wave with his stick and hat, and went.

A while later Lovelace found Blackwood sitting in his chair, his eyes closed and a finger and thumb pressed against the lids. He did not move for a moment. He had been turning over with a sorrowful heart Sedgwick's phrases about the want of likeness between him and Bob. How many people knew the truth, he wondered, or the half-truth that was worse? What use might not Sedgwick make of it, if he knew it and had the mind? The innuendo, the veiled sneer, the jibe over drinks? "The tempest in my mind doth from my senses take all feeling else save what beats there." But come—God giveth all good things in return for labour. Da Vinci knew all about it. Blackwood raised his head.

"Well, Richard?"

"I saw him going down the stairs. A pity he didn't break his blasted neck." Lovelace rolled a cigarette and looked out of the window. "Those sparrows out there are the fattest little sparrows I've ever seen. In a decent world all little sparrows would be fat, fat as hell. Has that ever occurred to you?" He saw that Blackwood had taken up his pen, thank God for that! "By the way, Oliver—how long did you say we've got?"

"One month."

"One month in which to save the world, eh?"

"*Our* world."

"One month in which to light a torch not all the seas of the western approaches in a howling gale can extinguish, eh?"

"That's about it, Richard."

"We'll have a cup o' tea on that, Oliver. A right cup o' tea." He got up and loped over to the electric kettle. "How about you having a night off, Oliver? I've got a drawerful of old leaders there—I'll never manage to get 'em into the paper unless you take a night off. One's a beauty—all about honours being diminished a stage in every generation unless the son does something spectacular—till finally the peerage comes down to the O.B.E., and then—nothing."

He went chattering on, but Blackwood didn't stop his writing. He said, as he wrote: "We'll use that one next Monday—Monday is a day for enlivening our readers for their week's toil. Always—remember—that. And now, Richard, silence! I am drafting something very important indeed—perhaps the most important thing I ever wrote—a private letter to stir the conscience and purse of some of the leading citizens of this great city."

"In that case," said Lovelace, "I shall put a little whisky in our tea. I was looking for an excuse."

CHAPTER XXIX

OLIVER BLACKWOOD DECIDED that one of the first features of his campaign to raise the needed £500,000 should be a talk to the staff in order that—like Cromwell's Ironsides—they should know what they were fighting for and love what they knew. No room in the office was big enough, so he took the Thurlow Hall beneath the town's chief library—a horseshoe hall, built in tiers; and he booked it for Sunday afternoon at four forty-five. They could hear what he had to say and then go on to work. The handful off duty could go home again.

He visited the cathedral on his way to the hall. It was a blusterous day, clouds high in the heavens, the wind pulling at hats and coats, jostling, playfully buffeting. Hannah drove down with him. Since the funeral and Sedgwick's departure, their relationship had been a good deal easier. Dryden had disappeared for another voyage. Blackwood himself, shaken a little by Bob's ordeal, knowing how distrait she, too, had been, and pulled asunder by warring thoughts, had striven doubly hard to be tender and considerate, ignoring her sharp remarks about the length of the paper's report of the police-court case, and thanking her when she had grudgingly conceded that she approved of much of his leading article. He was glad of a respite, glad of any easefulness, for there were times when it took all his inward resolution to keep going. The world was dark, and a house torn with dissension was a devilish dwelling-place for the hours of rest. If this seeking after an oasis was appeasement, then it was appeasement. He reflected that while he was a long way yet from Prospero, whose every third thought was of death or ruin, he understood him well enough. When Hannah had spoken with pleasure of meeting Mr. Sedgwick and had declared that his attitude towards Bob's case was completely her own, that Sedgwick was one of those cheerful, uninhibited extroverts with no pretensions of any kind and therefore the sort she was glad to meet for a change—while he had inwardly winced, he had not gainsaid her in any way. She must sail down the stream in her own fashion; the river of time would resolve all this as the years passed.

They had not been in the cathedral together for a long while— not, he thought, since one Sunday when Bob was on leave during 1943 and when, as the three of them had wandered round the city, looking at the bomb damage, Bob had suddenly said he would like to go to church. Blackwood had wondered what moved Bob: was he suddenly oppressed by the dangers he ran? They had walked up the hill to where the cathedral, this building of rosy sandstone, unfinished, looked down upon the city. Bob had said, looking up: "This one not completed by a long chalk and we're knocking down those that are. Too bad." Blackwood had seen that Bob knelt down inside—really knelt, not sitting forward on the edge of the wooden seat, and he and Hannah had knelt, too. He had wondered what words had passed Hannah's lips, for she did not believe in God in any conventional sense; perhaps they all sought to put themselves more in tune with the Infinite. He was profoundly glad to try. He had indeed himself been trying to achieve that for a year or two previously, during a struggle to make up his mind more firmly where he stood in relation to God. He had begun in those days to realise that, at times, and especially in the open air, he was in touch with some Force which orders this universe. And he had begun to open himself, as it were, to this Force as he journeyed to his work, as he trod the deck of the ferry-boats and lifted his face to the sky, half-unconsciously breathing more deeply. He had begun to feel, in the result, calmer, more confident. And part of the pain of his wound, and a sciatic pain in the leg, had gone. Faith, imagination, or a genuine healing power that could be drawn upon? Whatever it was, it had seemed true and real enough then. It had not always appeared so since.

But however that was, this majestic building imparted something of the calm and serenity that the sea held for him. The unearthly purity and beauty of the voices singing without organ, allowing the echo to die before they began the next phrase—this stirred him deeply, cleansed him. He looked down at Hannah with infinite sadness and compassion for what life had withheld from her. She was looking steadily towards the choir, listening, her face heavy in repose, breathing so gently that the rise and fall of her bosom was hardly discernible. Her unmoving solemnity was as that of one who slept. The preacher chose the text: "Be thou faithful unto death and I will give thee the crown of life." He spoke with immense confidence of the life hereafter, of our bereavements swelling the host of loved ones who would welcome us hereafter when our own time came. It struck Blackwood as too simple a version of what he thought the truth might be, but he allowed a part of his mind to listen while another part could go floating, as it were, among the high Gothic pillars, flying as a bird round the stained-glass windows, or hovering over the heads of the silent people the while pondering on the phrase, "O

how blessed a thing it is, brethren, to dwell together in unity."
Yes, that was blessed, thrice blessed. He took Hannah's arm as
they left the cathedral, going out into the wind, down the steep
flight of steps. She pressed herself against him, her arm tightening
against his, and he was glad of it—but whether she did it in
affection or because the wind buffeted her, he couldn't be sure.
She drove him down to the Thurlow Hall and there left him, and
he kissed her, she accepting his caress as a daughter might have
done.

The Thurlow Hall looked cavernous. About a hundred people
were assembled, seated at the front where Lovelace had drawn
them together. They sat smoking their pipes and cigarettes, a drab
crowd, who might have been delegates to any trade-union meeting. Only two women were there: Lavinia Ward, tremulous with
excitement and devotion; and Brenda Smith, making notes in her
microscopic pad, hoping they might be useful in fiction at some
unspecified time. The men were jocular, in a subdued fashion,
exchanging badinage: "Cricket forecasts were all wrong agen
this week" . . . "I propose Frank Knowles takes the chair" . . .
"Do we get time and a half for this, Frank?" . . . "Ask the Father
of the Chapel if he's brought the beer" . . . "Are the sentries on
the doors, Mr. Lovelace? Top secret, ain't it?" . . .
The buzz dwindled as Blackwood entered the hall; an inquiry
as to when they were all joining the Sedgwick circus being left in
the air, torn off, unanswered, as he strode to the platform. In his
dark clothes, black wideawake hat, dark beard, he looked the
leader of a revolution. He took the platform alone, took off his
light coat and placed it with his hat on the table. He stood in
front of the table, and as he spoke began to sit on the edge of it,
informally. He had never loved speeches and tried not to make
one now.
"I wanted you to come," he said, his voice a trifle harsh with
nervousness, "because you've more right than anybody else to
know what I'm doing, what I'm—up to. After all, we're a kind
of fellowship engaged in a serious business—not selling coal or
groceries but opinion and attempts to shape other people's
opinions. I've come from the cathedral, where a man is preaching.
Well, we do a certain amount of preaching ourselves. We try not
to be too solemn about it, we don't mind using invective or satire

or even a bludgeon—but we say what we think; we even carry on a crusade. Now what are we crusading about in the paper? At bottom, we're crusading for a better country, a better road of living, a better way of carrying on so that we shall all get more out of life —more fun, more knowledge and more dignity for ourselves. And by dignity I simply mean being proud of ourselves, holding our heads up, thinking we're as good as anybody else. I don't, myself, want there to be any slaves in the country, and I don't want any arrogant big bosses either. Neither the one nor the other is my cup of tea. And I'm not much good at toeing the line either. I never was, not even when I was in the army. Whenever anybody shouted 'Eyes right!' or 'Eyes left!' I had an almost irresistible desire to look in the opposite direction. I was a born member of the awkward squad." They laughed at that. "I didn't even like uniforms, or wearing buttons and badges. That's why I've never been a member of a political party. I know if I were I should soon be breaking out, leaping the traces, emancipating myself. The notion that everything your own side does is right, that all those in your camp are saints, and that all those against you are scoundrels incapable of doing a right thing—that is nonsense; nonsense for me, anyhow. I don't believe human beings are fashioned in that way. Whoever we are, rich or poor, black or brown or white, we are born and we die—and in between we joy and we sorrow, we are exalted and we are cast down.

"You see—" he paused in thought—"I'm an apostle of individuality, first, last and all the time. And I believe that's important today when, all over the world, men are being pushed around more and more, and invited to line up with this group or that, adopt this creed or that, and believe everybody outside the one group or party or religion is damned for everlasting. But because I try to make my creed—such as it is—tolerance and fairmindedness and justice and loving kindness, don't imagine I think nothing should be abused, attacked, scarified, pulled to pieces and torn apart. Let's be angry at stupidity, let's flog with scorpions what seems to us wicked, and let us turn on to the pompous humbugs, the charlatans, the swollen-headed bureaucrats the cleansing jet of laughter and ridicule." He took a pace or two along the platform and back and the audience moved and stretched its legs and grinned with approval. He started again, speaking sharply now:

"But you cannot refuse to toe the line unless you have independence. That is what I am coming to.

"The *Morning Star* cannot do its work unless it breathes free air. It is no new thing, of course, this view that I—and most of you —I hope all of you—hold, that a newspaper can only do its rightful work in the best way when it is free, free from any combine or authority centred hundreds of miles away, whether governmental or big business. That distinguished editor Mr. C. P. Scott has said—I've got it here somewhere. . ." He took a slip of paper from his vest pocket. " 'There are papers which will never be sold, which would rather suffer extinction. The public has its rights. The paper which has grown up in a great community, nourished by its resources, reflecting in a thousand ways its spirit and its interests, in a real sense belongs to it.' Well, I agree with that. The *Morning Star* belongs to this city. Imagine us being ordered about by somebody sitting in London! What I really want to see is the day when every town will have its own paper, owned by the town's citizens, reflecting the opinions of the neighbourhood—not a faint echo of what they think in Whitehall or Fleet Street. The heart of England is not necessarily in London—it throbs just as vigorously north-west of centre in the body— and that is here in Greycastle! I won't say that what Lancashire thinks today London thinks tomorrow—but I'll say that what we think and they think are often two different opinions altogether."

Frank Knowles muttered: "Aye, who should be captain o' the Test team," and a ripple of laughter swept over them.

Blackwood went on: "No; this notion of independence isn't new—it isn't even confined to England. Joseph Pulitzer, the well-known American journalist made this the platform of the *St. Louis Post-Dispatch*—" he fished out another scrap of paper—" 'It will always fight for progress and reform, never tolerate injustice or corruption, always fight demagogues of all parties, never belong to any party, always oppose privileged classes and public plunderers, never lack sympathy with the poor, always remain devoted to the public welfare; never be satisfied with merely printing news; always be drastically independent; never be afraid to attack wrong, whether by predatory plutocracy or predatory poverty.' It takes some living up to, of course, doesn't it, but it's good to see there are people on the other side of the world who think as we do—that we've got allies. There's the other saying, too, that truth is armed and can defend itself."

There were two or three "Hear hear's".

Blackwood folded his arms. "We have allies. We have long had allies. Even before the First World War Hilaire Belloc and Cecil Chesterton wrote a book drawing attention to the dangers of Press combines. The dangers of monopoly, of mass opinion, of regimentation, have not diminished since then. Quite the contrary. Emerson said, 'Whoso would be a man must be a nonconformist'. I don't imagine he was thinking of religion. And I would say— Whoso would run a good newspaper must be a nonconformist, too—a refuser to fall into line at the behest of financiers or politicians or the pullers of powerful strings. Vested interests must be fought whether they're those of brewers and landowners, religions —or trade-unions." Some of the printers stirred uneasily and Mr. Forsyth registered a mental reservation.

"Do you think this task of holding the scales justly, of speaking out impartially, of apportioning praise and blame where it's deserved—whether by Socialists or Tories, whether by Catholics or Protestants, whether by former enemies or former allies—could be performed by a newspaper that was a unit in a newspaper chain?"

There were murmurs of "No—no" . . . "Not on your life" . . . "Not b— likely"; and Lavinia Ward wiped moisture from her eyes.

Blackwood waited. Then: "No; not in a thousand years. But the independent line isn't very popular today. This isn't a very happy country today. Perhaps it never was. When I was a small boy writers were writing of the dwindling prestige of the House of Commons, the permeation of public life by indirect corruption, the Americanisation and plutocratising of England. But—all the same—I sometimes think there's a bitterness in the country today that is new in our own time—a political bitterness more akin to the United States than England; a growing anti-semitism—partly the aftermath of Hitler's monstrous sowing—a dislike of those who can see both sides of a question—and I ask you especially to ponder that! Imagine it—a hatred in England of fairmindedness—we, who flatter ourselves we're good sportsmen! It was Wellington who said: 'Next to losing a battle, the greatest misfortune is to win such a victory as this.' We're reaping a bitter harvest, gentlemen—we've all been dirtied and soiled by the war —and we need sending to the cleaners. We're not the dead honest people we once were. Who among us can lay his hand on his heart and say he hasn't fiddled a bit, hasn't dodged the column in some way or other? It's a bad business. And it won't be got better except by honest reporting of facts and straight talk about them. We shall have to do some twisting of the sword in our own wounds if we're to make them clean. We shall have to be self-critical, and castigate the vices and vanities we possess." He paused and a sigh broke over them and they stirred again. He looked at them a trifle sorrowfully.

"Our life," he said, "would be easy for us—we could be popular—if we came down heavily on one side or the other—if we were wedded to the Tory Party or the Labour Party. No lack of friends then. But as it is—it will be hard work. It has always been hard work. Every brutal fact we publish is disliked by somebody or other. Who among the Socialists likes to think the individual output among Lancashire cotton operatives has dropped by ten to fifteen per cent since pre-war, or that there are still a hundred and sixty thousand unemployed in the six development areas alone—in this time of full employment? Who among the Tories likes to know that there are villages in Durham where eighty per cent of the houses stood condemned when war broke out —and the people are still living in those houses today?—that from that county between the wars a hundred and fifty thousand people left, fleeing from unemployment as from a pestilence? That in this land of ours only one boy in six among those worthy of being sent to the university ever got there pre-war?

"No, gentlemen, every sore we reveal makes us hated by somebody or other, and every time we praise an act of courage somebody regrets that we have been generous. Politicians and Cabinet Ministers say—they have said it to me—'We never know whose side you are on—we never know when we can rely on you—you're just as likely to be against us tomorrow as with us today.' I have replied to that: 'Yes, of course. Why not? What does a judge do? A judge is not loyal to his friends or a punisher of his enemies. He has—on his judge's bench—neither the one nor the other. All he knows is that he is for those who are doing what's right according to the law. All we on the *Morning Star* know is that we stand for those who are doing right, as we see it. We may be often wrong—

perhaps we are—but we must act according to our lights—not other people's lights."

"That's the stuff," said Lovelace. "Good show, sir," called a voice from the back; and another: "Give 'em hell, sir."

Blackwood smiled: "Well, there we are. Hated sometimes—blessed at others. And—in order to keep on doing it—we need five hundred thousand pounds and we have a month to get it in."

A voice called: "Get it from football pools, sir. They're rolling in it!" And another: "I seem to have paid that much to Cripps myself."

Blackwood held up his hand, "All right! I gather you are with me."

A burst of applause and clapping greeted that.

"I can't offer you big money——"

A voice: "Too true!" and laughter.

Blackwood said: "Only long hours and hard work."

A voice: "Aye, we know!"

Blackwood continued: "Every day a battle. But it's a great fight. I believe we are winning. As a matter of fact our circulation is going up—twenty thousand more in the past year—most of them in the south of England."

A voice: "A bit of *nous* at last," and laughter.

Blackwood turned and picked up his hat and coat. "I think that's all. Now we'll go and print another—what is it?—a block-buster? Oh, by the way—any questions?" He stood there, hat in hand.

Frank Knowles got up heavily: "There's just this, sir—apart from saying 'Thank you for speaking to us'. I think we'd all like to say that?" He turned to the others.

"Yes, Frank" . . . "Good lad, Frank!" and some applause.

Knowles resumed: "Only this, sir—if we have any ideas on how to raise a bit o' brass—I know Brenda here happens to have a millionaire who's a fan of hers——"

"Now, Brenda!" . . . "Who is he, dear?"

Knowles went on: "Well, if Brenda asks him nicely, he might come across with something—even if it's only a hundred thousand, eh, love?"

Brenda said in her fluting contralto: "I'm quite willing to try him, Mr. Blackwood."

Blackwood said: "Certainly. And if anybody else has any ideas, send me a note. I forgot to say that I want to see the paper formed into a Trust controlled by half a dozen of the leading citizens of Greycastle to see it remains an independent journal with a liberal-minded policy—and an editor who'll edit with full responsibility. Anything else? . . . Good, then we'll go and do some work. Come along, Richard!" He strode off, Lovelace hurrying to keep pace. Outside they had to raise their voices in the lusty breeze.

"How did it go, Richard?"

"Champion! It'll make a good story—couple o' columns of it."

"What do you mean?"

"I didn't tell you, because I thought it might put you off. I had Prince behind that screen at the side taking a full note. Why not run it? The country will have to be told. Why not this way?"

Blackwood took his arm. "This is insubordination. But"—he smiled—"it's as good a way of kicking off as any other. Right! We'll do it." He felt singularly light-hearted.

CHAPTER XXX

THE PRINTING IN the pages of the *Morning Star* of Blackwood's address to the staff—he wrote no leader on the subject, just allowed the story to run in the end column of the main news page and turn over—had wide repercussions of various kinds and in various places. Mr. Sedgwick summoned Sir Frederick Pick to confer on whether and how it would be possible to invest enough money in the paper—say £300,000— to gain a controlling interest. "What a sell it would be for him, Freddy, to find he had to do what we told him after all."

"We should have to use nominees," said Sir Frederick.

"Well, what's the matter with that?" inquired Sedgwick.

"And this matter of a Trust——"

"Ah! A problem there certainly—a problem there all right. You'll have to live in Greycastle, Freddy, and pose as a leading citizen of the town and be *chairman* of the Trust. How about that,

Freddy? Now go and put your thinking-cap on—find ways and means. Talk to your friends in the city! Two things: either prevent him getting the money—that would be the best thing, in which case we buy the paper—Lady Molyneux will see to that; or we procure a controlling interest."

Sir Frederick puffed his wrinkled cheeks in and out, he tossed his coat tails up and down nervously, for he saw no daylight in this situation—none. His mind ran over wild ideas of bribing five hundred thousand people to subscribe a pound; he might try and persuade Blackwood to let him float a company on the Stock Exchange—and make a handsome profit on it, too. Really, half a million was a fleabite. And out of gratitude Blackwood might be amenable . . . But no, he knew he wouldn't agree. This terrible rectitude, this tommy-rot about Trusts. . . .

"Off you go, Freddy—find a *plan*!" Sedgwick almost shuddered at that awful word. "What do I pay you for?"

They parted, Pick in low spirits, Sedgwick jocose—but his playfulness didn't go deep. This was a ticklish situation. The time to talk about buying a newspaper was when you'd done it. Bargaining with a couple of searchlights playing on you and a roll o' drums going—no delicacy at all. Of a piece with this craze for open diplomacy, and where was that getting us to? The way he'd taken over the *Silchester Observer* was the way— nobody knew anything about that till midnight on the night— nobody but the two bargainers, himself and the old colonel who sold it. Neat, that was. Concise. Clean as a whistle. Ah well, there it was. He'd always known Blackwood would be a handful— like his uncle. And how much was Blackwood influenced by that bit of past history, he wondered, the remembrance that in the previous generation Sedgwick's father had been a compositor and Blackwood's uncle the famous editor? No telling what snobbery would do. Poked up its head in all sorts of ways and unexpected places. You'd have thought if you were an owner of newspapers, influencing the minds of millions of people, you'd have no more to ask for, no more to rise to, and yet there were all sorts of people with little titles who drew the lines of demarcation. . . . It was funny, it really was. Men he could buy up, condescending to him. Nay. . . . However, he would show them; he would demonstrate. . . .

At this moment Colonel Watson noiselessly opened his door and noiselessly moved over to his desk. "Mr. Fortinbras is on the telephone, sir."

"What did you tell him?" Sedgwick looked glum.

"Said I would inquire if you were in, sir."

"Oh well . . ." He lifted the phone and assumed his cheerful spirits. "Yes, Rupert; good to hear your voice again."

The noise at the other end seemed to suggest that that was as it might be. "Did you buy the *Morning Star*?" A deep chuckle and cough followed that.

"Not yet."

"I read Blackwood's speech to his staff. He's a fighter—I always like a fighter. Tell you what, Sam!"

"Yes?"

"If you can't buy the paper, buy the staff. Remember that poem which goes:

> You cannot hope to bribe or twist,
> Thank God, the British journalist;
> But seeing what the man will do
> Unbribed, there's no occasion to.

Of doubtful veracity, Sam. Buy some of Blackwood's leader-writers, Sam. They'd liven your papers up. Come and lunch with me on Thursday at Carlton House Terrace. I've got an idea for you."

And without further word, without waiting for an answer, Mr. Fortinbras vanished.

Now what was the old chap up to now? wondered Mr. Sedgwick. Some new mine he wanted to explode under the Socialists, no doubt; something to stop their Rake's Progress. By heavens, it was a good job Fortinbras hadn't spent his life in Fleet Street or his pace would have killed the lot of 'em.

In the purlieus of Downing Street and Whitehall certain Right Honourables were assuring one another that, "You see, we were right to set up that Royal Commission on the Press, after all, old man" . . . "Yes, but we didn't want too much to come out of it, did we?" . . . "Well, I wouldn't say that. Anyhow, this fellow Blackwood can be relied on to stir things up" . . . "Who, Blackwood? Oh, that chap! Doesn't sound very friendly to me—

thinks he's got a heaven-sent mission. I'd rather have the Tories any day of the week—less dangerous, anyhow" . . . "Has Sedgwick given his evidence before the Commission yet?" . . . "Don't think so" . . . "Well, he ought to have something coming to him—I suppose he's the chap mixed up in it?" . . . "Oh, I don't know about that—there are half a dozen newspaper chains active" . . . "As many as that? Never realised it. Time we had one of our own, old man" . . . "Aye, that's the answer, lad; what do the Yanks say? 'if you can't beat 'em, jine 'em.' In t' same way, if you can't squash 'em, outdo 'em". . . .

Blackwood's telephone was kept busy too.

Lady Molyneux began: "I didn't much care for that piece you had in the paper today, Mr. Blackwood. . . ."

The Lord Bishop of Greycastle began: "My dear Blackwood, I was delighted to read that speech you made. . . . I shall write you a letter for publication upholding . . ."

The Lord Mayor, Alderman Tom Stevens, began: "That you, Mr. Blackwood? . . . I liked that bit about not thinking t' same as Londoners do. If you'd like a town's meeting to be called, I should be glad to tak' the chair. . . . A bit later, like? I see. . . ."

Mr. William Moffatt, the philanthropist, began: "Good morning, Oliver. So you've turned orator. Always suspected you had it in you. What's the next move? . . . Count on me. . . . Eh? . . . Depends on the percentage you can offer. Most men who have a good deal of money want a lot more than four or five per cent. . . ."

Mrs. Amarilla Arbuthnot, ardent Socialist, began: "Oliver dear! What a lovely candidate you'd make! I shall be coming to see you soon. Keep an eye on the Honours list. . . . Not really, but something in the wind. . . .Yes, a blow between wind and water —I mean laughter and tears. . . ."

Colonel Henry Satterthwaite, shipowner, began: "Mr. Blackwood, 'tisn't often I read anything I agree with in your paper, but that bit about the awkward squad—damn it, you're an honest man. . . ."

Letters arrived in the ensuing days—letters literate, semi-literate and downright crazy, so that Lovelace, who handled most of them, was left wondering how it came about that such a remarkable number of lunatics were still at liberty. He reported to Blackwood that the paper's fight for its soul appeared to be supported by the Transubstantialists, the Holy Rollers, the Plymouth Brethren, the Swedenborgians, the anti-vivisectionists, the British Israelites, the single-taxers, the anarchists, the pacifists, the atheists, the disciples of Henry George, the Malthusians, the bimetallists, the flat earthers, the freethinkers, the vegetarians, the nudists, the sun worshippers, the bird watchers, the Pantheists, the utilitarians, the Zoroastrians, the Christadelphians, and the Peculiar People. "We are obviously," he said, "the bible of everybody who has a bat in the belfry." But both he and Blackwood were touched by the small cheques and postal orders that dribbled in from "Well wishers" and "Faithful readers".

And now there occurred an event which was clearly going to be of importance. In the birthday Honours list Mr. Ernest Jones, Member of Parliament for the Riverside Division of Greycastle was elevated to the peerage—a fact which illuminated Mrs. Arbuthnot's telephone message, and which heralded her visit to Blackwood. She lost no time in coming, for she had important news to give him both as editor and old friend—news that she was the Socialist candidate, and that to her a Press magnate was almost meat and drink. Blackwood said he would be glad to see her; she was eccentric, warmhearted, courageous, illogical and with a sense of humour. He wrote a short leader on the Honours list, drily pointing out that Mr. Ernest Jones had a son who, it must be supposed, would inherit his peerage, that many people in Greycastle had no doubt enjoyed some years ago Mr. Jones's denunciations of the hereditary principle and would be interested to know what had caused him to change his mind; and noting that Mr. Jones's appointment as chairman of a nationalised board commanded five times the salary he had earned hitherto as a trade-union secretary.

Mrs. Arbuthnot called on him the next day.

It may be wrong to say that she cared nothing for her appearance, for she dressed as though she would at any moment go on the music-halls. She wore on this visit to the *Morning Star* a plaid skirt that touched the floor, a black jacket over a red blouse, a rakish green-velvet hat with a curly brown ostrich feather and a green umbrella of enormous bulk befitting Widow Twankey. She greeted Blackwood by raising her umbrella aloft and declaiming: "Behold your champion, Oliver."

He came round his desk to shake hands. "You mean they've adopted you? How did you manage that?"

"Attrition, dear. I've worn them down."

"Did Lord Jones put in a good word for you?"

"His wife Lucy did."

"Lucy, yes. She's the one who wants to abolish first-class on the railways because it's undemocratic. I remember."

"She didn't like your leader, dear."

"Did you?"

"Oh, I didn't much mind. I'm in a grateful mood. I wanted a good plank in my platform and Providence has answered my prayer."

"Oh?"

"You, dear—you and your illustrious paper."

"Which most of your leaders hate."

"*I* don't hate you, dear. On the contrary . . ." She blew him a kiss. "That is a platonic, political kiss."

"The kiss of death, Amarilla." But he smiled.

"I don't believe you, dear. I have often wondered what we should do if we found ourselves suddenly deprived of our respective spouses."

Blackwood said: "I should inquire when the Clipper was leaving for America."

"Lovely! I have always wanted to go to America."

"Amarilla, I should be travelling alone."

She sighed. "I suppose I have never understood you. Long before we did fire-watching together at High Shields I venerated you——"

"*Venerated?* Am I so ancient?"

"You know what I mean—you and your paper have been a lamp unto my feet. Not a very glowing lamp, I agree, but I have always felt I could add an extra spark, and, with that, if you would only join our party——"

"Would you get me made an ornament of the Lords—along with your friend Ernest?"

"I daresay that could be arranged."

"Would you make me the Cabinet's chief adviser on how to

liquidate the Press?" He leaned forward across his desk and was suddenly grave.

Amarilla did not flinch. "You must admit, dear," she said, "that some of them could be liquidated with advantage."

"With advantage to your party?"

"To the cause of truth," said Amarilla. "And the Socialist State."

He sighed. He said: "I always wondered where young Charlotte got her ideas from."

"Charlotte! Has she been on to you?"

"Charlotte said to me that of course the Socialist State could not permit unbridled criticism."

"Good for Charlotte!"

"You see, Amarilla, you are hopeless."

"Not at all, dear. I see things as they are. Most of the Press will stop at nothing."

Blackwood asked drily: "Do you know what your leaders say about the *Morning Star*?"

Amarilla said: "Do you mean in public or in private?" She added: "And, anyway, that's because they take notice of you. They hope you will give them a word of approbation—as you used to. You have grown terribly acidulous, dear. You are like a lover who has grown cold. Our leaders are hurt. Mind you, I don't mean they are like spaniels playing round your knees waiting to be fondled. Those are the Liberals, as Mr. Fortinbras has described them. I do think that is awfully good—the picture of your giving the Liberals first a caress and then a cuff." And Amarilla leaned back and laughed.

Blackwood frowned good humouredly. He said: "Do I gather that in spite of my coolness towards your Party you are going to espouse my cause?"

Amarilla replied: "Anybody who fights the Press magnates is our man."

He said drily: "You mean just as Churchill immediately went to the aid of Stalin against Hitler?"

"Just like that, dear."

"Feeling you may have to fight me in the end when the first tussle is over?"

"I didn't say that, Oliver."

"That is how it will be." His eye had grown fiery. "Neither you nor Sedgwick are really in favour of the individualist.

Sedgwick wants to control enormous groups and fit me into one of them. Your own minds are less clear, but you are restive under criticism, you have a vague feeling that you would like to stifle us as the Tudors and Stuarts did. You think we imperil your State and, being of the breed of religious fanatics, you could gladly send us to the stake to save our souls alive. Like the Spanish Inquisitors your hearts would bleed for us—or shall we say for the first one or two? After that you would doubtless get used to it."

She said: "You are being brutal to me, dear, and I don't like it."

She was suddenly upset, all her gaiety gone.

Blackwood walked round his desk and stood near to her. He said, looking down at her, his face troubled: "I'm sorry, my dear, I don't want to attack you personally, but I'm serious about this. It's just possible we may be moving into a period when the old fights of Wilkes, Tom Paine, Milton and the rest will have to be fought again. Suppose your party was in power for the next twenty years? What would the Ernie Joneses and their friends be doing with all the power and privileges and money at their disposal? Would they look kindly on flying wasps like me? Already there are town councils that are virtually all Labour— and one or two have withdrawn advertisements from newspapers that dare to be critical. He put a hand on her shoulder. "So you see, Amarilla, why I view your championship with less joy than— for your sake—I should like to."

Amarilla took a disreputable lace handkerchief and wiped a corner of her eye. She said: "You may be a very lonely man, dear, in the new world."

He said: "I know."

"Shot at from both sides."

"Yes, of course."

"Much better to be in one camp, dear, than a foot in each."

"Better?"

"More comfortable."

"For the body—or the soul?"

"Hemlock is not a nice drink, Oliver."

"Don't glorify me, Amarilla."

She said in a low voice: "I do, I do—in the secret watches of the night."

He turned away, deeply stirred, and simultaneously a sudden spasm of pain in his loins shook him. He went and sat down at his desk again, resting his forehead on his hand. When he looked up she had lit a cigarette and was smoking.

She said, in her accustomed voice: "It will make it a lively election, Oliver."

"Yes, I suppose it will."

"You and I will be found speaking on the same platform."

"In that case, I may have to contradict what you say." He smiled.

She said: "The reporters will enjoy that. We shall make one another famous."

"As long as it is famous," he said.

She rose. "Give my love to Hannah," she said.

"Thank you, Amarilla. And my regards to Walter. How is he?"

She said: "I hardly see him. This nuclear fission. I think the Government have given him a problem to solve. His professorship is almost in abeyance."

Blackwood said: "I wonder how they keep sane—working in isolation—and knowing they are playing with the structure of the universe."

Amarilla stood very still and quiet. "Are there planes of sanity —as there are of thought? I think so. I fancy I move from one to another. Good night, Oliver. Thank you for giving me so much time."

"Good night, Amarilla. I hope you bring it off."

With a touch of her old gaiety she said: "*You* will get me in, dear. I shall shine in Westminster, like—like a morning star."

He smiled. "I used to watch them going out like candles at dawn when the night had been—— Oh well!"

She asked: "What were you going to say, dear?"

But he didn't answer. He looked at her quizzically, sadly, thinking she had never found anybody who matched her, who banished her loneliness. But then, did any of us?

Amarilla stayed for a second, waiting for him to speak, and when she saw he would not she went swiftly. Blackwood walked back to his desk, the cast of thought falling over his face. The night's work—the balm. Well, then . . .

CHAPTER XXXI

ALTHOUGH THE CRANKS and busybodies of Britain took an interest in the future of the *Morning Star*, and various editors on both sides of the Atlantic sent Blackwood private notes wishing him success and expressing admiration of the paper; and although some of Greycastle's leading citizens offered to come on to a public platform in support of the campaign, the sums forthcoming in the early days were small.

"They're better at lifting their voices up than getting their hands down," said Lovelace.

"It always takes the English a long time to move," said Blackwood.

"It takes dynamite to open safes," said Lovelace.

"I suppose," said Blackwood, "I ought to go to the bank for the money."

"That's what banks are for," said Lovelace; "and if you want a million or two you may get it. It's fellows like me wanting a fiver whom the commissionaires throw outside."

So Blackwood called on Peter Stead, the biggest local man in the Lancastria Bank, which did the *Morning Star's* business. He was a large and very genial man who conveyed the impression that money and business were a byproduct of life—that life was golf and yachting and wives and families. His enormous desk held two photographs of his wife and children, and two vases of flowers. The first thing he did was to make an appointment to play Blackwood golf the following Saturday afternoon and to discuss Bob's flying career and that of his son who was at Dartmouth naval college. On the subject of finance he was extremely genial but noncommittal. Of course, £500,000 was not an excessively large sum—but, on the other hand, the dividends paid had always been conservative—very conservative one might say, and on the new capital could hardly in the nature of things be larger in the future —indeed, they might well be much smaller. Investors were usually more influenced by earning power than anything else—earning power was the thing that interested *them*. He appeared to indicate that this might be very remiss of them, but there it was. Of course,

223

he said, you had to remember that some of the more prosperous papers in the provinces paid a dividend of twenty per cent—which was—er—rather more than that of the *Morning Star*—but they were usually Conservative in their politics. Investors looking for a property would more naturally turn to a Conservative paper of that sort, if they could get into it—which they usually couldn't. Family concerns, as a rule. Of course, there was the question of local feeling, local patriotism and all that. In the past, it would have been easier, no doubt—taxes today had a crippling effect, dried up the springs of philanthropy, but all the same he would not put it outside possibility—for instance, his family had taken the *Morning Star* for several generations, and he'd no doubt they would go on taking it. In one sense the paper was impregnable—in one sense. He thought the best thing he could do was to consult head office in Burnham, and no doubt they would sound their own financial house in London—no doubt that was what they would do. As to whether he was hopeful of the outcome, he found it very hard to say, really hard to say. Meanwhile, if Blackwood cared to make a direct approach to one or two Greycastle people who were not entirely short of this world's goods, well and good; could do no harm. Blackwood said he had thought of going to London to explore the situation there. Did Stead think that advisable? Stead said nothing could be better, nothing; excellent idea. For all his amiability Blackwood formed the opinion that Stead would be delighted to be rid of the responsibility. And he determined to go ahead with his plan of writing to those men who were cordial towards the paper and who had money—men such as Wilberforce the flour miller, McGrew the timber merchant, Hesketh the shipowner, and a dozen more he could think of. At Lovelace's suggestion they had had printed on first-class paper several hundred copies of Blackwood's speech to the staff; a copy of this could go with the letters. In this private letter Blackwood said it would be a strength to the paper and a pleasure to him personally if money to enable the *Morning Star* to remain independent in policy and control came from Greycastle men and women; it would be proof to the whole country that this idea of cities having their own journal closely identified with the town could be fulfilled.

Meanwhile Frank Knowles and certain other members of the *Morning Star's* staff were by no means idle. They turned over in their minds and conversations how to raise money. They thought raising money an easy affair—until they tried it.

As Forsyth said: "Look at the fellas who're rolling in it; you wouldn't send them round the corner to report a fire."

"Making money is like growing giant cucumbers," said Knowles; "either you can do it or you can't. My grandfather, now—whatever he touched turned to money."

"What happened to it, Frank?"

"Evaporated," said Frank. "My father could evaporate owt— he'd do the disappearing trick a treat with any sum from half a dollar to five hundred quid."

However, Mr. Knowles sounded various local trade-union leaders. The unions must have brass to invest, said Frank, and the *Star* as a Trust would be safe as the Bank of England. Besides, the *Star* always gave 'em a square deal—whereas Sedgwick's papers— well, they all knew what slant *they* had.

"And what response did you get, Frank?" inquired de Ferrers. (They were assembled in the reporters' room at the time.)

"A couple of 'em said they'd raise the subject at the executive."

"Why don't you try and raise the money at the T.U.C.?" inquired Prince innocently. "The Labour movement needs its *Times*."

"All right, all right," said Knowles. "That's enough o' that, lad. Here—how did you get on with the pools? Did you see that bosom pal o' yours?"

"Yes."

"Well, what did he say?"

"He was what you'd call *discreet*."

"Oh, he was, was he?"

"But he said he didn't think his boss was very sold on our articles hinting that all those girls they've got would be a sight better occupied in cotton mills."

"Well, you'd better go to the fountain head, Clifton lad. And listen, chaps"—he waved his pipe stem at the lot of them—"you all know about these northern industrialists and bicycle makers and woollen manufacturers who act as backers for mid-European film producers who can lose millions easier than you and me can lose our way in a fog. Well, who are these backers? Hunt 'em down. We're sleuths, aren't we? The paper is a good risk; we're a copper-bottom enterprise compared with films and West End productions. Who's the modern Jimmy White? Who's signing cheques today with gold fountain-pens studded wi' diamonds? Who's the new Young Man in a Hurry? Who got rich in the war catching that bloody-awful fish, and making jam and battledress and inventing bridges and Fidos and Mulberry harbours and whatnot? Don't say nobody got rich—I don't damn-well believe it. Ferret 'em out. Tell 'em they'll get knighthoods for being public spirited if they put their brass into this show."

"The trouble is we don't talk broken English, Frank. If we did, we could raise the Mint."

"I know all about that. All t' same—and you, Brenda love, when are you seeing old Satterthwaite—that boy friend o'yours? He spends half his time ringing you up—surely you can work the oracle there, love?"

"It's all right, Frank—I've got it all laid on."

Prince said, *sotto voce*: "You'd better have it buttoned up, too, dear."

They certainly had interesting moments while trying to raise money. Mr. Redvers Mornington, the brewer, for example, told de Ferrers he would be prepared to invest £10,000 if the paper would cease taking any notice of teetotal cranks and would support Tory candidates on the city council—a request which was a sufficiently good insurance against parting with a brass farthing. Then there was Mr. Fred Cheshire's hour in the company of Mrs. Angela Richardson. Mrs. Richardson was the widow of a cotton broker of immense wealth. She had spent £15,000 on her husband's marble tomb in the cemetery which was capped by flying golden angels and was better known and more looked at by the populace than any Old Master in the Hesketh Art Gallery. Mr. Cheshire found himself invited to go down on his knees in her drawing-room along with Mrs. Richardson to pray for the souls of Mr. Blackwood, whom she said she revered, and Lord Sedgwick, who was, she said, in danger of everlasting fire. And Mr. Cheshire had to do it, too. But she went no further on the subject of finance than saying she would consult the Lord as to what was the right thing to do.

But all those experiences paled into insignificance (in Brenda Smith's own words) alongside what befell her when she visited Colonel Henry Satterthwaite.

Colonel Henry Satterthwaite, J.P., was the man Knowles had referred to as Brenda's millionaire shipowner. She had once interviewed him on the shipping situation and from time to time since then he had rung her up to talk at length—notably about the decline, as he thought, of the merchant marine and ruination of seamen arising from their being given a cabin each and each man sporting his own electric razor. The colonel had read of this happening on a certain Dominion's line and he appeared to think it was widespread. He was very dogmatic that it would never happen on Satterthwaite ships. He had not himself ever served at sea. Nobody in his family had done so since the time of his ancestor Captain Fortunatus Satterthwaite, one of the old slavers. They had, however, owned fleets of ships and made a fortune from them, and those ships in two world wars had been one of Britain's standbys. He was as proud of their exploits against submarines, enemy raiders and Focke Wulf aircraft as if he had commanded all the ships himself. In fact, he often spoke as if he had. He was certainly prouder of his ships than his captains were of him. They swore about him, said the ships were ill-found and that you were doing well if you got eight knots out of some of the tramps. They said they wouldn't carry him as ballast, and that if they knew as little of sin as he knew of ships they would undoubtedly go straight to heaven. Nevertheless, they admitted he was a character. Partly, they admitted it, because of his garb. He frequently wore a red waistcoat, a stiff white cravat set off with a gold and diamond tie-pin, tight trousers and a check coat. His bowler hat was narrow with a curly brim. His moustaches were dyed yellow. Partly, they admitted it, because of the stories told of his private life, his women, his parsimony. He had shrunk now to the dimensions of a jockey —possibly an outsize jockey—and he was excessively light on his feet, so that he appeared to dance as he walked. His age? Nobody really knew—he kept it out of *Who's Who*—but it was thought he must now be over eighty.

Brenda dressed herself for the visit with great care. She had been to London for the royal garden party a month or two earlier and she wore the same dress today—a flowered dress, a wide black hat and a tight, black-satin jacket. She looked no more than twenty-one. It was worth getting yourself up to kill—and even running a risk or two, when the stake was large. The colonel had asked her for late tea or drinks and she arrived about five o'clock.

He received her in the shaded drawing-room—for it had been a brilliantly sunny day. His garb astonished her. He was wearing jodhpurs, white silk stockings and black dancing pumps, a white shirt and cravat and over it a yellow-silk dressing-gown. His cheeks were touched lightly with rouge and the small tuft of hair on the top of his head—astonishingly like that of a baby—had been curled and was dyed yellow like his moustache. His eyes were still faintly blue.

He took her hand and kissed it and she received, as he bent forward, an extraordinarily powerful whiff of eau de Cologne.

"How are you, my dear?" He took her hand again and held it.

It was, she thought, like placing your hand in dry leaves. He clapped his hands for tea, and when tea came he produced a decanter of whisky and suggested they should take a teaspoonful in their cups.

"Tea," he said briefly, "it is not what it was. The town's new water is to blame. As my mother used to say—it is poor stuff having neither taste nor smell." He indulged in a dry cackle that shook his teeth. He again inquired how she was, and she now took this opportunity of telling him that she and all her colleagues and their paper too were in imminent danger unless some patron of noble instincts and generous heart came to their rescue.

"Ah!" he said, "I saw a bit in the paper."

"Did it make you feel you must do something?"

"Oh no. No. I have never been moved by charitable instincts. My most powerful instincts are acquisitive. Otherwise I should not be a rich man. What I have never understood is that a man should spend most of his life growing rich, and then suddenly have a desire to part with his money. It shows instability. My wealth gives me an immense amount of pleasure and I have no evidence that anybody else would get half as much pleasure out of it. That being so, it would be wrong of me to part with it. Don't you think so?"

Brenda was a little taken aback, and she hardly knew if he were sincere or just stimulated by her company and the whisky. She tried again. She said she wished to say it with the greatest delicacy but even the finest things came to an end and would it not be a satisfaction to him before that happened to ensure that his wealth achieved great good?

"I gather," said the colonel, "that you are referring to my demise, which some appear to imagine is more imminent than I myself am inclined to think. Perhaps, however, that is because they are less well disposed to me than I am. No, no, the fact is I shall live a long time yet. I was out riding this morning and now I am quite ready to dance. Would that please you? It would afford me immense delight, I assure you. Excuse me a moment."

He vanished behind a green and gold curtain on the right and in a moment or two a Strauss waltz, which Brenda thought exquisitely modulated, filled the room. A moment or two later the colonel returned wearing delicate riding boots and spurs, which jingled as he walked. He bowed to her and she found herself rising and being taken into the dance. He danced, she had to admit, with remarkable skill, to and fro, swaying and swinging, taking her hither and thither, as lissom and firmly persuasive as a young man. The strange thing was that he found occasion now and then to stamp his feet and make his spurs jingle more loudly, and when that happened a small tremor of ecstasy ran through him and he grinned in a rather frightening way. The waltz died away and he bowed her into a Regency chair of black and gold and he himself took another.

He said: "Every year an added triumph—every dance a jewel in my crown. Will you take a little hock?" He clapped his hands once more and the butler appeared carrying the hock, iced, and they drank slowly and with careful deliberation.

Brenda did not regard herself as vanquished in the matter of the *Morning Star's* future and she now asked whether he did not think it would be unfortunate, indeed a public loss, were the paper to change hands and lose its character.

The colonel replied: "I am an old man, but one thing that is excessively clear to me is that the world is always a millionth part different in the evening from what it was in the morning. To-morrow you and I, my dear, will not be as we are today. Our minds will have slipped onwards towards a new outlook and our bodies will be imperceptibly older and wiser. Change is all around us—and why should the *Morning Star* escape? Everything is fleeting. Empires rise and fall—the deserts are strewn with the ruins of past civilisations. The Chinese have seen us of the West rise like a flower—yet the design on the button of the mandarin's coat is the same as it was when the British were painting themselves with woad. All this being indubitably so, I, who remember your more or less distinguished journal when it was the slave of the old-fashioned Liberals of the Manchester School, men who swore by Free Trade and thought, quite rightly, that the foundation of our fortunes was to buy in the cheapest market, carry the world's goods in our ships, and teach our lower orders to stand at their machines toiling like slaves from six in the morning till five-thirty in the evening—I who remember this cannot, even to please you, my dear young lady, feel any undue elation when I read your paper's encouragement to the workers to feel they are as good as I am. Because they are not. No—if for no more reason —although there are plenty—than that there are illimitable thousands of them, and there's only one of me. I am unique—and this unique person is enchanted to salute you—for you, too, are unique." The colonel rose swiftly, crossed to her chair, raised her hand to his lips, and kissed it. Then, to her momentary horror, he playfully bit the back of her hand. He resumed his seat, crossed his legs and filled up his glass. He now added: "So if the *Morning Star* is eclipsed, it will not be the end of the world."

Although it would be an exaggeration to say she was not in the least rattled or nonplussed, she was not as yet defeated. She put it to him that as one of the leading citizens of Greycastle he went to and fro in the world supported by his city and by the things his city was famous for—its ships, its vast trade—and its famous newspaper, which was quoted almost as readily in New York as in London. Without this newspaper, one of the pillars that supported him and his ego would be removed, he would totter a little, he would be a citizen of a meaner city, he would not be the man he was hitherto. Everything had its price, and therefore——

"I know," he said. "I know. We are accustomed to labour in ignorance of self-evident facts." And then to her astonishment he went on: "Take incest. Now most people think incest is a terrible thing and the Greeks wrote tragedies about it. But the fact is, my dear, and I ask you to ponder upon it, that if the stock is pure enough, incest—the incest of a son with his mother, improves it. The finest racehorse I ever owned was bred on incest. So were my dogs which won prizes everywhere. So, too, were the Pharaohs of Egypt. So is a race of Filipinos who are a head taller than anybody else in their vicinity. But if the stock is not pure, not fine enough, then incest emphasises the blemishes and the weaknesses. Now," he said, "this is all very important, but I never read a word about it in the *Morning Star*. The incestuousness that is no doubt prevalent in Greycastle may be on quite the wrong lines. Let me give you some more hock."

Brenda suffered her glass to be filled up and she drank almost greedily. She was feeling a little out of her depth. Was his mind seriously unhinged? Perhaps it was. But she made an effort. She said, after conceding that she was not very strong on figures and that she was not sure how many thousands of pounds would be a fitting contribution for so eminent a citizen to make, that if he did so make it, he could doubtless bring his influence to bear in getting incest brought under public scrutiny. On the other hand, of course, when he found himself in partial ownership of a family newsaper, he would have to ask himself——

"Ah!" he exclaimed, "this family newspaper indeed! Which buries so deep the topics of importance! Let us consider its work and what it omits. Why, I should like to know, did we lose India? We lost it because Englishmen began to take their wives to India, instead of procuring wives or mistresses from the Indians themselves and producing fine stock, as the old Mutiny leaders did. The *Morning Star*, or its forerunner, poured cold water—this being its favourite tipple—on the practice of marrying the natives and besought our erstwhile East India officials to take their spouses with them, so that India and elsewhere became over-run by English ladies who had the figures of five-barred gates or bags of flour, as the case may be, and the tongues of vipers. Moreover, these virtuous women, whose creed was that God loved all equally, and notwithstanding that they themselves had often been born in narrow streets or impoverished vicarages, now gave themselves the airs of princesses and looked down their Roman or knobbly noses at Indian ladies whose ancestors were noble when they themselves were eating the bark of oak trees. But none of this ever appears in the *Morning Star*."

Brenda said that might well be so, and yet she was sure that his views, were he one of the pillars on which the newspaper rested . . . would receive every attention. . . .

During her brief dissertation the colonel had not been idle. He had gone behind the green and gold screen and had carried into the room a dressmaker's box embossed with the name of

Montmorency, Paris, and had taken from it an exquisite gown of pure white silk with a high Empire corsage.

"I should like," he said, "to treasure a memory of your coming to see me. Would you delight me by putting it on?"— kneeling before her and holding the gown outstretched on his arms.

Brenda, thinking to herself in for a penny in for a pound, and with the reporter's powerful curiosity at work, at first demurred and then consented, although not entirely without misgiving. She retired behind the screen to change one dress for the other, finding there a small Sheraton table and chair with mirror and brushes. In next to no time she was ready. In those few moments a new piece of music, which she judged to be Chinese or Indian had begun softly to penetrate the room, and when she emerged the colonel was standing, still as a statue, with—of all things—a white dove in his hands. But it was his face which startled her more; it wore a grin that she could only think to herself was unearthly, a hideous smile, the light in the eyes that of a man looking at something far distant. With this look on his face, he slowly approached her, treading with infinitesimal steps and with an extraordinary lightness. He did not speak or make any sound—merely advanced upon her caressing the dove. She stood, herself motionless, spellbound, wondering what in heaven's name was about to happen, her impulse to run, or cry out, battling with her desire to remain and watch. He had now reached her and stood before her. With a sudden movement of his left arm he held the dove above her head and then, to her mixed incredulity, horror and dismay, he drew from his coat a small and slender stiletto and having poised it aloft for an instant, as she uttered a little scream, he pierced the dove's breast with the blade. Brenda shut her eyes and bent her head, and hardly had she done so than she felt a drop of warm blood fall on her neck and, opening her eyes, saw vivid splashes of blood on her dress. An exultant cry had broken from him and he was now pirouetting round the room, the bird thrown aside but the stiletto in his hand held high above his head. In a few moments he sat down, panting, looking extremely old, and murmuring: "Thank you a thousand times, thank you." Brenda had sunk down on to the couch, shaken and in tears; and she was still shaken when she left the house.

Colonel Satterthwaite, spent by his emotion, had retired out of sight, so that the hurried changing of her dress and her precipitate departure took place without hindrance or further incident. As she walked down the drive in the evening light, she might have imagined, but for the trembling in her limbs, that nothing whatever had occurred. As she said to Prince later over a double whisky, a fitting end would have been to find a fat cheque in her reticule, but in fact she didn't return with a sou.

CHAPTER XXXII

ALTHOUGH NOBODY ELSE equalled Brenda Smith's spectacular way of drawing a blank, nobody else, either, discovered anybody anxious to endow the paper with £500,000, or even to invest a quarter of that sum. Lovelace in his secret heart—and most of the reporters too—was convinced that they might have got on better had they asked for a million. A nation that had a budget of thousands of millions per annum, whose troops in Germany had diddled the British taxpayers out of fifty-odd millions in currency and black marketing, without apparently anybody turning a hair or getting sacked over it, couldn't be expected to grow excited over half a million. A film magnate could lose that much before he'd had his breakfast, said Lovelace. The Great British Public would expect the sum to be invested by some fellow who owned a dog track, or had won the Irish Sweep. Why, a couple of dirty old steam trawlers fishing from Fleetwood cost more than that! "Five hundred thousand," said Lovelace, "is neither here nor there——" Adding sardonically, "It certainly isn't here."

It was in these circumstances that Blackwood decided to make a journey to London and test financial opinion in the City; and he took Lovelace with him. They went by train.

"We go forth," said Lovelace, "like Don Quixote and Sancho Panza."

Both were enjoying a sense of being off the leash—Lovelace especially. He had several books to read—a novel by R. C.

Hutchinson and a piece of autobiography by O'Casey; he had his notebook in which he hoped to make jottings for his own novel (but over the doing of which he knew he might fall asleep— but what of that? Did not Cervantes say sleep covered you all over like a cloak, meat for the hungry and drink for the thirsty?) and he would enjoy looking out of the window. He had never got over being a boy in that, or in listening to the train's song—what someone called piddly dee, piddly dar, piddly dum. Above all, he had Blackwood with him. This was like old days. They had been having great talks lately—the jeopardy in which the paper stood had let loose a lot of conversation; it had also tightened various bonds—even the reporters and sub-editors had slackened their internecine warfare. You could almost thank God for Sedgwick, thought Lovelace—he had quickened the office, and, anyhow, he was as God made him, though doubtless a great deal worse.

Blackwood interrupted his thoughts: "You're like an old dog turning round six times before it lies down," he said. "What's the matter with you?"

Lovelace grinned. "I know," he said, "I know—I am doing what I please and therefore I have my will, and having my will I am content, and being content there is nothing more to be desired, and when there is nothing further to be desired there is an end on't. How soon will you be ready for a snifter?"

"Is that the mood you are in?"

"Whenever a war begins," said Lovelace, "one is justified in being a little tight—and nobody can say we are not at war—a war against the barons of Threadneedle Street and Lombard Street— or think you, master, they will have faces like a benediction?"

"I do not care, Richard, what their faces are like, if they take the padlocks off their safes. Happily you are as thin as a D.P., and they may take pity on us."

Blackwood settled down to his papers and his thoughts, while Lovelace went off to see how soon drinks would be available. Blackwood reflected that if good wishes had been diamonds, no journey to the City of London would have been necessary. The Lord Mayor, for example, had called a town's meeting at which the bishop, Dr. Brodrick, Professor John Clayton, the vice-chancellor of the university, Sir William Prentice, chairman of the repertory theatre, Mr. William Moffatt and all three political candidates

234

at the by-election had spoken—Mrs. Arbuthnot, Major Gore-Fleming, the Tory, and Mr. Llewellyn Morgan, the Liberal. The degree of unity had been astonishing. Speaker had vied with speaker in pronouncing the *Morning Star* one of the nation's best newspapers and in implying that they revered it almost as much as the Throne. Without freedom of the Press our democracy would be a vain thing—they had all been agreed on that although none of them inquired very closely into what the existing freedom amounted to. The Lord Mayor, Alderman Tom Stevens, had said he was sure every citizen would agree with him that the *Morning Star* should continue to be one of their guiding stars untrammelled by outside control. The darker the hour the more brightly it shone, etc. The Lord Bishop said that in these tempestuous days the searchlight of truth needed to play and the cold light of reason to be brought to bear, and of no newspaper could it more justly be said than, etc. Mr. Moffatt said he trembled to think what would befall if the time should ever come when it should happen that no *Morning Star*, etc. Sir William Prentice said that in artistic circles the paper was read with immense respect and, when artists knew their work wasn't up to scratch, with immense foreboding. Mr. Llewellyn Morgan said that whenever he wished to be reinforced in the great Liberal faith, all he had to do was to open the pages of this magnificent journal, than which, etc. Mrs. Arbuthnot, not to be outdone, said she had been taught to read at her mother's knee by spelling out the short leaders, and never a day had passed since, etc. Major Gore-Fleming, who was paying his first visit to the city and felt a trifle out in the cold in all this, said he had first heard of the paper from his batman in the jungles of Burma and he made a vow then and there to get hold of it. Imagine his pleasure therefore, etc. All three extolled its fairness in reporting them. Only Mrs. Arbuthnot had let herself go on the wickedness of Press magnates whom she likened to boa constrictors seeking whom they might devour. Blackwood had spoken last and briefly, thanking them for what had been said about the *Morning Star*, assuring those who found its artistic criticisms severe that even more biting remarks were often cut out, and saying that in his view independence of thought and writing was the lifeblood of the paper, and that without it it would—to all intents and purposes—die. He had been a little embarrassed, he said, by finding that his opinions in the paper appeared to be in line with those of all the three political candidates; but he would promise them to write something that very night they didn't *all* agree with, if, in fact, any of them agreed with it. However, when people told him he made their blood boil he always reminded them the fuel cost was almost negligible—two pence a day. And he was glad to inform them that that particular fuel supply could be ensured for all time at a very modest figure, for less than the price of one electricity generating station. After that, a resolution had been passed—it was a crowded meeting of a thousand people in the Thurlow Hall—pledging themselves to preserve the freedom and independence of the Press and in particular of the *Morning Star*.

But of offers of money, none that were spectacular were forthcoming as yet. Mr. George Wavertree, the business manager, had said a few days later that they didn't total a hundred thousand. George was not the best business manager in the world —indeed, Lovelace always declared that in many respects he must be quite the worst, judged on his propensity for discovering bargains in equipment only when somebody else had already obtained them—but at all events he could add up. George said the trouble was this small capital they'd had, this small dividend they'd paid, and this small circulation they possessed. It was really a family paper read by a coterie, said George, and if you doubled its capital overnight on the same buildings, machinery, paper and goodwill it was—well, it was asking them to have a lot of faith and idealism—and Greycastle folk weren't too good at mixing money and idealism. Mr. Wavertree had grown up with the paper and he was, if truth be told, a little sick of high falutin' integrity and running a family bible. He wouldn't at all have minded being given a few of the Sedgwick millions to play with, and he couldn't for the life of him see what was wrong with joining a firm that didn't always have to be minding its sixpences and shopping in the tuppenny ha'penny bazaars, so to speak. These were the days of mass production, groups, cartels, combines and whatnot—how could you stand up against 'em, he wanted to know? Why, the *Morning Star* didn't even have an evening paper to lean on!

This was the gist of what Mr. Wavertree had had to say to Blackwood, and it was not markedly different from what Willie

Travis, the advertisement manager, and Egbert Thompson, who looked after circulation, had said. Egbert was the most cheerful of the three, for Egbert could report a rising demand for the paper. He could draw you various small chimneys whose heights indicated what the paper's sale had been and what it was now. And it was encouraging—no doubt about that. The paper's policy and its bite were in tune with those folk who had wished the Socialist Government well—many of them had voted for it—but who were suffering some disillusionment. Unhappily, from the advertisers' point of view, these readers were not of high value, for they had precious little money—their standard of living had fallen considerably; their salaries had not risen but everything they bought had risen perceptibly. They were being gently but firmly ground down. All the same, the important thing, said Egbert, was that the paper was being read further and further afield. If only they had the resources they might become a national paper not only in political estimation but in a real sense. . . .

All this Blackwood reflected upon as he sat in his corner journeying to London. This was the irony of it—success greater than they had known was within their grasp if only they could raise the money. With increased capital they could carry out a vast advertising campaign, take the paper far and wide, install new machinery and——But could they, in fact? Could they? No, no; for, of course, the money would go to Lady Molyneux —every penny unless they were lucky—all they would have would be their existing resources in plant and equipment—and an inflated capital value placed on it. It would be akin to selling a Lancashire cotton mill at several times its value—as happened in the notorious boom which helped to bring about, or, anyhow, emphasise and make worse, the evils of the ensuing slump. Was Sedgwick right, then? Was he, Blackwood, venturing into an unknown and uncharted jungle? Was this an impasse—no way out? It was hard to see any daylight—unless it proved possible to raise not £500,000 but £750,000 and with the spare £250,000 improve the paper and give it an enormously greater sale and influence.

At this moment Lovelace appeared in the doorway with two large dry Martinis. "I've counted twenty copies of the paper being read between here and the buffet car," he said.

"I, too," said Blackwood, "have been seeing visions. I've worked out that if we raise 50 per cent more than the purchase price our troubles will be over."

"That," said Lovelace, "will present no problem. I shall let it be known I am writing for us a new serial. The rest will be easy. Master, your health!"

Two or three days later Lovelace amused himself by scribbling the following note:

"They went up and down Lombard Street and Threadneedle Street, sometimes accompanied by the city editor, Mr. Gustav McNaughton, and sometimes not. They explained, and expounded. They were lunched, they were dined, they were treated to expositions of where money came from and where it went to—but they were promised little. They went down into the City and they returned west again.

"They met financiers who said the *Morning Star* was their sustenance, the journal they read when they rose up in the morning and their favourite reading ere they dropped off to sleep. They met financiers who made it clear they had never heard of the *Morning Star*, had no overpowering desire to hear of it, and would not know what it meant if they did hear of it. They went down into the City and they returned west again.

"They talked to company promoters, half-commission men, editors of financial newspapers, members of Lloyds, members of the Stock Exchange, men who said money was plentiful, men who said money had seldom been so tight. They had sessions long or short with Scots from the Lowlands, Greeks from Athens, Jews from Beaconsfield, Englishmen from Haywards Heath, gentlemen who spoke in the terms of cricket, and gentlemen who spoke in the language of Wall Street. And they went down into the City and returned west again.

"They were received as guests and strangers in a strange land, handled tenderly, solicitously, while the simple facts of arithmetic such as two and two making four were written down for them on paper. They were also received as a pair of tough four-flushers who might at any moment sell a fleet of tankers to a country which had no possible outlet to the sea, or as men peddling shares in sheep farms at the South Pole. And they went down into the City and returned west again."

Lovelace tore the page out and passed it across to Blackwood. They had been to the second house at the Palladium and were now enjoying a final whisky and soda in their private sitting-room at the Suffolk Hotel, off the Strand.

"You are enjoying some literary licence, eh, Richard?" Blackwood smiled.

"Not much licence, master. Remember the Welshman in Throgmorton Lane? 'My principals are fery exacting men— it iss a matter of regret to me put they would not look with approbation on a yield of less than 10 per cent if any risk iss involved' And do you remember the three heavyweights of Finsbury Circus, whose guttural language we never deciphered? And tell me, Oliver, why is it that the City of London is now inhabited by bankers and brokers and financiers who are all farmers and who prefer to talk to us about their Jersey cattle and Welsh sheep and black pigs? And what was that we learned about the strange mortality that occurs among the animals whenever visitors are arriving or Christmas is coming? And about the way you can lose on your farm the profits you make in the city and thus you avoid some of your income taxes and yet have most excellent food. Is it that we don't know how to live in Greycastle?"

Blackwood said: "I know, Richard. By all means delve into this new farming racket—it will make a good article. But what's impressed me, too, is how many friends we've got—that old-fashioned financial house—Beauchamps—they were ready to stretch several points in helping us; and that youngish donnish fellow who's one of the directors of the Bank of England couldn't have been more sincere in trying to help."

"But, master, are we going to get the wherewithal?"

"God knows, Richard. But all is not yet lost—we have friends."

"It is time they girded on their armour. But let us have one more for the road and go out to see who is occupying that Embankment bench I see myself destined for when milord Sedgwick marches in and we march out."

Lovelace was enjoying himself. So, after a fashion, was Blackwood though he was in no doubt about the gravity of the outlook. Still, this watching the paper from a distance, this listening to the turmoil of Fleet Street, this tasting of new character and outlook in the City, this lightness of heart they were outwardly achieving despite the seriousness of their errand—pleasant enough

—and the peril in which the paper stood, gave an edge to every-thing. As Lovelace kept on saying, they were fighting their little war. They had run up against the name of Sedgwick and Pick several times— "We had a visit the other day from Sir Frederick Pick," men would say; or "Sedgwick is in the market for the paper, isn't he? Very shrewd fellow is Mr. Sedgwick"; and Blackwood was left wondering what strings the pair had pulled. Some of these very financiers they were talking with must have done well in their time out of Sedgwick's flotations—they would hardly wish to quarrel with him. Sedgwick's London evening paper had written a paragraph in its diary saying that the dis-tinguished editor Oliver Blackwood was to be seen in the City con-sulting various financial houses. Was he merely after finance for the *Morning Star* or was he intending to start an entirely new London paper? Mr. Blackwood was a man of strong will and original ideas, the paragraph went on, but he would doubtless find that the City of London was a hard nut to crack, especially by some-body so critical of the Tory Party, etc. etc. Yes, yes, so critical of the Tory Party. Several times the bland question had been put: "And what are the politics of your paper, Mr. Blackwood—not that that would affect our judgment, of course—we are not politicians here—but we wondered . . ." Sir Frederick Pick had done his work well, no doubt. This lonely furrow Blackwood ploughed—this middle of the road—no escaping the reminders, even if you wished to escape them. But did he?

The telephone rang. Lovelace answered it. "Yes, Fraser."

Ah, the London office, thought Blackwood

Lovelace was saying: "From the Prime Minister? Very well. On its way round? Good. Yes, I'll tell him. Good night, Fraser." He put down the receiver. "It's a letter from the Prime Minister's office, Oliver. Seems they rang up from Number ten to make sure you would get it tonight. Do you want to see the P.M., Oliver?"

"Not particularly. Always valuable, of course. I've no idea what it is—some months since I saw him."

The letter, when it came, was brief: "My dear Blackwood" (this written in the Premier's thin and irregular hand), "I know the notice is very short—but if you're free for breakfast would you come at 8.45 tomorrow, Thursday? One or two things I'd like to discuss. Sincerely yours, Cyril W. Wimpole."

CHAPTER XXXIII

IT WAS 8.30 A.M. and the sky pale blue when Blackwood drove down Whitehall to see the Prime Minister. Pigeons were fluttering in the light wind, a solitary aircraft, burnished silver, was in the high heavens, the morning as fresh as a young maiden. Crisis was abroad: Mr. Wimpole had recently said that only the nation's inherited skill and the labour of their hands stood between them and starvation. Mr. Fortinbras, for his part, had just prophesied poverty, hunger and disaster if the country stuck to Labour. Miners were being asked to work an extra half-hour a day, a fair number of timorous and poor-spirited folk were selling out Government stocks, and half a million people were anxious to emigrate to the Dominions. And yet, and yet . . . it was impossible for Blackwood not to enjoy the morning. He was in good spirits at the prospect of crossing swords again with the Prime Minister—light fencing swords they usually were, for both men held the other in good esteem—but all the same . . . He wondered if Mr. Wimpole would refer to the paper's comment on the Honours list—that it was hard to see what argument could be advanced for handing down, father to son, a peerage bestowed on a party hack, when the Victoria Cross and the Order of Merit were not so handed down. Wimpole would probably want to know what he thought of the coal situation—would the colliers deliver the goods? How would the industrial north take the cuts in petrol and films? He supposed Wimpole regarded him as a fragment of mass observation. Well, it was fair exchange—he always reckoned to leave Number ten possessed of a few pieces of knowledge that were highly confidential.

The Prime Minister wore an air of having been up a long time —remarkably suave and unruffled. Taller than Blackwood, pale and long of face, he had a clerical look—a kind of layman bishop, at first glance forbiddingly grave, but there was a sly humour there and, Blackwood felt, immense reserves of staying power. He was genuinely pleased to see his guest. Nobody joined them in this room at the top of the house with its dark-red carpet, its panelled walls of light olive-green.

They sat at a round dark mahogany table, Blackwood facing the fireplace and able to catch a glimpse through the windows in the east wall of the chimneys of the old Treasury building.

"I wanted," said Mr. Wimpole, after polite exchanges on health, weather and the morning's news, and when the bacon and kidneys were disposed of, "to discuss the future of the *Morning Star*. How are you getting on with finding the money?" He could be direct, a trait Blackwood admired.

Blackwood said: "We haven't got very far—hardly a quarter of the way. However . . ."

"You'll persevere?"

"Oh yes."

"Will you succeed?"

"I can't quite see how it is going to be done—and yet—I can't believe in my bones that it will *not* be done."

"Ah!" said Mr. Wimpole. "Like the war over again. No daylight to be seen, but all the same—the feeling that victory must come. Pugnacity—faith—shall we say some lack of imagination . . . the British stand-bys, eh?" He smiled down his long face. "Are you finding the City sympathetic?"

"As sympathetic as I expected—perhaps more so."

"But not sympathetic enough?"

"So far—no."

"Do I understand that if you fail to raise the money, Mr. Sedgwick may—be decidedly pleased?"

"Overjoyed, I should say."

"Would it be fair to say that he—bumped up the price?" The Prime Minister wrinkled his face as if the use of the colloquialism was a wrench.

"Yes—although, offered in the market, one group bidding against another, there's no knowing what might have happened—how high the price might have gone." Blackwood tugged his beard.

The Prime Minister said: "Yes, I agree. Prestige is an expensive commodity. The stamp of Lloyds. The name of *The Times*. The word of the Governor of the Bank of England. By the way——" Mr. Wimpole paused a long time; then he added casually, rising to give himself another cup of coffee: "I understand one of the financial houses you consulted had a word with the Governor of the Bank, and it's not unlikely, I believe, that the Governor may—

er—speak to Sedgwick to see—well, to see if anything is possible in the way of a Trust. He knows Sedgwick, of course—so he'll be able to talk quite frankly." Mr. Wimpole sat down at the table again and sipped his coffee thoughtfully.

Blackwood said: "An offer of a million was once made for the *Burnham Guardian*."

Mr. Wimpole asked: "A long time ago?"

"Yes."

Blackwood waited, and then, as the Prime Minister added nothing, he inquired almost in an undertone: "And what do you think will be the effect of the Governor's word with Sedgwick?"

The Prime Minister shrugged his shoulders. He said: "There are Press magnates—and Press magnates, those who will always study the country's interests as a whole as distinct from their own interests—and alas! there are one or two who are—shall we say—impish, wayward? It will be interesting to see which category Mr. Sedgwick belongs to."

Blackwood said slowly: "I am most grateful—for the interest that is being shown. If an opportunity occurs to inform those concerned——"

The Prime Minister nodded and stroked his chin. There was a silence for several moments. It was taking a second or two for the full import of the irony in the situation to be appreciated by Blackwood. Finally, he said: "You see——" and paused.

The Prime Minister looked up. "Yes?"

"I am afraid the amount is mentioned—fixed—in the will——"

"Oh?"—surprise and disappointment were in it.

"Perhaps I have been—hardly careful—enough. I asked Molyneux to give me time in which to find a sum equal to that offered by Sedgwick. This Molyneux did—he wrote a clause into the will. But in fixing the time—one month—he fixed also the sum. Lady Molyneux would be hardly likely to sell for a smaller amount."

"But if Sedgwick is—dissuaded—from offering this sum?"

"*If*——it is a considerable 'if'——"

"Agreed. But if he is——"

"I should feel in honour bound to try and raise that sum myself—since Molyneux could have sold at once before he died had I not argued with him and——"

"I see—you mean—yes—I see." Mr. Wimpole pulled a face.

"And, moreover, Lady Molyneux would be likely to put the paper on the market anyhow. She has no love for it under my editorship, I'm afraid, and if she knew—as she would learn from Sedgwick—that he had been dissuaded—that would hardly make her more amenable to reason."

Mr. Wimpole pondered, rose and walked to and fro, glanced out of the window, twisted his platinum-and-gold watch-chain between finger and thumb. He stopped. "Even so," he said, "even so——" and paused again. Then: "Even so—if she sold and the buyer proved to be somebody—not Mr. Sedgwick but somebody who owned no newspapers at all—or perhaps one newspaper—that might be preferable to seeing the paper enter a group or chain?" He looked at Blackwood inquiringly.

Blackwood said, cutting it off with a knife: "It might or might not. Besides—in any open sale how could Sedgwick be excluded?"

Mr. Wimpole said: "I am going to say something now that occurs to me at this instant—on the spur of the moment. Suppose —suppose the Labour Party acquired it, through your good offices—financed *you*, as it were, and the *Morning Star* became *The Times* of the Labour movement—would not that be infinitely better than its acquisition by Mr. Sedgwick?" The Prime Minister's face was lit up—it was as if he had seen a minor vision. But the illumination was brief, for Blackwood said, abruptly: "I'm afraid not."

"You really mean you see no difference?"

"Very little, I'm afraid. And then again, I am bound, so far as I have any power, to maintain the present policy and to turn the paper into a Trust—I've said so publicly."

"But supposing you *cannot* raise the money unless the Labour Party finds it—what then? Don't you agree that the Labour movement should have two national newspapers?"

"Oh yes—by all means. More than two, if you like. But——"

"Yes?"

"Not mine—not the *Morning Star*. To toe the Socialist line would kill the paper just as surely as being swallowed by the Sedgwick whale."

The Prime Minister, who was still on his feet, looked down at him. He said quizzically: "Your motto is—'Give me liberty or give me death'?"

"Certainly. Does that surprise you? Suppose you were told you could continue to be Prime Minister if you embraced the Conservative creed—not otherwise?"

Mr. Wimpole made an exclamation of incredulity. "That," he said, "that would be like asking me to take poison."

Blackwood said: "Your recoil is no greater than mine."

The Prime Minister sat down again. He placed the tips of his fingers together. "The old radical tradition," he said, "finds expression today in the Labour Party. You welcomed our accession to power——"

"Yes—we had great hopes of you."

Wimpole waved that aside. "Never in the history of the world has a revolution been carried out so quietly and beneficially. Never have so many million small lamps of hope been lit in the homes of the people—so much fear and insecurity banished, so much health improved, so many children and old people made happier. A vast amount that we have done is what you have always preached. You would agree with that?" Mr. Wimpole was bland, benign, sure that nobody could gainsay that. "Would it not be a fine thing, an immense public service to help us to keep those lamps trimmed and glowing, to keep the innumerable torches bright?" He leaned forward. "Suppose," he said, "suppose—your paper was printed in London also, your circulation many times what it is today, your influence immeasurable?"

"In the Socialist cause you mean?"

"Yes—why not?"

Blackwood shifted in his chair. "Sir," he said, "I am not a Socialist."

Mr. Wimpole said smoothly: "There used not to be much of a gulf between us."

"More than you think—and it has grown wider. I entirely agree that your Government has done excellent things—but running in harness with them are results that are less happy. Not easy to assess responsibility for it, but there it is. Shoddy workmanship more common, gambling spreading like a fire, churches emptier, hardly anybody a hundred per cent honest, and, when my paper has investigated it, not one firm in a hundred believes its workers are working as hard as they used to. Prime Minister—would you welcome the publication of those sorts of facts in a *Morning Star* that had turned Labour?"

Mr. Wimpole didn't answer that. He said coldly: "I think the emphasis is wrong."

"Naturally you do."

Mr. Wimpole went on: "Surely writers of responsibility have a duty to underline the good rather than the bad, in order that virtue may be encouraged."

"Sir, their duty is to be faithful to the facts. Some go farther. I could quote you one or two of our most distinguished novelists who have written lately of the writer's duty to cultivate an insolent irresponsibility, a disloyalty to convention, a contempt for honours and State patronage and to see even success and praise as dangerous to their integrity. What I feel strongest about myself is the need to support the individual in his struggle for survival against the groups and combines in private enterprise and against the weight of the State in his daily life. In that sense"—he smiled quite pleasantly—"I see Mr. Sedgwick on one hand and the Labour Government on the other as having something in common."

"Good heavens!" murmured Mr. Wimpole.

"In the essence of what they're both aiming at," said Blackwood. "Trying to absorb me or level me down, make me conform. Your party, sir, which began as rebels, now can barely stomach them."

Mr. Wimpole waited a moment politely to see if Blackwood had finished. Then he said: "Mr. Blackwood—if I may say so, you arrogate to yourself a degree of infallibility which cannot be sustained. We in the Cabinet reach our decisions by majority vote. You reach yours—alone—brooking no discussion, debate, vote or advice. Your method is essentially undemocratic. You claim the right to be judge and jury, to sap and mine, to present the laurels or wield the axe as the case may be. Remember what Cromwell said—consider lest you be mistaken."

Blackwood replied: "The prerogative of the individual is to be mistaken and to go to hell, if he wishes, in his own way. That is his divine right, and if he loses it, he is something near a slave. There is one further point—if I do not weary you——"

"On the contrary——"

"The *Morning Star* is of the north—its bone and sinew is northern—its thought is northern. Cotton, ships, coal, iron, steel, engineering—these are its trades, and its readers the men who

246

work them. Their speech, outlook, humour, way of going on are their own. You might as well try to turn Thomas Hardy into a Cockney as produce the *Morning Star* in Fleet Street—or control it from Fleet Street."

Mr. Wimpole ran a forefinger down his cheek. Then he began to fold his napkin. As he did so, he said in his suavest tones: "You will remember that the flight of fancy about your paper being acquired by—my friends—was a mere after-thought—and that, viewing it as you do, we shall say no more about it?" He rose and stretched his legs.

Blackwood rose too. "You have been kind—and patient. I am touched that you should have gone to this trouble."

"Mr. Blackwood, I seldom agree with all that you say, nowadays, but that doesn't mean I don't respect it. Let us remember Voltaire's dictum!" And as Mr. Wimpole extended his hand he did indeed believe that he shared the sentiments so commonly—if a trifle erroneously—attributed to M. Voltaire.

CHAPTER XXXIV

Lovelace sat in one corner of the compartment and Blackwood in the other. Lovelace had a pencil and writing-pad in his hands, but he was not writing. Blackwood had a book on his lap, but he was not reading. Lovelace was thinking: "So we're hard bound for home, as the sailors say, and our horn is blowing. But there's no joy in it for us. No rich cargo we're bringing home, no copper and salt and old tin trays; nothing but a shipload of resignation. Oliver has his hopes, but I—well—far less. All very well for the Prime Minister to be sympathetic and want to nobble the paper for Labour. What good is that? No future in that. No, no, I see Sam Sedgwick getting his own way in the end. Might is right most of the time. They want your souls, those guys, and if they don't get 'em they break you—or try to. Oh, he's a nice fellow, Mr. So-and-so—only don't get in his way." Lovelace went on ruminating. His sister Agnes would be pleased. Agnes had said they were crazy to think they could pick up the brass in London. All men were hopeless, Agnes said, and writers worse than most. As if anybody would earn a living by writing if he could do aught else, Agnes said. Agnes thought you took to writing because you'd failed to get a job in the town hall or on the railway—something steady. What good had writing done him? she would enquire. Did they even own the house they lived in? Of course not. Did they possess a thousand pounds to buy a little business with—Agnes's dream—a baby-linen shop or a good tobacconist's? They did not. If he sacked himself from the paper—as he knew he would if Sedgwick took over—oh, he'd have to write then—write his heart out. But could he do it, could he? Had he got it in him now? Or was he as a barrel at which too many mouths have drunk? Ah! there was that spell he'd had before he joined Blackwood, that spell when he'd decided to be a real man of letters and he'd written *Son of the House*. It took him a year to write and it made £275—the critics spoke well of it, too, those who acknowledged its existence. The next book did worse—*Slump* didn't earn its advance, although in his opinion it was a better book. And he had begun to try and get back into journalism. But it was tough. He wasn't an easy man to fit in—too distinguished or too old they said—or too cranky—though they didn't of course say that. He remembered his feeling of being cold-shouldered, ostracised, brushed off. Hell! An invitation to an assistant editor to have a drink ignored. An attempt to speak on the telephone to the local programmes director of the B.B.C., fruitless—he was in conference, always in conference. The theatre producer who had his play, and had had it three months, was, of course, rehearsing—at every hour of the day he was rehearsing. He, Lovelace, was in the humiliating position of wanting something—and of knowing they knew it well. He came to realise what the out of work, the down and out, the sensitive soul who crossed the road when he saw a friend approaching, felt like. There was the day when he had counted his money like a miser and calculated that, if he were to earn no more, he could live for the best part of a year as he was living then. And after that?—the dosshouse, the roadmender's hut, the envelope-addressing? Oh, his imagination had worked overtime —even thinking of the day when, as Henley said, Death, with his well-worn lean professional smile, would come to his bedside, unannounced and bland. But even as he wallowed in the slough,

looked in the mirror of a morning and thought he could see the
hand of time writing ever-deepening lines on his visage, he had
known that all this experience would come in useful one of these
days. But alternating with that was the knowledge that the scrap-
heap held too much old iron to be a comfortable bed for long.
And then in a moment of intuition he had written to Blackwood—
Blackwood who had had some faith in him, buoyed him up more
than once, and had, on one occasion when they were covering a
by-election together soon after the First World War, written
Lovelace's first paragraph to get him started—for that was an
awful day when Lovelace's mind wouldn't work. And Blackwood
had said he could have a dogsbody job if he wanted—doing odd
leaders, a bit of drama, book reviews, specials about the waterfront—"but none of your damned Bolshevism, Richard," he had
said; "keep your feet on the ground—one foot, anyhow." It was
a pang—and a triumph—for Lovelace to realise how happy he'd
been on the *Morning Star*. He had been able to say, as his
namesake said three hundred years back:

> If I have freedom in my love
> And in my soul am free
> Angels alone that soar above
> Enjoy such liberty.

Aye, he'd been free in his soul all right—Blackwood had done
that for him. Blackwood had given him what all artists wanted—
a chance to work and to know where the next meal was coming
from, and a pat on the back and a kick in the pants now and
then—had lent him assurance, fortified him, loved him; aye,
loved him. Passing the love of women? Maybe, maybe. And he'd
written a good book or two—not much brass in 'em, but good
work, so when the universe and he were one, as the python said
to the rabbit, folk would still be reading his *Night Without Moon*,
drawn in tatters out o' the public library up Litherland Road.
And what could a fella want more'n that, eh? As for t'other sort
o' love, he reckoned he was free at last—he could look at a
bonnie woman now with a triumphant feeling, safe behind the
barricades of age, no longer in danger of flying off in pursuit
of that will-o'-the-wisp that . . . Well, nearly safe, pretty-well
safe. True, he'd had a momentary relapse a day or two ago—

that woman in St. James's Park the other evening—watching the waterfowl—a woman of early middle-age and great handsomeness, radiant, dark hair, lustrous eyes sparkling with mischief. She had never known he admired her, for, as he pondered whether to address to her a remark on the subject, let us say, of the unfairness of God in giving drakes all the plumage, Oliver—unknowing too—had linked his arm in his and borne him off. Just as well, maybe just as well. But he really *was* safe, oh yes, perfectly safe. And if the worst came to the worst and he and Oliver walked out of the *Morning Star*, well, give him a wad o' copy paper and a pencil and a bottle or two of Guinness and what masterpieces might he not turn out? He reckoned there'd be a ghost o' Lovelace found writing novels in the small hours perched in his old corner, Sedgwick or no Sedgwick. But what would Oliver do, aye that was the rub, what would Oliver do? Oliver had written no books and he couldn't see him doing it. He'd poured his blood into the old rag, made it his life, work and pleasure rolled into one, built it, slaved for it, and if he lost it he reckoned he'd die. Men have died and worms have eaten them, but not for love. Yea, but they had, for love o' this sort, love o' the thing fashioned out of your bones; aye, died for it. Lovelace looked across at Blackwood, who was leaning back, eyes closed. In repose the face had a remarkable serenity, albeit a deep pallor. Was it sleep that had wiped away the cares—sleep, that little child of death? But no, Blackwood coughed and stirred but did not open his eyes. Blackwood was withdrawn from him and he, Lovelace, suffered a pang in consequence and blamed himself for so doing; it was childish, adolescent, even female, this resentment of another's privacy and secret life. But he found it hard to overcome, this jealousy which sprang from his deep affection. Blackwood was the one stable, certain thing in a crooked world, the rock, the anchor, the one completely honest and reliable man he knew, the measuring rod—what would Blackwood say, what would he do? Put alongside him, most men were riffraff. What problem of the *Morning Star* was he wrestling with now, he wondered?

But Blackwood was not at that moment trying to resolve any of the intricate problems of the *Morning Star*; he was living in his thoughts with Hannah and to a lesser degree with Bob. For he had seen Hannah in London in company with Sedgwick in the Savoy grill where he and Lovelace had dined before the Palladium. He had noticed them only when he was leaving, and Lovelace, with his short sight, had not seen them at all. Nor had he spoken of it to Lovelace. Whether Hannah or Sedgwick had seen him in return he didn't know, but he thought not. It was strange, he thought, that they were dining in this public room, Sedgwick being as well known as he was, but perhaps Hannah had preferred it or insisted on it. He knew she had received one or two notes from Sedgwick, reminding her of his wish to meet again. "My dear Mrs. Blackwood," he had written (Hannah had pushed it across the breakfast table to Blackwood), "I don't know if you will be up in Town soon, but there is a play I am interested in—*Forgotten Episode*—in which Mrs. Tremayne is playing. I should be delighted if I might take you to see it. I think you would find it amusing—Polly is rather good. With kind regards, and to your husband, Yours sincerely, Saml. Sedgwick." Hannah had asked Oliver if being interested in the play meant that Sedgwick had backed it, and Blackwood had replied that it probably did. She had commented: "I should like to see what Polly Tremayne is like on the stage." She had not definitely said she would go to London and he had not inquired. It had long been a point of honour with him not to appear too closely interested in her movements. The torment was there in this counterfeited indifference, and the hiding of the torment made it no easier, but he vouchsafed no sign. Sedgwick's letter was unexceptionable, of course, just so might a man begin a campaign when bent on injuring or humiliating a rival. But was he so bent?—was Sedgwick, in fact, doing anything beyond behaving as a man of business who was intent on gaining a business end and using any means available—and glad at the same time to indulge his delight in having attractive women round him? Difficult to say. He had written to Bob, too, inviting Bob to call on him, "especially", said Sedgwick, "if any unpleasant results crop up from the case in court where, as you know, you spoke very much what was in my own mind". Bob had quoted that sentence in writing what was for him a phenomenally long letter to Blackwood and Hannah of two pages. He, Bob, had had a somewhat "shaky do", he said, when seeing his flying chiefs, who were not at all excited—except in the upside-down way—by what he had said in court or the incident as a whole, but he thought it was all over now. Sedgwick had offered him a job on the circulation or advertisement side of the Sedgwick Group whenever he liked to have one, and those branches of a newspaper were just as important, said Sedgwick, as any other; without them the paper couldn't exist. "After that," wrote Bob, "we had a large whisky and soda together and he gave me two seats to see Mrs. Tremayne's play. Not a bad old stick! I even told him to lay off buying the *Morning Star*. Took it all right—said if he did buy it, he'd consider letting me in on the managerial side. That was after a second drink. So long, folks, and love."

Bob sounded in good spirits and at thought of that Blackwood's heart lifted. Bob had taken the court case surprisingly well—a shoal they'd all floated off much easier than might have been expected. Bob had said the *Star's* leader on the case was "fair enough"—and that for him was high praise. With luck Bob might now have a quiet spell, beset only by the hazards of flying—and normal living. Hannah had said, with one of her secret smiles, that Bob had been getting on famously with Mrs. Tremayne when dancing at Greycastle, and now, with a sudden flight of fancy, it struck Blackwood that the situation that existed that night could recur in London—a quartette in which Sedgwick partnered Hannah, and Bob Mrs. Tremayne; and how admirably that might please Sedgwick. But, even so, what depth would that comedy have, how subtly be played; what would be the effect striven after? How much laughter in it, how much of tears? No knowing, no knowing. How far was Sedgwick the instrument and product of his times, the unwitting tool of events, of his power and money? Hard to say. Nothing original in him, merely the off-shoot of men like Northcliffe, but with less insight and love of the craft, using newspapers like merchandise, himself swayed by politicians, drugged by power and fascinated by his title. Not a bad old stick, Bob said. Right enough in its way as a summing up. Sedgwick—or so Blackwood imagined—saw about half the problem of individual man—saw that he needs protection in the many fields the State has invaded, but didn't see that his best protection—or anyhow one of the most important—was the constant enunciation of the inherent dignity and worth of the human person, that it was human culture that was man's divine right and that it was artistic creation in the shape of music, science, painting, sculpture and letters that gave us our pride in the human race and which best testified to our pilgrimage on this earth; and that it was this artistic creation which stood the best chance of achieving mutual understanding and encouraging the faith that the brotherhood of man was not a vain hope. It was this blindness in Sedgwick to nearly all save politics and money-making that made him rank the editorial writers as no more important than sellers of advertising space or men boosting circulation. Therein lay the danger of him—not wickedness but lack of vision.

And yet, and yet—with money, power, and a physical bullishness, what advantages he possessed! And if Hannah succumbed to his bland, persistent onslaught, what then, what then? What then for him, Blackwood, save the deeper immersion in toil, the application of the freezing, numbing constriction to his nerves that he had practised down the years?

CHAPTER XXXV

A FEW DAYS after his return from London Blackwood decided since London financiers were a most doubtful quantity, that he must make a more direct approach to the leading businessmen of Greycastle—those men and women he judged to be sympathetic to some extent, anyhow, and who had the means to assist. He therefore wrote a second personal letter to a round dozen men and women to whom he had written once before, now asking if they would meet him in conference to discuss the future of the paper. He invited them to come to the office, feeling that the atmosphere there—simple, without frills, would be conducive to business. The bishop and Lord Mayor and vice-chancellor on this occasion he left out. They had sympathy in plenty but their means were small. He would concentrate on those who were doubtful in attitude but were well-to-do—Satterthwaite, Henry McGrew timber importer, Raymond Wilberforce flour miller, John Picton marine engineer, Mrs. Angela Richardson widow of a cotton broker, Redvers Mornington the brewer, William Haslam leather manufacturer, Arthur

Hesketh shipowner, Thomas Bolton builder and contractor, Edward Mallalieu wholesale clothier, Jacob Rosenstein mammoth caterer. He invited also Sir William Prentice and William Moffatt, both extremely friendly but neither, so far, having decided to invest in any noteworthy degree.

All but John Picton accepted, and now, which room at the *Morning Star* would do? The so-called board-room was excessively small and mainly used for storing bound volumes of the paper. His own private room wasn't big enough either. It would have to be the sub-editors' room—so he had the long rectangular table cleared and the best chairs they could muster placed alongside together with notepads and pencils. Austere certainly; he smiled over it. Some of the visitors looked astonished when they saw the room into which they were ushered. He explained what the telephoto apparatus was, the tubes for pumping copy upstairs, and the spikes for rejected news. They sat down, most of them placing their hats in front of them, Colonel Satterthwaite saying the place reminded him of the saloon of one of their early steamers, Mallalieu adding you could cut out a suit o' clothes all right on a table like that, and Jacob Rosenstein declaring it would do for a wedding breakfast. Mrs. Richardson adjusted her hearing aid and all waited expectantly.

Blackwood, who had Lovelace and George Wavertree sitting behind him, began: "It's most kind of you to come. I wanted to say this: I think you all know the *Morning Star's* position—either we raise half a million pounds in the next week or two—or the paper will be sold to Mr. Sedgwick. I've been up in London consulting various financial houses. The outcome is uncertain—to say the least of it. I want to clear the air and see the position as it really is. Let me be perfectly blunt. So far we haven't raised a quarter of the money. We are all northcountrymen—you won't object to plainness from me and I shall welcome it from you, however uncomfortable it is. Are you—any of you—thinking of investing any considerable sum in this journal? If you are, could you tell me within the next day or two. If you are not, could you tell me that, too. I don't expect you to say here and now— although if you do, well and good. There must be many things you want to ask me—things you are not clear about; it's to give you the opportunity of cross-examining me that is the second reason why I asked you to come. I have really no more to say. The outlook is grim—unless a number of minor miracles occur. And now, ladies and gentlemen, I am at your disposal. Ask me anything you wish." He sat down and waited.

There was silence for a moment or two. Then Jacob Rosenstein asked: "Vhy don't you print the racing news and make the paper more liked?"

"Not in our tradition," said Blackwood. "We've never printed racing. Racing is linked with gambling."

"Ye print the Stock Exchange news—plenty o' gambling there," said McGrew. "And plenty on the cotton exchange—or used to be."

"Agreed," said Blackwood. "But I don't believe racing news would help us. We should have to give less parliamentary news. People buy us for the parliamentary report—not many papers give it so fully."

Colonel Satterthwaite asked: "What does Lady Molyneux want all this money for? She is not like a man who wants to keep his racehorses, his yachts and his mistresses. If you suggest it to her, she will probably leave at least three-quarters of her money in the paper."

Blackwood said: "I'm afraid not. She dislikes the paper and its policy. And she charges me with having robbed her of money, inasmuch as she believes Sedgwick would have been willing to raise his bid still further."

Thomas Bolton, the builder, said: "Ah've never been able to understond why Sedgwick is so spokken against. I read his Sunday paper—no worse than t'others. He owns a lot o' papers and Ah own a lot of houses. Can't see much difference."

Blackwood said: "Mr. Bolton, you like to speak your mind?"

"Aye, and Ah'd like to see t' chap as 'ud stop me."

"Mr. Sedgwick would stop you—if you were his editor."

"Ah'd like to see him try."

"You and the *Morning Star* are in the same boat, Mr. Bolton— you refuse to be muzzled."

"Oh, that's it, is it. Well, Ah'm wi' you there."

Arthur Hesketh broke in: "At the same time, Mr. Blackwood, I think the paper could be more popular, without losing anything. More photographs, cartoons, comic strips—wouldn't they pay dividends?"

Blackwood said: "If *The Times* competed with the *Daily Mirror* which of you would buy it? The *Morning Star* similarly couldn't compete with the *Express*. No middle-aged woman can peroxide her hair with success."

Mrs. Angela Richardson nodded her head vigorously: "I can agree with that, certainly I can. But this is a Conservative city and I think we ought to have a Conservative paper. That's what I say. At the same time I always agree with what Mr. Blackwood says and I asked God last night if I ought to invest twenty thousand pounds in the paper and He said to me 'Yes,' and I am going to do it." She looked round the table, her small head trembling so that her bonnet shook. "There must be several of us," she said, "who cannot have long to go and we can't take it with us." She was staring at Colonel Satterthwaite.

"Ma'am," he said, "I know you think I am walking about to save funeral expenses. But I shall see a lot of people out. Mark my words."

"Very true, Colonel," murmured Sir William Prentice. "Now I should like to ask Mr. Blackwood if he thinks the Royal Commission are taking cognizance of what is happening? Have they communicated with him? Has he given evidence yet?"

Blackwood said: "I've had no communication with them beyond submitting some written evidence. They cannot, of course, exercise any powers to prevent the sale of a paper, although I imagine the Commission's existence is already restraining various tendencies—as a policeman's eye controls mischievous boys. I shall give oral evidence in due course."

Redvers Mornington cleared his throat and pulled down his brows. He turned to Blackwood. "I know you, sir, regard Mr. Sedgwick's action as reprehensible. But it's good business—and it's a compliment to your paper."

Blackwood replied: "Mr. Mornington, if a London firm tried to take over your brewery you would fight. Especially if they tried to put beer brewed in London into your Greycastle barrels under your name. You'd call that deception. It's the same with the *Morning Star*. Our wisdom and wit—such as they are—are home brewed. We believe people have a taste for them."

Mornington said: "Yes—but our beer makes a good profit. Does yours? How much dividend will you pay me if I provide ten thousand pounds?"

Blackwood said promptly: "Rather better than the Post Office."

Mornington shook his head. "Not good enough. You're not gilt-edged."

"Neither," said Blackwood, "is a university—or a repertory theatre."

"I don't understand." Mornington puckered his brows.

"A repertory theatre doesn't make the profits of a cinema showing gangster films. The dividends of a university are paid in scholarship and learning and instilling the humanities—a long-term job. The *Star* is in the repertory and university class. We do well to make any profit at all."

"If ye're educational," said McGrew, "why doesn't this Welfare Government back ye up? They poke their fingers intae enough pies."

Blackwood said: "I'm in a difficulty there. I've had certain meetings. And I've reason to believe some of the leaders of the Labour Party would like to take the paper over. But——"

They all looked at him intently.

"—but we should be smothered under the Socialist blanket as surely as under the Sedgwick one. One's as bad as the other."

This drew several "Hear, hears" and smiles.

Blackwood said: "You are all individualists—unless I'm mistaken. So am I. There's a great fight for the individualist going on all over the world—can he survive? That's the pre-eminent question today. We're fighting it here on this paper. We'll either win—or go out."

Wilberforce, the flour-miller, said: "Right—right as rain is that. They tried to absorb me—*me!* Eh?" He looked round challengingly.

Thomas Bolton said: "Ah like a fight—Ah'm always in favour of a fight. I'm wi' you on that."

It was at this point that a telegram shot up the tube from Wilfred with a vast clatter and Lovelace went over to pick it up. It was addressed to "Oliver Blackwood, Star Office, Greycastle". He handed it to Blackwood, who apologised and opened it. After a moment he said: "You'll be interested in this, gentlemen. It's from Jonathan North, proprietor of the *London Independent*— a Lancashireman, as you probably know. He says: 'Congratulations your fight stop If seventy five thousand is any use it's yours

Is

provided six other Lancashire lads will find twenty five thousand each stop Can't have Yorkshiremen running Lancashire papers stop Up the rugged individualists and blow the combines out of the water Good luck from J North.'"

Thomas Bolton said: "You can put me down, Mr. Blackwood."

"And me," said Mrs. Richardson in a shrill quavery voice.

"I can't keep out o' this," said Wilberforce. "That'll make three of us anyhow."

"I'm deeply grateful," said Blackwood. "I ought to say that I know the boards of two or three other independent papers are watching the position closely and if our fate is in the balance for a score or two thousands I believe they will fill the breach. As you're probably aware, papers like *The Times*, the *Yorkshire Times*, *Burnham Guardian* and leading Scots papers have written leaders wishing us good fortune. Well, ladies and gentlemen, if there are no more questions——" He looked round at them.

"I take it," said William Moffatt, "if we don't find twenty-five thousand, we're not ruled out."

Blackwood said: "We're getting postal orders for half a crown. That's so, Lovelace?" He turned round to look at him.

"Quite right, sir. A street-corner orator who says he often quotes our leaders sent us his collection—one and fivepence ha'penny. And a woman in Llandudno sent us her sweet ration."

On this note the meeting broke up. Two or three, as they shook hands with Blackwood, said they would be writing to him.

When they had gone, Blackwood said: "The Almighty staged the intervention of Jonathan North very well."

"The Almighty—and your humble servant," said Lovelace.

"What do you mean?"

"It came, master, during lunch when I looked in. I opened it according to orders when you're not here. And I had a brainwave: stuck it up again and gave it to Wilfred to do the needful at the right time."

"You're a scoundrel, Richard."

"God has His own mysterious ways. Who gave me the brainwave? It was inspiration."

CHAPTER XXXVI

Meanwhile the visit of Mr. Fortinbras to the by-election at Greycastle imparted its own air of raillery to what was developing into a serious debate on the British Press. Not that Mr. Fortinbras was lacking in his praise of the Fourth Estate. By no means. It was his custom to speak as a former member of that august profession which, as he reminded his audiences, had been described as one that, when it arrived on the scene, caused the past to re-enact itself and persuaded the future immediately to occur. He was equally firm in his praise of the *Morning Star*. This journal, he said, was one of the few daily papers that could be read with pleasure a day late, so enlightening and timeless were its articles, and, indeed, he added with a chuckle, its lofty attitude to what the vulgar called spot news was such that if by mistake you picked up last month's issue, you were likely to derive as much pleasure from it as the one moist from the press. And then he would gaze blandly down at the reporters' table and smile benignly upon them. The *Morning Star*, he said, was high up on the list of the newspapers he thought it essential to glance at while he was engrossed in his English breakfast which the Socialist Chancellor had so miraculously transformed from eggs and bacon to sackcloth and ashes. But at the same time he managed to convey that this question of ownership of the Press could be taken rather too seriously; that there was nothing very much wrong with the British Press, that you must take it as it came, that to err was human and to forgive divine, and that it was naïve and adolescent to look for perfection. Something would have been lost to English life, he suggested, if one or two of our Press magnates had not exhibited those eccentricities which found vent in so admiring a theatrical play in which their friends appeared that they caused a flattering paragraph to be written every day of its run, or, on the other hand, found a barrister who had appeared in a case against them so detestable that they ordered their sub-editors to use only his initials when he did well and his name in full when he found himself engaged in a wordy brawl with the judge. Let us not depreciate those Press magnates, he said, who might appear to have a distant kinship with the madness of genius. For, just as many of us are likely to remember more easily the Emperor Caligula who made his horse a consul than we are emperors of more pronounced virtue, so the Press owners of extravagant behaviour are likely to be more firmly written into the history of our times than those who are austere and impeccable. English life was justly famed for its eccentrics, and none but the churlish and narrow-minded with no sense of history would regret them. And as with the Press magnates, so it was with the Press. We lived in arid times, and if the newspapers saw their principal function—as many obviously did—as entertainers and amusers, was that, after all, entirely a disadvantage? He had to confess that when a very young man he had indulged his fancy when working as a journalist in coining sayings or aphorisms, attributing them to fictitious sages of Greece or Rome and seeing them solemnly printed in the pages of the highly respected journal with which he was then associated—and nobody, so far as he knew, was any the worse. What was equally important, he had never been found out. He had also contributed in his time a number of letters under various names to various grave journals venturing to make a number of astonishing and imaginative statements which he always prefaced by the remark "It is well-known that . . ." In this fashion he had stated that Napoleon's guards were mostly Irishmen, that Garibaldi's Chief of Staff was a Cockney six feet two inches high, and that it was in the concerted neighing of the horses that the Scots Greys were so superior to most other cavalry regiments. It was true that some of these statements were justly challenged, but the resulting correspondence was invariably lively and made excellent reading. Great changes had occurred in the Press during his lifetime, but who among them would dare to say they were all for the worse? He was familiar with the charge that headlines were often now so large and overpowering that you felt, as some critic had said, that the very type lied. On the other hand he could not himself have anything save a warm corner in his heart for the sub-editor who put up the heading: "Mosquitoes scatter tanks round Nancy", or that the "Government plans crisis", for who could call in question the veracity of that?—or the one which appeared in this great seaport and was erroneously attributed to the *Morning Star*—namely "Adrift in Atlantic—four days on a piece of chocolate". Headings could be misleading, of course, to those who were not altogether acquainted with our methods and ways of speech, as in the case of the Frenchman who was concerned for our stability and who was confronted on picking up his evening paper with a great banner-line which announced "Collapse of Kent"—but that was by the way. As Cocteau had remarked—tact in art lay in knowing how far to go in going too far; and journalists unquestionably had been known to blunder—but who had not? Sometimes reporters acknowleged they were so little artists that they mistook themselves for private detectives and became so determined in their hunting that a friend of his had spent three days riding on top of a London bus to escape them. But wasn't riding on a bus the most agreeable thing in the world? You could say that among our public men there were two sorts, those who pursue the Press and those whom the Press pursues. In his time, he was constrained to admit, he had been something of both. Yes, the Press had unquestionably undergone vast changes, and pressmen too. When he was a young man the most important man in the newspaper office after the editor was the foreman printer and you kept on the right side of him. Today perhaps he was the advertisement manager; and although Northcliffe used to scorn advertisers so much that he was credited with the remark that if he had thrown three advertisers down-stairs during the morning he could then enjoy his lunch, the advertiser of bargains which conjured the spare cash from our pockets provided the newspaper's sinews of war. In his young days Fleet Street was occupied by an army of young men wearing top hats and frock coats—these were reporters—who looked like gentlemen—and some of them were; though more than one had to remind himself not to remove his coat and disclose that he couldn't afford a waistcoat underneath. But however that was, they were men of immense imagination who thought nothing of sallying north to a colliery disaster and writing a two-column description of the pithead scenes as they travelled up in the train. He much doubted if the scribes of the present day could improve on that record, although he had heard of the modern dictum that a wrong story is better than no story at all. The point which was desirable to make, he thought, was that however much we might condemn the journalist who sat in the office and wrote a letter to the editor signed "Mother of six" in order to stir up a controversy, or the reporter who wrote a description of Hitler's entry into Prague several hours before it had occurred in order to catch the early editions, it was not altogether a new manifestation. That great Englishman Sir John Falstaff had his flights of fancy too, but what a joy he was! And could you, by the way, imagine Sir John being a disciple of Sir Stafford Cripps, or voting Labour?

No, no, there wasn't very much wrong with the Press, if you looked on it with a tolerant eye and a sense of humour. And it was in this spirit of raillery that Mr. Fortinbras, his grey locks blowing in the wind, his moustache lending him the air of a benevolent sea-lion, his wide panama hat giving him a relationship with Missouri, called on Oliver Blackwood early one evening. Mr. Fortinbras had not announced his coming. He elbowed his portly way through the door, inquired of Wilfred whether Mr. Blackwood was in and learning he was—he scarcely paused—began to puff his way up the stairs saying over his shoulder: "Send somebody with me and tell him I'm coming up." Wilfred telephoned up in some consternation and Blackwood came down the corridor to meet his visitor.

"Well, young man," said Mr. Fortinbras, "I've come to pay my respects. You're very uncivil to me sometimes in this paper— very uncivil—but I bear you no ill-will. It is a very good paper, although, I daresay, I could make it better. Don't you think so? No, I don't suppose you do, but it's quite true nevertheless, eh? Eh?" And he sat down and puffed his pipe with immense enjoyment.

Blackwood said, smiling, that an occasional contribution would be warmly welcomed, wasn't that so, Richard?

Mr. Fortinbras turned to look at Lovelace and growled out that he looked like the brother of Cassius. He then added that he thought he ought to be paid for that amusing column they had got out of his speech the night before. "Now about this newspaper business," he said, levelling his pipe stem like a dart at Blackwood's waistcoat. "When I was a young man—before your time—the best news was so private as to be unprintable and the stuff printed was unusually unreadable. Nowadays the private stuff is printed or concocted, a lot of it is readable provided you are not too fastidious, and most of it you need not unduly burden your mind with in trying to remember. Your paper, of course, is

262

an exception—you are a kind of intellectual exercise—I rank you with *The Times* crossword on an easy morning, eh? Eh?" He chuckled, and resumed: "I know—or suspect, what you think of Press magnates. Some are tame tabbies, some are roaring tigers—and I shall not divulge to you which animal tribe Mr. Sedgwick belongs to. I would say only this: I would rather have him than have newspapers owned by political parties, even by the illustrious party to which I have the honour to belong—and I need not tell you it is by far the best party and the only one in England today that has a good word to say for liberty, eh? Eh? I do not deny that on the national papers the editor is now no more—with some rare exceptions—than the executive instrument of the proprietor—but since the proprietor is responsible for millions of other people's money—none of my own I am glad to say—he must be cautious and have a sense of duty. Now the provincial paper in a group like Sedgwick's, by spreading the financial risk, by modernising plant and all the rest of it, by sending its foreign correspondents over the globe at enormous expense—which you, my dear fellow, cannot afford to do—has manifest advantages. And if a paper is dying on its feet, as a good many have been and will be again if things continue as they are with the Socialists driving us to ruin, it may be better for Sedgwick to take a paper over and give it a blood transfusion than permit it to die, for a dead paper cannot print my speeches which, in turn, are needed to save this country, eh? Eh? Now I know you have a great deal to say in reply to this, but I have no time to listen to it. I did not come here to listen to you but to make you listen to me, eh? Eh?" He chuckled and puffed his pipe and his blue eyes almost vanished as he smiled more broadly than ever. "And I have this further to say to you. You must both listen." He waved his pipe to embrace Lovelace. "The man to find you the money to save this paper—to which I bear the utmost goodwill despite the rough way you handle me"—he smiled again—"is a young man of my acquaintance named Barclay Boddington. Ever heard of him?" As Mr. Barclay Boddington was heir to a famous soap manufacturing business it was by way of being a rhetorical question. Mr. Fortinbras shot a look at them. "I see from your faces that you have. What you do not know, however, is this: Mr. Boddington, who throughout all his comparatively brief life has called himself a Conservative, now, alas! calls himself a Liberal. Do not ask me to account for this sudden conversion—this alarming mental aberration—I cannot do so. It would be painful for me to try. Nevertheless, it is a fact. He has made this appalling confession to me personally. Whether the madness will pass or whether it will go even further and he will in course of time become a Socialist, I cannot say. But at the moment he stops at Liberalism. Like most Liberals—and there are a few Conservatives who feel much the same—I happen to be aware that he finds no remarkable pleasure in the reflection that he is no more than the custodian or trustee on behalf of Mr. Cripps for the greater part of the personal fortune he possesses, in short that when he dies the Chancellor will snaffle the bulk of it. In these circumstances it would be no great surprise to me if he found the idea of rescuing this journal of yours like a brand from the burning just as attractive to him as giving his money to the Treasury. Indeed, I have dropped a hint to him that he would be a public benefactor were he to do so, and that, when my party returns to power, it would not be altogether strange if we were to recall who perpetrated so signal a good work. Whether this—I shall not call it poison, for it is nothing of the kind, as you will readily agree—whether this—advice—will have its effect I do not know. But the seed is admirable—and the soil is reasonably fertile. I have also pointed out to Mr. Boddington one further fact, namely that if he does indeed embark on this wise adventure, he will be an historic figure—he will become almost a legend, for this—I ask you to mark this carefully—this is the last generation of Englishmen who will ever have it within their power to engage in such a munificent act. The Socialists have done their nefarious work too well. In a short while the possibility will have vanished, ended. Men like Mr. Boddington will be as extinct as the dodo, eh? Eh? That is all I have to say. No, no, do not thank me. I am moved by self interest. I should miss those prayers for my soul that I read between the lines of those admonitions and pejorative remarks that are addressed in my direction from time to time. Goodbye, Mr. Blackwood—and your friend Cassius. You will be wise to send a good reporter to my meeting tonight. I should not like you to miss what I have to say." And with this he shook hands with Blackwood, nodded to Lovelace, and took his departure.

CHAPTER XXXVII

THE VISIT OF Mr. Fortinbras was not the only one to which Blackwood was treated following the publication of Jonathan North's telegram. The bishop, Dr. Brodrick, came to see him. Mr. Llewellyn Morgan, the Liberal candidate, called. The Lord Mayor, Alderman Stevens, looked in. These and many more. Colonel Henry Satterthwaite visited the office once more. He, however, called in the forenoon, and on being informed that Mr. Blackwood did not usually arrive till late afternoon, formed an even lower opinion than hitherto of the efficiency of the *Morning Star*. What they all wished to know was: How is the fund going? Why don't you . . . And then followed a number of suggestions for still further rousing the city and the nation. Mr. Llewellyn Morgan suggested that the paper should print under its title the slogan "The paper standing alone", which would be one in the eye for Mr. Sedgwick; the Lord Mayor had the venerable notion of erecting a tall thermometer outside the office with £500,000 at the summit and the ball of mercury showing where the fund had got to. The bishop thought it would be well to print an article pointing out how much it cost nowadays to build a battleship—between six and ten million pounds, he supposed—and thus show by comparison how paltry a sum was required to preserve the integrity of the *Morning Star*. With a sudden brainwave he added that it was less than a half of the cost of making the British film *Caesar and Cleopatra*. Blackwood listened to all these suggestions with great courtesy and he thanked them all warmly. But he had a slightly divided soul about them. It was one thing to approach financiers of the City of London whose business it was to raise money and float companies, and there was no loss of dignity in holding a town's meeting or approaching a handful of citizens personally as he had done. And, of course, every by-election meeting indoors or outdoors heard a reference made of some sort or other to what Llewellyn Morgan had called, "Our paper's fight for life". "It is our little David against a Press magnate Goliath," said Mr. Morgan. Mrs. Amarilla Arbuthnot, for her part, said: "It's the attempt to crush the Little Man; it's like the smashing of the little corner shop by the multiple stores. Give me my corner shop every time—give me my free public house against the tied house. Let me imbibe whatever beer I like—yes, and let me imbibe whatever opinions I like, not opinions of this or that Press dictator. The *Morning Star* is our North star, the fixed star—and it's going to stay fixed, too. Grapple with the Press Groups! Curb the Press Combines! Pulverise the Press Moguls!" Amarilla certainly let herself go! She assured her audiences that her election at the head of the poll would be a message to Press magnates that the days of expansion were over, that the great British public wouldn't stand for a favourite paper being swallowed up. "If the *Star's* such a bloomin' favourite, why doesn't it sell a million?" a voice shouted at one of her meetings. She retorted: "Because people like you haven't enough gumption to buy it." Yes, Amarilla saw herself as the special champion of the paper. And she, too, had ideas about a campaign to raise money. She proposed to Blackwood the formation of a women's committee to hold bazaars, baby shows, and beauty competitions and she wanted the paper to manufacture scores of thousands of tiny stars that people could wear in their buttonholes. Blackwood could have groaned at the prospect. He said to Lovelace: "They want me to outdo Northcliffe's sweet peas and standard bread."

"You may have to do it, Oliver. If it's that or extinction, I'll carry placards round myself."

George Wavertree, the manager, Willie Travis of advertisements, and Egbert Thompson of circulation, bobbed in and out with bright notions. George Wavertree, who never took off the bowler hat worn on the back of his head, floated in one evening to announce that John Picton, the marine engineer, had now offered to invest £10,000 if ten other citizens would do the same, and he had already tapped Sir William Prentice and William Moffatt and they hadn't had the nerve to refuse. "After all, they'll get a better divi. than they do in Dalton's gilt-edged," he said. The small cheques and postal orders were still dribbling in. "If every reader gave us a couple o' quid," said George, "we'd have a hundred and forty thousand."

"Good old George," said Lovelace, "you remind me of the Salvation Army—'throw your pennies on the drum—we're only nineteen and elevenpence off the pound'."

Willie Travis and Egbert Thompson had ideas that ran to fêtes and fireworks—"and burn the effigy of a Press magnate," said Lovelace—and to a university students' rag, to a regatta on the river, to a celebrity concert to which the Fleet Street choir might be invited, to a competition for their old and faithful readers with prizes for the oldest copies of the *Morning Star* in their possession.

What finally decided Blackwood to agree to some of the plans —not all by any means—was a visit from Frank Knowles and Seth Entwistle, Fathers of the editorial and composing chapels.

"We're a deputation," said Knowles.

"That's right, Mr. Blackwood," said Seth.

"We're a deputation from both chapels," said Knowles.

"That's right," said Seth, "from both chapels, composing and editorial."

"Editorial and composing," said Knowles firmly.

"A pretty serious business when both chapels come together," said Blackwood gravely.

"Unprecedented," said Lovelace. "Do you want me to take a note of what goes on?"

"A full note," said Blackwood. "Now, gentlemen!"

"The members of our respective chapels ——" said Knowles.

"Quite right," said Seth.

"—have passed resolutions——" said Knowles.

"Nem con," said Seth.

"—unanimously," said Knowles, "that they propose to work a week without drawing their wages."

"No wages at all," said Seth.

"But I don't——" said Blackwood.

Knowles held up his hand. "Excuse me, sir—without drawing their wages so they can invest those wages in the paper." He finished the sentence at a gallop to avoid any misunderstanding.

Blackwood got up. "Well, gentlemen, I hope you'll tell them— how grateful I am." He was both amused and touched.

Seth said: "We know it's a good investment, Mr. Blackwood."

"Safe as the Bank of England," said Knowles.

"It's just one week's pay," said Seth.

"That's all we're authorised to say, but I know some of the editorial'll put a bit more in than that," said Knowles.

"Depend on it," said Seth, "whatever the editorial do, the compositors'll not be far behind—in fact, I reckon they'll be in front."

"They should be, seeing how well they get paid," said Knowles.

"They don't get paid, anyhow, for the time they spend in pubs picking up gossip," said Seth, winking at Lovelace.

"We've every confidence—now we've set the ball rolling—that other chapels on the paper will follow suit," said Knowles.

"In fact, one or two are having meetings tonight," said Seth.

Blackwood took off his spectacles and polished them. "Thank you, gentlemen—and thank your members. We shall have to see they don't lose their money." That was all he found to say before they withdrew. But afterwards he sat looking at the ceiling and smoking his cigar for an appreciable time.

CHAPTER XXXVIII

"My dear Oliver," Mrs. Arbuthnot wrote, "I should like to come and see you privately—could I come soon after my lunch-hour meetings? I know you're not usually in as early as that, but it is rather important. What a wicked old man Fortinbras is—all this codology about the Press. Why do you give him so much space? I'm the one you should report *verbatim*. Send a message to my committee-rooms. With love, Amarilla."

He wrote in reply: "My dear Amarilla, Come at three tomorrow. Yours ever, O.B." She was, he supposed, in a somewhat wrought-up state. Every woman candidate he had ever known became something of a prima donna when fighting an election and, in addition, got worn out. You made six or seven speeches a day, were managed in the style of a prize fighter, rosetted like a winning mare, your time apportioned as if you were royalty, your words reported like those of a Cabinet Minister—how could anybody withstand the impact and remain normal? However, he could easily come in to town earlier. Hannah was still in London —she was returning in two days' time when Bob would be up for the week-end—both she and Bob had written about seeing Mrs. Tremayne on the stage. Bob said the play wasn't up to much but she was all right—if she were able to sing and dance he thought she'd give Cicely Courtneidge a run for her money. Hannah was detached on the stage performance—thought Mrs. Tremayne hadn't made up her mind whose school she belonged to—Marie Tempest's, Athene Seyler's, Yvonne Arnaud's or Hermione Baddeley's—not that she approached their class. They had had supper together afterwards, Hannah said, and had driven down, accompanied by Sedgwick's nephew and heir, Harry Sedgwick, to Mr. Sedgwick's country house where, she said, the sheets were a palish-green and her maid was French. "The nephew and Mr. Sedgwick were, of course, keenly interested in whether you will be able to raise the money and asked what I thought. I simply said you had never been interested much in money until now. We played poker for an hour before going to bed and I won two pounds. I didn't sleep much—the room seemed too hot and the sheets too luxurious, apart from everything else. The men left early for the office, but Polly and I stayed till the afternoon, bathing and reading. She likes you, I fear, a great deal better than me. She was very annoyed to find that he had given me a cigarette-case—I didn't tell you, but I lost mine in the train on the way down—I must have left it on the table in the restaurant car and it vanished—as things do nowadays. She thinks you one of the most distinguished men she has ever met—says you could play Abraham Lincoln to perfection. Bob is the next man on her list of beaux—but she cannot get over his being so different from you. She harped on this a vast deal—especially after she found out about the cigarette-case. I suspect Bob has taken her out to supper once or twice—she has the woman of forty's passionate delight in the man of thirty—but even this could not account for her volubility on this subject of lack of resemblance. She let fall Rex's name, but I did not take her up on it. He danced with her, you will remember. Bewitched with you and Bob, angry or jealous of me, I wonder what she will say when she next meets Bob. I should think she may say anything. But perhaps it does not matter. I have sometimes thought how strange it is that one's body, being so soft and vulnerable, should endure so long unbroken in this world of iron and steel objects rushing to and fro wildly; and in some way, you and I have been vulnerable to gossip yet seem to have escaped fairly well—until now! I've been thinking while I've been away of what you will do if you do not manage to raise the money. Queer—how little I've thought of that so far. I suppose we could live very simply and travel a little

—and you could write a book—if you could unwind yourself. All these years you have been as a clock too tightly wound, always with the hand of duty screwing you up before you have a quarter run down, and striking the hours and the quarters with inexorable regularity. I could have screamed sometimes, and I suppose I have done—metaphorically. To carry it a stage further, we've been a clock with a man and woman attached—when he goes in, she comes out. Do you know what I mean? I don't know why I ramble on like this. Sometimes I think I've made a discovery about myself —and then again I know I probably haven't. And yet again I don't know at all. Goodbye, dear. I shall see you on Friday—or I suppose I mean when you wake up on Saturday morning. With love, Hannah.'' Blackwood had received this letter and Amarilla's note on the same day. Hannah did not usually write at this length and he wondered if anything had happened to her—something between her and Sedgwick perhaps? That phrase—the heat of the room *apart from everything else*—did she write it without purpose or meaning—or was it deliberate and, if deliberate, brutal? She had not been devoid of brutality in the past, when he had sensed she was suffering acutely, and lashing out like an animal wounded. It was true what she said about not thinking much of what would befall if he left the paper; they had discussed it little; he, too, had shut it out. And, of course, he had been engrossed in the fight, and still was. Time enough to look to the future if the worst happened. A long rest?—a time unbroken by days and the day's work and exacting tasks? To grow old and read and read yet again and study—and learn all those things life had given him no pause to find? To dive deep down into history and the past, to feed on books like a hungry man who found himself in a valley of plenty, a valley of sunlight and warmth and soft airs? To spend night after night at the theatre and to journey abroad listening to fine music, to wander in the art galleries of the world drinking it in, not with the stern critic's eye who will write of it, but absorbing it, slowly, gently, restfully. Would he ever want to see a newspaper again, hear a radio announcement? Not for a long while, not till the river of time had been bearing him away for endless days, not until he had had enough of nothing; and it was hard to think that that would ever be.

CHAPTER XXXIX

LOOKED AT FROM Mr. Sedgwick's point of view, the evening when he took Hannah Blackwood to the theatre and afterwards down to his country house was rather confused; in its way rather exciting, rather amusing, rather—illuminating?—well, illuminative of women's character. Up to a point everything went remarkably well. The dinner at the Savoy was delightful; nothing could have been more charming than the way in which she accepted his modest gift of the gold cigarette-case. She had been surprised, of course. It had been only three hours earlier that he had learned over the telephone of her loss—that had been rather well-timed too, that little conversation with her at her hotel soon after she arrived. She had not, of course, intended to tell him she had lost her cigarette-case—he knew women well enough for that—the fact had slipped out in momentary irritation, in comment on the general state of the nation's honesty, a view he thoroughly shared. Why! in some of the West End clubs you read notices these days warning you to be careful of your clothes! Imagine that! However, here was a gesture of Fate, a heaven-sent opportunity for him to repair the loss; and Colonel Watson had within an hour brought back to Sedgwick's room at Sedgwick House three or four gold cases to choose from. Ah! how delightful it was to be able to do this sort of thing, how much more blessed to give than to receive! Within a second hour her initials were engraved on it—with a flourish—a flourish on that completely plain but delicate case. "H.B." They looked very fine, very fine indeed. Rather better, he must confess, than his own, "S.S.", which, especially during the late war, had borne an unfortunate connotation and had led, he was told by his spies, to many ribald comments in the reporters' room. Ah well, the price of fame! The time had come during the dinner that he had offered her a cigarette, and after taking one himself had gently but firmly placed the case alongside her plate. "Do you like it?" . . . . "Lovely," she had said. She was radiant, after the champagne, her complexion rosy and tinted most hauntingly with blue, her eyes holding that yellow tint of golden wine in them. That was what he had thought then, the vein of—was poetry too strong a word?—rising in him. "I'm so glad, Hannah," he had said. "It's for you." . . . "For me?" . . . Did anybody ever catch her breath so frankly, so charmingly? "Oh! but——" He thought for a second she was going to say she couldn't possibly—and was immediately ashamed of himself for attributing such conventional thoughts to her, for what she in fact said was: "But how perfectly charming of you! How on earth did you—in the time?" . . . "Ah," he had said, "to do something for you, Hannah, the swiftest aircraft in the world would be all too slow!" So there it was, executed with—finesse? the Sedgwick touch? And presently she had offered him another cigarette from the case with an amused air of pride and proprietorship. No wonder he had ventured when placing her wrap about her shoulders in the car to allow his arm to linger for a moment or two round that beautiful shoulder so firmly—yet how profoundly excitingly—moulded. His thoughts flew .to Blackwood for a moment—how had he kept his sanity in his tragic predicament? As for Hannah, how cruel the gods had been, how unutterably cruel; and with what genuine feeling of generosity, compassion, doing a fellow mortal a good turn, might not a man act as, well, up to a point, possibly that lightweight character Dryden had acted. He sighed, and placed the lightest of rugs across her knees. She had not, of course, made any response to his caressive touches, his use of her name Hannah, his most obvious—he hoped they were obvious—manifestations of feeling, affection, regard. But he had not been altogether surprised at that, although disappointed perhaps. At the same time she had vouchsafed no signs of displeasure, of finding his attentions too—demonstrative? He was sincerely moved, very sincerely moved indeed. Neither Alice Collins nor Polly Tremayne had ever moved him in quite this way—for one thing they had not the—maturity? the strength? the abounding vitality? to match his own. He suddenly said—it was almost forced out of him—"Did you read that book on Ruskin lately?—that poor unfortunate woman. Could you imagine anything more awful? A marriage that is no marriage—these poets, intellectuals, artists of indeterminate sex. . . ." Hannah had said: "Yes, I know. . . ." He had continued: "Of course, any man worthy of the name would release a woman at once—when he found himself . . ." She had said: "Perhaps she didn't wish it—not for some time—she may have thought he had work to do in which she could help him. . . ." "Oh," he had said with great heartiness, "I don't think a fellow should trade on a woman's loyalty—and—well, heroism—to this extent. And," he had said, "any woman finding herself in this tragic situation could be forgiven for seeking such consolation as her spirits and nature demanded—in order to keep her sweetness and good humour." That sounded to him the soul, the acme, of reasonableness, and he would have liked to know what she thought of it. But the Fates had arranged that at roughly this moment they should arrive at the theatre. What seemed of importance—then—was that she didn't demur to what he had—with such feeling, being on women's side—enunciated. The evening continued to be an immense success—*Forgotten Episode* touched lightly on illicit love, investing it with the aroma, the glamour, that is customary in the theatre, making amusing and innocent that which in real life can be touched with the sardonic. Yes, Hannah, he was sure, had enjoyed it all quite as much as he did. Looking back, his mind was inclined to leap over the visit to Polly's dressing-room, and the vivacity of Polly, edged, he thought, with a sharpness in her badinage that was not altogether usual—to leap over the journey home during which, with a feeling of magnanimity, he sat closer to Polly than he did to Hannah; to pass lightly by the game of poker during which he did his level best to see that Hannah won a trifling sum; and to go to the final walk in the garden he had contrived to secure with Hannah before they turned in. Polly, with what he suspected was a little pique (was her sixth sense at work, he asked himself?), had said yawningly that she was tired and had gone to her bed remarking—rather pointedly—that she hoped nothing would disturb her. He had thought this rather uncalled for, but, really, of course, nothing suited his mood better, nothing. A late walk in a garden inevitably enables you—nay, it almost demands that you should—throw a protective shield of support and warmth round any lady—that is, if she is reasonably young and not biting your head off in argument. If the evening had grown chilly—as this had—that, in his opinion, was no disadvantage; and he had every excuse for holding her arm with some firmness and bending his head towards hers. Moving in and out of the path of light, their feet crunching the gravel, their hips lightly brushed against one another—and how delicious he had found this experience, how inexpressibly stimulated and kindled he was! The words leapt into his mind—

it was not, of course, the first time he had used them on such an occasion as this:

Let those love now who never loved before
Let those who always loved, now love the more . . .

and he had murmured them, giving her hand an additional squeeze. She had laughed softly and then had, rather inexplicably —or was it truly inexplicable?—might it not have been deliberate? —yawned lightly and murmured that the hour grew late. He had been solicitous at once, had upbraided himself, apologised for his shortcomings as a host, and, putting an arm round her, had guided her towards the Gothic door as though devils or footpads might at any moment spring upon them. The house was quiet, awfully still and silent, so that as they parted on top of the Regency staircase, he was constrained to whisper his hopes that she would sleep well. "And you," she had returned gently. . . . "I have a most amusing book," he had said, "I would like to lend you—in case you are restless—the new Evelyn Waugh. . . ." She had smiled and gone her way. And now with what amazing speed—and yet what immense care—he had prepared himself for this visit which might prove a voyage to the stars, to Elysium, to—no matter! How slow his fingers were, how stiff the collar, how intractable the shoe laces, how fast the stubble on his chin appeared to have grown since the morning—had he time?—yes, he really must shave! Oh, ten thousand devils—a cut! And where in God's name was the eau de Cologne—damn that valet, he had often thought of sacking him and now he must veritably go! Ah! There! Oh, rather too much, but still. . . . There now! He hadn't been very long—softly, softly —really, how absurd, in one's own house—Polly, after all, would be asleep—damn it, she ought to be, unless the little beezum had purposely lain awake, but if she had, confound her, she must take the punishment that the eavesdropper meted out to himself—herself. . . . Well, now, the book under his arm, negligently, almost humming a bar or two—this was the door—damn it, *was* this the room—the Villier's room—they had put her in? Why in heaven's name had he not made sure? Never for long years had his heart pounded like this. Extraordinary—fantastic—it was too absurd. Was all still? Yes, yes, all still. . . . What was it Henry VIII said in that film? "The things I have done for England!" The very antithesis of this occasion. Ah, that was better—now he could smile, now he was his accustomed self—well, almost, almost. He would tap discreetly—no, damn it, he would not. He would turn the handle boldly—so. And yes—he was in—and this indubitably was the room; and Hannah was there, sitting up in bed, looking quite adorable—and reading—quietly, calmly reading, as though there was all the time in the world! She had turned and smiled at him. "Oh," she had said, "you really should not have bothered— Sam." With what ecstasy he had heard her use his name! With what a sense of triumph he had advanced upon her, gazed down rapturously at her, inquired playfully what she was reading. She had held the book up for him to see—Tolstoi's *Anna Karenina*. That, he realised now, was the first intimation of things going a little astray—the reading of that tragic tale of illicit love—that wretched creature who had flung herself in front of the train. . . . "Thank you so much, Sam," she said again, "you have given me a lovely evening." And she had yawned in the middle of it, so that a little water—a tear or two occasioned by the yawn—came into her eyes. "I'm so sorry," she said; "I suppose it's because I'm so tired. You must be tired, too—Sam." "Oh no," he had said, "not at all—I never feel tired at this hour of the night." And then the second intimation—a feeling that standing here motionless he was making himself just the smallest trifle—ridiculous, was it? He had placed the book he had brought down on her table, and looked long at her and she at him, and then, once more, she had begun a yawn and placed a hand before her mouth—not, mark you, a slender hand, yet a hand he had an almost uncontrollable desire to seize—but alas! she had suddenly moved it to her table and adjusted the bedside clock—turned it a trifle so that she could see the time. And now, on an impulse, feeling the opportunity was positively racing away, he had taken the plunge, and said rather hurriedly: "You remember, Hannah, what I was saying just before we got to the theatre—that no woman who had been harshly dealt with by Fate could—that she might well feel justified —in accepting the devotion. . . . Hannah, my dear—my heart, all my heart would go out to such a woman. . . ." And he had turned his burning eyes—he had had no doubt afterwards that his eyes had certainly burned. . . . And then—he recalled what she said—and what he had said. So far as he could remember, it was this:

"Yes, I knew that was what you had in mind."

"And you realise my sincerity, Hannah?"

"Oh yes."

"And well . . . my dear . . . it would give me inexpressible delight to prove my . . . devotion to you. . . ."

"I am—deeply touched—and were I—in such a position—as the woman you have in mind—I do not know how I should be able to withstand you . . . but as it is . . ."

At that precise moment—it stuck in his mind, the drama of it—the curtain had moved, rustled by the wind, and the noise had startled them—only in an infinitesimal way, certainly, but all the same. . . . And he had realised that the adventure—no, hardly an adventure—was over without having truly begun. And then, with a strange—an extraordinarily strange—feeling of —rectitude?—he had said: "Good night—then—Hannah," and had stooped over her to kiss her, and she had turned her cheek to him—in the friendliest way, but yet, her cheek—saying, "Good night, Sam—and thank you so much—for the book. Would you —would you mind putting up the window just another inch or two?" "Certainly," he had said, and he had gone to the window and made a great noise pushing it up—gloried in the noise, revelled in it, as if he were announcing: "There—all of you listening! Nothing has happened, nothing at all, Hannah and I are the best of friends, but no more, not in the least, nor had we—I—ever the least intention of being anything more—no!" He had turned then and smiled broadly at her, his composure restored, had touched his fingers to her and withdrawn. But the desire to make a noise had suddenly left him. He opened the door discreetly, walked softly back to his own room, looked at himself in the glass and thought: "Well, by God—that was very interesting, a new experience; we live and learn. And—she was lying like hell, unless I'm a Dutchman. Have I been had, as Old James would say?" He examined the cut on his chin. He hoped Polly would not visit him very early in the morning and notice it—Polly, he was afraid, was at the moment capable of taking the worst possible view of it. He climbed into bed and lay pondering. Ah! There was one thing—he could now use any devices he could think of to outwit and defeat Blackwood with a freer conscience than if he had—well, if he had had a rather more sleepless night than he was now going to enjoy. And with that he smiled and rolled over.

CHAPTER XL

The editorial offices along the corridor of the *Morning Star* were deserted at the time Mrs. Arbuthnot called to see Blackwood. It was about three o'clock. Not till about four would strange, odd characters with a worn, casual, hard-up air, pockets bulging with newspapers and books, begin to climb the stairs. The place slumbered in the warmth, and shafts of sunlight turned the dust into a haze of diamonds.

Blackwood, who was feeling slumbrous too, walked down the corridor to meet her. "Well, Amarilla, I suppose you've been leavening the unleavened bread?"

"I hope so, dear. These meetings at the dock gates—I was in competition with a shunting engine which had a clanging bell." She took his arm and held onto it. "I'm worn out, dear. Thank God there's only another few days to go!"

"Never mind, Amarilla. You're going to get your heart's desire." He sat her in the ancient leather armchair on the right of his desk and took scrutiny of her. She certainly looked tired. She had rouged her lips and cheeks a little, a task at which she was never expert, and she now resembled a broken-down old actress. Her clothes were rather more sombre than usual as if she had held down her wild tendencies, but this was offset by a flaring red bow in her hat and an enormous red rosette on her bosom. When she closed her eyes for a second and her mouth opened, it showed the inner side of her lips free from paint, lending her, he thought, a ravaged look. He got up and went over to the electric kettle.

She heard the chink of cups and opened her eyes. "What are you doing, dear?"

"I have an overpowering desire for a cup for tea."

She said quickly: "You think I need one. Thank you, dear. But I never believed you could do it."

"The immortal Lovelace is usually in charge—but I can just manage to do it—when I have to." He put the kettle on and came back. "What have you been telling the dockers?"

"That when the devil is sick, the devil a saint would be."

"And who's the devil in this connection?"

"Fortinbras—and lesser little Satans, the Press magnates."
She was sitting up now with a light in her eye.

He said, smiling: "Mr. Fortinbras has his points, Amarilla."

"Points, dear? His only points are the two on the end of his
horns." She laughed. "I must use that."

He put his feet up on the desk. "He made an interesting
suggestion to me the other evening."

"You mean he came to see you, Oliver?"

"Yes."

"I hope you used a long spoon, dear."

"He had an idea of how I could get the money for the paper."

"The wicked old hypocrite!"

"You must not allow your inveterate dislikes to throw things out
of focus, Amarilla." He spoke banteringly and went back to the
kettle and began to put tea into the pot.

She called across: "You don't know the half of it, dear."

"Why?"

"You ask your precious Welsh Liberal. He's been nearly
knocked sideways twice in his little loudspeaker car by their
lumbering publicity van."

"Deliberately?"

"Oh, they always apologise afterwards—but he *thinks* it's
deliberate."

"I'll send somebody down to see him. Have they gone for
you?"

"Nothing worse than placards torn down and disturbances at
meetings."

He said drily: "Your friends are usually very good at those
things themselves, Amarilla." He poured out the tea and brought
it over.

"You're too good to be alive," she said; "seeing both sides all
the time."

"You mean your party would prefer me dead?" he said,
smiling.

"I didn't mean that," she said seriously, looking out of the
window.

She sipped her tea and he sat watching her, feeling warmed
by her company and her frank regard for him—sometimes em-
barrassingly frank. His own affection was genuine enough. He

278

drank his tea, smiling quizzically to himself, glad that she would soon be an M.P., for there seemed no doubt she would get in. She'd be better than most, for all her wildness.

"I don't know how to begin," she said. He saw she was troubled. She put the cup down on the floor and dabbed her mouth nervously, so that her lipstick smeared her cheek.

"What is it? Take your time." What on earth was it? Was she going to leave Walter?

"It's about you, dear."

"Me? Well, don't worry about *me*."

"It's something they're saying about you." She was leaning forward, fiddling with her handkerchief.

"I daresay they say a lot about me, bricks from both sides. Don't worry—truly, Amarilla."

But she kept on peering up into his face. "It isn't like that, Oliver—it's—it's about you and Bob and Hannah—and, I suppose, somebody else."

"I see." He was grave now. He knew he had begun to suspect this. His heart thudded more slowly, more heavily. "All right. Tell me, then." He cupped his chin in his hands and stared at her moodily.

"It's being said you are not Bob's father at all—that it's all very well to——" She stopped, and looked down at her restless hands.

"Go on, dear." She flushed at his use of the word "dear"—he had never used it before. She knew he must be deeply disturbed, which upset her the more.

"That it's all very well to be so high and mighty—so superior—putting everybody in their place in your articles——"

She stopped again, took a breath and let it go in dribbles.

"Yes, Amarilla—go on, please." He was already calmer—so this was really it—well, it had been a long time coming——

"First, they say, there was your son—fined for assault—no better than he should be—a bit of a Fascist——"

"Sounds like the Communists getting busy. Yes?"

"And then—then your pretence that your son is yours when he's not. . . . Oh, Oliver, such foulness, such baseness, how dare they? How dare they?" Tears were in her eyes and began to run down her nose and cheeks. She stared at him, not heeding them. He was perfectly calm now—surprised at himself. He leaned forward, took the soiled handkerchief from her fingers and wiped the tears away himself. He didn't say anything. He got up and walked across the room, returned and crossed again. He was thinking: "I wonder what set this going *now*? Who could profit by it? What purpose——" He could look at it now, quite outside himself, almost enjoy the drama in it.

He returned to his chair, cupped his chin again.

"Amarilla, how do you come to know about this?" He spoke like a cross-examiner.

"I had to tell you, dear." She was half expecting anger.

"I know. You were quite right to tell me. Where does it come from?"

"My agent, Bill Stafford. Bill got it from one or two canvassers —it's being said in pubs."

"Does he think it's malicious—or just gossip for the sake of gossip?" He was examining it now judicially.

She opened her eyes wider. "But, Oliver, how could it be anything *but* malicious—done to injure the paper's campaign for money, to injure me because I'm standing up for the paper. . . ."

A trace of a smile crossed his face. "All *three* candidates are standing up for the paper."

"Oh, but, Oliver——" A troubled frown crossed her face. "You must see, dear—this doesn't happen at this time for nothing—it can't be just an accident——"

"Why not?"

"Why *not*? But, Oliver—this is politics—this——"

"It *could* be an accident—almost—I mean that it happens at this time. Of course, I'm in the news far more just now—we're making people take notice of the paper—and then Bob's case in court. You weren't there—you won't remember—Dryden was mistaken by the magistrate for Bob's father—a number of people heard and saw that—took a good look at them— that could have set it off. You see?" He had gone on ruminatively, piecing things together.

Amarilla heard him, watched him, spellbound, uncomprehending—disappointed. She said, but now in a quiet, small voice: "But it's a horrible slander, dear—on you—on Hannah— it's a wicked lie—it's the worst thing I've ever heard done in an election." Tears were in her eyes again.

He sat brooding now, his face heavy and sorrowful.

She said: "Something ought to be done, dear."

He shook his head. "I don't think so."

"But it's actionable, dear, if we can pin it down to some-body."

"No, no. More harm than good."

She said, exasperated: "You'd fight if it were anybody else, dear —you've always fought—to get justice done."

He didn't answer.

"If it were me they were saying it of—you'd flay them alive—or try to."

He smiled for an instant at her.

She said: "If they get away with this they'll go on saying it for years, dear. Every time you do or say anything they don't like, they'll rake it up."

"They'll get tired."

"They may not. And those who love you will want it stopped."

He thought: "Those who love me—yes." He looked at her almost sternly.

She met his eyes. She said quietly: "*I* love you, Oliver. Did you know?"

He saw her eyes suffused with tears, her face stricken. He leaned over and placed his hand on her hers and she gripped his hand convulsively. He nodded, then: "I knew you had an affection for me—as I have for you. But—it's no good, Amarilla—no good at all." He rose and walked across the room, there and back swiftly.

She said as he came towards her again: "It's always good to love somebody, dear. Surely." Her voice was choking her.

"Not in this case, dear."

"I have asked for nothing, Oliver—nor do I."

He went and sat in his chair again and put his head in his hands resting his elbows on the desk. He spoke down to the desk. "You see, Amarilla——" he said.

"Yes, dear." She spoke eagerly, trying to help.

"You see, Amarilla—what they say is true."

"True?" She scarcely breathed it.

"True, Amarilla. I was wounded in the First World War, so that—it was impossible for me to have children. Hannah and I were very much in love—had been for some time. She was—heroic about it. I was—weak perhaps in allowing her to marry me." He

281

paused there, still staring at his desk, noting the doodle he had drawn on his pad the night before.

"Yes, Oliver—yes, dear. . . . Oh, I'm so terribly sorry, Oliver." The voice came to him from what seemed a long way off.

He went on: "So—there came a time—Hannah wanted children—needed children. And we both decided—she should have one. So you see, Amarilla——"

Amarilla moved off her chair on to her knees and slid forward gropingly, arms outstretched, until she rested on his lap and lay there weeping.

"Come, my dear," he said. "Come—it's not as bad as that." But even as he said it, he knew it was.

CHAPTER XLI

WHEN BLACKWOOD AWOKE on the Saturday morning, his mind was resolved. From the time Amarilla had broken down and wept, he had turned it over. Perhaps Amarilla would be, in her fashion, more comforted now, knowing that even if things had been different between them, even had he loved her, frustration would have been her lot. She had wept and he had held her in his arms—for the first time in their lives he had held her, sitting in his chair, soothing her like a child. He saw how incomprehensible it would have seemed if any member of his staff had walked in; they had not; and, anyhow, when the event was grave enough, nothing mattered in the shape of what people thought. He could remember as a subaltern shouting at a major of artillery who was wheeling his horse among troops in a reckless fashion—near Guinchy corner on the Somme, that was—a winter's day in 1916. What a lifetime ago! Yet, in its way, mixed up with all this, for it wasn't long after that that he was wounded and narrowly escaped what Milton called—"Grim Death, my son and foe". Well, this piece of death which had fallen on him and robbed him of his son, in yielding him, Blackwood, the portion of his life, had killed his son. Aye, killed him. Well, there it was; and they had made a counterfeit, an impostor, played a kind of trick, a trick in its fashion on Bob and the world, defrauded the law, falsely registered him—for how could they do otherwise? Call him born out of wedlock, stamp him at birth, put a seal on him? No. Who was it called a lie the truth in masquerade? He had remembered that thought at the time. Fate had dealt harshly by them, and they had reacted—forcibly. Yes. Too violently? Perhaps. But suppose Hannah and Dryden had been married before he knew Hannah —unpleasant enough thought—and Bob had been born to them and soon afterwards they'd been divorced and he had married Hannah? The position would have been much as now, and Bob might well have grown up till school age, looking on Blackwood as his father. And then, no doubt, one day, with names to be signed, used, the truth would have been told him. But, as it was, the arguments against had always reared their heads: why meet troubles halfway? Why upset the boy? Why take from him that feeling of security and trust? Why throw his mind into ferment over his mother and another man, for who could tell how an adolescent boy might take that? But now the situation was different. Bob was a man of the world, versed in the follies and frailties of mankind. Moreover, if what Hannah had hinted at was true, then Mrs. Tremayne might traffic in hints and probings and suspicions which Bob would find of the intensest discomfort; and Sedgwick himself. If the money to buy the *Morning Star* were forthcoming and the paper eluded him, would he in his irritation, wittingly or unwittingly, say something which might enrage Bob?—for his temper could be ungovernable. That danger existed now in Greycastle. Suppose Bob, drinking in the Grand Hotel bar, over-heard gossip. . . . No, no, he had better be told. "The tempest in my mind doth from my senses take all feeling else save what beats there." Well, the tempest was eased once the question was resolved.

This was the first time he had seen Bob since Bob had returned to his flying after the magistrate's court case. In the afternoon they went down into the garden together—a blazing hot afternoon. They both liked sun. A fighter aircraft was cavorting in the sky, noisy, venomously playful.

"Getting ready for it," said Bob laconically, shading his eyes. "Makes me feel old." He stretched himself luxuriously. "An old 'bus driver—that's all I am—all I am. Good show!" He smiled and closed his eyes.

Blackwood said: "I'm glad it was no worse over the fining business, Bob."

Bob grunted amiably. "I dare say it's set me back a bit. But—can't be helped. Life in the raw." He was talking with closed eyes, enjoying the heat. "Have you met old Frederick Pick, father?"

"Just met him."

"I'll bet he's got a nasty taste in his mouth through licking his master's boots—I'll bet he has. I say, what a place Sedgwick's is compared with the old *Morning Star*—all commissionaires and concrete. Seeing Sedgwick was like seeing the Grand Mogul— surprised me the doors didn't open before me of their own accord as they do in Hollywood. He himself isn't so bad—I rather like the old sod. Fine little cocktail bar in his room." He grinned to himself. "Like an Air Marshal who's never been off the ground—if such a thing existed."

"Could you work for him?"

Bob pondered that. "Well, easier than you could, I daresay. But—no, I shouldn't think so—unless I were starving. I should be no great shakes anyway; my sales-talk would be hopeless. It's a gift, that sort of thing. Now *I* had a rear-gunner who, prewar used to sell sets of wonderful account books to little iron-mongers—books the ironmongers couldn't have used in a million years. He damn' nearly sold *me* a set. But he wasn't keen on going back to the job—it didn't arise, actually—he got shot up."

They fell silent. Over the hedge, on the links, they heard a voice saying: "I don't know what's the matter with me today. . . . Last week my irons weren't too bad . . ."

Blackwood said musingly: "From links all over the country an omniscient Being could hear that plaint going up—'I don't know what's the matter with me today' . . ."

He was reluctant to begin this talk—and it seemed a little fantastic to plunge into grave matters in this sunlight, with golfers passing outside the gate. Yet he had chosen the garden deliberately—he had had a desire to get out of the house where his talk with Hannah had been uncomfortable. She had been against telling Bob. Late in the forenoon, while Bob was tinkering with his car—which gave him more pleasure than anything else—Blackwood had asked Hannah if she would come into his study for a moment.

He had begun by speaking of what she had written in her letter about Mrs. Tremayne and Bob—the hints Mrs. Tremayne had let fall. To his surprise Hannah now said she thought it didn't matter—Mrs. Tremayne was a garrulous lady. He had then told her of his visit from Amarilla and of the gossip running through the Riverside constituency which had led him to the conclusion that Bob should be told. Hannah had taken that more seriously, had pondered its origin, had said she supposed it sprang from something Dryden had said to Polly Tremayne—"for," she had said, "I have never told a soul in my life—have you?"

For a moment he was startled by this question. Then, his impulse towards frankness always being strong, he had said: "Not until Amarilla came to see me."

"You told Amarilla?"

"Yes."

"But why? You could have denied it—as I have always done." She felt he had let her down—betrayed her—she saw again the scene when she had stoutly lied to Sedgwick—she forgot now that she had done it partly in self-defence, to ward him off. "Why did you tell her?" She faced him accusingly.

Outside he could hear Bob whistling "Lili Marlene". He hated the subterfuge but he could hardly reply that it was because Amarilla said she was devoted to him and that he thought it best, once for all, to prove to her how hopeless it was. He didn't feel he could reveal Amarilla's confidence in that way. So that he said: "She was trying to persuade me to take action about the gossip, action to which I was opposed—besides, she's a good friend of ours and can be trusted completely."

"Not much good," she said, "my lying my head off when you —go and do this."

"Why, Hannah? Have you been asked point-blank questions, too?"

Hannah wished she hadn't said what she had, but she couldn't withdraw now. So she said: "Next door to it."

"Not by Amarilla?"

"No—of course not."

She was silent and walked to the window, where she began to straighten the long velvet curtain with vigorous tugs. When she had finished she stood looking out on to the garden, her back taut, her thumbs held tight inside her fingers.

He asked: "Was it Sedgwick?"

She turned and faced him. "Yes, it was." There was a touch of defiance in it which depressed him. His thoughts ran to her letter—"sometimes I think I've made a discovery about myself —and again I know I probably haven't."

He said: "Well, with all the fire directed on us from—various quarters—Bob had better know where he is."

"Not necessarily."

He groaned inwardly. Here was the old Hannah back again, as if the cordiality in her letter had never been.

He repeated her words irritably: "Not necessarily? Do you agree or don't you?" He knew this was provocative but, anyhow, reason seemed to be wasted on her.

She replied savagely: "No, I don't. And I wish you'd remember he's more my son than yours."

He said fiercely: "That's the pity of it." They had stared at one another, Hannah surprised at the speed with which he had lost his temper, Blackwood surprised, too, but not altogether regretting it—might do no harm in the long run and, anyhow, it was an agreeable feeling, letting himself go.

Hannah had suddenly asked, coldly, abruptly: "Do you mind if I use the car? I want to go into Greycastle."

He hadn't answered that—she knew she need not ask. He had merely rejoined: "I shall tell Bob. It has to be done."

She had said: "You'll please yourself, I suppose."

There had been a long space of quietness in the garden and Blackwood now said, his thoughts going back to the rear-gunner: "Was he killed, Bob——"

"Who? Oh—old Washbrook—yes—well, died of it later on. He was better out of it—too knocked about."

The chink of golf clubs came from beyond the hedge and the mutter and sharp cackle of voices. A burst of laughter rang out, brittle. The aircraft zoomed down the sky. Blackwood waited till the garden was stiller. A low hum came from bees among the roses. He said: "I wanted to have a talk with you, Bob——" He stared long at Bob, who still sat, eyes closed. This was it, as Bob would say. But Bob had no idea.

"Yes, I know—is it about going back into the R.A.F.?"

He had to answer that. "No—why, were you thinking of doing that?"

286

"Somebody'll have to, I suppose—but I decided against it for the present, anyhow. I thought that might be what you wanted to know."

Blackwood said more urgently: "No—it's about you and me and your mother." That seemed appallingly vague. He brought himself nearer, almost gritting his teeth: "I got hit—a devil of a time ago."

"Yes—I know—it still gives you hell sometimes."

For half a second Blackwood wondered if Bob were stalling, wincing away. He said: "Well—it put me out of action—in certain ways. Made me no catch in the marriage market."

Again it was as if Bob were glancing the shaft away. He said: "Oh, I don't know. I think you've done darned well—you've made the paper——" Bob stopped there, and now he turned in his chair and looked hard, through his creased eyes, at Blackwood.

Bob now sat up slowly in his chair and Blackwood decided this was the first moment that Bob had really grasped the seriousness of what was being said. He felt better for knowing that—they knew where they were now. He said, his heart for a moment banging dully at his chest: "I hope it's not too much of a surprise and shock, Bob, what I'm going to say. . . ."

Bob rubbed a forearm and looked a long way off. "No," he said, "that's all right. Carry on, father." He was frowning a little.

Blackwood said: "Knowing what you know—about the damage I got—did it ever occur to you to wonder if I really *was* your father?"

Bob's frown deepened and he screwed up his eyes more narrowly. Then, as if he had dismissed something, his face cleared. He said, "Yes, I have—off and on. A long time ago to begin with—I suppose fellows often *do* wonder if their father really is the chap. At school—when you begin to talk smut. . . . And then I was such a dud at some things—no sign of you—no brains—and—— Of course, I didn't take it seriously—not for a long time. But sometimes—thinking it over—darned little likeness between us—and—and all the rest of it." He had rambled on, Blackwood feeling he was talking to ease the situation, letting the engine run. Then Bob said: "You mean you're *not* my father —father?"

It was the repetition of the word that suddenly touched Blackwood and he said: "No, Bob." And then he added with an intensity he had hoped to keep in check, "I wish to God I was."

Bob, who seemed now much easier than Blackwood, said almost casually: "So do I, by God, so do I." As if belying that easefulness he stared up into the blue heaven and said: "Those aircraft are hopelessly out of date."

Blackwood was aching inside but, in a way, glad of the pain. He was drained, no words left in him. He lolled back in his chair and they both fell silent. After a while, a thought occurred to Blackwood and he leaned across and placed a hand on Bob's knee, lightly: "I hope this will make no difference, Bob—it won't to me—not the slightest."

"Christ, no," said Bob. "Why should it?"

No, Blackwood thought, why should it? But it might all the same. He said: "Good, Bob. After all, we've had over twenty-five years of it, haven't we?" He could smile now.

Bob looked at him and smiled, too. "Just about," Bob said.

Another silence fell for a while. Bob sat nursing an arm again and looking over the hedge. Blackwood saw him out of the corner of his eye. He didn't want to disturb him. If Bob felt he'd had enough. . . .

But Bob presently said in his abrupt, quiet fashion, without preamble of any sort, as if his mind had just got to this point: "Is Dryden the man?"

Blackwood was struck by the impersonal withdrawn tone and word—"the man". It was almost sardonic or denigratory. He replied: "Yes, Bob, as a matter of fact he is."

Bob said musingly: "I had thought that once or twice. It does explain one or two things." After another pause, Bob said: "He's a bit of a card, isn't he. I see where my wild character comes from."

They went on talking for some time, feeling a sense of release.

CHAPTER XLII

Lovelace carried in the first edition of the paper and laid it, rather damp and moist, on Blackwood's desk. He stood behind Blackwood's chair and they looked at it together. The centre column of the main page was headed:

"Socialists hold Greycastle—Majority increased 1,521— Victory for a Free Press—Mrs. Arbuthnot."

There followed a note of what she had said after her victory was announced: "Riverside has struck a resounding blow against Press monopoly, against the power of the Press magnates, against their practice day after day and month after month of colouring the news and putting it into the focus that suits them best. I have stood for the lone fighter, the *Morning Star*, against mediocrity organised in groups, I have stood for the individual and robust and independent voice of the north against the gramophone, metallic, tannoy of the south. And Greycastle has supported me in no uncertain fashion. . . ."

Mr. Llewellyn Morgan, who had lost his deposit, said that it was typical of the Socialists to have sailed to success on a raft whose planks were stolen from the Liberals and with a sail bearing a Liberal device. . . .

Major Gore-Fleming said the country was not yet fully awakened to the dangers that confronted it. The Socialists had fought the election as usual on a spurious issue. Nobody had been more cordial towards the *Morning Star* than he had. As for Mr. Fortinbras, he had not concealed his affection in spite of the way the paper had, at times, the effrontery to call him to account. . . .

Lovelace said: "The old girl did well."

Blackwood said: "She's a good fighter—if at times a wrong-headed one."

"We shall lose some publicity now the election is over." Lovelace rolled a cigarette and dribbled tobacco on to the edge of the desk, picked up fragments and began to chew them. He lit his cigarette and loped over towards the kettle. "Could you stand a cup o' tea?" He looked at Blackwood, thought he was looking tired—as he was; suspected he was weary—as he was. They on the *Morning Star* had had a lot of attention one way or another; they had, as Lovelace had said one day, been battered to death with bouquets—but nobody had come forward as yet with the other two hundred and fifty thousand pounds they still needed. Lovelace had heard—as who on the paper had not?— the gossip running through the Riverside division about the parentage of Captain Robert Blackwood.

Seth Entwistle had discussed it with him, asking: "Does he know what they're sayin', Mr. Lovelace?"

"I expect he does, Seth."

"I told one chap I'd take the nuts and bolts out of him if he said one more word."

"Good for you."

"There's been a bit o' gossip even in the machine-room."

"That's human nature, Seth."

"Disgustin' I say. Can nothin' be done?"

"It'll die down."

"I'd tie 'em in bundles o' six and throw 'em off the pier-head, I would, Mr. Lovelace."

"Good show."

"I'd fasten 'em atop o' the Rock Light and let the seagulls come and pick the flesh off their ugly faces, the eyes out o' their ugly heads and the tongues out o' their ugly mouths."

"You'd have no mercy on them, Seth?"

"Not a ha'porth. They crucified a chap a long while ago— remember? And there's them livin' 'ud crucify another."

"Too true."

"Come to somethin' else: are we goin' to get the brass, Mr. Lovelace?"

"Hope springs eternal, Seth. We've raised over half of it."

"Aye, Mr. Lovelace, but there's not much eternity about this, is there? How much time is there left—a week?"

"No more, I'd say."

"A week to—what is it?"

"Save our souls, Seth—save the world, eh?"

"It's a funny thing, Mr. Lovelace—I've often noticed it— when you get a good thing in this world, summat tries to kill it, strangle it. I've seen it in my garden—get some good roses and them green-flies are extra special terrific."

"The Almighty putting 'em to the test."

"That's right enough, Mr. Lovelace, but what if they go down under it? What if they're not strong enough? They're no worse for not bein' strong—not their fault, I mean. Look at weeds—tough as hell. I often think about it."

"Law of life, Seth."

"Law of the jungle, Mr. Lovelace."

"Braces you up, lad—makes you fight. Weeds out the frail ones."

"And the evil flourish like the green bay tree."

"They do, Seth, they do."

"Well, we shall live and we shall die—if t' dogs don't worrit us, Mr. Lovelace."

"Not much doubt about that."

"Would it—would it be any good us chaps springin' another week's wages—investin' it, like?"

"I'll ask O.B., Seth—it's a nice thought."

"Nay, it's life insurance, you might say."

"I'll ask him, Seth. . . ."

So now, as Lovelace walked across the room carrying Blackwood's cup, and spilling tea into the saucer and thinking his hand had no right to be as shaky as this, he said: "I'd a talk with Seth Entwistle last night."

"The news would be if you didn't have a talk, Richard—pour that slop into the waste-basket—that's better. Well, what had the prophet Seth to say?" He stirred his tea and sat back.

"Wants to know if the chapel should have another whip round to save the old bone-shaker."

Blackwood drank his tea, said, "No wonder your hand shakes, drinking this black stuff all day. . . . No, Richard, very kind of Seth—but we need to tap a new seam—a few hundreds get us nowhere." He smiled. "You didn't find a letter from Mr. Barclay Boddington among the correspondence today, I suppose?"

"Not a syllable."

"How much longer have we got?"

"That's another thing, Oliver. How long *have* we got? When did the old scoundrel die?"

"The twenty-third of last month."

"Sure it was the twenty-third—not the twenty-second?"

Blackwood chewed his pencil. "It was close on midnight when I left here. Must have been well after midnight when he died."

Lovelace screwed up his eyes and cast them at the ceiling.

"That gives us to the twenty-third of this month, then?" said Blackwood.

"Does it?"

"Of course. We were given a month."

"A calendar month—or a lunar month?"

"Damn it, Richard, what are you up to now?"

"It's only just occurred to me. It's very important, master."

"Yes, I suppose it is. Fetch the *Oxford Dictionary*."

Lovelace carried the tome over and found the place. They read several definitions of a month: "A measure of time corresponding to the period of revolution of the moon"—"Used as an indefinite measure of time."

"Here's a good one," said Lovelace: "'Usually the term denotes the synodical month, the period from one new moon to the next, the length of which is 29 days, 12 hours, 44 minutes, 2.7 seconds.' It 'ud be a pity if we lost the old paper by a fraction of a second, eh?"

Blackwood then said: "This is more like it: 'A month in law is a lunar month, or 28 days, unless otherwise expressed.' Our old friend Blackstone says that, confound him. But wait—what's this next bit? 'The word month to mean Calendar Month unless words be added showing Lunar Month to be intended. Act 13-14 Vict. c. 21.' Well, that's a generation or two after Blackstone, and, I take it, washes him out."

Blackwood looked at Lovelace and Lovelace ran his upper lip down over his bottom one till it nearly reached his chin. "Damned if I know," he said. "If the magistrate sends me to gaol for a month, how long is that? Isn't it four weeks? What is certain," added Lovelace, "is that if they can do us down—Sedgwick and the baronet's widow—they will. Much better raise the wind in the twenty-eight days, master."

"You have my full authority."

"Yes. The crock of gold is always at the end of the rainbow."

They lapsed into silence. Lovelace knew that Blackwood's mind in these moments was in the habit of resolving things, and coming out with a decision made, so he was not surprised when Blackwood said: "Reach that *Who's Who*, Richard." And when he had turned up the letter B, "Here we are—'Barclay Boddington: eldest son Christopher Boddington of Marley House, Rochdale, Lancashire; born 1907; educated Winchester, New College, Oxford; Captain, M.C., Royal Armoured Corps; clubs Garrick, Carlton, Beefsteak; recreations, billiards, model yachting, politics. Publications: *The Use and Abuse of the Spinnaker; Political Effervescences* (light verse); *Disrupting Influence of the Telephone on Thought Processes* (an essay). Address: Carlile Square, Chelsea; The Old Stone House, Rye, Sussex.'

"It may well be, Richard, that on this man our future depends."

"On an iridescent soap bubble, so to speak, Oliver."

"Seriously, Richard, I think you'll have to go and see him. I don't like tackling people in this way—but I see no way out."

"He won't lose his money. To hell with him! He ought to be proud to do it. I shall tell him if he wants to buy immortality, this is his safest bet. You really want me to go?"

"Yes. The situation is serious."

Lovelace growled: "This city is made o' brass. Why don't they stump up?"

"In a way they've done well enough—over a quarter of a million—it's a lot of money. And maybe I haven't banged the big drum enough—I expect they all feel sure the money will be found. What's everybody's business is nobody's business. And they don't feel passionate about the judicial line we take—not many ever do. By God, Richard, we've got to find this money. Tell London end to find out if Boddington's in Town."

"Yes. Right away." Lovelace scribbled an urgent s.g.

"When you find him—and you've got to find him wherever he is—tell him we need a quarter of a million. I daresay we could do with less at a pinch because money is still coming in—but better seize his imagination. Tell him he'll get a return on his money although we can't guarantee him how much. Tell him he'll get no control of policy, which will remain as it is absolutely, but that a Trust will be formed of which he can be one. Quite clear?"

"Shall I mention Fortinbras?"

"Yes. He put us on to him and I don't think he wanted any secrecy about it."

"Can't understand—if Fortinbras was right—why Boddington hasn't come to life off his own bat."

"I agree. But he may be an odd young man; and people are behaving strangely these days—extremely casual; put out of gear by the war, I suppose." He pulled his beard, thinking of Bob.

Lovelace asked: "If Boddington fails us, are we sunk?"

"No; but it may be very tough indeed. There are various possibilities. We could call on two or three of the independent newspapers I spoke of—in Burnham, Leeds, Edinburgh, Glasgow. I've had a mysterious letter from Henry Satterthwaite—he sent it home—asking me to make an appointment. Don't know what the old madman wants. May be something or nothing. I believe at the worst Jonathan North would throw another lifeline. I believe, too, that in extremity this city would really find the rest of the money—if we delivered an ultimatum, as we may have to do if Boddington falls down. But try him first— and let me know instantly."

"I go forth like the dove seeking a morsel of land."

"You go forth, Richard, on possibly the most important assignment of your life."

On this same evening Mr. Sedgwick spoke to Lady Molyneux by telephone. After the usual compliments had passed, he said: "My spies tell me Blackwood has raised something over half the money."

"It is shameful," she said, her voice vibrating, "the way he is touting round. I wrote to tell him so—Redvers Mornington told me how they were invited to a meeting—and positively dunned for money."

Sedgwick said: "So I hear. Hard as nails, these nonconformists, where money's concerned. But the outlook isn't very promising for him—half the money to find and less than a week to go. Did Mornington put up any, I wonder?"

"Not a penny—I advised him against it. Even *we* have never had any dividend worth mention. Greycastle people aren't so stupid as Mr. Blackwood seems to think. Who is this Jonathan North, Mr. Sedgwick, who is putting his oar in?"

"Oh, one of these radicals—a wild character. Pitboy at one time. Hates the peerage. Disappointed himself, I suppose. Is there much feeling in the town?"

"My friends sympathise with me—all the horrid publicity— and knowing you would have paid me more than this sum."

Mr. Sedgwick frowned: "Well—um—er——"

She was going on: "Can nothing be done to stop Blackwood, Mr. Sedgwick?"

"Time—inexorable time—will do it, I think. Let me see—how many days is it now? Six or seven?"

"Yes. The bishop asked me if I would consider granting an extension. Really . . . I think I was rude to him."

"Quite right. Quite right. At my end a few strings have been pulled in high places, hints that a Trust would be a good thing—and wasn't my price a little excessive? I inquired did they know a million pounds was once offered for the *Burnham Guardian*?"

"Really, Mr. Sedgwick—what business is it of theirs?"

"Exactly. Blackwood's influence, I suppose. However—won't do him any good—or avail him anything. Time marches on, as they say."

"Oh, Mr. Sedgwick—how long it takes six days to be six days in these circumstances! And if—as I pray every night—Mr. Blackwood doesn't succeed and you obtain the paper—as I profoundly hope you will—would you—consider—increasing your offer at all, Mr. Sedgwick?"

"I'm afraid the sum is clearly laid down in the will, Lady Molyneux."

"I am advised, Mr. Sedgwick, that that is only so far as Mr. Blackwood is concerned. When he is disposed of I believe it would be quite in order. . . . I was thinking of what you said about the *Burnham Guardian*—the million——"

"Of course, one doesn't really know if that was a copper-bottom offer—but I assure you, Lady Molyneux, that when Blackwood is out of the picture, I shall give the whole matter—and anything you say—my very closest consideration."

"Thank you, Mr. Sedgwick."

"Not at all. Good night, Lady Molyneux, and we will keep in touch."

"Good night, Mr. Sedgwick, good night."

Well, by God, he thought, as he put down the receiver, what a grasping old vixen she is! And what a hope she has got!

CHAPTER XLIII

M<small>R. L</small>OVELACE'S SENSE of the dramatic and the theatrical was fully engaged when he set forth on his quest. It was, as Blackwood had said, the most important mission he had ever had entrusted to him. He was an ambassador seeking a modus vivendi with a troublesome potentate; he was a salesman of an objet d'art to an American millionaire; he was a hospital superintendent seeking to move the heart of an eccentric lady of vast wealth; he was the Prime Minister bound for the Kremlin and a secret talk with Mr. Stalin; he was a foreign correspondent setting out to investigate the drug traffic in Egypt; he was a reporter given the assignment of interviewing an atomic scientist who loathed newspapers and looked on reporters as fools or liars or both; he was Montgomery going to Cairo to take over the Eighth Army; he was Jellicoe leaving harbour to intercept the German fleet; he was Nelson on the eve of Trafalgar; he was Marshall Hall entering court to defend a notorious poisoner; he was Laurence Olivier in his dressing-room making up to play Hamlet; he was the King on the morning of his coronation; he was a bridegroom driving to church for a wedding to a woman he now knew he did not love; he was the opening batsman in the deciding Test match; he was about to attempt to hole the putt that would decide whether he won the open championship; he was a young man waiting to hear the results of his medical finals; he was a playwright watching the curtain rise on his first-night—and with a distressingly large overdraft and an importunate bank manager; he was the leader of a new Government going to kiss hands on his appointment—with a war in the offing. By God, when you came to think of it, this task of his was nothing—nothing at all. All he had to do was to get Mr. Barclay Boddington to give to him, Richard Lovelace, a cove who looked as if he hadn't got change for a five-pound note—or ten bob if it came to that—the modest sum of quarter of a million pounds. Now what was this quarter of a million? First, it was money made out of soap, money made by charging all the folk (like himself) who bought soap rather more for it than it was worth. Were it otherwise, of course, Mr. Boddington would not be the rich man he was. Every time he, Lovelace, bought a shaving-stick for eighteenpence, he contributed maybe sixpence towards that quarter of a million. Whereas he, Lovelace, got his sixpences less easily. To wit, when a public library bought one of his novels he got about a shilling as his royalty and that book was read to bits for years and years—he didn't get much more than a penny a year, and probably twenty people read his immortal work for that sum—ten readers for one ha'penny. Not that he was really disgruntled about that. The wind and sun were free and the moon and the stars also, and if he were put in their class that was quite right. Mr. Shakespeare was cheaper than he, Lovelace. On the other hand, neither the wind nor the sun nor yet Mr. Shakespeare had to eat and drink. But now, the quality of the quarter of a million being clear, it was obviously desirable to deflect it into an honourable channel, use it for a purpose that would lend it distinction. Nobody could deny that the *Morning Star* would rank pretty high on the list of benefactions suitable for rich men—such as church organs, stained-glass windows, clinics, dogs' homes, ballet, art galleries, deer parks, bird sanctuaries, ancient monuments, the introduction of the metric system and the reform of English spelling. Mr. Boddington would be saving his soul alive by parting with his money. Mr. Lovelace having reassured himself in this fashion—it took very little doing—he asked himself what his best method of approach was. He was aware that his personal appearance was not impressive. Once, when entering a restaurant laden with books for review, on pausing to exchange in the goodness of his heart a greeting with the lady in the pay-box, he had been told he could not sell the books in there—"Not in here," she had said sternly. And yet—he felt in his bones that approaches by telephone or letter were not in the spirit of this quest. No. He would take his chance, arrive unheralded, like the overdue load of coal or the D.P. domestic from Austria. If he were mistaken for the man who wound the clocks or read the gas meter or, alternatively, for the tramp poet or the curate in plain clothes, he would not be mortally offended. The great thing was to make contact. As Nelson had said, no captain could go far wrong if he were to lay his ship alongside the enemy and board and take her.

A lesser man or a man wiser or a man more circumspect would have first proceeded to his hotel to leave his bag and wash his hands. Mr. Lovelace did nothing of the kind. He fortified himself with a bottle of stout at Euston and, having arrived at 6.45 p.m., he was before 8 o'clock riding down the King's Road, Chelsea, in a bus, holding his diminutive suitcase on his knee. He was bound for Carlile Square and trusting in the Almighty or his guardian angel to do the right thing. They did not fail him. The concourse of motor cars ringing the square but more particularly abutting on Number IIa, indicated that something was afoot, and when he entered the house, without explanation or hesitation, on the door being opened to his knock, he saw at once that a party was in progress. The room on the left into which he was guided by a young man who might have been either a butler or a Cabinet Minister's secretary was strewn with hats and light coats and dispatch cases, thrown down as carelessly as if the world were still an honest place, and from the rooms above came that fearful hum and crackle of conversation and laughter which makes it self-evident that you can drive motor cars on alcohol, and that the recorders of gossip, the weavers of romances, the disputants of theory, the retailers of scandal are no more downcast or disconsolate than ever they were. Mr. Lovelace entered that sea of noise, gesticulation, bumping, barging, half-hearted apology, muttered imprecation, mistaken identity, flashing teeth, grasped cocktail glasses, bolted savouries, trodden toes, delectable association with warm, soft breasts and buttocks, nods, smiles, frowns, overheard and disjointed remarks, confidences, asides, arguments, disputations, appeals, arrangements for conjugal or illicit meetings, intercourses and assignations that are the life and soul of such assemblies as this. Mr. Lovelace fitted in admirably. He appeared eccentric, rapt, benign, and he was the perfect recipient of whatever drinks were going. The menservants and maidservants blessed him, nothing passed him by, nothing was refused. In such an array of scornful and fastidious recipients Mr. Lovelace was a boon. He made the servants feel they earned their handsome wages. From time to time a few odd remarks were addressed to him. An old gentleman who looked like George Moore confided to him that "we are done away with —we are less than the ladies in Piccadilly——" A young lady of abounding charms asked him how long he thought his Irish play would run; a Polish woman of immense vivacity informed him that she had implored somebody for God's sake to turn off that loudspeaker only to find that it was not a loudspeaker at all but Mr. X., the publisher; and a wild man with a shock of grey fuzzy hair asked him if he didn't agree that M.I.5 was overdoing it and what was the right attitude to adopt when you knew your private love letters were being photographed, and did he think this arid Government was to be relied on in that sort of thing? Occasionally Mr. Lovelace, between one dry Martini and the next would murmur that he hadn't caught sight of Mr. Boddington yet, and then with a flurry of head turnings and pointings and up-spilled glasses and apologies a friendly soul anxious to help would say there he was—oh no, sorry, he wasn't—yes, by the window—no, damn it, he'd vanished. . . . During the evening it became manifest that Mr. Boddington was in turn a tall man with a beard and eyeglasses who resembled Mr. Parnell, a young elegant man with a stoop, a hectoring man with a black moustache, a shuffling Scotsman who spent his time serving a springy pair of pince-nez at his nose and seldom hitting the target; and, alternatively, that Mr. Boddington was in bed with a cold. Lovelace had one horrid moment when it occurred to him he might be at the wrong party altogether so elusive or unknown did Mr. Boddington appear to be. It was nine o'clock by the time the last guests had gone. By this time most things on which Lovelace fixed his eyes appeared to be a vast distance away and receding rapidly like shy comets. He sat himself down gingerly on the edge of one of the solitary chairs and waited, quietly and with immense dignity, albeit hiccuping softly. Nobody took any notice of him. The menservants and maidservants went on tidying up and clearing away, moving round him and about, until presently he observed another figure perched on a chair opposite much in his own attitude of dignified thought. For a moment he thought it might be his own reflection in a mirror, but no—this figure was much too fat. Mr. Lovelace turned on the figure his beatific smile and the figure beamed in return. The figure rose and waddled over. It had a high voice and small blue eyes and a large round cranium on which sparse bristly hairs grew. The clothes were of some light fabric such as tussore silk, open at the neck. The figure said: "You're not drinking anything. William, let this gentlemen have something to drink."

For the sake of peace Mr. Lovelace took another dry Martini, lifted it to his nose—and shuddered.

"I agree with you," the figure said. "It is a barbaric drink." He took the glass from Lovelace's hand and put it down on the table. "Are you feeling all right?"

"I am feeling superb," said Lovelace—"although not altogether of this world."

"I hope you are not sorry you came."

This remark placed Lovelace's wandering feet firmly on the ground.

"No," he said, "oh no. I came for the special purpose of seeing Mr. Barclay Boddington. Was he here?"

"Yes and no."

"Oh!"

"He made a liberal compromise."

" I understand he has embraced that faith."

"Embraced may be too strong a word. However . . . he was here and he was not here. That is to say he does not enjoy these parties very much and once he saw that he and his guests were of one mind about the date—it is so easy to be mistaken—he went to his club for a swim. He returned just before the end and was gratified to find that nobody had missed him. The English are an independent race—give them all they require and they ask for nothing more. They are, in that respect, like that most estimable creature, the cat. The cat is a far more suitable emblem for the English than the bulldog. Or perhaps you don't agree?"

"Not being English," said Lovelace, "I regard them with an amused and unrelenting eye. They are less than human but have godlike qualities. Realising they are at their best in adversity, God hurls His thunderbolts upon them. Whereupon they are apt to complain bitterly. By the way, is Mr. Boddington still here?"

"Sir, that is my name." Mr. Boddington bowed and Lovelace rose and bowed in return, although a trifle unsteadily.

"In that case," said Lovelace, "my quest is at an end." He added: "Though not my mission."

Mr. Boddington now brought a chair and sat down facing Lovelace in a manner that reminded the latter of the two gangsters in Mr. Edgar Wallace's play *On the Spot*. Meanwhile the clearing up went on around them. "Are you," inquired

Boddington, "from the Society of Buddhists, or the Fellowship of Model Yachtsmen or the Revolt of the Men of Letters Group?"

Lovelace said: "I am afraid I shall disappoint you. I am from the *Morning Star*. And it is very important."

"To me—or to you?"

"To both of us."

Boddington said, observing Lovelace's somewhat glassy eyes: "If you will allow me to say so, I have you at some disadvantage which a prairie oyster may remove. Or if you would prefer a swim at my club that might achieve the same purpose. By the way, what is your name?"

"Richard Lovelace."

"William, bring Mr. Lovelace a prairie oyster in the first place. Bring it up to my study. Did you write—'stones do not a prison make nor iron bars a cage'?"

"That was my namesake."

"Of course. Did you write *Stone in the Heart*?"

"Yes."

"Why did you—let us go upstairs—why did your heroine attach so little importance to chastity? That was rather old-fashioned, wasn't it? And why did you kill her off in the docks in that air raid? Down a step there and turn right."

Lovelace fell down the stairs, and when he had recovered himself, said:

"I was sick and tired of her and I was damned hard up, and wanted some money and the publisher said, 'Don't, whatever you do, let it go over a hundred thousand words'."

"Those are excellent reasons and very clearly put. Did you ever read my *Use and Abuse of the Spinnaker*?"

"No."

"Does it mean anything to you? . . . That's the best chair."

"No. Is it indecent?"

"I don't think so—although you put an idea into my head. Ah, there you are, William. Try this, Mr. Lovelace. I hope he hasn't put too much vinegar in it. Your mind will be quickly as clear as that of Mr. Fortinbras when he orates. Better? Good. What is this mission of yours? Did Mr. Blackwood send you?"

"He did."

"Do you want to interview me on why I have become a Liberal?"

"Oh no—although of course we know that people at times profess the strangest reasons. If you cared to take us into your confidence, I am sure Mr. Blackwood would be delighted to know."

Mr. Boddington's eyes roamed over the book-lined walls, his corner devoted to the poets, his remarkable collection of books on Dante, his fifty books on Napoleon and seventy-five on Horatio Nelson, his Nonesuch and Golden Cockerell treasures, his two long shelves crammed with first editions of living novelists among whom Lovelace was numbered, his five hundred books of plays, his four hundred on the two world wars and—near the floor— the lives of the British prime ministers, sandwiched among innumerable blue books. He said: "My history is a humdrum one. My father, as you know, kept a grocer's shop in Rochdale where it was borne in on him that the truth in the old adage 'where there's muck, there's money' really lay in the fact that the money could most readily spring not so much from making the muck— as most people thought—but from washing the muck away after it was produced. So he invented soft soap—hence the term soft-soaping people, meaning getting the best of them by flattery— and he hit upon soap flakes. Indeed he persuaded those hard-bitten Lancashire housewives that Monday, instead of being purgatory, was really paradise. Being unquestionably a benefactor of the truest kind, having at heart the interests of the kingpin of the community—I refer to the housewives who are being ground to powder under the heel of the successive governments of today—he undoubtedly deserved to make a fortune. Many other benefactors have deserved to make fortunes without doing so. Coming, however, from Rochdale, he took care that he was an exception. He was, as you will have surmised, hard-headed and close fisted, a teetotaller and non-smoker, a sidesman at the chapel who did not hesitate to ask for divine guidance in his business transactions. It goes without saying that he was, of course, a pillar of the Liberal Party, an adherent of the Manchester school of economics, and a man who might have become a peer of the realm had he been willing to pay Mr. Lloyd George's price. I was never quite sure whether it was that his principles were too strong or whether he thought the price too stiff; he was a man who all his life bought things wholesale. It was not unnatural, I suppose, that I should have had a slight recoil from his way of life, that I should have taken—at first—no more than a cursory interest in soap—that commodity close to godliness that has made me what I am—and that I should have turned from Liberalism to Conservatism. Greater men than I, of course, have done that. But the time came when my faith in the Conservatives was shaken. When I found, as a humble member of the Royal Armoured Corps in the Western Desert that our tanks mounted no more than two-pounder guns while the enemy had six-pounders, I was disturbed. Your faith has to be very strong when the enemy can shoot at you for a thousand yards before you can poop off at him—and there was no doubt in my mind that it was my friends the Conservatives who were principally responsible, by their failure to rearm efficiently and in time, for my being in that unfortunate predicament. It is all very well waiting in the traditional British way until you can see the whites of their eyes, but in the Western Desert the whites are very difficult to see indeed, especially when the sun is behind them, as it usually was. However, I digress. It became increasingly borne in on me, as my lamented father would have said, that, apart from my illustrious friend Mr. Fortinbras, the Conservatives are not men of any pronounced genius and that the working class to which I may be said, despite my wealth and erudition, to belong, have no strong faith in them. On the other hand, it would be hypocrisy to pretend that I lean towards Socialism. I am a patron of the arts in my modest way; I do not really enjoy laborious or boring work; I am quite certain that I was intended to be a dilletante amateur of games, politics and letters; that I am a born disciple of any Socrates or Plato who is going; and that I am quite as good a channel as any Government department—indeed, far better— for spreading light and leading and learning. I am, in fact, completely opposed to being nationalised. For me, therefore, only Liberalism remains. Mind you, I must confess to having mental reservations. I am only too well aware that the Liberal Party has a predilection for being led by Welshmen or Scots or aliens— whereas I am English to the core. I know that the party would be a more vigorous and likeable group were it to number among its leaders and devoted followers men who smoke cigars, drink brandy, own racehorses, and did not pretend they never kept their mistresses. I could wish they were not so prone to think those who take up arms against us—or, alternatively, those whose skins are yellow, brown or black—were always right and ourselves miserable sinners. I should be glad, too, if they did not fall so ready a prey from time to time to eloquent twisters, Smart Alecs and four flushers—many of them from Central Europe—whose discerning eyes perceive how gullible Liberals can be. But all this is really by the way. The Liberals are the only ones who are likely to allow me to go my own way, whose ranks will tolerate such individualists as I, who will grind down neither the rich nor the poor but damn them all indiscriminately when the need arises, and who will govern the country—if ever they get the chance, which I gravely doubt—with the judicial sense of the Lords Justices of Appeal. I would add to that, if you could bear to hear it, that the Liberals are the only people who could ever—or will ever—produce journals like the *Burnham Guardian* and the *Morning Star*—or editors like your Mr. Blackwood. But I am afraid I have been wearying you. I do apologise."

"Not at all—oh dear no."

"Then why were you asleep?"

"I was not asleep. Whenever I listen to great music I close my eyes. I, Mr. Boddington, have been listening to a Bach concerto, a Beethoven sonata, a Mozart minuet. I am uplifted, I am intoxicated, I am now screwed up to the sticking point. I am going to astonish you."

"I do not think it will be easy, but pray go ahead."

"I am going to ask you—nay, I am now asking you—at this very moment—in this very breath—for a quarter of a million pounds." Mr. Lovelace breathed hard and his eyes grew large with excitement and expectation.

"Is that all?"

Mr. Lovelace gulped. "All? Did you say—*all?*"

"Yes. Mr. Fortinbras warned me it would probably be much more. I thought it might be half a million."

"And you would have found that much?"

"Oh, I did not say that. I went no further than accustoming my mind to the idea. Like Monsieur Carpentier, I like to take a glance at the ring I am going to fight in."

"I have no doubt," said Lovelace with a wistful and placatory air, "that if you were more attracted by the larger sum than the smaller, that we could raise the request."

"Such blood of my father as still moves in my veins demurs a little to that, Mr. Lovelace. On principle, you understand."

Lovelace nodded. "I appreciate that. Either sum seems to me more money than there is in the world. I cannot believe it exists."

"My own reactions," said Mr. Boddington, "are much the same. I suppose that is because we are artists to whom a succession of noughts merely multiplies zero. But does, in fact, the money exist? I much doubt it. Businessmen easily delude themselves. At times a child could take them in. When my father floated his company he bought for himself most of the one-pound shares. Each of those shares is now worth, on the market, four pounds. To raise a quarter of a million pounds, all I should have to do would be to throw on the market—that is the term which, I must say, has an attractive note of licentious abandon in it—throw on the market just over sixty thousand one-pound shares. The public—that voracious, acquisitive, credulous entity—will, in an instant, pay the quarter of a million—in other words the anonymous public among whom will be hundreds of astute businessmen, brokers and so forth, will subscribe three-fourths of the sum the *Morning Star* requires, and I shall subscribe a quarter. Doing so I shall acquire the whole of the éclat, esteem and virtue attaching to the transaction. Perhaps that is what is meant by doing good by stealth and blushing to find it fame."

"I am sure," said Lovelace with great earnestness, "that your father—looking down—would approve of it."

"I think he would, too—a purpose so noble and the cost so cheap. Indeed, what Liberal could *not* approve of it?"

"And you will do it, Mr. Boddington?" Lovelace leaned forward until his cadaverous face was within a foot of Mr. Boddington's own, fat, serene, imperturbable.

"Of course. Why not? Do you see any reason against it? Why are you distressed?"—for tears had leapt into Lovelace's eyes.

"I—I am not distressed. I am—overwhelmed, overcome. Mr. Boddington, you don't know what you are doing, what you have done." Lovelace placed a lean hand on Mr. Boddington's and gave it a convulsive squeeze.

"I trust you are overcome with pleasure, Mr. Lovelace, and not remorse."

"Oh yes, oh yes. I feel like a drowning man pulled out of the river—limp, but living."

"I am glad of that, Mr. Lovelace, because although my mind is made up—indeed, I made it up a couple of days ago subject to Mr. Blackwood approaching me—at the same time a little war goes on within me between my father's commercial blood and my artistic own. And his ghost will not be entirely quiescent until I have put to you one or two questions. I put them to you as a man of business, but you must answer as an artist—that is, with appalling frankness. Is that agreed?"

"Answering in any other way is constitutionally impossible for me, Mr. Boddington. I take no credit for it. It has nearly ruined me several times."

"Very well. Shall I receive any dividend?"

"About the same as the post-office savings bank."

"Excellent. What could be fairer than that? Mr. Lovelace, will the paper review my publications?"

"Have we done so in the past?"

"Only the few lines—neither signed nor initialled—by which you fill the gaps at the bottom of columns on the literary page."

"That is all you will get, then, unless you improve."

"The fact that my action will receive some acclaim and I shall be better known than heretofore——?"

"Nothing to do with literary merit, Mr. Boddington."

"And my speeches on politics and affairs?"

"Unless you become an M.P., or prospective candidate, not much hope. We take a firm line on eccentrics and mad-hatters—forgive the words, just an office phrase."

"If I were to offer to do notes on billiards and model yachting —free?"

Lovelace shook his head: "We should insist on paying you, if we used them, but in fact we never should use them."

"You are certainly uncompromising, Mr. Lovelace."

Lovelace sighed. "The voice is the voice of Lovelace, but the spirit is the spirit of Blackwood. I will own to you that, as an artist, I think a little log-rolling in our favour would not be out of place. But on the *Morning Star*, alas . . ."

"I begin to understand, Mr. Lovelace, why the paper shines with a celestial radiance. I hope my approaching proximity to heavenly virtue will not unduly scorch my wings. I feel already one of the immortals—or, rather, I should do so were I not so hungry. Could you eat a steak? I know a place—and if you will lie down on this sofa while I change my clothes? Admirable. Put your feet up. I shall not be ten minutes. William, put a rug over Mr. Lovelace's knees."

It was close on midnight when Lovelace spoke to Blackwood from the telephone box in his hotel.

"Master," he said, "the deed is do-done."

There was a pause at the other end.

"You don't sound remarkably sober, Richard. Are you?"

"Not entirely, master. But I have dined with Mr. Boddington—a most estim-estimable man, and he will let you have all the mon-money you want."

"You have done well, Richard, if what you say is true. . . ."

"As God is my judge, master—a quarter of a million—whenever you want it——"

"You are sure you have seen the right man, Richard?"

"As God—is my——"

"Yes, I understand that. Where did you find him?"

"Cock-cocktail party—long talk—then we dined—Maison Basque—very beautiful wine."

"Better take two Alka-Seltzers now and go to bed. Ring me up at home at ten-thirty in the morning—better still, ask Mr. Boddington to ring me up."

"Yes, master, without—the slightest—fail."

He lowered the mouthpiece to the end of the cord and left it hanging. This seemed rather strange but he didn't quite know why. He pulled himself up the stairs by the banister. He wished he was feeling better than he was, but all the same this was a memor-memor-memorable day.

Blackwood, for his part, had not much doubt that Lovelace, for all the drink in him, was right in what he said. Blackwood was both elated and calm—he supposed that, after a fashion, he had always expected that the miracle would happen. For the moment he had no desire to tell anybody. Anyhow, he must wait for confirmation. He continued writing, a smile curving his lips, his heart singing within him. Seth Entwistle came in and stood waiting. "Don't go, Seth. What do you think of these married women going back to the mills in the evening to work from five-thirty to nine-thirty—at about sixty mills that is happening, Seth. Puts us to shame, eh?"

"Is that what you're writing about, Mr. Blackwood?"

"Yes."

"If only the young 'uns were as good as the old 'uns, Mr. Blackwood."

"Perhaps humans are like fruit cake, Seth, improve with keeping."

"Some, Mr. Blackwood, some."

"There it is, Seth." He handed him the pages of writing. "Like a cigar?"

"Thank you, sir. The missis will enjoy that." He put it in his waistcoat pocket. "You'll not be writing any more tonight?"

"No."

"And nothing coming from Mr. Lovelace?"

"Not for publication, Seth."

Blackwood looked at Seth and Seth could have sworn he saw a special glint in the eye. But he said nothing. He thought the cigar might be significant—Mr. Blackwood hadn't given him one for six months, but he didn't mention that either. When the assistant overseer asked him if there was any news—did O.B., give a hint of anything, Seth said no, he didn't—he was as he always was and as he reckoned he always would be; he'd go on being O.B., and he'd die of being O.B., being O.B., and doing enough work for half a dozen. Aye. What is the good, thought Seth, of having my job if I don't know a bit more than anybody else?

CHAPTER XLIV

At ten o'clock the next morning Blackwood took a mashie and two or three golf balls and went out on to the links.

"You're very early today," Hannah said, eyeing him curiously.

"It's a lovely morning, dear. I'll be back in less than half an hour if anybody rings." He spoke lightly, casually.

He conquered his impulse to tell her the news. Time enough when the news was certain. She knew already that Lovelace had gone to London in search of Boddington, and how much hung on it. She had been sceptical. Women's caution, he supposed, was greater than man's, the sense of daring and adventure less pronounced. Natural enough, and no use stirring up her doubts of Lovelace's reliability. He had minor doubts himself; the man's imagination was inflammable. By heavens, he thought, as he dropped a ball and glared at it, I haven't quite realised how much depends on this. We've got about five days to go—and here I am—— He struck the ball as if it were an enemy, struck it with a searing crunch and tore up a piece of turf after it. Well, that was good. Here he was behaving as if time were of no moment. Well, no, not quite that. Things had moved in the last day or two. They had received promises now of close on £350,000 from citizens of the county and town. Old Satterthwaite had called yesterday and between his pleas that the paper should campaign for birth control among native peoples and that the world should revert to a wholesale system of barter, he had offered to find £50,000. Sir Amos Kendrick and Dame Ethel Hesketh had added their names to the investors of £10,000. He had found this evidence of faith in the paper harder to bear than abuse; and as he thought of it now he struck the balls more fiercely to exercise the constriction in his throat, and then, picking the balls up off the green he strode as hard as he could towards the dunes and the sea. That was better. The sea everlasting; the wind everlasting; the dome of heaven the same yesterday, today and for ever. Be quiet, thou spirit, and be deeply and quietly thankful for this. If Lovelace was right, a door was opening before him, a path straight before his feet down which he could walk for the rest of his days. Oh, it would be mixed slavery and kingship, mixed anxiety and exultation, mixed frustration and fulfilment. Endless work, exhausting work, work quietening for his own tumult. All this for him, but for Hannah—what? Dedication in some measure for him —but for her—what? What door could he fling open for her? Travel?—The finding of a different house?—for there had been too much unhappiness in this one. Would she be sad to think they would be chained to this town majestic in its ugliness, the smoke-hung heavens, the greyness, the jagged broken buildings that were testimony to war? Had she been hoping that a Sedgwick conquest would spell escape for them? He turned inland from the sea and walked swiftly back.

He was in his study when the telephone rang. Hannah, who had not heard him return, came to answer it and, seeing him, asked if he would like coffee? He nodded gratefully and lifted the instrument. For an infinitesimal moment there was a tremor in his hand then it was gone.

"Hello, master." It was the flat Greycastle intonation, so homely and familiar that it brought a smile to Blackwood's lips.

"Hello, Richard. How are you this morning?"

"Wax to be moulded as you please, master."

"Were you dealing in fact or fiction last night?"

"My customary understatement, master. I have Mr. Boddington here in the flesh to speak to you."

"Good. I am ready."

A high voice then came on, crisp. Lovelace, standing nearby concluded that the blood of Mr. Boddington's father was in the ascendant at that moment. "Good morning, Mr. Blackwood."

"Good morning, Mr. Boddington."

"Short of Mr. Fortinbras I'd liefer speak to you than anybody living."

"You put me in good company."

"You have a great responsibility on your shoulders, Mr. Blackwood."

"How so?"

"You are principally responsible—you and your newspaper—for my crossing my private floor, Tory to Liberal."

Blackwood thought he discerned a rustle of laughter at the other end. He said: "In reality, Mr. Boddington, you have now joined the great majority. No, I don't mean that all Liberals are dead—though some of them, I daresay, give that impression. I mean that the British are mostly liberal at heart but don't vote that way."

"Mr. Blackwood, I am casting in your direction a quarter of a million pounds' look—as I understand Lovelace has already told you."

"We are more than grateful."

"It is an honour. My solicitors will be writing to you one of their somewhat incomprehensible letters, but you can take it the purport is as I say."

"Thank you. Will you be willing to be a member of the Board and one of the Trust to be set up?"

"I shall be proud. I understand I shall function rather like constitutional royalty—listen to what you say but leave all the editorial decisions to you?"

310

"Perfectly correct."

"Would you be averse from printing in London?"

"Not in principle, but I do not think we shall be able to afford it."

"We shall see. More and more soap is being used, and that may lead to something. Although as a hardheaded Rochdale fella you will understand I am making no definite promises."

"Of course. Not beyond the quarter of a million."

"As you say, Mr. Blackwood."

"I should like to see you. Both I—and the staff—I think I can speak for them—would like to thank you in person. And I should like to agree with you on any public announcement to be made."

"I will come up on the night train. By the way, would you have any objection to my informing Mr. Sedgwick of what I am proposing to do?"

"I would rather you waited," said Blackwood, "until we are on the eve of making the announcement. We are not unduly impressed by scoops, but we would rather we had it than he had, especially when it will be—unlike most of his—accurate."

"Mr. Blackwood, you are right—as always. Is it not strange that we who write can be so wise, and that those who govern us can be so excessively foolish? If the *Morning Star* and the *Burnham Guardian* ran the country, has it occurred to you how justly and rightly all would be done."

"Justice is respected, Mr. Boddington, but it is seldom much liked."

Blackwood was aware that Hannah had come in with a cup of coffee and placed it at his elbow. On an impulse he put out his hand and took her arm and detained her. She stood alongside, waiting.

"Then I shall see you tomorrow morning, Mr. Blackwood?"

"Would you come out here and breakfast with us? I am sure my wife would like that, Mr. Boddington." He looked up at Hannah, seeking her agreement, and she shrugged her shoulders, meaning: Have it as you like.

Boddington said: "Most kind. Mr. Lovelace can tell me how to get there."

"Goodbye till tomorrow," said Blackwood.

"Goodbye, sir. Would you like another word with Mr. Lovelace?"

"Thank you. Hello, Richard."

"Yes, master."

"You can come back."

"I thought, perhaps, if I came on the night train with Mr. Boddington . . ."

"No, catch the one about lunchtime. I've a job for you here."

"Yes, master."

Blackwood rose and turned to Hannah.

"That was Boddington."

"So I gathered." A faint smile crossed her face.

"He says he'll find the money."

"Can you trust him?"

"I think so." He smiled in turn. "He comes from Rochdale."

"You're as pleased as if you'd been pensioned off instead of getting a life sentence." She was thinking that all at once he looked years younger.

"Yes," he said. "Yes, Hannah. The end of one part of a journey for me—and the beginning of another. Say you're glad, too—I do hope you can be glad." He spoke the last words in a voice not easy to hear, so full his throat had suddenly become, and he held out his hands to her.

She tried to smile, but the smile quivered and broke, and in the same instant she went into his arms. He strained her to him with an intolerable yearning. After a time she lifted her face, down which the tears had coursed. She said, her voice choked, "Journeys end in lovers' meeting——" He held her fiercely to him and lifted his head and could have cried out. She said: "It's all right—darling—it's all right. We're older now. . . ." and buried her head in his shoulder and wept again.

CHAPTER XLV

On the afternoon, a day or two later, that Blackwood once more addressed the staff in the Thurlow Hall, he received a letter from Mr. Sedgwick:

"My dear Blackwood," (he wrote)
"A word of salutation!

"The fight, so far as I am concerned, is now over, so that I can congratulate you with all sincerity on having acquired the *Morning Star* and having achieved the wherewithal to turn it into a Trust. It is not for me to question whether you put rather too much faith in this magic word 'Trust' and this formula you believe you have found for ensuring that, down the ages, the policy of the paper shall not change. Although I am a Conservative with the liveliest respect for tradition I should never think of laying it down that nothing must change. The Conservatism of today is the Liberalism of tomorrow, as you know. It will be an awkward moment for you when the Liberal chrysalis bursts forth into the Socialist butterfly, as has so frequently happened, and as, in your case is, I fear, inevitable.

"But now that you have achieved your heart's desire, I must congratulate you, if you will allow me, in another capacity—I mean almost as your godfather, your *deus ex machina* who has made all things possible for you. For, as you will see on reflection, had I not been momentarily dazzled by the brilliance of the *Morning Star* and turned my mind towards owning it, Sir Thomas Molyneux might well have died with no plans made for its disposal, and in that case can you doubt whose wooing—yours or mine—Lady Molyneux would have found the more acceptable? You may not owe me everything in the world, but the degree to which you are indebted to me is almost embarrassing—for both of us. I trust you will bear that thought with an equanimity equal to my own.

"One further thought occurs to me, that my faith in Providence being possibly greater than your own, I can accept the turn of events as being all for the best. There can be only the smallest doubt that the fitting of the *Morning Star*, under your guidance, into my group would have required a major operation and either more forbearance than comes altogether readily to me or a drastic lopping off of some of those portions of your mental anatomy that must have caused excessive pain to you. In short, I daresay the taking over of your distinguished self and your most esteemed paper, would have proved a damned nuisance.

"With these consoling reflections on what might have been, I bid you adieu.

"Yours very sincerely,

"Samuel Sedgwick.

"PS. Since writing the above, I have had an idea that I trust will be of enlivening interest. My *Daily News-Letter* which at present is published only in London has, as I am sure you will be glad to know, an increasing public in the north. Why should I not therefore print it also in Greycastle? That will enable me to conform to your wishes that the reading public should have the widest diversity of news and views put before it to choose from, and will enrich that free competition and enterprise to which you are so rightly devoted. It will do more—it will allow me to maintain and deepen those associations—personal and otherwise—that I have found so agreeable in Greycastle and which it would grieve me to sever.

"This is an idea which, once thought of, improves on acquaintance. Indeed, I cannot imagine anything that will deflect me from putting it into execution. So, in the sure knowledge that we shall soon be, as it were, fellow citizens and vigorous competitors and that under that stimulus the *Morning Star* will be inspired to show still more vividly what it is made of, I now bid you a *comparatively brief* adieu. I should be grateful if, at the same time, you would convey my kindest regards to your wife and son, of whom I cherish the warmest and most ineffaceable memories."

Mr. Sedgwick had written the postscript with unusual satisfaction. That, he had reflected, would take care of Blackwood to some tune. If Providence shut one door she invariably opened another—provided, as his father, Old James, would have said, you took a strong enough crowbar to the lock.

It was a private meeting that Blackwood addressed, but he had invited to it those who had expressed their wish to invest sums that mattered in the paper, and all those who had lent distinguished support to its campaign for independence. He had with him on the platform in addition to leading members of his staff, the bishop (Dr. Brodrick), Sir William Prentice, Dame Ethel Hesketh, Mr. William Moffatt, the Lord Mayor (Alderman Stevens), Mr. Llewellyn Morgan, Mr. Thomas Bolton, Mrs. Angela Richardson, Mr. Raymond Wilberforce, Mr. John Picton, Sir Amos Kendrick, Colonel Satterthwaite, Mr. Henry McGrew, Mr. Jacob Rosenstein and, of course, Mr. Barclay Boddington. Blackwood had had several talks with Mr.

Boddington during the previous day or two, during which they had discussed, on Boddington's initiative, various plans for printing the paper in London and Glasgow and in the meantime flying it to London so that its morning delivery could coincide with that of London newspapers. Lovelace, present at some of the discussions, found this was a new and different Mr. Boddington—a man with, apparently, the ghost of his father, the Soap King, prompting his words. No decisions were taken—there were far too many complex problems to consider, and, certainly, unless a very large further sum of money were raised, printing elsewhere was out of the question. But Blackwood had no objection to Boddington's imaginative flights—he was quite capable of keeping them within bounds, and a little controlled dynamite in exploitation would be no disadvantage. Mr. Boddington, on his side, was delighted. He confided to Lovelace several times that, next to Mr. Fortinbras, Blackwood held his admiration more than anybody he knew. "What a pair they would be," he said, "what a pair! Imagine Blackwood as his Chief of Staff!" To which Lovelace replied that Blackwood would be no good as second in command—he had to have his head.

Blackwood had asked Hannah to accompany him, and they drove down together, the warmth of their new relationship filling them both with composure. Neither knew how long it would last —how far the excitement of the changed situation regarding the paper was the cause of it—but they were both grateful for the respite, and both taking a new pride in each other. They arrived at the hall especially early that they might welcome the guests. The hall was filled with a subdued chatter and gaiety when the Lord Mayor led the platform party on and Frank Knowles started a flutter of applause. Since this was a private meeting called simply to hear his own statement Blackwood acted as his own chairman. So soon as his guests were seated, he rose at once.

"You must not think," he said, "that I have turned Communist if I begin: My Lord Mayor, My Lord Bishop—friends and comrades —because that is what we are——"

Lavinia Ward, who was in the front row with her eyes travelling from Blackwood to Hannah and back again, found her eyes suddenly dim with tears.

Blackwood went on: "In this same hall four short weeks ago, we were faced with the task of raising half a million pounds; with either raising it or facing what would have seemed—to most of us—a disaster, the passing of the newspaper we have served to a new owner with a new policy—a new owner for whom I, and I daresay a lot of you, could not have worked. My own personal fortunes would not have been of any great account—and in the light of history probably yours neither, for I'm not going to flatter you—better men than you or me were killed in the last war and mankind goes on—but the death or stilling of the *Morning Star*—yes, that would have mattered. Milton said he who destroys a good book kills reason itself. I shall make bold to say that's true of a good newspaper also.

"But that disaster has not happened." (Applause broke over the benches.) "And it is not going to happen." (The flutter of applause became a crescendo.) "The money has been found.

"We can be sure now that as long as England stands, money is worth anything, and paper and ink and metal continue to exist, so long will this paper endure, like Longfellow's

> goodly vessel
> that shall laugh at all disaster
> and with wave and whirlwind wrestle.

In other words, we've still got our job—not too well paid" ("No, sir," and laughter) "—but one that needs to be done, to tell the truth that shines—and sometimes hurts; to tell exactly what happened, how it happened and why it happened, and what men said. Of course, we can't always do it—we can't always find out. And it's certain, anyhow, that unless all the heavens were paper, all the rivers ink, and all the forests were our pencils, we couldn't find the space and materials to set down the story; all we can do is to choose a particle of it, what swims into our ken, and deal faithfully with that.

"There are those who say people don't want the truth, won't buy it, find it wearisome. It isn't altogether correct. When the scoffers say it to you in future, you can remind them how the citizens of this county and neighbourhood, or those native to it, put on record by finding half a million pounds that they, at all events, thought otherwise. We're profoundly grateful. Some of them are here on this platform." (Applause.) "They're meeting most of us for the first time, though of course it may be they have felt they had a slight acquaintance from perusing our handiwork occasionally. We shall be a serious disappointment in the flesh, I have no doubt. We're not to be distinguished in appearance from seamen or bank clerks or carpenters or dog fanciers or anybody else. Our lineaments set down in cold print are the only ones we've any liking for or take any pride in. We hope we've got a glint in the eye and a ring in the voice there all right—once in a while; and that our word there, what we say, can be relied on and is our bond. We'd better be judged on that.

"Well, there it is. What they've done, of course, by this expression of approval of what we do—and they'll have been able to see how far it falls short—is to determine that we've got to go on. No release or respite for us. They've signed a kind of death warrant for us—with a reprieve attached for life. No getting away from it. 'Work apace, apace, honest labour wears a lovely face.' It might have been written specially for us. Similarly with, 'God giveth all good things in return for labour'." (A voice: "Let's hope so, sir.") "I agree. We have got to not only work for the night is coming, but work when the night is on top of us. In an ideal world this permanent nightshift would earn us time and a half or double pay, but the world isn't ideal—yet; it's part of our task as seamen of a ship called Britain to edge her towards that paradisal shore—if we can do it.

"Those of us who are gathered here are really writing the end of Book One of the *Morning Star*. And tomorrow's issue will see, in its fashion, the beginning of Book Two. The chapter heading is— Towards a New World. We don't know what its history will be except that it will be chequered, filled with comedy and tragedy, with disasters, triumphs, exaltations, despairs, mechanical inventions, experiments in the arts, the entry of new and magnificent works in the temple of literature, the placing of new masterpieces in the halls of painting and sculpture, and the sending forth through the spheres of music that has not heretofore enchanted the ears of men. On all that happens in this emergent world we shall be privileged to express our opinion, praise the noble, lacerate the contemptible, encourage the fainthearted, pulverise the bullies, assail the torturers, lift up the needy, pour ridicule on the pompous, stand with the pioneers, always uphold freedom of thought and speech and the sacredness of the individual, believing the State is his servant rather than he the State's. This is a high privilege; no man's is higher. The Prime Minister and his Ministers speak their opinions from time to time; we speak ours six days a week. There's an ancient saying that words are the daughters of earth and things are the sons of heaven. We write of things done and other men do them, but in writing of them and judging them we too influence and mould them in our fashion.

"And in this writing and judging—the independence we have always claimed—and had—is now assured to us by this half million pounds so long as we live ; so long as this nation stands. For no government of Englishmen by Englishmen will ever dare—or, anyhow, succeed—in filching that liberty and independence of mind from us. I cannot believe any group of such men would ever attempt it. If they attempted it, they would certainly fail. Englishmen have not died for those rights in the past to lose them now. As for the Press groups and chains and petty monopolies, our own danger from them is over.

"So far as we on this paper are concerned, then, this is an important day in our lives; none will ever be more important. I am proud, and deeply thankful. We have won through to it together. It is no idle phrase on my part that calls us a band of brothers. Of course, we're not as monastic as once we were." He glanced at Lavinia Ward and Brenda Smith, smiled, and went on. "The making of a newspaper is not quite like the manufacture of merchandise or even the building of a fine ship. There goes into the paper every day the thought and character and blood and sinew of the men working on it. It is a living thing, trembling with life, easily losing, if care isn't taken, its health and virility, its morning face reflecting faithfully the intentions, the failings—or the qualities—of the men behind it. Only a unity of men working for a common purpose and with a good heart can make it a fine thing. We have striven to do that and, up to a point, I think, we've done it. By God's help, we will go on." ("That's right, sir—we will an' all.")

"Just before I came here I received a letter from Mr. Sedgwick—a letter of congratulation" (Laughter.) "with certain mental provisoes and reservations, I daresay." (Renewed laughter.) "The operative paragraph was in a postscript in which he says he intends to print his *Daily News-Letter* in this city to give us the stimulus we sorely need—or words to that effect. We shall not, I imagine, be unduly disturbed by that." ("The fish-and-chip shops'll be glad of it," and laughter.) "The more contrast we get the better. I mention it to remind us that the fight isn't ended—will never be ended—I mean the fight to gain the ear and attention of the public. We want nothing better than that. I shall tell Mr. Sedgwick that our motto is the old Lancashire dictum 'Let 'em all come'. I think that's all. We shall meet again shortly—in another place, as they say."

There was more laughter, and Frank Knowles started to sing "For he's a jolly good fellow", and this chorus swept the hall, while Blackwood stood on his feet wondering what to do next and feeling as awkward as men do in these circumstances.

The guests stood on the platform chatting for a while, Blackwood busy introducing Boddington to those who had not already met him, including the bishop, who said he regarded him as the instrument of Providence, and Mr. Boddington responding that Mr. Fortinbras had something to do with it also.

"Ah," said the bishop, "Mr. Fortinbras—I always look on him as the very son of Destiny." He walked Mr. Boddington to the edge of the platform. "I am not at all sure," he said, "that Mr. Blackwood is not singled out in a much similar way. Not at all sure."

"Sir," said Mr. Boddington, "my conviction on the point is absolute."

CHAPTER XLVI

THE REPORTERS' ROOM discussed the situation an hour later when Frank Knowles brought in a bottle of sherry and a bottle of port from Sam Sharp's dive.

"Now then," he said, "you can all stop work for a bit—that is if anybody is doing owt. It's an important occasion, is this. Who says sherry and who says port?" He stood beneath the small statue of Mr. Shakespeare and eyed them as a father does his erring children.

"What are we celebrating, Frank?" inquired de Ferrers innocently, spilling a cup of tea over the old table he was working on.

"We're celebrating," said Knowles, "for them as don't know

it, the fact that we've made history. Here Brenda, sherry or port, love?"

"Port, Frank. Who's paid for it? Expenses?"

"Never you mind who's paid for it. Fred Cheshire, what are you having? You can stop addling your meagre brains wi' that *Times* crossword a minute."

"I don't mind, Frank, what I have."

"Come on, come on, for God's sake—make up your mind. Do you realise you're safe from the sack at last?"

"The paper," said Mr. Cheshire mildly, "hasn't been made that couldn't sack me, Frank. Sherry, please. Suppose, for instance, O.B. gets run over by a tram?"

"Run over by a—nay—Jesus!" said Knowles in disgust. "Now then, Clifton, what is it?"

"Could I have a mixed?" inquired Prince.

"Why, what's the matter?—diarrhoea over having a column to do? Now then, Forsyth, port? There you are then! Now then—everybody got one?—to the new *Morning Star*!—safe as the Bank of England and the best bloody paper in the country bar none—begging your pardon, Brenda."

"Don't mention it, Frank. Hear! hear! Up the *Morning Star*!"

"Up the *Morning Star*!"

"*Morning Star*! Lead in your pencil, Frank!"

"And to hell with Sedgwick's *News-Letter*!"

"I should damn-well think so."

"Fill up your glasses again!" said Knowles "Here—Clifton, Ferrers——"

"Allow me," said Prince, "to throw a contentious bone—whose wage packet was increased this week? When does the office get its fleet of reporters' cars? I'd been looking forward to Sedgwick taking us over."

"Now, now," said Knowles, "you don't mean a dam' word of it. It's a triumph, I tell you—tho' I shall say nowt about how Brenda had to fight like a tiger for her honour with old Satterthwaite. Here, Brenda, what did you do to get that fifty thousand out of him?"

"Told him I'd had one of those pocket cameras in my pocket all the time—snapping everything he did——"

"Front-page news-girl, I know. Port or sherry, Forsyth? Here——" Knowles took the bottle over.

"Why should that old bitch, the late lamented's widow, get all the brass, that's what I want to know?" said Forsyth. "She fixed it with old Sedgwick, I'll bet a quid—easy money—bump up the damn price, split the proceeds. Half a million raised and the old rag doesn't get a penny of it—not a penny better off. All to the old bitch who loathes our guts. And then Sedgwick brings up the *News-Letter* to take the bread out of our mouths. . . ."

"You ought to be glad—more union subs. for you to collect," said Brenda.

De Ferrers said: "Not bad stuff this, Frank. Give us another sherry. What I say is—I hope we start doing racing and expert advice on the pools and a nice bit o' keyhole garbage—that's what people want. And no error."

"Sacrilege, Ferrers, sacrilege!"

"All right, I'm telling you. I have three mouths to feed—for we that live to please must please to live, as Dr. Johnson said."

"Who says we live to please, Ferrers?" asked Prince "We do them a favour by letting them buy us at the dirt-cheap price of two-pence."

"Wrong again, Prince—you're always wrong," cried Forsyth. "You must be the original of Shaw's reporter who always got it wrong—wrote it down and got it wrong. Port for me, Frank, and don't be so damned stingy this time. Ah, here's our guide to the gates of heaven. How goes it, old Jonesy?"

"What are you doing, celebrating? Well, that iss right. It hass been the Lord's doing and iss wonderful in our sight."

"I say——"

"Shut up, Ferrers," shouted Prince, "I'm working."

"I say what I would have liked——"

"Give Ferrers some more port——"

"I say, I'd have liked a finish on the winning post—with an old miser arriving with a cab filled with one-pound notes——"

"All your black-market pals, Ferrers——"

"A cab filled with one-pound notes—that's how they'd have done it if they'd had a drama—a dramatic—sense——"

Forsyth said: "Sedgwick's *News-Letter* is written for those who can't damn-well think—with pictures for them who can't read".

"Listen!" said Cheshire. "I've just found this in a book—listen to this—'most newspaper owners I have met have been men of small education, repellent manners and suffering from atrocious megalomania. Having heard an opera for the first time, one of them wanted to ask Wagner to dinner'."

Ferrers said: "Never mind that. We shall never have a real financial success till we have a successful racing tipster. Even the nonconformist papers have racing tipsters——"

"Shut up, Ferrers. Who's talking about financial success? On this paper you go into the church."

Prichard Jones said: "When I heard Mr. Blackwood say that the *News-Letter* wass coming up here I thought to myself, I thought, of the old saying 'Where God hath a temple, the devil will haf a chapel'. Yess, that iss what I thought. May I haf another sherry, Frank?"

"You'd better put those bottles away, Frank," said Forsyth—"what's left of 'em—or that column of O.B.'s speech will never get done. Who's doing it—Ferrers?"

"God forbid," said Knowles; "he'd get a wreck in the middle of it. You're doing it, Clifton, aren't you?"

"I would be if you ladies and gentlemen would allow the peace of God to fall upon you. Who got the names of those on the platform—you, Cheshire?"

"Yes, but I don't know whether Barclay Boddington's name is hyphenated or whether——"

"Well, for the love of all that's wonderful go and look in *Who's Who*—or did you never hear of the thing?"

Ferrers said: "The greatest day in our lives—and here we are behaving normally—apart from a drop o' port everything going on just as usual——"

"Did you know," asked Prince, "that there's a paper to come out tomorrow called the *Morning Star*?"

"The *Morning Star*? You don't damn-well say!" said Ferrers.

"The *Morning Star*—that's the name——"

Tap tap . . ."The *Morning Star*, eh?" muttered Knowles . . . tap tap . . . "Well, who'd have thought" . . . tap tap tap . . . "Aye, well, now"—tap tap tap . . . tap tap tap . . .

The clatter gradually filled the room.

Towards eleven o'clock Lovelace's reflections on the quiddity of life in general and of the Press in particular were interrupted by the entry of Seth Entwistle.

"Mr. Blackwood not in?"

"Down in the subs. room. What is it?"

"Wondered if I ought to have set his leader on us in bigger type—seeing its historic, like?"

"He'd think that was too—demonstrative, Seth."

"Aye; I suppose he would. I thought he could have let himself go a bit more—he's won a battle—and he's entitled to shout. Montgomery would have had more to say."

"There'll be the column report of his speech."

"Aye—but still—it's historic all right. I'd begun to think we should go up the spout. We run it pretty close."

"A damned close-run thing, as the Iron Duke said."

"Did he? Aye. Well, he ought to know. God—not always on the side o' the big battalions. Never believed He was. Them little Napoleons o' the Press, Mr. Lovelace. Ah! When Northcliffe went to Paris he tried Buonaparte's hat on. I read about it. Waistcoat-pocket dictators, Mr. Lovelace, that's what."

"We've struck a blow, Seth."

"We have, Mr. Lovelace, we have. Mixed up, isn't it, the Press. Good and bad. It's a funny thing—when I know all about something, the papers never seem to get it quite right—wonder why it is?"

"Bending light, Seth——"

"Eh?"

"Things don't look the same from both ends, Seth. London Press at one end—us at the other. Different angles."

"Nay, Mr. Lovelace—you don't believe that. You and me's worked on papers where all they want is bitchy stuff. It's got to be strong meat to attract—and if the odour's bad—all the better."

"You're in a crusading mood, Seth."

"Aye—well—what Mr. Blackwood said at the meeting— stirred me up. If everybody in the country read our paper it 'ud be a different place."

"We shall sell more yet—if we can get the paper."

"That 'ud be like it, wouldn't it—more demand and no paper."

"They can pass it round."

"Lot o' bread and butter that'll give us."

"You can't expect it, Seth. You're signed on for plain living and high thinking——"

"I know—I know. When Mr. Blackwood's talking I feel I'd be proud to starve—but my missis always says uplift makes folk hungry—makes heavy demands on the emotional system.

Anyhow, the grocer has to be paid. No use giving *him* a couple o' copies of the *Morning Star*. But I'm rambling on. I'm as proud as punch, really. There'll be a few people climbing on the band wagon now, if I'm any judge."

"Right there, Seth."

"Letters and things coming in!"

"Telegrams from the Prime Minister down."

"Going to use them?"

"Day after tomorrow, I expect."

"If you could let me have some of 'em later on tonight I could get a few set. Worst o' this job, Mr. Lovelace, whatever happens the paper has to come out. If we were just a factory we should shut down—go on the spree."

"We're like the tides—keep coming in."

"Like the river—rolling along."

"Right, Seth."

"Well, I guess I'd better be rolling too. But it's historic, Mr. Lovelace—it is that."

Downstairs in the subs. room Blackwood stood talking at the head of the long deal table.

Charles Greenhalgh, glistening with sweat, was saying: "That special report of the conference of cotton-mill managers—it's a bit long——"

"Don't cut it unless you must, Charles. Throws a lot of light on the situation. Did you realise output could rise by twenty-five per cent without either more operatives or machinery? No? Nor did I. And that remark— 'everybody expects somebody else's wife to go back into the mill but not his own'——"

"Those crisis paragraphs? They're pretty grim——"

"Yes, I know they are. But keep them on the main page. The facts'll have to be got into people's heads with a hammer and chisel. . . ."

Blackwood stood eyeing the men at the table. Something was in the air tonight—an added touch of resilience, of high spirits, a cheerful note in the shouts for boys to put copy up, a smile shot at him sideways from heads lowered over telegrams. "Evening, Mr. Blackwood—enjoyed your speech" . . . "Evening, Mr. Blackwood, Royal Commission will be pleased" . . . "Evening, Mr. Blackwood—interesting to read what Sedgwick says in his papers tomorrow." Charlie Greenhalgh had said: "I haven't felt so cheerful since the end of the war."

Upstairs in the corridor Blackwood ran into Lavinia Ward.

"Why, Lavinia—what are you doing here so late?" Lavinia was wearing a smart little hat and was holding a page proof in her hands. "I wanted to see this page before it finally went down. And somehow I couldn't keep out of the office tonight. Oh, Mr. Blackwood, I can't tell you how delighted I am!" She clasped her hands to her breast, crumpling the proof and not heeding it, looking up at him as if he were the light of the world.

"Well, thank you, Lavinia—very kind of you. I read your page —that's a good piece about the enormous gulf between the price of cloth when it leaves the mills and the price of shirts and dresses in the shops. Keep at it."

But Lavinia's thoughts were elsewhere. "I know one woman who will be thrilled when she hears the news, Mr. Blackwood— Mrs. Arbuthnot—she's doing an article for me on Westminster impressions. She said in her letter——"

"Yes, Lavinia, she's a good friend of the paper, I know——"

"Oh yes, Mr. Blackwood—she feels about you—" Lavinia blushed—"about the paper just as I do."

Blackwood thought, "Yes, this letter in my pocket——" He said: "Well, Lavinia, don't stay too late. Read that cotton conference carefully—one or two ideas there worth following up."

Exeter ran into him a yard or two further on: "Want me any more, O.B.?"

"No thanks. The stuff reads all right."

"I've drafted something on Trieste."

"Good—that will do tomorrow."

"Good night, Oliver. It's been a great day."

"A challenge for us, Randolph."

"I guess it'll be taken care of."

"I hope so. Good night."

Blackwood was glad to get back into his chair.

"Anything fresh, Richard?"

"A few more private telegrams. The news gets around."

"I wonder if the Governor of the Bank ever spoke to Sedgwick, Richard?"

"We'll ask Sedgwick when he comes up." He noted the touch of pallor in Blackwood's face. "I'll make a cup o' tea." He put the plug into the electric kettle. His heart quivered for a moment. Suppose anything happened to Blackwood—all this edifice—— He asked: "Have you been round the machine-room, Oliver?"

"Yes, I looked in."

"And the foundry, packing-room and everywhere?"

"Yes. Why?"

"You've had a day."

"Nothing, Richard—nothing."

Nothing. All the same he was glad to be sitting down. This warmth flowing towards him—he hadn't expected it—turned bones to water. These letters: Amarilla's—"I do not love you less because I know the truth. It explains so much. I came across Amelia Earhart's, 'Courage is the price that life exacts for granting peace'. I'm finding some peace, Oliver, in the hurly-burly here and in the fighting there is to do—and in my love and pride in you—and in the knowledge that the *Morning Star* will go on shining down the years."

Lovelace brought his cup of tea over.

That was better.

"The paper's gone to bed, Oliver?"

"Yes."

"Chapter One of Book Number Two—as you said."

"Yes." They both looked at the clock.

"They're late," said Lovelace. But even as he spoke the old building trembled—a shiver in its fabric—and from a distance came the faint rumble and hum.

END OF *Morning Star*.